SPIKED

JENNIFER LANE

PSYCHED PUBLISHING

Published by Psyched Publishing

First published, October 2016

The characters and events in this book are fictitious.
Any similarity to real persons, living or dead,
is coincidental and not intended by the author.

Library of Congress Cataloguing-in-Publication Data

Lane, Jennifer.
  Spiked / Jennifer Lane – 1st ed.
  ISBN: 978-0-9979970-0-2
  1. Swimming — Fiction. 2. New Adult Romance — Fiction.
  3. Sexual Assault — Fiction. 4. Psychology — Fiction. I. Title

10 9 8 7 6 5 4 3 2 1

Book Design by Coreen Montagna

Printed in the United States of America

To survivors of trauma:
may you tell your story and heal.
May you honor the past as you embrace the present.

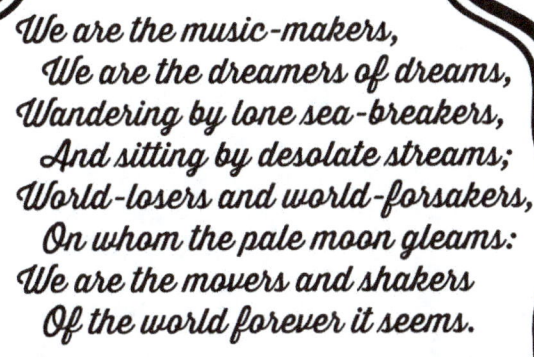

We are the music-makers,
  We are the dreamers of dreams,
Wandering by lone sea-breakers,
  And sitting by desolate streams;
World-losers and world-forsakers,
  On whom the pale moon gleams:
We are the movers and shakers
  Of the world forever it seems.

~ARTHUR WILLIAM EDGAR
O'SHAUGHNESSY
★ ★ ★

Jessica

★ ★ ★

The stale odor of spilled beer and unwashed laundry assaulted me as I walked down the humid hallway, confused by the blown-up Disney images of Elsa, Anna, and Olaf lining the dorm walls. Was this a university or a preschool?

Next to me, Mom wrinkled her nose. "I wish Highbanks had placed you in one of their newer dorms."

"No, this is perfect," Dad said, behind me. We'd piled my stuff into a cart that he now pushed, and it was difficult to hear him over the squeaking wheels. "The quintessential college experience: fifties architecture, no air conditioning."

I pursed my lips. Why had I wanted my parents to stay together again? They disagreed on everything.

"Guys," I said. "We already went over this. Canfield Hall is where most of the freshman swimmers live, 'cause it's close to the pool." I rolled my wheeled suitcase to a stop in front of room 220.

From our online chats over the summer, I knew my roommate had planned to arrive on campus yesterday. She'd said she'd need to adjust to a new time zone. Australia was a long way away. I knocked on our door, but there was no answer. A thrill zinged up my spine when I extracted my key from my pocket. *My new home.* The key signified freedom and fun.

When the door opened, the contrast between the two halves of the room startled me. One side was ugly, sterile, plain. The other, which was clearly now Mackenzie's, exploded with color and energy. She'd lofted her bed frame to provide more space, and posters of shirtless men covered every centimeter of wall below and above the mattress. A fan on her desk rotated, pulsing the warm air.

"Well." Mom set down her handbag and approached a muscled sportsman with a critical eye. Despite the heat, she looked perfectly put together in a pale pink silk blouse, black pencil skirt, and beige pumps. "Alex Rance, Richmond Tigers," she read. "From the AFL. What's that?"

"Australian Football League." I heaved my suitcase onto the naked mattress. A bead of sweat slid down my spine. "Mackenzie's boy crazy. She wants to become Australia's equivalent of Erin Andrews so she can get up close to hottie athletes."

"Who?" Dad asked.

"She's an ESPN reporter," Mom said, her eyes still on the poster. "I met her once at a fundraiser." As a US senator, Mom attended plenty of those. "We discussed the challenges of working as a woman in a man's world."

Dad and I shared a smirk. Mom was a staunch feminist.

He scanned the bare walls, hands on his hips. "You need to spice up this room. Want me to paint something for you?"

I straightened. He would do that for me? "Sure. I guess."

He fiddled with the collar of his light blue button-down shirt. "If you don't like it, you don't have to display it."

"I love all your paintings, Dad." He'd inspired me to major in art at Highbanks.

"That will get you going again, finally," Mom said to him. "You always love immersing yourself in a new piece of art."

Dad didn't reply, but from the tightness around his eyes, I could tell what he was thinking: *Get off my back.* His last gallery show had been almost a year ago, and Mom had been on his case to start painting again. But his muse wouldn't be rushed, especially since the arguments between him and Mom had increased. Their spats poured ice water over his creative flame.

Mom fanned herself. "You sure we can't convince you to live with your brother, honey?"

Before I could reply, Dad said, "Jessie wants her own life, Lois. She doesn't want to live in Dane's shadow. Plus, she'll be closer to the art building here."

"Don't lecture me like I don't know my own daughter." Mom folded her arms across her chest, and my stomach clenched. "I appreciate the value of struggle for building resilience." She waved her hand toward the chipped wood bedframe. "Like living with this cheap furniture. But Patrick, she'll have enough stress as a college student-athlete. Do you have any idea how packed her schedule will be?"

Dad scowled. "This is a dig about how I haven't been involved with Dane's volleyball career?"

I stifled a groan. Two years ago, right before my mother lost the presidential election to Adolfo Ramirez, we'd learned my dad had cheated on her. He'd been distant for some time, and after that revelation, it all made sense. But he'd ended the affair, and my parents had committed to saving their marriage. They'd gone to couples counseling, and for a while I'd been simultaneously embarrassed and relieved to see them kiss and hold hands. But after my dad's gallery show didn't do so well last September, he'd become grumpy. They'd started to bicker more. And I couldn't stand listening to their arguments.

Tuning them out, I texted my brother. Maybe his flight from Colorado hadn't left yet.

Save me. They're fighting again.

Fuck. They suck.

I grinned, grateful Dane didn't act like the twenty-one-year-old college senior he was. He texted again:

Just boarded in CO Springs.
Layover in Denver then home at 5.
I'll rescue you.

This was the second Olympic developmental camp he'd attended, and he had a good shot of making the national volleyball team after he graduated from Highbanks next May. I would *kill* to be on the national swimming team. I had less than two years of college training before the Olympic trials—two years to prove I was the best breaststroker in America. Just thinking about it made me giddy.

I replied:

> *The rents will be long gone by then.*
> *Mom has a thing at the Statehouse.*

Not too late to change your mind and live with me.

I sighed as I looked at the scratched linoleum floor. Dane lived in a sweet off-campus two-bedroom condo with probably ten times the square footage of my dorm room. But living with him meant I wouldn't get to know my teammates or other students as well. I wouldn't live a normal college life. And after all the publicity of my mother running for president, I wanted normal. Besides, I didn't want to be a third wheel.

> *You and Lucia don't want me around.*

Luz loves you, you know that.
We're psyched we both have our sibs here.

I gulped, picturing olive skin and dark, soulful eyes. Lucia's younger brother, Mateo, was new on campus this year, too.

My choice to attend Highbanks had been a no-brainer, given I'd grown up here in the Midwest, and the school had a top-ten NCAA swim team. Mateo's decision had been more of a surprise. He reportedly liked the music school, but I bet it had come down to security. Secret Service already had Highbanks figured out. They planned to house him with Lucia in a safe off-campus house.

> *Did Mateo move in yet?*

Not sure. Sec Serv won't tell Luz anything.
Boarding door just closed. Will call when land.
Tell Dad to stop being a dick.

It was more like Mom was being the dick, but I'd have to save that discussion for later.

I felt Dad's hand on my shoulder as I texted good-bye.

"Bested by the cell phone once again. We're clearly not needed here." He smiled.

Mom looked in the mirror and brushed her fingers through her hair. Hers was blond, short, straight, and perfectly coiffed. Mine was blond, long, curly, and imperfectly feral.

"Sorry we got heated, honey." She patted her hair, then looked at me. "I know you don't like it when we argue."

Then why do you do it?

"You'll be okay, then, Jessie?" Dad's deep blue eyes assessed me.

"More than okay." I grinned. "I've been waiting for college for forever."

Mom approached me. "I remember feeling the same way, my first day at Yale. You too, Patrick?"

"Sure." Dad paused and shook his head. "Actually, I was scared shitless. The other art students seemed so sophisticated, and here I was, this poor kid from Ohio."

"Aw." Mom rubbed his shoulder. "I didn't know that. I wish I could've been there for you back then."

Dad nodded. "Me, too." He reached for her hand.

I exhaled.

"So your mother didn't take you to school?" Mom asked.

Dad shook his head. "She couldn't get off work. I had to make the trip to New York by myself."

As much as my parents annoyed me, I had to admit I was glad they'd helped me move in. But now it was time for them to leave. "Thanks for helping, Mom and Dad."

"That's code for *Get the hell out*." Mom laughed and hugged me.

Dad squeezed me tight. "I'll miss you. Can't wait to watch you swim here."

Butterflies fluttered in my stomach as I thought about my first college swim meet.

Once my parents left, I finished unloading the cart and returned it to the dorm lobby. I was stuffing my last shirt into the overcrowded closet when the door swung open.

"Roomie!" Mackenzie squealed as she bopped in.

She was about five-five with a dark brown ponytail. What I would give for that straight, sleek hair…She wore a Highbanks Swimming T-shirt, and her gym shorts showcased tanned, muscular legs.

"Hey. I'm Jessica." I reached out my hand.

She frowned at my hand and scooped me into a hug. "Blimey, you're tall!" She looked up at me. "You're almost two meters, then?"

I chewed on my lip. "Um, I'm six feet."

"Beaut." She scanned the room. "So, whaddaya reckon?"

"Too hot in here." I grimaced. My curls had seized up from the humidity, and I felt sweat at the nape of my neck. "Love your posters, though."

She brightened. "Right? He's my favorite." She ducked under her bed and patted the muscles of an intense-looking guy with a shaved head. "David Zaharakis, from Essendon." Her hand fluttered over her heart. "He's scored over a hundred goals."

"Awesome." I had no idea what she was talking about. Were goals like touchdowns?

She straightened. "Hope I meet a guy as cute as him here. You're coming to the swimmer party tonight, right?"

"I didn't know about a party."

"Now you do. It's at the swimmer house. We're going."

The giddy feeling returned. My first college party!

She held up her phone. "Elyse texted me about it. She wants your number, too. What is it?"

Elyse was a senior on the team who had followed me on Instagram. After I told Mackenzie my cell number, I asked, "What's the swimmer house?"

"A bunch of senior guy swimmers have a house on south campus." She stripped off her T-shirt and turned to her closet. Like most swimmers, she had no need for modesty. "Is your mum here?"

"She had to leave."

"Shit. Dad wanted me to meet her." She tugged a camisole over her bra. "He reckons she's famous."

She didn't know my mother? "You know she ran for president, right?"

Mackenzie blinked at me. "President of the United *States?* Rack off!"

I laughed. How could she not know that? "She lost the election two years ago."

"Bugger. That must've sucked."

I shrugged. "It's not too bad. I wouldn't have been able to live in the dorm if I had to have Secret Service all the time, like Lucia."

"Lucia?"

"I told you about my brother, right? He's a senior on the volleyball team here. His girlfriend is President Ramirez's daughter."

"I'll be buggered. Dad didn't tell me that." She tossed her backpack onto her desk chair and rummaged through it. "I wonder what it'd be like to date the president's kid."

I wonder, too. I'd met Mateo at the presidential debate two years ago, but hadn't seen him since. Back then, Secret Service agent Johnny Zucko had guarded me, and Dane told me Johnny was now on Mateo's detail. I hoped I got to see them both soon, as well as meet the hot men on the swim team. The sweetness of eye candy awaited me.

I studied my closet, wondering what to wear to the party. "Hey, what's up with *Frozen*-palooza in the hallway?"

Mackenzie snickered. "Zoe—she's the RA—she said our wing theme is *Frozen*."

"Whatever."

"Right?"

As I selected a turquoise-sequined halter top, I thought about Anna, the younger sister in the movie. First she fell for the handsome and confident Prince Hans, but then the unassuming Kristoff wormed his way into her heart. One betrayed her, and the other earned her love.

"Love your shirt," Elyse told me. Thankfully she'd leaned in to shout in my ear so I could hear her over the pounding bass.

I was glad I'd stuck with sequins despite Dane's arched eyebrows when I'd met him for dinner. His only advice: *"Don't drink too much."*

"Yours, too!" I yelled back.

Elyse's crimson cap-sleeve top complimented her long, vampire-black hair and dark-framed glasses. We both wore jeans. Her high heels brought her almost to my height.

"Want a beer?" she asked.

I nodded. I despised the taste of beer, but tonight was a chance to whip my taste buds into shape. When she left, I felt self-conscious, standing by the wall alone. A cute blond guy had captured Mackenzie's attention, and I hadn't met anyone else yet. I tried to fade into the woodwork, which was hard to do as a six-footer.

"Hey, beautiful."

I turned toward the deep voice, and my breath caught in my throat. He towered over me, his gaze pinning me to the wall. He'd gelled his short brown hair into a peak over the middle of his forehead.

"Um, hi," I said.

His smile revealed perfect, white teeth. "About time you got here. The girls' team needs a fast breaststroker." His eyes flicked down to my chest.

My heart revved—he knew who I was. "You're a swimmer, too?"

"Of course. This is my house." He opened his arms, and I noticed a crack in the plaster behind the beat-up, striped sofa. "Instant swimmer, just add water."

I grinned. "What do you swim?"

"I'm a sprinter."

I should've figured that. Sprint freestylers tended to be tall. And cocky.

Elyse sidled up to me and thrust a can of beer into my grasp. "I see you've met Blake." Her voice dripped with disgust, but he didn't stop smiling.

"How was your summer, Lyse?"

"Fine." She gave him a tight smile.

I took a swig of beer and couldn't hide my shudder.

Blake's chuckle was low and deep, resonating in my toes. "Not a fan of the brewsky?"

"It's great," I lied.

Elyse latched onto my elbow. "I want you to meet Hailey."

Blake shook his head as he smirked. "Catch you later, Jess."

I allowed Elyse to lead me away, but I knew I wanted to talk to him again. My spine tingled, and when I looked back, his eyes still tracked me. Woo! Eye candy sugar rush.

"Elyse!" a girl shouted, grabbing her for a hug.

A little while later I was chatting with a couple of juniors on my new team when a commotion at the front door drew my attention. A red-haired woman in a business suit entered, and the second I noticed her earpiece, I gasped. Why was Secret Service at a college party? Had someone threatened my family? When I saw a spike of black hair behind her, I had my answer. Mateo was here!

A blond agent swept into the room, and as he neared me, I tapped his shoulder. He whirled to face me. When I noticed the alarm in his eyes, I jumped back. "Johnny, it's me!"

His eyes flashed with recognition. "Miss Monroe. You've, ah…" He looked me over. "Grown up."

"It's so good to see you!" I'd spent over three months with him before the election, and I bounded into his arms for a hug. I felt him stiffen before he chuckled and patted my back. He let me go and scanned the scene around me. Elyse and the two juniors I'd been talking with gawked at us.

"How're you liking Highbanks, Miss Monroe?"

I'd missed his warm, blue eyes. "It's amazing." From the corner of my eye, I caught movement. Mateo now stood nearby, with the redhead behind him. He frowned at Johnny and me.

I gulped. "Hey, Teo."

His frown morphed into a smile, and I noticed a dimple on his right cheek. "That's what Dane calls me."

"Is that okay? I mean, I wouldn't want to use a name you hate."

He nodded. He'd shot up in height since I'd seen him.

"Mr. Ramirez, please join Agent Kennedy so you're not out in the open." Johnny pointed to a corner where the redhead now stood after clearing the area of partygoers.

Mateo's dark eyes studied me. "Will you…come with me?"

"Sure." I followed them. As I passed by Elyse, I waved at Mackenzie next to her. They both looked impressed.

We stood near the wall with the agents a few feet away, barricading us from the prying eyes of the party. When a new song started, a girl screamed and started to dance. Just like that, we were no longer the center of attention, and I let out a breath.

I turned back to focus on Mateo. He had a five-o'clock shadow and perceptive eyes that seemed to see through me.

"Why're you here?" I asked.

He blinked at me for a moment, and I felt the urge to brush away the black hair hanging over one of his eyes. Finally he shrugged. "Probably stupid to come, drag Secret Service here. I'm not an athlete or anything."

"Did you know I was here?"

He nodded. "Dane told Lucy, and Lucy told me. I just thought I'd say hi, but she didn't want me to come—said it was too dangerous." He shrugged again. "Obviously, I didn't listen."

Mateo glanced at the beer in my hand, my second of the night and just as nasty as the first.

"Oh, you want one?"

He shook his head. "Somebody will take a photo of me drinking and use it to embarrass my dad."

"That's awful." I couldn't imagine dealing with such scrutiny. And now that I thought about it, standing next to a Ramirez put me in the spotlight, too. I didn't want to get into trouble with my coach, so I set the can aside.

"Everyone here's a swimmer?" he asked.

"Most of them, I guess. I heard there were some rowers, but I haven't met any."

"When do you start practice?"

"Not sure. We have a team meeting and physicals tomorrow, but we'll be in the water for sure by the time school starts."

"Three days." He shook his head. "What are you majoring in?"

I smirked. "You sure ask a lot of questions."

His eyes widened. "*Lo siento.* Sorry, I, uh…"

"*No problema.*" He was so cute! "I'm majoring in art."

"Really?" His head cocked to one side like he was surprised. "What medium?"

"Not sure. They told me it'll be tough to swim and major in art, but I have to try. Maybe painting? Or three-D? What about you? What do you want to major in?"

"Music performance."

"Wow." He was artistic, too.

"Hey, Jess?"

I turned to see Blake peering around Johnny. "Wanna call the dogs off?" He tilted his head toward Johnny, who didn't look pleased. "I got you a real drink." He held aloft a glass of clear liquid on ice. "You want it?"

Smoking-hot boy was offering me a drink? Of course I didn't want to turn him down. "Sure."

Johnny's mouth set into a firm line as he let Blake through.

I took a sip through the small straw and tasted sweetness and lime…and a lot of alcohol. "Vodka tonic's my favorite."

Blake's face lit up. "I like a girl who knows her booze." He knocked back a swig of his own drink.

I realized Mateo was frowning again. "Uh, Teo, this is…Blake, right?"

"Blake Morrell." He shook Mateo's hand. "The president's son at my house. Epic. Why are you slumming with us commoners?"

Mateo started to speak, but Blake interrupted him. "How rude of me. What can I get you to drink, man?"

"I'm good," Mateo said.

Blake squinted. "You don't drink?"

"I…" Mateo looked at me for help.

"He doesn't want to get caught drinking underage." I looked around as I lowered my vodka. I didn't want to get caught, either.

"How old are you?" Blake demanded.

Mateo raised his chin. "Eighteen."

That was my age too, and I smiled.

Blake laughed. "Really? You look fifteen." He shook his head, and Mateo's eyes narrowed. "But it's a stupid law. If you're eighteen, you're old enough to die fighting for your country. You should be able to drink."

I agreed.

Blake draped his arm across my shoulders, and I smelled his musky aftershave. "This one gets it." He gestured to me. "Swimmers are strong. They can handle anything. Right, Jess? Five four-hundred IMs, descend one to four, number five all-out. Piece of cake."

I watched Mateo inch back, uncertainty flitting across his face.

"Swimming isn't everything," I said feebly as I took another sip. Blake's body heat was getting to me, and I felt sweat beading at my temples.

"I better go," Mateo said.

Crap! I didn't want him to leave. I wiggled out of Blake's hold. "You don't have to."

"It's okay." He gave me a sad smile. "Lucy was right. I don't belong here. I'll see you around."

"Teo —"

But he'd already signaled his agents, who led him to the door.

"Glad the kid knows his limits." Blake took my hand. "C'mon. I want to show you something."

I felt dizzy — how much vodka was in my drink? I allowed myself to be tugged along up the stairs, careful to climb each one without falling. At the top Blake pulled me into a room and shut the door. *Ah.* A blessed decrease in music volume up here.

I swayed a bit as I took in the navy duvet on the bed — a neater space than I expected for a college boy. "Wow, I'm tired."

"Yeah, move-in day can take it out of you."

That must've been it.

"But now the real party starts." He grinned as he crossed over to his dresser. After closing the drawer, he held up a small cigarette. "Time to get high, baby."

Oh, shit. That was a joint? I swallowed.

He sat on the bed and patted the spot next to him.

"What about drug tests? I don't want to get in trouble."

He shrugged. "They never test the freshman athletes. You'll be fine." When I remained perched by the door, his eyebrows drew together. "C'mon, Jess. I was sixth in the country in the fifty last year. You really think I'd do something to jeopardize my career? Studies show weed helps your lung capacity. You'll see. It actually helps your swimming."

The bed *did* look inviting. I floated over to him and set my drink on the floor.

"I rolled this myself." He lit the joint and handed it to me. "This is your first time, right?"

I chewed on my lip and gave a small nod. He probably thought I was lame and naïve. I'd turned down weed in the past because I'd heard it would hurt my swimming, but now he was saying the opposite. "Smoking can't be good for you."

"Then why do they give it to cancer patients? This comes straight from the hemp plant, with lots of medicinal properties." He nudged my shoulder. "We're teammates now. I wouldn't do anything to slow you down. I just want you to feel how awesome this is; have a little fun."

The sweet, earthy scent invaded my nostrils. It was hard to think straight. *Should I?*

"Just relax. Getting high is so much better than getting drunk. No hangover, no calories. Breathe in and hold it."

I tried to hide the tremble in my hand as I inhaled the scalding smoke. Of course I started coughing, which made Blake laugh.

"You'll get used to it." He filched the joint from my fingers and took a hit.

We passed it back and forth several times—I lost count—and in a flash I found myself looking at the ceiling. When had I fallen back on the bed? The walls undulated around me as the air took on a hazy quality. Blake entered my line of vision, hovering over me.

"How're you feeling?" he asked.

I was too tired to speak. As my eyes closed, I thought I saw a smile spread over his face.

2
Mateo
★ ★ ★

Way to go, chico. My first college party couldn't have been more of a disaster. First a stud upperclassman swimmer thinks I'm a child, then he swoops in to steal Jessica away from me. And of course she liked him better. Who would want a sick, scrawny loser like me?

"Do you need anything from the store?"

I looked up to see Karen staring at me from the front seat. Next to her, Johnny turned the vehicle onto the main campus drag on our way back to the greenhouse, where I now lived with Lucia. My sister had nicknamed the house because a Highbanks professor who was an expert in green energy had lived there.

"Uh…" I shrugged. "I think I forgot to pack shampoo."

"We shouldn't stop," Johnny said. "Too many people out."

Karen took that in. "Could you use your sister's for now? I'll run to get you some tomorrow."

So I couldn't even enter a store here? Or attend a party unaccompanied? I'd thought security would be looser outside of DC. "This is how it's going to be?"

"'Fraid so, Teo." Johnny met my eyes in the rearview mirror.

Despite my frustration, I did enjoy hearing him use that nickname. It reminded me of Jessica. She'd looked so hot in that turquoise shirt. Her long arms were tan and strong, with the muscular curve of her triceps reminding me of her swimming talents. Lucy had told me Jessica was one of the top swimming recruits in the nation. Highbanks had been lucky to sign her. And her blond curls were so spunky. Since meeting her on the debate stage two years ago, I'd longed to tug one of those thick curls and watch it spring back. *Boing.*

She'd asked why I came to the party, and I'd considered telling the truth. I did. But I chickened out and mumbled something stupid. The truth? *I wanted to see you.*

Would she still have ignored me for that older guy if I'd been honest?

I sighed as we drove through the greenhouse gates. *Probably.* What on Earth did I have to offer compared to that suave swimmer shithead? A lifetime of nurses and needles could hardly compete.

"Come see me before bed," Karen told me as we walked in the house.

Johnny looked up after resetting the alarm and waggled his eyebrows.

I rolled my eyes. Coming from any other woman, that comment would be full of sexual innuendo. But I knew Nurse Practitioner Karen just wanted a blood sugar check.

"Thanks, but I got it."

Karen frowned. My parents had encouraged me to leave my endless diabetes care up to her so I could focus on school, but I wanted to do things myself.

"Since you've refused to get the pump, I thought we'd agreed *I* would check your blood sugar," Karen said.

I shook my head. "I never agreed to that, especially at college."

Johnny slid his hands into his pants pockets. "Hey, Kar, how 'bout we table this discussion for later? We should go review the latest death threats."

"*Death* threats?" Lucia paled as she looked from Johnny to me. I hadn't seen my sister enter the foyer. She held our cat, Escuincle, in her arms.

"Hey, Lucia." Johnny grinned. "Security threats, I should say. Just a little joke I have with Mateo. He thinks sniffing out terrorist plots is a cool part of my job."

Lucia glared at me. "Yeah, real cool. Hilarious."

"C'mon, Lucy, lighten up." I reached out to pet the cat, and he leaned into my touch. "How're you liking your new home, Squinks?" Sated purrs were his only response. Our older brother, Alejandro, had been the one to name him Escuincle—Spanish for brat. Señor Squinks wasn't very fond of Alex.

I headed to the kitchen with Lucy on my heels, leaving my agents behind. As I checked out the pantry, I told her, "It's not like we can do anything about people trying to kill us. Might as well joke about it."

She watched me open a bag of chips. "Alex's scars aren't a joke."

My heartbeat kicked up as I crunched on a chip. Two years ago, in a hate crime against Latinos, a deranged man had shot Alejandro while he was here visiting Highbanks. I forced down a swallow of salty grease. "Having scars from getting shot? Now *that's* cool. Instant street cred."

Lucia's lips pursed. "Give me one of those, *idiota*."

I offered her the bag, and to my surprise, she grabbed a few—proof she'd come a long way in healing from her eating disorder.

"How was the party?" She bit into a chip, then offered the other half to Escuincle. He sniffed at it but turned his head and wiggled in her arms. She set him down. "You didn't stay very long."

I sighed as Jessica's sparkly top bedazzled my memory. "This is the part where you say 'I told you so,' huh?"

Her face fell. "You didn't have fun?"

"Adult chaperones and fun don't really go together. 'We're not normal college students,' remember?"

"I'm sorry, Matty. I shouldn't have said that. I shouldn't have told you not to go."

My eyebrows rose.

"Truth is…" She sighed. "I was really lonely my freshman year until Dane and I found each other. Until Maddie became my best friend, too. I'm lucky they understand what it's like to be protected by Secret Service."

Jessica wasn't under protection now, but she likely remembered how the government guardians squelched any sense of social life.

"Of course you wanted to go to the party," Lucia said. "There's nothing wrong with that."

I ate another chip. "But you were so against it. Why the change of heart?"

"Dane talked to me about it, made me remember what it was like to start at Highbanks. I don't want you to be lonely like me."

"Luz!" Dane hollered from somewhere deep in the house.

"In the kitchen!" She smiled at me. "I bet he's mad I left him watching the movie all alone."

"Where've you been?" The six-foot-eight blond giant stalked into the room, scowling at Lucia. "You're missing the trash compactor scene." He snatched the bag of chips from my grasp. "Hey, Teo."

Lucia's lips parted as she watched him stuff about ten chips into his mouth. "Gross."

"Whooaat?" He paused mid-chew.

I shook my head.

"Matty was eating those, *cerdo*."

Dane grinned at me, likely because his girlfriend had called him a pig. "Hey, was Jess at the party? Did you see her?"

"Yeah."

"Did she seem okay?"

I shrugged. "I guess."

"What was she doing? Did you talk to her?"

"She…was kind of busy."

Dane squinted. "Doing what?"

I chewed on my lip. "There was this older swimmer guy she was with. I don't know…seemed like I was intruding."

His blue eyes clouded as he stared down at me.

"It was a swimmer party, and I'm not a swimmer or anything," I added.

Dane was quiet for a few moments. "I wonder if I should go over there."

"What?" Lucia bumped his arm with her shoulder. "You are *not* going there."

"Why not? What if this guy's a creep or something?"

Her hands found her hips. "What'd you call Alejandro when he tried to interfere with my life?"

He closed his eyes. "Overprotective control freak on a fucking power trip."

"*Exactamente*. You don't want to be that way with Jessica, right?" She smoothed her hand down his forearm.

I considered the responsibility of being an older sibling. I only knew the experience of being bossed around by mine. They'd never seemed to care one iota how controlling they were, so it was strange to watch Lucia and Dane deliberate now.

"Let's get back to the movie," Lucia suggested, then looked at me. "Want to join us? We're watching Star Wars episode one."

"It's actually episode four," Dane said.

Lucia rolled her eyes. "Way to fly your geek flag."

"How dare you." He tossed the bag of chips onto the table and hoisted her off her feet.

She shrieked as he slung her over his shoulder. "Put me down, *gigante!*"

I shook my head as he manhandled my muscular sister, who was only a couple of inches shorter than me.

"Could a geek do *this?*" He patted her bottom affectionately as he turned toward the TV room. He glanced over his shoulder. "Coming, Teo?"

They seemed so happy together, and I didn't want to bring them down as a depressed third wheel. "That's okay. You guys go ahead. I'll unpack."

Lucia's upside-down position muffled her voice. "Feel free to change your mind!"

As he walked away, I heard Dane say, "You really think Jess is okay?"

I followed them out of the kitchen to hear Lucia's response: "It's gonna be a long year if you're freaking out about your sister the first night."

She was right. I sighed. It *would* be a long year if Jessica consumed my mind after only one night.

I headed to my new bedroom. It wasn't as big as the one I'd had in the White House, but it was more modern. It was painted a kind of olive khaki, and I liked the sage green duvet. I also appreciated the sleek, contemporary furniture. My acoustic guitar rested against the black chest. I'd already checked to make sure it was unharmed in the move.

I stacked some socks and underwear inside a drawer. My jaw clenched as I placed syringes and glucose test strips in the drawer above. Supplies to maintain my status as a human pincushion. It was probably time for me to check my blood sugar yet again.

Meow. I looked up to see Escuincle saunter into the room. He leaped onto my bed and curled up on the duvet. Lucia had been thrilled that I'd brought him from the White House. Mom had said she was glad to be rid of him and his destructive ways, but I knew she and Dad would miss the First Cat.

"Hey, Squinky." I plopped down next to him and scratched his ears. I wanted to hold him, but he only visited laps of his own volition. My mind drifted as his purr lulled me.

The room had been dark, the music thumping. Her pink cheeks had glowed. "Why're you here?" she'd asked.

I wanted to see you, I'd almost answered. Instead, I'd stared at her like a dumbass.

I heard a chord, followed by the phrase *shouldn't give in to fear.* The beginnings of a new song? I unbuckled my guitar case as more lyrics tumbled into my mind. *Shouldn't give in to fear. Shouldn't even be here.* But why not? I was a college student. It was a college party. I had every right to be there.

With a smile, I patted the signature on the guitar's shiny surface. I strummed some E minor power chords, stopped to jot down a few lyrics, and repeated the process countless times over the next half hour. Soon, I had the skeleton of a song.

Shouldn't give in to fear
Shouldn't even be here

The sequins they blind me
With bursts of possibility
This sequence can't find me
Too hard to figure out

It's all a damn calamity
I hoped to bring you into me
The truth is the absurdity:
I wanted to see you

I wanted to see you
I wanted to know you
I wanted to hold you
You didn't want me

Hey, man, you want a beer?
No way, can't have that here

The rules diminish me
Now the boy's got to flee
This game finishes me
Too hard to figure out

Where is divine divinity?
I hoped to bring you into me
The truth is my flaccidity:
I wanted to see you

I wanted to see you
I wanted to know you
I wanted to hold you
You didn't want me

You didn't want me. Usually I got a charge of energy after penning a new song, but tonight I only felt deflated. College was off to a stellar start.

My phone dinged with an incoming text. *Whoa*, Alejandro was still up? It was almost midnight.

How's it going at Highbanks?

It fucking sucks. But I didn't type that. My twenty-six-year-old brother didn't approve of swear words.

Isn't it past your bedtime?

Oye, it's Friday night. Not an old man yet.
What're you up to?

I didn't want to tell him about the party, either. He would definitely disapprove of the safety risks I'd taken.

You know, unpacking.

Getting settled in the greenhouse?

Yeah.

This conversation was boring the hell out of me, so I added:

Kind of tired, think I'm gonna go to bed.

Oh. Actually, I have a question for you.

If he dared to ask about my blood sugar, I'd whip my phone at the wall.

Maddie's with me. She wants to say something.

I squinted at my phone. His fiancée Maddie was at Johns Hopkins? Alejandro had just started his fourth year of medical school there, and I'd thought Maddie was still in Turkey playing volleyball for Team USA.

Hey, Matty, it's Maddie. ☺

I managed to smile at that.

**I'm psyched you're at my alma mater!
How's Highbanks treating you?**

**Not great. Went to a party…was a shitshow
bc of my agents.**

Once I pressed send, I kicked myself. Maddie was easier to talk to than my brother, but I had to remember he was right there with her.

I'm sorry. That sounds tough. ☹

**I'm back (Alex). You went to a party?
Did Lucy know?**

My shoulders tensed. Would he lecture me? When I didn't respond, he said:

Be careful, okay?

That wasn't too bad. He *had* been shot in public, after all.

Okay.

So, Maddie and I set a date tonight.

A date?

For the wedding!

Duh. They'd gotten engaged a year ago, so I'd sort of forgotten about the ceremony part.

That's great. When is it?

Your semester's over December 13, right?

I guess?

**We picked December 15.
In Cleveland. It's a Saturday.**

Why was he telling me all the details? Mom would make the arrangements to get me there. She lived for shit like this.

**It's not much time to plan, but we wanted
to seal the deal before Maddie plays in China
and I go on residency interviews.**

Okay, cool.

He didn't respond for a while, and I wondered if I should say something else.

Mateo, will you be my best man?

My mouth hung open. Hadn't seen that one coming. I'd thought for sure he'd choose his best friend. But maybe Jake couldn't leave Iraq or Afghanistan or whichever desert they'd stationed him in.

Not Jake?

**I want Jake to be a groomsman, if he can be there.
But Maddie & I want YOU to be my best man.
Will you?**

Of course, hermano.

Gracias. Means a lot to me.

*Me, too! (This is Maddie).
Thanks, Matty. *hugs**

I wondered who else they'd ask to be part of the wedding party. Maddie's brother, Braxton? He seemed pretty cool. Would her mother attend? She'd been estranged from Maddie and her brother for a long time, but I'd heard Maddie was trying to build a relationship with her.

Alex again. Is Lucy still up?

Probably not. She has weights tomorrow.

Man, I do not miss those early morning practices.

I'd never know what those were like. Then I realized why he was asking about my sister.

*Wait—you're going to ask Lucy
to be the best woman, right?*

**Maid of honor, sí, but don't tell her.
Maddie wants to ask her.**

Lucia was Maddie's best friend, so of course they wanted her to be maid of honor. I frowned. Had they asked me to be best man just so I wouldn't feel left out? But then I smiled.

*Are you obligated to ask Dane
to be a groomsman, then?*

Unfortunately.

My smile grew bigger. Alejandro and Dane weren't exactly BFFs, though my brother had been less hostile since meeting Maddie.

Maddie said I should "be nice."

Yes, you should.

**Hey, Dane's little sister
is at Highbanks too, right? Jessica?**

How could I forget?

What's she like?

Gorgeous, I thought.

Is she as liberal as her brother?

Don't know and don't care.

**Mateo, you can only get away
with being uninformed for so long.**

*I can't help it Dad's president.
How about I choose what's important to me?*

Another pause—he was probably typing a lecture.

**That's fair. You don't have to be involved in politics
if you don't want to.**

I gaped at my phone. My brother *had* chilled, that's for sure.

**You said you were tired, so I'll let you go.
Thanks for saying yes.**

You already are my best man in life.
But now it's official for the wedding, too.

What a cheeseball. I shook my head.

Congratulations, big brother. TTYL.

My first wedding. Was I supposed to bring a date? I knew who I wanted to ask. She'd probably wear a sexy dress, and I hoped it would be turquoise. That color looked incredible on her. But then I remembered the swimmer guy by her side tonight. She'd probably much rather date him than go to the wedding with me. *Ugh.*

3
Jessica
★ ★ ★

"Jess!" Something touched my shoulder and jarred me awake.

Can't breathe. I rocketed upright as I gasped for air.

Mackenzie jumped back and stared at me with wide eyes. "You okay?"

I blinked and looked around, wondering how I'd ended up in my dorm room. The blanket covering me had slid down when I sat up, and I kicked it fully off me now that I noticed how stifling hot the damn thing was. I was in my bra and panties, and my hair was wet like I'd been swimming. But I hadn't been in the pool, had I? "What time is it?" My throat killed. Did I have strep throat?

"Eight thirty."

"In the morning?"

She squinted at me, and I realized what a dumb question that was when I saw slats of sunlight reflected on the linoleum.

"*I'm* the one from another time zone, remember?" She continued to study me like I was a mental patient.

I attempted a smile as I lifted my hair from my neck. "Sorry." I tried to swallow but my throat was so dry. "Think I blacked out last night."

"You were passed out when I got back. I was looking for you at the party. How'd you get here?"

I have no freaking clue. The thought kicked up my heartbeat.

"I wasn't sure if I should knock you up."

I shook my head. I was totally disoriented, and now my roommate wanted to impregnate me?

"Oh!" She laughed, reading my confusion. "I mean wake you up. My dad told me not to use that slang in the States." Mackenzie crossed to her mirror and brushed her hair. "Kaylee asked if we wanted to hit breakfast before the team meeting." She gathered her hair in one hand.

"Who's Kaylee?"

She spun around and let her hair fall to her shoulders. "Our *teammate?* You're going troppo—you met her last night. She lives down the hall."

"Oh." I squirmed under the heat of her stare. She must've thought I was a total whackjob. "I met so many people—hard to keep them straight."

Her mouth relaxed. "Indeed. But I definitely won't forget Christian. Shit, hot! You remember him too, right?"

When I closed my eyes, the pressure inside my skull seemed to compound my fog. *Add a killer headache to the list.* How much alcohol had I consumed? As I massaged my damp temples, a flash of blond hair entered my mind. "Christian's a blond guy, right?"

She smiled as she slipped her hair into a ponytail holder. "You *do* remember!"

A knock on our door increased the pounding in my head. Mackenzie opened the door, and I lunged for the balled-up sheet at my feet as two girls entered the room. The taller, bigger one looked at me as I drew the sheet to my chin. "Jeez. Rough night, Monroe?"

Crap. She looked familiar, but I didn't know her name, just like I couldn't identify the thin blonde next to her. My face felt hot. "I'll be fine, Kaylee."

"Jessica!" Mackenzie stepped up and clasped the thin girl's shoulders. "*This* is Kaylee." She pointed to the brunette who had spoken to me, and now was scowling. "That's Emma, her roommate."

I winced. "Sorry, guys."

Emma grinned. "It's okay. You obviously had way more fun than I did last night."

"Obviously," Mackenzie said, then gestured to my desk. "Her phone's been buzzing nonstop, probably with messages from all the blokes she met. I'm surprised that didn't wake her."

When I glanced at my phone, my skin crawled for some reason. I gripped the sheet.

"Who's texting you?" Kaylee crossed over and picked up my phone.

My throat tightened, but I got out, "Don't—"

"It's that yummy senior, Blake!" Kaylee held up my phone with a triumphant stab in the air.

My heart and mind competed in a race of fear. My mind filled with an image of his leering eyes hovering over me... *Oh, God—had he...?* I couldn't finish the thought.

Kaylee marched toward me, and I flinched back. She gave me a strange look before handing me my phone. "Enter your passcode. There's good stuff in there. I want to read the rest of his texts."

My hand shook as I stared down at his name: *Blake Morrell*. When had I entered his number? Had he taken me home? Had he seen me in my underwear? Had he...*raped* me? Bile pressed up my throat. I didn't know what had happened, but I wanted his name off my phone. It only showed the beginning of a text.

Hey, did I do something wrong?
Why don't you text back?...

I looked up to find three swimmers watching me. My stomach roiled, and my eyes darted to the wastebasket under my desk. I forced down a thick swallow.

"You need a sickie?" Mackenzie asked.

I couldn't think straight, and I didn't want to falsely accuse a guy I barely knew. I just wanted to be alone, try to remember what happened, try to sort this out. I strained to swallow again. *Please don't barf in front of them.*

"I don't feel so well. Sorry."

Mackenzie's tone softened. "So you probably don't want to go to breakfast?"

"Hey, guys." Emma glanced at her phone. "We better go if we want to make it to the dining hall before the team meeting."

The team meeting? I touched my matted hair. I couldn't show up like this or my coaches would know I'd been partying. Plus, I smelled. I needed a shower.

"See you at the meeting, Jess?" Mackenzie asked as she headed to the door.

Kaylee frowned at me. "I want details. We can sort through those texts later."

Her parting comment reminded me of the messages I needed to read. Maybe they would offer a clue about what had happened last night.

Shudders climbed my spine once my teammates left. He was just a guy, right? Why did I feel terrified every time I thought of him? The feel of his touch on my body…I turned my hand, palm facing up, and peered down at my shaking wrist. Was that a faint bruise? I closed my eyes, and all I could feel was a dark shadow pressing down on me, my arms trapped over my head…

I tumbled out of bed to stop the image, but waves of dizziness hit me once I got to my feet. As I scrabbled for the headboard to steady myself, an ache pulsed from a place deep inside of me. I'd slept with my high school boyfriend, Duncan, a couple of times—fumbling, giggling, unsatisfying sex—and this was a similar sensation, though more painful. Maybe I'd had sex with Blake. No big deal. I stumbled to the wastebasket. *No.* The nausea, dizziness, and complete state of panic… this was different. This wasn't a playful roll in the sheets with Duncan.

Tingles of disgust crept up my scratchy throat, the threat of impending vomit. I heaved, but nothing came. "Please," I moaned as tears welled in my eyes. *Get it out of me.* I had to find relief from the pressure in my gut.

Hunched over, I looked at my phone. There were five texts from him. *Did he rape me?* The thought made my knees buckle, and I crumpled to the cool floor. That's when I noticed the oval bruise on the inside of my ankle. Where had that come from? My shaky fingers entered my passcode, pulling up his texts. The first one was from an hour ago.

Hey, Jess. Thanks for adding me to your phone, beautiful girl. Did you sleep okay?

Had I slept okay? More like passed out. Navy blue swam in my mind. Had I passed out on his bed? I read the next text.

> I thought we should wait,
> get to know each other first,
> but you kept coming on to me.
> You're so fine, I couldn't resist.
> You're a tiger in bed, baby!
> But your pussy's so tight.

My mouth dropped open in revulsion. I clutched the wastebasket and heaved. Tears rolled down my face as I threw up. I wanted to die.

The words of his texts circled my mind with each convulsion of my body. He didn't sound like a man who'd just raped me. So I must have seduced the first guy I'd met at Highbanks. *Awesome.*

Through blurry tears, I read the next text.

> You want me. I want you too.
> Only way this works is we're exclusive.
> I'm a little possessive that way. ☺
> When can I see you?
> I hope it's soon, baby.

I cringed at the thought of being with him, and soon I retched again. The dinner I'd eaten with Dane was long gone, and the empty heaves produced shock waves of pain, but they kept coming. Oh, God—what would Dane think? I didn't want him to find out I'd already slept with a guy.

It seemed like forever before my body stopped convulsing. Minor aftershocks coursed through me as I read another text. What was this, his fourth? Stalker much?

> Where are you? Maybe your meeting's later?
> On my way to ours—starts at 8:00.

I looked at my watch. 8:52. I had to be at Griffin Athletic Complex, way across campus, by 9:30. My throat burned with acid, and I wanted to crawl back into bed, but I couldn't miss our first team function. Sobs wracked my body as I clutched my aching belly. What would I say when I saw him? His last text had come at 7:59.

> Hey, did I do something wrong?
> Why don't you text back?
> Thought we had such a good connection.
> Talk to me, baby.

I threw my phone on the bed and pushed myself up on trembling legs. A cloak of blackness shrouded my vision, but I blew out a breath and managed to stay conscious. *Shower.* I needed a shower in the worst way.

As I grabbed my bathroom caddy, I made the mistake of looking in the mirror. Wilted mascara streaks stained my puffy cheeks, turning me into a character from a Tim Burton film.

Once I stumbled into the communal shower — thankfully empty — I started crying again. I didn't want to go to the meeting. I didn't want to see him again. I didn't want to be *here*. Cool water streamed down my face, mingling with hot tears.

Crap, I'm late. I wiped sweat off my forehead and tried not to wince as I hobbled into the athletic training classroom of the Griffin Athletic Complex. When my head coach frowned at me, I looked down as I scooted past her. Mackenzie's eyes widened when she saw me, but she gestured to an empty chair she'd saved. *Love my roomie.*

A small gasp escaped as I slid into the hard plastic chair. I'd never been so sore before, and hustling across campus in the heat hadn't exactly helped my situation. I felt Mackenzie's questioning eyes on the side of my head, but I kept my focus glued to the stack of papers sitting on the curved desk attached to my chair.

"Sign that one," she whispered as she pointed to the top paper.

I scribbled my name without caring what I signed. A guy in a suit and tie stood at the front of the classroom, droning on about NCAA policies. I wondered what the NCAA would think about me banging a teammate my first night on campus. Was that against the rules?

Mackenzie lifted one corner of the top page of my stack and whispered, "That one, too."

I followed her instructions to sign five more times. As I turned the pages, a few words registered about academic credits, extra benefits, and eligibility, but mostly it was a blur.

"Okay, this next form's about NCAA drug testing," the suit said.

I slunk down in my chair as I realized why my throat felt raw. Though the memory was hazy, I knew I'd smoked weed. My hand had seemed under someone else's control as I'd accepted the joint from

Blake and taken a hit. Maybe the beer, vodka, and weed together had made me pass out. *Fucking idiot!*

"The NCAA has two types of testing. If they test you on campus, they only test for performance-enhancing drugs."

Phew. No steroids for this *girl.*

"If they test you at NCAA championships, they're looking for PEDs *and* recreational drugs."

My stomach clenched until I remembered that wasn't until March of next year. No way weed would last over seven months in my system.

"Sign at the bottom to allow the NCAA to drug test you."

Did I have a choice? With my coaches perched near the door, no way I'd ask my question out loud. Like good little foot soldiers, all twenty-three of my teammates and I signed the form. I watched Elyse rest her ear on her hand, her elbow propped on the desk. The team captain couldn't have looked more bored. Following her lead, I tried to exhale. This was routine stuff that shouldn't freak me out.

"The next form is for Highbanks drug testing," he continued.

Freak-out, recommence.

"We conduct year-round random tests for recreational and performance-enhancing drugs. Know this: you *will* be tested. Don't roll the dice."

My heart hammered. *But they don't test freshmen.* Wait—where had I heard that? A niggling sense I was missing something tugged at the corner of my mind.

Jessica Monroe, I scrawled on the form. This signature looked shakier than the rest.

"Thanks, Bill," another guy said as he shook the suit's hand. This man looked younger than Bill, and not just because of his casual maroon short-sleeved polo and khaki shorts. With his smooth, earnest face, he could pass for being in college.

He turned toward his audience of college swimmers. "We also have some medical forms for you to sign."

I leaned toward Mackenzie and whispered, "Who's that?"

"Our athletic trainer. Can't remember his name."

I hadn't realized I needed to sign my life away just to swim here. After yet more forms, the athletic trainer said, "We have some great resources for you at Highbanks." He looked right at me. "Freshmen, you're probably too overwhelmed to remember much of this right now..."

Understatement of the year.

"...but I want you to meet our awesome support staff. First up's our sport psychologist, Dr. Valentine."

I sat up when a woman with straight blond hair and a polka dot shirt faced us. Dane had met with her on and off for a couple of years, and he seemed to like her. She was a little shorter than me with a solid build, like a softball catcher.

"Thanks, Zeke," she said. When she smiled, her hazel eyes crinkled. She wore a silver necklace with a huge medallion. "Hey, swimmers! I'm Carly Valentine. How y'all doing this hot August day? Who wishes Highbanks had an outdoor pool?"

Laughs and murmurs echoed around me, but I scowled. Plunging into cold water in the sunshine sounded exquisite right now. Stanford and USC had wooed me with their gorgeous outdoor pools, but I was kind of scared to go to college two thousand miles away from home. And after Highbanks had hired Coach Fredericks last year, Mom thought I would enjoy swimming for a female coach.

"Well, I can't offer you a sunny swim, but I *can* offer you free counseling at Sports Medicine," Dr. Valentine continued. "Quite a few student-athletes have met with me over the years. We talk about mental toughness behind the blocks, so you're not too pumped up or too chilled out, or other stuff like managing stress and relationships."

Judging by last night, I definitely needed help with relationships. But I didn't want anyone to know I'd jumped into bed with the first guy I'd met. The media hadn't cared as much about Dane and me since Mom lost the presidency, but she was still a high-ranking senator, and I didn't want to embarrass her.

Now the sports dietitian was talking. She was tiny—probably a former gymnast. "I love working with swimmers," she said. "I was a diver at Highbanks."

Ah. Swimming and diving were often lumped together as one sport, but the two activities were oceans apart. I couldn't dive gracefully for the life of me, and no way I'd even jump off the ten-meter platform, much less do flips from that crazy height.

"With your intense training, it's hard for swimmers to meet their nutritional needs. I can develop an individualized plan for you."

Now that she mentioned it, I would typically be starving after skipping breakfast. But my stomach was still in a tight ball, clenched by nausea. I closed my eyes.

When the meeting finally ended, we had to wait our turn for physicals. As I stepped into the hallway, I watched my coaches walk out of the building. They'd just informed us we had an optional practice in the afternoon, and I hoped I would feel better by then. Puking in the gutters wasn't exactly a way to impress my new team.

Mackenzie asked, "Why are you limping?"

"Um." I blinked rapidly as I tried to come up with a lie. "I carried in so many boxes yesterday. My hamstrings are killing me."

"You should've used the carts they have in the dorm. I got mine chockers with all my crap."

"Good idea." Thank God she hadn't been in the room when we'd wheeled my cart in.

Elyse leaned back on the wall next to me. "Optional practice, my ass," she grumbled. "We'll catch hell if we're not there."

Mackenzie laughed. "Good to know swim coaches are the same in America as in Australia."

Kaylee sidled up to us. "How many yards a day would your team swim, Mackenzie?"

"Meters. Around twelve K, more if Coach was in a ripper mood."

"What happened to you last night?" Elyse asked me.

Her question startled me. Mackenzie and Kaylee continued their conversation, but Elyse kept staring. "I went home, I guess."

"You guess?"

My face flamed. "I think I blacked out. Kind of embarrassing."

"But you didn't drink that much."

"I know, it's weird. Maybe I was just tired or something."

She frowned, then after a beat she grinned. "Who knew a Republican could be so cute."

"Mateo?" When she nodded, I smiled, too. I wondered what he'd done the rest of the night.

"So he has to travel everywhere with Secret Service? That would get old, real fast."

"It does." I sighed. "Johnny—one of Mateo's agents—he protected me before the election."

"Wild. He's kind of hot, too, but Mateo…*yum*. He could turn me into a cougar."

I smirked. "You're not *that* much older."

"Nah, I'm over the hill. Besides, it's clear he only has eyes for you."

When I whipped my head toward her, I reeled from dizziness. I tried to breathe. "He just wanted to check out a party, like a normal freshman."

"Uh-uh. Nothing normal about that jalapeño."

The prickling of hairs on the back of my neck stopped my chuckle mid-stream.

"What the fuck?" Elyse said as she looked over my shoulder.

"Jess."

That deep voice zinged a frisson of fear through me. I rotated to see Blake standing there. His royal-blue T-shirt hugged his muscular frame and brought out the blue in his eyes, but I didn't feel turned on. I felt trapped. I couldn't breathe.

"What're you doing here, Blake?" Elyse asked.

He ignored her and stared at me. "I want to talk to you."

My heart was like a jackhammer, and my feet wouldn't move.

"Elyse Jones, you're up." The athletic trainer stood at the door of the training room, holding a manila folder.

She looked at Blake, then at me. She shook her head.

"Elyse, let's go. The doc's waiting."

She blew out a breath and entered the training room for her physical.

"C'mon." Blake cocked his head down the hallway.

My throat hurt when I swallowed, and I shoved my hands in the pockets of my shorts to hide their tremble. As I passed my teammates to follow him, Mackenzie winked at me.

When we were alone, he reached out to touch my hair, and I quailed.

He frowned. "Your hair's still wet — did you shower?"

Why did he care?

"You didn't text me back."

"I was sleeping." My voice was raspy, and I cleared my throat. "Then I was late to my meeting, so I didn't have time."

He offered a lazy smile. "You live across campus from here. I'll drive you next time."

No way I'd ever get in a car with him, I realized. Then I wondered why I didn't want to. He was incredibly handsome, and a senior to boot. He was into me. Why did I want to get the hell away from him?

"You took me home last night?" I despised the tremble in my voice.

His eyebrows pushed together. "Don't you remember?"

"Did you take my clothes off?"

He leaned in really close. "We were naked together, baby."

Don't barf.

"You got nothing to worry about. You're beautiful. Can't stop thinking about you." He brushed his fingers down my arm.

I pulled back on instinct, but he inched closer. My heart exploded, and my queasy stomach rocked.

"When can you come over again?"

I shook my head. "I can't." My voice sounded shrill.

"We have amazing chemistry. You said we could be together." His forehead creased. "You can't change your mind now."

"I…" I licked my lips. How could I get out of this without causing a scene? I had to find a way to keep him away from me. "I'm just starting at Highbanks, and it's too soon—"

"I won't tell anyone about the weed."

I gaped at him.

"I won't tell your coach, if that's what you're worried about."

He'd tell my *coach?* I couldn't breathe.

"Jessica Monroe?" The athletic trainer beckoned me from down the hall.

Blood rushed in my ears as I turned back to Blake. "I gotta go."

"I'm not giving up on you, Jess."

I really wish you would.

"Text me," he demanded.

"Okay." *Hell, no. Get out. Get away.* I panted as I zoomed to the training room. When I approached, my athletic trainer held out his hand. "Ezekiel Woods. You can call me Zeke."

My legs shook as I followed him to a padded table. He asked me to hop up, and somehow I made it. He slipped a blood pressure cuff on my arm and pumped a few times. The suffocating pressure of the cuff suddenly mimicked the force of Blake pushing himself on me. The memory stole my breath.

Zeke frowned at the number. "Is your blood pressure always this high?"

4
Mateo
★ ★ ★

Thirty sets of eyes stared at Johnny and me as we entered the classroom. *Welcome to the first day of school.* At least Karen had stayed by the classroom entrance. She'd yelled at me this morning for forgetting to check my blood sugar the past few nights, and I didn't want to be anywhere near her right now. I already had a mom.

The room seemed pretty full, but a couple of guys in the back waved at me and pointed to some empty seats.

"Can we sit back there?" I asked.

Johnny's mouth twisted to one side. "Gotta do some recon first."

What did *that* mean?

He led the way to the rear of the classroom, and students gawked as we passed. *Take a picture, it lasts longer,* Joey would've said. I missed hanging out with my snarky best friend. But she'd gotten into Berklee — the premier school for musicians — and I had to settle for Highbanks.

The guys who'd waved at me smiled as we neared. One of them wore a Chicago Cubs baseball hat, and he looked up when Johnny said, "Please remove your hat, sir." He shrugged, then slipped it off to reveal shaggy, brown hair.

"What's your name?" Johnny asked.

"Fitch." His delivery was slow and easy. "Ryne Fitcherson."

Johnny tilted his head. "Spell that." As Fitch dictated, Johnny typed the name into his phone, then read: "Born in Chicago, moved to Cincinnati four years ago when parents divorced. One younger sister. Methodist. Three point two high-school GPA. Drummer."

Fitch's mouth hung open. Combined with the lingering indent of hat head, it wasn't a good look for him.

I heard something behind me, and watched Karen stop the professor as he entered the classroom. She spoke to him, then gestured in my direction. He frowned when he looked at me. *Great.* He probably didn't welcome the circus freak show I brought with me everywhere I went.

Johnny turned to the guy next to Fitch. His eyes looked Asian—Japanese, maybe? But his light-brown skin threw me.

Johnny nodded. "Name, please, sir."

"Who wants to know?" Japanese guy said.

"US Secret Service." Johnny's tone was clipped.

He ran his hand through his black hair. "And if I don't tell you?"

Johnny glanced at Karen, then back at Japanese guy. "We go for a chat outside."

That didn't seem to faze the guy, but Fitch shook his head. "Class is about to start. Just tell him, Itch."

Their names are Fitch and Itch? Locos.

"Ichiro," he finally said. "You know what? You coming in here and demanding to know our names, then broadcasting the information—it's plain rude."

"Nothing personal." Johnny scrolled through his phone. "We've done background checks for all the students in Mr. Ramirez's classes."

Itch eyeballed me. *Not my choice, dude.* I shifted the backpack on my shoulders.

"Ichiro Kahanawke," Johnny read aloud, though he did lower his voice so that I could barely hear him. He adjusted his earpiece. "Also from Cincinnati. Japanese mother. Father a descendent of the Mohawk tribe. Two older brothers. Four—"

"I know who the fuck I am," Itch growled.

"—point four GPA," Johnny continued.

A GPA of 4.4? Dang, he might be smarter than Alejandro.

As our professor fiddled with something at the podium, I noticed Karen's gaze bouncing from us to her phone and back to us. Johnny was probably reading aloud to let her know the names of the guys I'd be sitting next to. If he ever let me sit down. The entire class continued to stare at us.

"Plays keyboard and bass guitar." Johnny nodded at me. "Okay, they check out. Have a seat, Mr. Ramirez."

I slid into the chair next to Itch, and Johnny sat on the other side of me.

Itch leaned across my desk to glare at Johnny. "Mateo seems cool. He can sit with us. You, not so much."

Johnny stared straight ahead.

"We're kind of a package deal," I said. "Sorry."

Itch drummed his fingers on the desk, then sat back in his chair.

"How long you been playing bass?" I asked.

He rolled the tip of his tongue along the inside of his cheek. "Since the band started. We didn't have a bass guitarist, so I had to teach myself."

"You're in a band?" I'd die to be in one.

"With Fitch." Itch's thumb popped toward his bandmate, who was wearing his Cubs hat again. "Started a few years ago in the 'Nati."

What the heck was the 'Nati? I gauged Itch. "You're the lead singer?"

Fitch chuckled.

"Fuck, no," Itch said.

"His voice is like a honking goose straining to take a dump," Fitch offered. "*Ehreehreeuh.*" He tensed his arms at his side and squeezed his eyes shut.

Not a visual I need right now.

Fitch dropped the pooping-goose act. "I'm backup vocals. Our lead—he's still in Cincinnati. He's too stupid to go to college."

"What's your instrument, man?" Itch asked me.

"Vocals and guitar."

"Acoustic or electric?"

As I leaned toward Itch, my heart fluttered. Joey played the flute and could talk nonstop about classical music, but I'd never had the chance to discuss my kind of music, my passion, with anyone before. "Mostly acoustic. I play a steel-string Ovation."

"Ovation?" Itch cocked his head. "That's kind of old-school. Where'd you get it?"

I paused. Here I was trying to fit in like a normal college student, and answering his question wouldn't help me much. Next to me, Johnny held his wrist to his mouth, likely saying something to Karen on the comm-link. Who was I kidding? I was *far* from normal.

"Uh, Neil Diamond gave it to me when he performed at the White House."

Both Itch and Fitch gawped at me.

"You met Neil Diamond?" Fitch asked.

I shrugged. "He's my dad's favorite. When he agreed to give us a private performance, my dad lost his shit."

Itch said, "Don't know which I'd want to see more—Neil Diamond sing or your dad lose his shit. Seems like *el presidente* is so cool under pressure."

I remembered Dad yelling when he'd caught me drinking beer last year. "He has his moments."

Itch sniffed. "What's that smell?"

"Probably you," Fitch answered. "It's called a shower. Use it."

"Communal showers aren't my thang. My petition still has a chance."

"They're not gonna let freshmen live off campus, dude." Fitch shook his head. "Give it up. You don't shower by tonight, and I'm throwing your ass in there."

"Empty threats." Itch looked down his nose at him. "You're, like, four feet tall."

"Hey, I'm five-five."

"Not something to celebrate, Leprechaun."

Fitch muttered, "Freakishly tall Japanese person."

Itch looked at me. "None of this dorm crap for you. You get to live in luxury, right?"

I shrugged. Living in the dorm would actually be fun if I could live near these guys. Or maybe near Jessica. I wondered what her first art classes were like.

Itch wrinkled his nose. "That smell's driving me crazy. It's, like, coconut or something."

I tensed as he leaned toward me, and Johnny must have sensed my unease because he straightened in his chair.

"It's *you*," Itch said. "What, you wearing girly lotion or perfume?"

Shit. "This is your fault," I hissed at Johnny.

He recoiled. "What'd I do?"

"You didn't let me buy shampoo. I had to use Lucia's."

Johnny tried to keep a straight face. "It's coconut-scented, huh?"

"Oh, baby," Itch said. "That coconut shampoo sure smells sexy."

Fitch laughed.

Traitors. "We're stopping at the store to buy guy shampoo."

"Not sure that's on today's itinerary," Johnny said.

"Do it," Itch ordered. "I'm sporting a woody from that smell, and that's not cool coming from another guy."

The professor spoke up. "Welcome to Music Two-Two-Two-One, Music Theory."

I turned to face him, careful not to move my head and waft out more coconut fumes.

"I'm Dr. Linton, and I've taught at Highbanks for twenty-three years."

He must have been older than my father, though his dark blond hair hadn't grayed yet.

"Meeting bright-eyed music majors is always an exciting time for me. You're full of optimism, unlike the jaded seniors I teach in my applied class." He grinned. "This semester we'll embark on a journey of melody, rhythm, timing, and harmony — the cornerstones of life itself, wouldn't you say?"

He walked to the podium to gather some papers. "Today we'll review the syllabus, so you know what to expect. I see some of you have your laptops up, maybe open to the syllabus on CougarNet?" He hoisted the papers above his head. "But I have print copies for you. Go ahead and power down those computers."

Itch groused as he turned off his laptop.

"I find my students pay much better attention without screens in their faces." Dr. Linton distributed the printed syllabi. "Did you know students retain lecture material better when they write the notes instead of type them?"

Yeah, I do. Alejandro had learned that during his neurology rotation. He'd shared all kinds of study tips. *Lucky me.*

When the class ended thirty minutes later, it was time to head to math. On the way out, Itch clasped my arm.

"I want to see that Neil Diamond guitar. Weston's coming up this weekend to rehearse. Can you stop by?"

Ripples of happiness flowed over me. "Sure."

"Awesome. What're your digits, dude?"

I turned to Johnny, who frowned. For security purposes, very few people had my cell phone number.

"How 'bout you give me your number, and we'll get a hold of you," Johnny said.

When Itch hesitated, I wondered if he'd put a kibosh on the whole thing. But then he rattled off his number. Maybe the start of my first Highbanks friendship?

After two more classes, my cat and I sprawled on my bed. Lucia wasn't kidding about naps being the best part of college. When there was a knock on my door, I groaned.

Karen didn't wait for me to answer, but marched in and prepared a glucose test strip. I was too tired to fight her. Escuincle, on the other hand, growled.

"Good cat," I said, as she pricked my finger.

A moment later, she shook her head at the result. "Sixty-eight."

"That's not that low."

"Eat something before you take a nap." A protein bar materialized in her hand.

My eyelids weighed a ton. "Too tired."

"You're tired because you haven't eaten. We need a better plan if you're going to have three classes in a row multiple times a week."

To get her off my back, I accepted the bar and took a bite. *Gross.*

"Come to the kitchen when you wake up. I'll make lunch."

I closed my eyes once she'd left. Bossy much? It hadn't surprised me when I heard she'd been in the Navy before the Secret Service. Squinky's purrs lulled me as I sank deeper into the mattress...

The shrill beep of the smoke alarm woke me, and I bolted out of bed. Was the greenhouse on fire? But where were my agents? I jogged to the kitchen, where Karen waved her hand over a pan on the stove, which only seemed to amplify the smoky haze. "Take out the damn battery!" she hollered into the TV room.

"I am!" Johnny stood on a chair as he fiddled with the smoke alarm.

Finally, the piercing blast stopped. Karen glanced at me. "Sorry." She shoved the pan to the back burner. "I was trying to make quesadillas."

"Oh." I coughed. "I thought there was a fire."

"Should've known it was Karen cooking again." Johnny smirked as he walked through the kitchen.

Karen narrowed her eyes. She'd already burned one meal since we moved in.

"It's the thought that counts, right?" I opened the freezer and pulled out some burritos.

She gave me a small smile. "Right. Leave those burritos out, and I'll heat up one for me."

"And one for me, too!" Johnny hollered from the other room.

She shook her head. "Jerk insults my cooking then expects me to make him lunch? Fat chance."

Once I removed my steaming plate from the microwave, Karen said, "Hold on." She brought over the pan and lifted the edge of the charred tortilla to reveal gooey cheese, chicken, mushrooms, and zucchini slices. She scooped some onto my plate.

Actually, the quesadilla innards weren't bad — just a little smoke-flavored. I'd eaten most of them and had started on my burrito by the time Karen and Johnny joined me at the kitchen table. Despite her protest, she'd made a plate for him, too.

"Did you grow up in poverty, Karen?" he asked.

Where did that question come from?

She eyed him warily, like she'd had my same thought. "Why do you ask?"

"Oh, sorry. Didn't mean to pry. Just noticed you don't let food go to waste, and wondered where that came from."

She grunted. "Irish Catholic family, seven siblings. Dad worked as a beat cop, and Mom stayed at home. What do *you* think?"

"I think you learned the value of food early on."

I looked at her. "Is that why you shove food at me all the time?"

"No. I do that when you skip meals, like you know diabetics shouldn't do." She stared at me until I took another bite.

"Where are you in the birth order?" asked Johnny. "Wait—let me guess. Oldest, right?"

Her eyes narrowed. "How'd you know that?"

Because you're bossy.

"Because you take care of people," he said.

Judging by the way her fair skin glowed, his response was much better than mine would've been.

Johnny continued. "Sometimes if feels like Teo and I are your younger siblings, and you try to take care of us."

"Lord knows what you two would be up to if I didn't." She cut a neat piece of burrito and popped it in her mouth.

"I think we'd be okay," Johnny said. "We have the backup team, too."

Two agents lived in an apartment between the greenhouse and campus. I saw them once in a while, but mostly they operated behind the scenes in coordinating protection for Lucy and me.

"There's a reason they're the *backup* team." She wrinkled her nose.

Johnny dipped his chin. "You should give them more credit."

"You guys bicker like an old married couple." I shook my head. "Hey, why do all our protection teams have a male and a female agent? Alex has Brad and China, Lucy's got Frank and Allie, and I'm stuck with you two."

"The director likes it that way for our younger protectees," Johnny said. "Sort of like a second mom and dad."

"One's enough," I grumbled.

"We'll try to stop arguing like we're married," Karen said. She dipped her chin as she aimed a stern look up at Johnny

"She only wishes she could bed a young stud like me." He grinned.

They did look about twenty years apart. "How old are you?"

He shrugged. "Almost twenty-six."

My eyes bugged. "You're younger than Alex? So you were only what — twenty-three? — when you were protecting Jessica?"

"You haven't heard about Wonderboy?" Karen asked.

"I guess not."

"Johnny was on Senator Monroe's advance team right after he finished training at Glynco. He busted up a terrorist plot to bomb her campaign bus. When Senator Monroe found out, she asked him to protect Jessica."

I'd considered Johnny sort of immature and sort of awkward at times, but never a super agent. "I hadn't heard that story."

"That's because our boy's modest."

Johnny looked down as he shoveled in a bite of burrito.

"How'd you bust up the plot?" I asked.

He finished chewing and shrugged. "Idiots left a trail on social media. Anyone could've figured it out."

"But *you're* the only one who did." Karen rose and took our plates to the sink.

Johnny sat back in his chair and patted his belly. "Bastards are getting sneakier these days, encrypting their messages."

I wasn't sure I wanted to know that.

Karen returned with a test strip. "Okay? We forgot to test before the meal."

"Sure."

After seeing the number, she prepared an injection.

"Do you plan to work out later?" she asked.

I nodded. The gym in the basement was almost better than the one in the White House. But not as great as running outside, which I hadn't been able to do since Dad got elected.

Johnny looked away as she gave me the insulin. The injections seemed to make him uncomfortable. I noticed the dose Karen gave me was lower than normal, probably titrated for my exercise. I didn't need as much insulin on the days I used the treadmill.

Johnny looked back at me. "Want me to run with you?"

Fortunately we had two treadmills downstairs. "I think, given what I've learned today about your mad skills, I'd rather you work on the computer than on your fitness."

He grinned. "But once I identify the ISIS douchebags, I gotta catch them."

"True that. Four thirty work for you?"

"Perfect."

I supposed that meant I should study until then. I retrieved my music theory textbook from my backpack and sat at the kitchen table. *Tonal Harmony*. Sounded riveting. Escuincle stalked into the kitchen and leaped soundlessly onto a chair next to me. I scratched the top of his head, and he purred his approval.

After a while, I heard the beeps of the front door alarm resetting, then Lucia swept into the kitchen. Her hot pink T-shirt had a volleyball on it with the saying:

I DON'T SWEAT…I SPARKLE

She smiled when she saw me. "Hey, best man."

"*Hola*, maid." Lucia had been thrilled when Maddie had asked her to be maid of honor. And I cracked myself up every time I used her new title. "You want a frozen burrito?"

"We have a team meal in a couple of hours, before the game."

"You didn't tell me you had a game tonight. Do you want me to go?"

"Oh, it's just an exhibition game. The other team sucks. You don't have to waste your time."

I nodded.

"But I'd love if you could make our first home game this weekend."

I shrugged. "Sure." Then I remembered Itch's invitation. "As long as it's not the same time as band rehearsal."

Her eyebrows lifted. "You're in a band?"

"Well, no…but I met these two guys in music theory class…"

Lucia was positively beaming.

"What?"

"That's so great, Matty! You're making friends here!"

"Let's not go too fast. They already made fun of how I smell from your damn shampoo."

She laughed as she approached and took a whiff of my girly essence. "Yummy." She shimmied her hands through my hair, ruffling and tousling it. "Oh, Mateo! Your hair's so sensual."

"Stop it, maid." I ducked away but couldn't help smiling. Grabbing the cat off the chair, I held him up in front of my face. "Save me, Squinks!"

Lucia scratched under his chin and cooed, "*There* you are, Mr. Squinkster! How's my wittle muffin bratty baby?"

Gag. I hated her baby talk. I replaced Escuincle in his chair.

With a sigh, she sat at the table on the other side of me. "I think Dane left some shampoo here a while ago. I'll try to find it for you."

I pretend-gasped. "Don't let Dad find out Dane sleeps over."

"I know, right? Dad would need the White House doctor to revive him."

"I wonder if he'd be cool with Alex and Maddie getting it on, now that they're engaged."

Her head tilted as she studied me. "You know that ship has sailed, right?"

"Oh, right. You hear the details from Maddie."

Her nose scrunched. "Not the details, because…*eww.* But I do know they didn't wait long. Dad's not being realistic to think we'll wait until marriage. He's so archaic sometimes."

"So I'm the only Ramirez not having sex. Awesome."

She frowned at me. "That's a *good* thing. You're the youngest, and there's no rush."

I ignored her reassurance. "Just like I'm the only one who isn't a stud athlete."

"Matty, we've talked about this. Even with diabetes, you could've stayed in baseball or soccer."

I looked down.

"I know what you did," she said. "I know the sacrifice you made. Mom freaked out every time you went to the hospital, so you stopped playing sports."

I remembered Mom's whole body shaking when she held me after one collapse. I'd felt awful for making her so scared. "She couldn't handle it," I muttered.

"We'll never know." Her earnest brown eyes blinked up at me. "But, Matty, that's in the past. Now's the time you can focus on you. College is great for that. You don't have to worry about pleasing Mom and Dad, or Alex, or me, even. It's about finding your own path."

I twisted to look into the TV room. "Is there a hidden camera somewhere? Filming a motivational commercial?"

She gave me a look. "*Puta.*"

"Ohh, *that's* not very nice language from the president's daughter."

"I think even Dad would approve in this case, sarcastic ass." She removed her phone from her pocket, and a line creased on her forehead when she looked at it.

"What is it?"

She blinked. "Maybe nothing. Dane's worried because Jessica hasn't returned his texts. She's probably just busy."

Probably busy with Suave Swimmer Shithead.

5

Jessica

★ ★ ★

A glob of yellow paint dripped down my thumb as my paintbrush swept under the foam curlicue. I didn't bother to wipe it off. The chlorine bath that awaited me in a few hours would clean my skin.

Other than the soft music from my phone, Hopkins Hall was so quiet at night. I relished the solitude. It had been a little less than a week since the swimmer party. Since Blake...

"Great movement—"

I jumped at the sound of a male voice, and the brush flew across my face.

"Damn!" The guy stepped back from my table, his brown eyes huge. "Sorry 'bout that. Didn't mean to startle you."

My heart thrummed, and my body shook. I panted like I'd just swum a race.

"You've got some paint..." He gestured to my face, then brushed his fingers across his cheekbone. "Here, um..." He swiveled around and walked to his table, then returned with a cloth.

I shrunk back when he reached for my face.

"Oh." He held his hands up like I had a gun on him. "Here?" He handed the cloth to me.

He must think I'm insane. I forced a swallow down my dry throat and accepted his offering. After I scrubbed my cheek, I attempted to smile. "Thanks. Sorry."

"Should've known better than to come into your space at two a.m."

I glanced at my watch. No wonder I was so tired.

"You were really into it. I admire your focus."

It took me a moment to realize he might be flirting. He was about my height, with light brown hair gathered in a tiny man bun. His shirt was bright orange, and he wore skinny jeans held up with a braided belt. Gay, maybe? Or art student hipster?

He continued, "Me, I've barely started my sculpture." He pointed at pieces of foam board on his table. "But you're almost done, and it's not due till next week. Why're you here so late?"

Because I don't want to go to sleep. "I've got a busy schedule. Trying to stay ahead of the game."

"You work, too?" He slid his hands into his pockets.

"Work?"

"I teach yoga at the PAC."

Yoga? My gaydar beeped louder — Mom wouldn't be pleased by my stereotyping. The PAC was the Physical Activity Center, located right next to the natatorium.

"I guess you could say I work there, too," I said. "My teammate Elyse complains that swimming for your scholarship is just like a job."

"A swimmer, huh?" He offered his hand. "I'm Van, by the way."

I took a breath, then shook his hand. "Jessica."

His smile lit up his eyes, and I felt my shoulders lower an inch as I exhaled. A thin, artsy, man-bunned yoga instructor wasn't a threat, right?

"I wasn't bullshitting you, Jessica." Van pointed to my sculpture. "Your piece has good motion."

I'd cut the foam into a tall shape with sweeping curves and whirling dervishes winding around and through it. It reminded me of a windstorm or hurricane, like the sculpture was about to lift off the table and spin across the room. One sharp line that stabbed through the midsection was now bright red after two coats of paint. I'd been working on the top curves when he'd scared me.

Van stepped closer and cupped his hand under a yellow curlicue. "Looks like you're running from something."

What? "That's not *me*."

"It's not?" His hands circled toward his chest, mimicking the curves on the top of the statue. "These spirals here...they're your curly blond hair, right?"

My stomach tightened. "I..."

"And see, this is your leg." He pointed down to an angled piece of foam I'd painted denim blue. "Like you're running away, trying to get the hell out of there."

That *did* look like a knee. A leg poised to fight, to run, to flee. Just like the nightmares I'd been having—no matter how fast I ran, I couldn't get away. As I imagined the dark shadow chasing me, my entire body tensed. No fighting or fleeing for me. All I could do was freeze.

"You okay?" His head tilted, and his eyes scanned my face.

How much time had passed as I'd stood here like a zombie? "I need to go." I lunged for my backpack and headed for the door. "Got practice in a few hours—need to sleep."

"Aren't you gonna clean up?"

I spun around and noticed the caked paint drying on my abandoned brush. "Oh." My feet were pulled to the exit, but I knew it was bad form to leave out paint supplies. Professor Schneider had lectured us on the importance of taking care of our space.

"I'll do it for ya," Van offered.

I blinked at him. "You sure?"

He shrugged. "It'll give me a good reason to procrastinate some more." He frowned at his table. "See you in class tomorrow."

"See you!" I had to get out of there. I sprinted down the stairs and flung open the door. The humid day had bled into a cooler night, and I gulped in fresh air as I leaned against the brick. Spasms overtook my chest like that time I'd swum in Lake Michigan in early June, when the lake still remembered being frozen in the winter. My hands shook as I guided headphones into my ears, then connected their wire to my phone.

I looked both ways before starting toward my dorm. Highbanks wasn't far from downtown, and Mom had warned me about the crime statistics. Maybe it wasn't the best idea to walk alone in the middle of the night, especially with earbuds in. *Screw it.* I had other things to worry about. Like trying to slog through four-thousand meters without sleep. My feet dragged just thinking about it.

As I opened the door to our room, the light from the hallway slanted across Mackenzie's loft bed. Her face was turned toward me, her jaw slack against the pillow. The soft sound of her breaths filled the room. I bet she was drooling. I'd discovered she slept like a champ during the countless hours I'd stared at the ceiling. *Bitch.*

I crept inside and winced when the door squeaked as it closed.

Her breathing stopped, and she rustled under her sheet. "What time is it?"

"Two thirty." I set my backpack down.

"How're you going to wake up for practice in three hours?"

Excellent question.

"Where've you been? Making out with Blaaake?"

I closed my eyes as my heart rate spiked. Mackenzie couldn't stop talking about the "fine senior" pursuing me. I couldn't bring myself to admit we'd had sex.

When I didn't answer, she said, "You left your phone, so I couldn't ring you up."

"Sorry." Blake had texted so many times that I hadn't even looked at my phone the past few days. I clutched the hem of my shirt, but then realized it was pointless to change into my pajamas with practice so soon. After grabbing my shower caddy so I could wash my face and brush my teeth, I turned to the door.

"Could…"

I looked over at her. "What?"

"Could you take your phone with you next time?"

I glanced at the offending object plugged into the charger on my desk. "Why?"

"It kept buzzing when I was trying to fall asleep."

"Sorry." I gulped. "I've been a crappy roommate." Tears welled in my eyes, and I tried to fight them off. I was just so tired.

"No, you haven't—"

I was out the door before she could finish. I hoped she'd fall back asleep by the time I returned from the bathroom. I wasn't so good around people these days.

After taking extra long in the bathroom—I might have drifted off for a few minutes while washing my face—I exhaled upon finding Mackenzie's eyes closed when I returned to the room.

I glared at my bed. *Okay, who's going to win tonight? You or me?* My heavy eyelids drooped. It had been like this the past four nights: I was so exhausted I could barely stand, but when I climbed into bed, it was like I'd just downed five energy drinks. And the few times I *had* fallen asleep, nightmares had blasted my hope of peaceful rest to hell.

Maybe if we lofted my bed, it would feel different, cozier. Dane had promised to come over to help me, but I hadn't heard from him in a while. He was probably too busy with his classes, practices, and Lucia.

The bed looked so innocent, so inviting. I knew it was a trick, though, luring me in before keeping me up. My teeth clenched. I shook out my muscles and cracked my neck from side to side. *Let's do this.*

After sliding under the sheet, I had to admit how relaxing it felt to let my body sink into the mattress. My neck was sore from hunching over my sculpture, and my lats ached from a tough weight workout.

My watch alarm was set for 5:40, and I doubted I'd fall asleep before then. I prepared for another night of staring at the ceiling, kicking off the sheets, feeling lonelier than ever in the darkness...

Where was the freakin' door? I was in Hopkins Hall, and the door should've been at the end of the hallway, but instead there was a mural on the wall—a hot pink demon with a thousand tentacles swirling around it.

Excellent movement, I thought. *But I need to find the door.* I was late to something. Maybe practice? Coach would be mad at me.

I turned down another hallway, then one more. It felt like I was walking through thick, wet sand, each step sucking up all my effort. Eerie snake-charmer music drifted out of one classroom. I wiped my slick forehead.

Finally I found a door and stumbled outside into the black night. I looked down and noticed I wore wedge sandals with massive heels. No wonder I couldn't move quickly—the heels must've been four inches at least.

I heard a deep exhale behind me, and spun around, but nobody was there. *Practice.* I had to get to practice.

To the side, a cruel laugh echoed, rocketing fear through my veins. But again I saw nothing. I tried to hurry, but my girly shoes slowed me.

Then I felt it. The shadow behind me. I knew it was there. A sickening shudder crept down my spine, like someone had dropped an ice cube down the back of my shirt. *Run,* I breathed. But my legs wouldn't move. I lifted off my feet and started swimming through the air. The dark grass swayed below me as I flailed my arms in a freestyle sprint. My pace was agonizingly slow, and I knew he was catching up to me. *Faster.* He was coming—I heard him. When he grabbed my foot, I gasped.

I bolted upright, hyperventilating and panicked. I kicked my leg straight, and it thudded against the footboard. *Ow.*

My eyes darted around me. I was in my bed? It was a dream? As the shape of my dorm furniture slowly came into focus, I clutched the sheet to my neck. There was the dresser, and the small fridge on the stand.

When I looked over at Mackenzie and found her still sleeping, I exhaled. Thank God I hadn't woken her a second time.

I looked at my watch. 5:20. No point trying to go back to sleep now.

By the time Mackenzie's alarm blared, I was sitting on my bed, ready to walk to the pool. She groaned, then rolled over and looked at me. But she didn't say anything until she returned from the bathroom.

"I wish *I* could get by with such little sleep," she told me.

I closed my eyes. *I wish I could actually* get *some sleep.*

We hustled through the dark, quiet quad, slipped on our suits in the locker room, and made it to the pool deck before 6:00. Most of my twenty or so teammates were already there, sitting or stretching. We all wore the same black swimsuits with a Highbanks Cougar logo on the chest. Nobody spoke.

I unclenched my fists when I noticed the far end of the pool was empty. The guys' team must have had the morning off. The opportunity to avoid Blake's grins and stares made the morning slightly more tolerable.

"My arms are so sore," Emma said as she hugged them to her chest.

My entire body was sore.

"At least we don't have weights today," said Mackenzie.

Just two swim practices, I thought. It wasn't even September yet. Typically training would build in intensity throughout the fall, even though we'd start competing in meets in October, and culminate in hellacious practices over winter break. It wasn't uncommon to swim ten miles a day in late December. There was no way I'd make it, feeling like I did right now.

Our assistant coach, Mike Henry, emerged from the office onto the deck. He was tall and lanky, with light brown hair that stuck up at the crown, likely from bed head. I'd considered becoming a swim coach, but waking up before six every morning didn't sound like a dream career. He meandered to the white board and scribbled our warm up.

Kaylee muttered behind me, "Please let this practice be short."

I closed my eyes and silently echoed her prayer.

"We're getting our kick on this morning!"

I stifled a groan as I turned to see my head coach bounce out of the office. *Morning people...ugh.* Kathy Fredericks sported short, dark hair and wore the same polo and shorts combo as her assistant. Her broad shoulders were a testament to her excellence in the butterfly events years ago.

"We've got a great kick set for you," she said with a smile. "Isn't that right, Mike?"

He gave her the thumbs up. I'd noticed he didn't speak much.

"Great," Emma whispered. "So now my legs will be destroyed, too."

"Okay, in by the five!" Kathy shouted.

I glanced at the pace clock as I dragged my equipment bag over to the middle-distance lane. As I twisted my unruly mane to stuff it under a swim cap, Elyse plopped her bag next to mine. She also swam individual medley and shared my lane. I felt her stare.

"You don't look so good."

I shrugged. "Yeah?"

"You look exhausted." She squinted at me—she didn't like to wear her contacts for morning practice.

I tucked stray curls beneath the rubber cap. "Everyone looks exhausted at six a.m."

"Hold up!" Kathy yelled.

When had our athletic trainer come on deck? Zeke stood by my coach, along with a tall woman I hadn't met.

Elyse sighed. "Crap."

"What is it?" I asked.

Before Elyse could respond, Kathy said, "Michelle Farris is here from Athletics. Listen up, people! Michelle?"

"Would the following swimmers come with me." She looked down at the paper in her hands. "Cameron Myers, Elyse Jones…"

A junior next to us started laughing. I was pretty sure her name was Hailey.

"Shut up," Elyse hissed at her.

"And Jessica Monroe," the tall woman finished.

All eyes turned on me, and somebody said, "Oooo."

Elyse ripped off her cap. "This is bullshit. C'mon." She tilted her head toward our coaches and marched off. I hustled to catch up.

"Why's Hailey laughing?" I asked. "What do we have to do?"

"I get randomly chosen Every. Freaking. Time. And I've *never* tested positive."

I halted in my tracks.

Elyse turned around. "What?"

"We're getting drug tested?" I squeaked.

"Welcome to Highbanks, freshman."

"I thought freshmen didn't get tested."

"Where'd you hear that?" She scrunched her nose. "It's more like *seniors* shouldn't get tested. This is ridiculous." The panic must have shown on my face, because she patted my shoulder. "Relax. It's embarrassing to have someone watch you pee, but it's no big deal."

She hadn't seen me smoke weed with Blake in his room. This was a very big deal. I was going to lose my scholarship and embarrass my mother in the national media. My hands trembled as I slid off my swim cap.

A teammate I didn't know — she must have been the other girl, Cameron — walked ahead of us. We followed Zeke and the tall woman to the training room off the pool deck. Behind me, I heard splashes of my teammates diving in to start warm up.

Kathy's voice boomed behind us. "If you're not in by the five, we're staying late!" I heard rapid splashes after that.

We filed into the training room, and Zeke went to sit at his computer.

The woman turned to me first, and offered her hand. "I know Elyse and Cameron, but haven't met you, Jessica. I'm Michelle Farris, associate athletic director." As I shook her hand, I noticed her classy business suit and stylish jewelry. How did she pull off a polished look so early in the morning? "Welcome to Highbanks."

They sure had a crappy way of rolling out the red carpet. My stomach dropped.

"This is Debbie from the drug testing company," Ms. Farris said as she gestured to a mousy-looking woman holding an iPad. "This should be quick. We never have drug problems with women's swimming."

Until now.

Debbie handed us some forms to complete, then took photos of the bar codes that would label our urine specimens. "Chain of custody is very important," she said. I felt like I was in a courtroom, as the defendant of course.

I followed her to the unisex bathroom off the training room. When she asked me to take off my bathing suit, I tensed. Would I have to pee in front of her naked? Then she gave me a team sweat jacket to wear. It took a while for my bladder to get over its shyness, but soon I produced my dirty urine.

After running some tests on my pee, Debbie screwed a cap on the plastic cup and sealed it with my bar code sticker, all right in front of me.

In other words, she sealed my fate.

Once she released me, I couldn't get in the water fast enough. I'd probably be kicked off the team once I tested positive, so I had better enjoy practice now. All my Olympic dreams were being sucked down the drain. But practice was too tough for me to wallow in self-pity.

"Time for animal kicks," Kathy told our three middle-distance lanes.

What the fuck? Kaylee and I exchanged worried looks.

"Ten one-hundreds kick, your best stroke, on the fastest interval possible. Yeah, baby!" Kathy raised her chin and howled like a wolf, which made Elyse laugh. "Elyse, what's your interval?"

She grinned. "One thirty. Bring it on."

My eyes widened when I heard her response. That was *fast* for kick. I clutched my kickboard.

"Jessica, don't look so scared. You can hold that for breaststroke, no problem," Kathy told me.

My heart raced as I fake-smiled. I didn't want to let her down, but how the hell would I make that interval?

We had sprinted through seven hundreds, with me barely getting two seconds rest between each, when Kathy said, "Jess, hop out."

I swear I'm trying my hardest. She was going to yell at me. Tears prickled my eyes, but I blinked them away. My chest heaving, I pulled myself out of the pool and braced myself for a tongue-lashing. Instead, Kathy pointed to my athletic trainer. He stood next to a woman with a dark-blond ponytail.

Zeke waved me over. *Oh, shit.* Had they already discovered THC in my pee? It hadn't seemed to work that quickly when they'd drug tested me at US Nationals.

"I'm Tina, the trainer for volleyball," the woman said. "Dane couldn't get a hold of you, so he asked me to pick you up."

I stepped back. "Pick me up? Why?"

"He had an accident. He needs your help."

6
Mateo

★ ★ ★

Dang, it was loud in here. I'd watched Lucia play in the NCAA quarterfinals the past two years, where there'd been a lot of crowd noise, but I hadn't expected her first regular-season match to be so raucous. There were even cheerleaders. At least people didn't stare as much as they did when my parents were with me.

"How about over there?" Karen pointed to an empty section of the arena close to the opponents' fans.

I scanned the Highbanks' student section until I found Dane's blond head, sticking up above the other spectators in his row. "No, I want to sit with Dane." I headed that way, pleased when my agents didn't put up a fight and followed me. But when I got closer and saw who sat next to Dane, I stopped.

Jessica.

I would've arrived much earlier had I known she'd be here. I hadn't seen her for a whole week.

"Everything okay?" Johnny asked.

"Yeah." I resumed walking and tried to hide the stupid grin threatening to erupt.

But Jessica didn't seem as happy to see me. She'd turned to Dane, a curtain of curly hair hiding her face. They were arguing about something and didn't even notice me standing there.

"Dane?" I finally said.

He looked up. "Oh. Hey, Teo." He didn't crack a smile, and his tone seemed deflated. Crutches leaned against the seat next to him.

I looked at Jessica, and she rolled her eyes. "He's grumpy from his injury."

I nodded as I took in the black rehab boot on his right foot. "Lucy told me about it. You hurt your foot in the weight room?"

"Josh dropped a fucking forty-pound plate on my foot."

"Ouch." I sucked in air through my teeth.

Jessica stood. "And now I'm his chauffeur everywhere—can't get away from the grumpinator. Thank God you're here so I have someone else to talk to."

Her comment filled me with happiness. But when she clasped my wrist, the elation multiplied.

"Want to sit?" she asked.

My butt found the seat next to her in a nanosecond.

"Hey, Johnny." She waved.

He nodded as he and Karen took seats behind me.

There was a media whore on the court who turned his camera to us, but I ignored him. He didn't look our way for long because Lucia and her team jogged out from the locker room. The crowd roared when the home team took the court. I noticed Lucia's agents behind the Highbanks bench.

"Go, Luz!" Dane hollered.

Through all the cheers, she managed to hear his voice, and looked up at him with a grin. Her gaze drifted over to Jessica, and when it reached me, her smile widened. She patted her chest as she winked at me. Was she suggesting something with that wink? Had Jessica spoken about me to her and Dane? Her smile dropped when her coach said something, and she dashed to the huddle.

"Don't be an ass, Holter," Dane muttered. He'd never liked Lucia's coach.

I glanced at the boot on his foot. "So, your foot's broken?"

"Yep."

"Sucks, man. How long are you on crutches?"

Dane looked down. "Four shit-tastic weeks."

"Wow."

Jessica shook her head. "You'll be fine."

"No thanks to you," Dane said. "Why weren't you answering your phone?"

Her shoulders tensed as she looked down. "We already discussed this. I've been busy."

"Uh-huh." Muscles rippled in his jaw. *Right.*

She was obviously downcast about something, and I didn't like his sharp tone with her. Didn't they get along? They reminded me of Alex and Lucy going at it when they were younger.

Thinking about my brother, I remembered Alejandro staying home for a week or two after his elbow surgery in college. Talk about grumpy. He'd screamed at Lucy and me for making too much noise in the house, for having friends over, for *breathing*, basically. I'd been so relieved when he returned to TCU. But he hadn't returned as a promising baseball star. He'd never pitched again.

I studied Dane as he watched the teams warm up. He rubbed his thumb over the back of his other hand, and his mouth tightened. There seemed to be a longing, almost a hunger, in his eyes.

I cleared my throat. "You're gonna make it back for your senior season, don't worry."

His eyes darted to me, and he exhaled.

"When does your season start?" I asked.

"January," Jessica replied for him.

I cocked my head. "But that's four months from now."

Dane's face reddened. "*This* is the important time! You got to put the work in now!"

I recoiled. Jeez, what was his problem?

Jessica leaned closer, and I smelled clean chlorine mixed with a floral scent. She whispered, "Sorry he's being a douche."

She gave me a thin smile, then covered her mouth when a yawn overtook her. She shook her head, seeming to try to wake herself up, and blinked a few times. When I saw dark smudges under her eyes,

I took a closer look. Her blue eyes didn't sparkle like they had at the party. She wore dark jeans and a maroon Highbanks Swimming T-shirt that seemed to hang off her tall frame.

The announcer introduced the players, and I noticed the black and red uniforms of the opposing team. "Who's Highbanks playing?"

"University of Cincinnati," Jessica said.

Fitch and Itch were from Cincinnati. They'd continued to entertain me in class this week, and I couldn't wait for band rehearsal tomorrow. I was stoked I could make both the volleyball match and rehearsal this weekend, though waiting all week to meet the lead singer had increased my anxiety. What if he didn't like me? I so wanted a chance to join the band—if there *was* a chance.

"Ladies and gentlemen, please rise for the national anthem."

"Fuckballs." Dane gathered his crutches, then balanced on one foot.

Jessica and I shared a smirk and stood as well. I placed my hand over my heart and silently sang along.

"Very patriotic," she teased.

I glanced down at my chest, then over to her amused eyes. Her hands were at her side, and for the first time I felt self-conscious about covering my heart during "The Star Spangled Banner." It was just something we did in my family.

She asked, "Aren't you going to sing?"

I looked at her from the corner of my eye. "No."

"Thought you were a music major."

"That doesn't mean we belt out songs everywhere we go. And some of us don't sing at all." I thought of Itch.

"C'mon, sing."

I smiled. "No."

"You don't want me to hear your voice. I bet it sucks."

My mouth popped open. "Rude. Did *you* bring me a painting?"

"No." She leaned away.

"Thought you were an art major."

Applause and cheers ended the national anthem, and Dane collapsed back onto his seat. Jessica and I followed.

"Cou-cou-cou-cougars!" the cheerleaders chanted.

I shook my head. "Can't believe they're at a volleyball match."

Jessica huffed out a breath. "We *never* have cheerleaders at swim meets."

"When's your first meet?" I asked.

She seemed to stiffen. After a beat, she said, "October."

"How do you like your coaches?" Dane interjected. "Kathy and Mike, right?"

She looked down, her voice sounding sad. "They're great."

Dane nudged her shoulder. "You okay?"

"Yeah."

But she seemed as dejected as her brother had been a few minutes ago. I fought the urge to wrap her in a hug. She appeared to need one.

When the crowd cheered, I noticed the first game was underway. Cincinnati served, and a Highbanks player in the back row passed the ball. Another girl set the ball to Lucy, who spiked it down the line for a kill.

Dane stuck his index fingers in the corners of his mouth and whistled, blasting my eardrums.

"Damn, Dane!" I covered my ears. "That's louder than an air horn."

He chuckled. "Just want my girl to know I appreciate her skillz. Ain't nobody can block her!"

Jessica said, "He does that whistle thing at my meets all the time. The parents hate him for it."

"But you hear me during your races, right?" Dane's elbow nudged her. "Huh?"

She shook her head but smiled. "Especially during breaststroke."

I chewed my lip, wondering if I should admit my lack of swimming knowledge. My curiosity won out. "Why can you hear him more in breaststroke?"

"Oh. Well, your head's out of the water every stroke." She sat up and thrust her arms straight out in front of her with her thumbs locked together and her hands touching. Her head dipped between her arms, and I had to lean in to hear her. "So you're in this streamlined position, after your whip kick." She pushed her hands out at a forty-five-degree angle to her body, then pressed down her palms and scooped them to her chest as she kept her elbows high. At the same time, she lifted her face. "This is the part of the stroke where you breathe."

"And where I execute my rip-roaring whistle," Dane added.

She shot her hands forward and her head dipped once again, returning to her starting point. Then she dropped her hands in her lap, looked at me, and shrugged. "That's the breaststroke."

As she brushed a curl off her face, I realized I was grinning at her. She'd seemed to come alive during that little air-stroke demonstration. I would love to see her tall, lithe body power through the actual water.

"Hell, yeah!"

Lucia must have gotten another kill, because Dane did a fist pump. I was supposed to be watching the match.

"It all starts with a good pass," Dane said. "Kaitlyn's kicking ass."

"Is she the one with the spiky black hair?" asked Jessica.

"Yeah — the libero."

I nodded. Lucia had taught me the libero was a defensive specialist.

"But damn," Dane marveled. "That sophomore setter's the real thing. That set Alexis just pushed to Luz? Impressive. She's almost better than me."

Jessica and I looked at each other with raised eyebrows.

"Actually, she *is* better than me." He crossed his arms. "Considering I can't fucking play."

I wasn't sure what to say to him. Maybe silence was best.

When Karen tapped my shoulder, Jessica jumped. I scrunched my eyebrows as I studied her, trying to figure out her reaction, and she looked away.

"I'm getting you something to eat," Karen told me. "What would you like?"

Now that she mentioned it, I was feeling a little shaky. But I didn't want Jessica to think I was an invalid. "I'm good."

"You didn't eat much dinner," Karen said.

Johnny piped in. "Yeah, and you ran pretty hard with me today."

Jessica looked at me. "You run?"

"On the treadmill." I shrugged. "No big deal."

"Listen, I'm getting you something," Karen said. "Last chance to choose what it is."

"Fine." I blew out a breath. "You can get me a pretzel and a coke, as long as you get something for Jessica, too."

Jessica's head shot up. "Oh! That's okay—"

"I totally heard your stomach growling," I said. "Aren't you hungry?"

She looked sheepish. "Yeah, I guess I am."

"And some for me, too," Dane chimed in. "I'm starving."

Karen grunted but didn't say no.

"She's pretty overprotective, huh?" Jessica said, once Karen left.

"Yeah." I scowled. "Karen told me they assign male-female teams, like a married couple, to younger protectees—another set of parents to keep an eye on them."

"No kidding." Dane laughed. "They sure missed the boat when they paired China with Brad."

His chuckles continued as I considered Dane's former agent and Alejandro's current agent, China. Her hard-ass personality was hardly the motherly type.

"A marriage made in hell, right there," Dane said with a grin.

I smiled, too. "You know you miss them, Monroe."

"Oh, hell no." He stretched his arm across the back of Jessica's seat, something I wished I could get away with. "China's a nightmare. Though I wouldn't mind the door-to-door SUV service with these fuckin' things." He gestured to his crutches.

"China's actually gotten cooler—less aggressive—since the shooting." I bristled as the words came out of my mouth. I shouldn't have brought everyone down by mentioning that.

The Cincinnati coach called a time out, and the awkward silence that descended over us became more noticeable without cheering in the background.

"China's one tough chick, I'll give her that," Dane said. "Can't believe she's still in the field after taking a bullet to the head."

When Jessica bolted up from her seat, I stood, too. From the corner of my eye I saw Johnny get to his feet.

Her eyes were wild, and she seemed to be panting. "I'll be…back." She zoomed away in the direction of the bathrooms.

I looked at Dane, who appeared as puzzled as me about her abrupt departure.

"Is she okay?" I asked.

He frowned. "She's been acting weird. Could be trying to balance everything as a student-athlete. She's got a lot on her plate."

I looked over my shoulder at Johnny, who was still standing. He seemed to want to follow Jessica, but he couldn't leave me alone. He turned back to me and held out his hand, inviting me to return to my seat. Once I sat, he walked to the end of the row, which placed him closer to the door Jessica had exited. He stood with his back against the wall as he scanned the crowd.

"Or maybe this talk about shooting freaks her out," Dane added. "Did you know there was a plot to bomb my mom's campaign bus?"

My stomach clenched. "Yeah. I just found out Johnny busted it up."

"Jess overheard the agents talking about it, I guess. She was only sixteen, and it traumatized her. She had nightmares, but didn't tell anyone. I didn't find out she knew until after the election. Sucks she had to deal with that by herself."

I felt sad, too, and wished she'd confided in someone earlier. But if I'd known her then, would she have let me in? She'd alternated between being friendly and aloof tonight.

Karen returned. She handed me a soft pretzel with a plastic cup of melted cheese, and a bottled water. I scowled. I *knew* she wouldn't get me a coke. She also had a pretzel for each of the Monroes. Dane had scarfed down half of his by the time Karen could ask, "Where'd Jessica go?"

"Here I am." She gave a shaky smile as she took her seat.

I felt shaky, too, so I scooped a bite of hot, doughy pretzel into the nuclear orange cheese. *Yum.* Jessica stared at her food for a while, then took a bite.

"God bless the Secret Service," Dane said as he patted his belly. He stretched toward Karen with a twenty-dollar bill in his hand. "Here you go."

"That's okay," she said.

"I know you paid your own money for Jess and me. Take it. Gramps can afford it."

His grandfather had amassed a real estate fortune.

Karen paused. "But it didn't cost that much."

"You can buy me more food later. I'll never turn you down, sweetheart." Dane gave her one of his charming smiles, and finally she accepted his money.

Once Jessica started in, she ate almost as quickly as her brother. I liked that she wasn't a dainty eater. When she finished, she glanced at her empty cardboard box. The prettiest blush rose on her cream skin. She'd lost some of the suntan she'd had at the party.

"Didn't realize how hungry I was," she said.

"Dorm food's pretty bad, huh?" I popped another piece into my mouth.

She exhaled. "Yeah."

I wondered if she ate with Suave Swimmer Shithead. "Who do you go to the dining hall with?"

"My roommate, Mackenzie. She swims, too. And two swimmers who live down the hall, Kaylee and Emma."

The crowd roared again. Highbanks won the second set and only needed one more to win the match. A smaller school like Cincinnati didn't have a chance against my sister's team.

"Shit," Dane said as he gathered his crutches. "Gotta hit the head." He towered over us, then crutched off.

Now that we were alone, I summoned the courage to ask the question on my mind all night. "How's that, uh, how's that swimmer guy?"

She stilled, and seemed to pale. She didn't say anything for several moments.

"Jess?"

She looked at me and exhaled, like she hadn't been breathing. "What?"

Maybe she didn't know who I was talking about. *I hope.* "The guy at the party? Who got you a drink?"

"What about him?" she snapped.

I leaned back. "Sorry, I…"

Her chest heaved like she was trying to catch her breath. Did he turn her on that much? Just thinking of him?

When she rubbed her hands against each other, they trembled. Had I upset her?

"I didn't mean to pry. You're right—I ask too many questions."

She shook her head. "Not your fault. I'm being a bitch. Sorry."

"No, you're not!"

She kept looking down, and we didn't speak until Dane returned.

"One trip to take a piss and I'm wiped out." He lowered his body and set the crutches aside. "Fuck these cripple sticks."

Highbanks was up in set three, and it looked like they'd sweep the match. Lucia did a jump serve, but the ball shot into the net.

"Shake it off, Luz!" Dane yelled.

She looked up at him and smiled. Kaitlyn came up to her, said something, then smacked her butt. As Lucia giggled, I shook my head. *Athletes are weird.*

The next play, Kaitlyn's pass veered off to the side, so Alexis had no choice but to set the back row. Lucia approached and screamed the ball cross-court, where it smashed down at the far corner, just in bounds. The Cincinnati defender didn't even touch it.

"Look at that!" Dane pointed to the court. "Look how well she bounced back from that service error!" His big claps echoed around us. "That, my friends, is mental toughness. Good use of nonjudgment."

"Nonjudgment?" I asked.

"It's a mindfulness skill. Seeing but not evaluating. Just the facts — not judging something as good or bad. Instead of yelling at herself, Luz probably thought, 'Everyone makes mistakes.' So she could let it go." He scowled at the side entrance of the arena. "What the fuck?"

I turned to where he was looking and saw a tall, tanned, gray-haired man stride in. Wait — was that Dane's father?

"What's that asshole doing here?" Dane hissed.

Apparently he'd discarded the nonjudgment.

"Dad!" Jessica bounced over and gave him a hug.

I stood as they approached.

"This is Mateo," Jessica said.

Mr. Monroe shook my hand. "I've heard good things about you from Dane."

But not from Jessica?

He peered around my shoulder. "How're you feeling, Dane?"

"I told you not to come."

Mr. Monroe sighed. "Your mother and I decided I'd take care of you. Jessie's too busy with school and swimming."

"So you're here for Jess, not me."

My eyes widened. My father and I had our share of differences, of course, but I would never speak to him like that.

Jessica pulled her father down to sit between her and Dane, and I took my seat on the other side of her.

Applause rang out, and I realized the match had just ended.

"Let's get out of here," Dane said. His dad tried to help with his crutches, but Dane brushed him off. "I guess you're coming with us, then?"

Mr. Monroe glanced at Jessica and then back at Dane. "Yes."

"Awesome." Dane's mouth was tight.

"Ready to go?" Karen asked me.

I didn't want to leave Jessica, but I didn't have much choice. "Yeah." I fidgeted as Dane crutched by me, with Mr. Monroe following him. Jessica turned to me.

"Good to see you, Teo." She clutched my wrist again, and I liked it, even though her hand was cold and trembling. "Sorry I've been such a mental case. I, I've had a lot going on." She swallowed, and her eyes glistened. Was she about to cry? When Dane barked at his father, she looked over her shoulder. "I better go. Stop these two from killing each other."

"Right. See you."

I watched her walk away, shoulders slumped, seeming lost in a world of her own.

How would I stop thinking about her now? I'd hoped not seeing her for a week would decrease my obsession. But after tonight, that hope vanished. Something seemed off about her, like a fragile shell had enveloped her and obscured her bubbly spirit. I hoped she wouldn't break.

7
Jessica
★ ★ ★

"Hey, Jess."

I gasped when Blake touched my bare shoulder. *Son of a bitch.* I'd been up late after Lucia's volleyball match, and I didn't need this so early on a Saturday. But I knew he wouldn't just go away, so I forced myself to turn around and face him.

He stood too close, clad only in his black swimsuit. Rivulets of water dripped down the curves of his pecs, slipped over his thighs, and left a small puddle on the pool deck. Why did the guys' team have to end practice at the same time as us? *Damn it.* I'd almost escaped to the locker room.

"We're having another party tonight." He smiled as his gaze lowered to my swimsuit. "You're coming."

My heart was on overdrive. I crossed my arms over my chest and reached up to clutch my shoulders. I knew my shiver wasn't just from standing on deck in a wet suit. The flickers of his tongue across his lower lip seriously creeped me out.

"I'll pick you up at eight." He nodded and turned.

"I can't," I breathed.

His scowl froze me in place. "Of course you can."

"My dad's visiting." I looked up to the stands above the pool, but he wasn't there yet. And I didn't see anyone else on deck to save me. Most of my teammates were already showering. "We have plans after the game."

"The old man will be in bed by ten for sure. Then I'll come get you."

He turned to leave again, but I blurted, "Can't. We're staying at my brother's tonight. He, uh, broke his foot, and he's on crutches, and my dad came to help…"

As Blake's scowl returned, I tried to think of a better excuse.

"Jessica," Kathy said.

When I looked at my coach, my stomach dropped. Her hands were on her hips, and her mouth was tight. But it wasn't her angry expression that made it hard for me to breathe. Next to her was Michelle Farris, associate athletic director. Drug test overseer. Grim reaper of my swimming career.

"We need to speak to you in my office," Kathy said.

I gulped.

Blake's eyes got big. He clasped my elbow as he leaned in and whispered, "You got drug tested?"

I shrugged out of his hold and stepped away as my face flushed. *This is* your *fault, asshole.* I should've screamed that, but the two women about to end my career were within earshot.

Ms. Farris narrowed her eyes at Blake, then looked at me. "I'm late for an alumni breakfast. Let's go."

I couldn't feel my feet as I followed them to Kathy's office. Behind me, Blake said something, but I didn't make it out over the buzzing in my ears.

I'd started swimming at age six. Twelve years later, it was all I knew. How would I survive without my beloved sport? I cast a longing look at the crisp, blue water before I entered the office. *Adios, chlorine dreams.*

My assistant coach, Mike, was already inside. *Great. More people* to witness my demise.

Ms. Farris and I joined Mike at the round table in the corner of the office. Kathy rummaged in a cabinet and pulled out a fluffy towel. She draped it over my shoulders before she sat next to me. As I drew its warmth around me, I wondered why she'd done such a kindness right before kicking me off the team. The gesture made me want to cry.

"Do you know why we're here, Miss Monroe?" Ms. Farris asked.

My dry throat made swallowing difficult. "I failed a drug test."

Ms. Farris's eyebrows arched. After a beat, she said, "Correct. You tested positive for metabolites of THC."

I couldn't look at Kathy or Mike. They must've been so disappointed in me.

"Here's a letter outlining the consequences of your positive test." Ms. Farris offered it to me, but I didn't take it right away—I wanted to be a swimmer a little longer. The letter would revoke my scholarship and boot me off the team. Nausea stirred in my gut just thinking about it.

"Jessica." She rattled the paper, and I took it. "You are to schedule an appointment with Dr. Valentine within the next week."

My forehead wrinkled. Why would I have to meet with the sport psychologist if I wasn't a Highbanks athlete anymore?

"You'll be tested more frequently now," Ms. Farris continued. "And if you have a second positive, you'll lose two weeks of the season."

I stared at her.

Her head tilted. "Do you understand?"

"Wait." I blinked. "I'm still on the team?"

"Of course you are," Kathy said.

I'm still a swimmer. My blinks picked up speed as I tried to fight off tears. But I lost the battle and soon I was bawling. All the fear and tension I'd been holding spilled out of my eyeballs and nostrils. I was grateful when Mike handed me some tissues.

"This reaction's a bit unusual," Ms. Farris said. "Most athletes deny using drugs. And I've seen tears, but not a total meltdown like this."

"No, this fits. Her last coach told me Jessie's a good girl. She's just lost her way." Kathy nodded at me. "I wondered why you haven't been swimming well. I knew you couldn't be out of shape, not with Gary as your coach."

My last club coach, Gary, was known for his tough practices.

"But if you've been smoking pot all the time, that makes more sense."

I cleared my throat. "I only smoked once."

Ms. Farris rolled her eyes. "Now *that* reaction's more typical."

"It's true." I sniffed. "I'm not a pothead."

"Regardless, you will meet with Dr. Valentine, and she'll assess the situation." Ms. Farris reached for her handbag. "I don't want to have this meeting again, Miss Monroe."

My eyes widened. "You won't."

"I need to get to the Cougar breakfast at the PAC." Ms. Farris stood, and the rest of us got to our feet. She looked at me. "Are you going to the game?"

I'd almost forgotten there was a home football game this afternoon. "Yes. My dad's here."

"That sounds nice."

A worry entered my mind. "Will you tell my parents about the drug test?"

"That's up to your coach," Ms. Farris said.

I looked at Kathy, who frowned. "I haven't decided," she said. "If you get your shit together, I won't tell them. But if I think you're not on the right track, you can bet I'll have them on speed dial."

I exhaled. I didn't want anyone to know about my stupidity.

Ms. Farris stared at me from the doorway. "Oh, and Miss Monroe, stay away from negative influences."

Was she talking about Blake? If so, I would have no trouble following her advice. Now that my THC trip-up was out in the open, Blake couldn't threaten to tell my coaches about it. I wouldn't have to talk to him at all, I hoped.

When I emerged to the natatorium lobby, I was surprised to find Dane standing next to our dad.

"What the hell?" Dane looked at his watch. "Did you fall in? We've been waiting forever."

Dad shifted, looking uncomfortable, and I noticed he carried a canvas with its back to me.

No way I'd tell them about my meeting in the coach's office, so I chose deflection. I pointed to Dane's crutches. "I didn't think you were going to the game."

Dane shrugged. "Dad pointed out that it's my senior year. I might regret it if I don't hit up all the home games."

"We didn't have a nationally ranked football team at art school," Dad said.

"Or a football team at all," Dane added.

Dad grinned. "Right. Or over a hundred thousand fans at the games."

There seemed to be a lighter mood between them, and I wondered what they'd been up to since they'd dropped me off last night.

"Plus, I want to watch your reaction to the painting." Dane gestured to the canvas in Dad's grip. "He was up all night finishing it."

"Dad!" I studied him, but he didn't seem tired. If anything, he seemed bright-eyed. "You didn't have to do that."

"You know what it's like, Jessie. When the muse graces you with her presence, you need to welcome her with open arms — stay up all night, if that's what it takes. You can always make up sleep."

I hoped that was true. Last night had been another rough one with the nightmares. I felt my eyelids droop.

"Staying up all night seems like a manic episode to me," Dane said.

Dad frowned. "You sound like your mother. Just because I'm an artist doesn't mean I have bipolar disorder. And you haven't even started grad school. It's way too early to fling around diagnoses."

Dane sagged against his crutches and moaned, "Don't remind me about grad school applications."

"Besides, bipolar's highly heritable. Maybe *you* were in a manic episode when you stayed up most of the night watching *Days of Our Lives*."

Dane blushed.

Dad looked at me. "Did you know your brother's hooked on a soap opera?"

"Uh-huh." I giggled. "He got Lucia to start watching, too."

Dane jutted his jaw. "Yeah? Who was the one asking me all about the show as he painted, hmm?"

Dad shook his head. "Now the jerk's got *me* addicted. Fuck."

Dane laughed, and Dad joined in. I marveled at them.

"Just wait, Jess," Dane said. "I got Luz and Dad to watch, and I'm going to get you addicted next."

"No way." I shook my head.

"And Teo, too."

A smile played on my lips as I remembered sitting so close to Mateo last night. I'd felt safe with him and his agents. But my smile faded as my freak-outs came to mind. Why had Mateo asked me about the "swimmer guy"? I never wanted to think about Blake again. Mateo probably thought I was cracked.

"Is Lucia going to the game?" Dad asked.

Dane shook his head. "Her coach won't let them go because they have another home match tonight. Says it drains their energy."

"Is Teo going?" I asked.

"Nah. Luz said he's meeting up with some guys in a band."

He was in a band? *That* sounded sexy. I craved more information but didn't want to appear too eager. My phone buzzed, and I read the text.

What happened with Kathy? You okay?

Blake. He wanted to know if I'd implicated him as my supplier. I decided not to answer, and powered down my phone. *Make him squirm.*

"Who was that?"

I looked up and met Dane's inquisitive eyes. "Nobody." He kept staring at me. I swallowed, then gestured to the canvas. "So, are you going to show me my painting or what?"

Dad blanched, and he tapped the corner of the painting. His apparent nervousness was cute. He flipped it around to reveal a sea of light blue and silver. He'd combined white and blue so artfully that it looked like waves undulating off the canvas, like the painting was alive, pulsing with energy. I stepped closer to peer at the creature in the middle. A flash of silver, like scales on her body — a fish, perhaps? Pale yellow tendrils flowed from her head, swelling and rolling with the waves. I made out faint lines of eyelashes and a serene smile, as I looked closer. *Peace.* The sea creature had found the peace I coveted. I wanted to dive into the painting to be with her. I wanted to *be* her.

When I touched my face, it was wet. I was crying again? What the hell was wrong with me?

"Wow, Dad," Dane said. "Your painting really moved her."

They watched me as I stepped back and sniffed.

"You like it?" Dad asked.

I smiled at him through my tears. "I love it."

"Well, I love watching you," said Dad. "I was trying to recreate the feeling I get when you swim. You're so beautiful. So powerful. It's like you belong in the water."

And I'd come so close to losing swimming. *Dumbass.*

"You don't seem like yourself, Jessie." Dad set the painting down. "You're edgy. And sad. Like you were two years ago."

"Two years ago?" Dane asked.

I looked down. "The terrorist bus thing."

Dad continued, "Are you having trouble sleeping again?"

"A little," I confessed.

"Did anything happen?"

Dad's question ratcheted up my heartbeat, and my tears stopped. I couldn't tell him or Dane about my first night at Highbanks. "No. Maybe it's being in a new place, trying to sleep in the ugly dorm."

"Let's go hang this in your room, then." Dad looked at his watch. "Dane told me you want to loft your bed, so maybe that'll help, too. We have time for that and a bite to eat before the game, if we hurry."

I shifted my backpack and nodded.

The sunlight blinded me as we walked out of the dark pool lobby. Dane's long stride allowed him to keep pace pretty well next to me, with Dad behind us. "Dad knew about your nightmares after the terrorist plot?"

I noticed his grimace. "Yeah."

"He helped you?"

I nodded, wondering why he was asking.

"Sorry I wasn't there for you."

Oh. Mr. Budding Psychologist felt guilty he hadn't helped me deal with an emotional crisis. "It's okay. Mom was busy with the election, and you were busy pretending you didn't like Lucia."

He barked out a laugh.

The metallic shifting and blunted thud of the crutches on the pavement lulled me as we continued our progress toward my dorm. We passed scads of people excitedly chatting or pointing to campus landmarks. The first game of the season brought out all the fanatics.

Dane looked at me as we stopped by the entrance of my dorm. "You know you can tell me anything, right?"

I sucked in a breath but tried to look cool. Did he know about Blake? About the drug test? "I know." I swiped my ID, and we went inside.

Five hours later, Dane and I collapsed on the sofa in his condo. We'd left the game early for two reasons: Highbanks was crushing Bowling Green, and Dane's foot was hurting. At least we hadn't had to walk far to the car since Dane had a handicapped-parking hangtag.

"Here you go." Dad handed him a bottle of pain pills and a glass of water.

"*Gracias, padre.*" He closed his eyes after swallowing a pill. "Can't believe I forgot these."

Dad picked up a pillow, fluffed it, and propped it under Dane's foot on the ottoman.

"Who knew you were such a good nurse," I said. He'd nursed me, too, by bringing the painting. It really brightened my room and now hung right under the lofted bed Dad had built. Dad had even promised to get me a small sofa for under the bed.

Dad smirked. "I took care of your mother when she broke her leg."

"Mom broke her leg?" asked Dane.

"Before Jessie was born. You were only one. She was carrying you in from the car and slipped on the ice."

Dane leaned back. "Yikes."

"She managed to protect you when she fell." Dad looked out the window. "She's good at that. Protecting her kids."

The sadness in his voice made me look over at Dane, who stared back. Was Dad implying he didn't do so well at that?

"Jeez, it's hot out there." Dad wiped his forehead. "I need a drink."

So do I. Alcohol sounded so good.

He looked at Dane. "You got anything?"

"Uh, there's some beer and wine in the fridge."

Dad headed to the kitchen. "Any liquor?"

"Vodka's in the cabinet over the microwave, I think."

"Want a drink?" Dad called.

Dane and I looked at each other again.

"Better not mix it with my pain meds," Dane said.

"Jessie?"

If my dad was cool with me drinking underage, then I was, too. "Sure."

Dane clicked on the game, which had five minutes left in the fourth quarter. The Cougars were up 45-0, and the stadium was starting to empty.

Dad handed me a glass of white wine and sat on the other side of me. "Here's some Riesling. I couldn't find any tonic for the vodka."

"Sorry, guess I'm out." Dane took another sip of his ice water.

As the wine slid down my throat, the sweetness awoke my taste buds, and the coolness relaxed me. *Yum.* I'd hated the red wine I tried last year, but I could get behind this drink.

Five minutes later, Dad glanced at my empty glass. "Whoa, guess you were thirsty."

I blushed when I noticed his was still full.

He smiled. "A little too sweet for me. Why don't you take my glass back to the kitchen and pour yourself another? I'll go out and get some sauvignon blanc later."

I was already feeling a pleasant buzz, so I didn't hesitate to take his suggestion. Maybe if I kept drinking, I wouldn't have nightmares tonight. I polished off his glass in the kitchen. After I topped off mine, I snuck a glance toward the family room. Dad and Dane couldn't see me, so I took a long pull from the bottle.

Thirty minutes later, I was decidedly drunk. The postgame show was on, but Dane was texting Lucia instead of watching it. Dad snored next to me, and I wanted to sleep, too. But I needed one more glass of wine first. Off to the kitchen I went.

I sulked as I poured the last drop in my glass.

"You drank the whole thing?"

I jumped and almost dropped the empty bottle. I turned to glare at Dane. "Jesus. Why'd you sneak up on me like that?" And *how* had he snuck up on me? He didn't have his crutches—he must've hopped over without me hearing him. "Dad had some, too." An edge of defensiveness laced my voice.

"He had a few sips. What's up with you?"

"Nothing." I looked away.

"Dad's right. You're acting weird."

I tried to steady my hand as I drew the glass to my mouth. I wished he would go away and leave me to my sweet serum.

"Jess, come here."

I peered at him. "Why?"

"Just come here."

With a sigh, I set down my wine and shuffled over to him. I tensed when he gathered me in his arms. "Why are you hugging me?"

"Luz said you need a hug."

"You talked to Lucia about me?"

"She cares about you. Mateo, too."

Mateo wouldn't want anyone as damaged as me.

"You're so tense — just relax."

I closed my eyes. I couldn't let myself relax, or...*Shit*. I was crying again. I was just so tired. I rested my cheek against his chest, and his hold felt solid even though he balanced on one foot. My breaths came ragged and shallow.

"You're crying again?" His arms tightened. "Something *is* wrong. I've never seen you cry like this." He was quiet for a moment. "Did Johnny do anything to you?"

I lifted my chin and gawked at him. *"What?"* I stepped back and swiped at my cheeks. "No."

"He's the common denominator for both times you had sleep problems. You're having nightmares again?"

"My nightmares would be a lot worse if Johnny hadn't stopped the bomb."

He frowned. "True. But if he ever hurt you, I don't care that he carries a gun. I'd take him down."

Dane's fierce look warmed my heart. But I couldn't have him questioning a man as honorable as Johnny. "If you must know, I'm freaking out because I had a positive drug test."

Whoops. The way his eyes bugged made me second-guess that disclosure. *Damn wine.*

"For what?" he demanded. "Alcohol?"

My stomach dropped. "You can test positive for alcohol?"

"Yeah, but you'd have to drink a shit-ton to show up on a drug test the next day."

"Phew." My heartbeat crested its peak and began to decelerate.

"So if it's not alcohol, what'd you test positive for?"

I sighed. "Weed."

His jaw lowered. "Since when do you smoke weed?"

"Since a week ago. I smoked once on Friday and got tested on Wednesday." I peered around the corner, but Dad still looked asleep.

"You used once in your life, and got tested right after?" He covered his mouth with his hand, but his shaking shoulders made it obvious he was laughing at me.

"Shut up." I marched over to my glass with the intention of slugging it down, but then paused.

He chuckled. "That is classic. I gotta tell Luz."

I spun around. "No, you can't."

"Why not?"

Because I don't want Mateo to think I'm a druggie. He hadn't had one sip of alcohol at the party. I wished I'd been as smart. "Just don't tell her. It's embarrassing, okay?"

"But Luz wouldn't judge you. She and I used to meet with Dr. Valentine. That's who you have to see, right?"

I pursed my lips and nodded.

He grinned. "She's cool. Don't worry."

"If she's so great, then why don't you still see her?"

He angled his head. "You know, you're right. I probably need a tune up. This injury's a punch to the nuts."

"Thought it was your foot, not your nuts," I muttered.

He laughed. "Now *that's* the Jess I know. Welcome back. You'll get over this stupid mistake and go on to have an awesome career." He hopped back over to the sofa.

I swirled the wine in my glass and felt my nose burn. I wished I felt as optimistic as my brother.

8

Mateo

★ ★ ★

"What was your BG this morning?" Karen's eyes met mine in the rearview mirror.

Of course I'd forgotten to check my blood glucose, so I aimed for a number that wouldn't alarm her. I was too nervous to eat, and my fingertips were sore from countless needle pricks. "One twenty-two."

"So the exact same number as yesterday, right before you spiked to three-sixty." Her gaze tightened with apparent suspicion.

"But it came back down before the volleyball match."

She shook her head as she continued driving.

I wished I knew why my blood glucose was all over the place. It hadn't been this erratic since I was sixteen. Back then the doctor had told me it was hormones. Maybe I was hormonal now, too, given that I thought about Jessica all the time.

"The streets are empty," Johnny said from the seat next to me. "I like this."

I noticed all the open parking spaces at the Kroger we passed. "Lucy told me the best time to go shopping is during home football games. The entire city shuts down."

Johnny frowned. "We could've made it work for you to go to the game, you know."

"Yeah. It's cool." I patted my guitar case. Music beat football any day of the week, especially when dealing with security at the game would be a huge hassle. My phone buzzed with a text.

Sorry took me so long to reply.
Lame. How's life?

I smiled. My best friend Joey was finally texting me back.

You ARE lame, wench.
Berklee's kicking your ass?

OMG. My fingers are falling off.

That didn't sound fun, but I knew she loved it. Not that I was jealous or anything. I hadn't auditioned at Berklee, but I probably wouldn't have gotten in. Things were all set up for me with security at Highbanks, anyway. Another message came in.

What're your classes like?

I thought about Itch and Fitch, who I would see in a few minutes.

Music Theory is pretty cool.

I'm in theory too! What else are you taking?

Voice, keyboard skills, English,
calc, freshman survey

Listing my classes reminded me I had to write a short paper for English by Monday. I also had calculus homework. *Ugh.* I already felt lost in that class, only one week in. I typed:

Can't understand my calc teacher.

Why not?

He's Chinese—major accent.
Think he's in grad school.
I suck at math as it is.

Lies, all lies.
You got an A in calc at Friends.

Joey and I had both attended Sidwell Friends School, located near the White House. Her parents didn't have nearly as much money as mine, but she'd earned a scholarship. I asked:

What're you taking besides theory?

2 woodwind labs—techniques and improv,
flute repertoire

That would be strange but welcome to take only music classes—at least she didn't have to suffer through math. She texted again.

Did ya hear my dad got on your mom's detail?

Interesting. Joey's dad had been a Secret Service agent for fifteen years. His security clearance was a big reason they'd let Joey hang out with me in the White House after we'd met at school. Apparently it was quite a coup for an agent to land the presidential protection gig.

A promotion, right? Congrats to him.

Yeah, he's stoked.

Good luck handling my mom, though.

LOL. She's better than MY mom.

Her mom was always pushing for Joey and me to date. But we just didn't have any chemistry. We'd tried several times, but she always felt more like a sister than a girlfriend.

I need to tell you something.

I tensed. *That* sounded ominous. A minute went by.

How would you feel if I met someone?

My eyes opened wide. *Already?* She'd just revealed the real reason she hadn't texted all week. Yet another person in my life had found a significant other.

Really happy for you, Jo.

Oh, thank you! I thought you'd be cool with it—just
wanted to check. You have to meet him.
He's awesome! He's a cellist.

Can't wait.

And I wanted her to meet Jessica, though I'd be introducing her to just a friend, not my boo. I exhaled a long sigh and noticed how tired I felt. Joey had met someone in less than a week, and I would probably never have a girlfriend.

We pulled into a lot next to a beat-up warehouse. I didn't want to tell her about the band rehearsal in case it crashed and burned, so I typed:

Better go. Good luck with the dude.

Adios!

The car stopped, and I waited for Johnny to give me the signal that it was safe to come out. My hands trembled as I clasped my guitar case. Dang, I was nervous.

Coming in from the bright sunlight, the dark interior of the warehouse felt like a cave. A hot cave. Fitch had told me his uncle owned the warehouse, and evidently he didn't believe in air conditioning. The scent of sweet smoke hung in the air.

My agents and I weaved through stacks of lockers — Fitch's uncle sold them to schools or something — to find the corner where three guys were setting up equipment.

Itch looked up at me from his keyboard. "Hey, Coconut."

Not the shampoo thing again. I glared. "*Cállate.*"

"What?" Fitch asked from his kneeling position near the drums.

"I think he just told me to shut the fuck up." Itch grinned. "Come meet Weston." He circled around the keyboard stand and gestured to a guy with long brown hair sitting with a guitar in his lap. Red blotches lined his light blue eyes.

Weston held a thick pen in his mouth and smoke poured out both nostrils. What the hell was he smoking?

"Hey, man." He extended his arm, and I bumped his fist. His gaze floated behind me, and his eyes narrowed. He turned to Itch. "You didn't tell me the copstapo was coming."

My heart hammered as I realized my agents were about to screw this up for me. I heard them whispering.

"They're not cops," Itch replied. "They're Secret Service. I *told* you they'd be here."

Weston cocked his head. "Yeah?"

Itch blew out a breath. "That weed's messing with your memory, West."

"It's not *weed*." Weston dropped his chin as his eyes rolled. "It's herbs." His chuckle turned into a hacking cough.

"Mr. McCloud," Johnny said as he stepped around me. "We need you to put away your vaporizer."

I stifled a groan. So he and Karen had decided to make this a thing. And of course they knew his name. They probably knew more about him than his own mother.

"And if I don't?" Weston challenged.

Johnny glanced behind me, and I twisted to look at Karen. She shook her head as she patted her face with a tissue. She looked like she was sweating, and I felt uncomfortably warm as well. When she took off her suit jacket and turned to drape it over a chair, she revealed the crisscross gun holster molded to the back of her shirt.

I looked back at Weston to find him lowering the vaping thingy as he noticed her weapon. She hadn't said a word, but she'd communicated quite effectively.

"This state's decrimalized," Weston said.

Huh?

"Decriminalization means you won't go to jail for possessing less than one hundred grams," Johnny said. "But cannabis is still illegal."

Fitch pointed a drumstick at Weston. "Dude, just put it away. We're about to start jamming, anyway."

Weston scowled at me, but he finally clicked something on the device and set it on the floor. He gestured to my guitar case. "Let's see it. Your chick magnet."

I unclicked the clasps.

"Whaz your name, man?" Weston asked.

Itch sighed. "His name's Mateo. Mateo Ramirez, the son of the president of the United States?"

"Whoa. That's sick." Weston looked at me through half-lidded eyes.

Did he seriously not know my dad? Alejandro's constant railing about the uninformed electorate seemed to have merit in this case. Of course, Weston probably didn't vote—except maybe for laws to legalize marijuana.

When I removed my guitar, Itch materialized by my side. "That's it there?" He pointed to the silver signature on the curve of the black guitar body. He leaned in. "What does it say?"

The scrawl *was* rather difficult to make out, so I translated: "Hang on to a dream, Neil Diamond."

Itch's head shot up. "That's a lyric from 'America.'"

I nodded, impressed.

Fitch took off his Cubs hat as he came closer. "Sweet."

"Bullshit." Weston rose and set his guitar on the stand. "Your guitar's not signed by Neil fuckin' Diamond."

"See for yourself," Itch said.

A waft of skunk odor hit me as Weston leaned over. "Can't even read it."

"Neil Diamond is President Ramirez's favorite artist," Itch explained as he headed back to his keyboard. "He played a private concert at the White House, and Mateo got to meet him."

Weston's squint left him still looking suspicious. "What's he, like, ninety?"

I bristled. "I think he's in his seventies. But he can still rock."

"Let's get started so we can get out of here," Itch said. "It's hot as fuck in this place."

"You said it, brotha." Fitch moved to his drum set.

I noticed Karen had stepped to the side, fanning herself, and Johnny had disappeared. He was probably canvassing the perimeter of the warehouse. The heat made me sleepy.

"I got 'Gaijin Dream' programmed into the keyboard," Itch said. He slung the strap of his bass guitar over his shoulder. "I'll play bass for this one."

They clearly needed another member if Itch had to play two instruments. I was a better guitarist than piano player, but I wondered if I needed to offer to play the keyboard.

Itch nodded at my guitar. "Mateo, how 'bout you join in at the hook after you've heard it a couple of times."

¡Hijole! Going into a song blind like this would definitely test me. At least they didn't have a mic or amps to magnify my mistakes. And at least I didn't have to sing. My mouth felt as dry and shriveled up as my love life.

Weston shook his head as he strapped on his guitar, and I worried he'd object to me playing in. Instead, he said, "Been working on a new song. Let's start with that."

"No." Itch wiped the heel of his hand across his sweaty forehead. "We'll do that later, when we're warmed up."

Weston strummed a discordant chord and sang, "Itch is on a power trip. A power trip, an acid trip, he's gonna flip…"

Fitch grinned and added a kicky beat on the snare drum.

"Fuckers!" Itch shouted over the din. "We have a guest, assholes. We should start with a song at least three of us know."

Fitch shrugged, but nodded. He turned his hat around backward.

Weston grunted. But he did look at Itch, who hit a button on the keyboard to start the song. The piano melody sounded like a perversion of "Chopsticks." Weston's guitar kicked in, followed by Itch's bass. Once Fitch began a standard four/four rhythm, I found my head pulsing forward with each beat. Weston closed his eyes and sang:

Ohayo, pretty badie
Commo ava me
Oh hi yo, panda panda
Snore sah on wif me

I dug his gravelly voice, but I couldn't understand one damn word. He mumbled something fierce. I glanced at Itch, who rolled his eyes but kept strumming his bass. At least I could understand the rather simple melody, so I joined in at the next stanza.

You're sowey sahn
Alecking dawn
Holland in bahn
My gangeh drain

Itch stormed to the keyboard to stop the recorded tune and sliced his hand through the air to silence us. "What the fuck, West? The song is 'Gaijin Dream,' not 'Ganja Dream.'"

Weston's only response was a low chuckle.

"It's about a Japanese guy who falls in love with an American movie star," Itch continued. "Not about toking it up till you're so obliterated you can't see straight."

Weston was singing about weed? I had no freaking clue. I realized I was thirsty and wished I'd brought some bottled water. Maybe the stifling heat was making it hard to breathe, too.

"We agreed you'd stop mumbling when you sing," Fitch said.

"All the legends do it, man." Weston smiled.

Itch threw his hands in the air. "You're not a *legend!* You're a stoner!"

Fitch laughed. "He's a legendary stoner?"

Whoa. A wave of fatigue washed over me, leaving a tsunami of trembles in its wake. I needed to sit down. I eyed the chair Karen had used to hold her suit jacket, but I worried she'd think something was wrong if I went over there. I snuck a glance at her and blanched when I found her staring at me. She approached as the guys kept yelling at each other.

Karen frowned. "You look awful. I need to test you."

"No. I'm fine."

"Then let me get you something to eat."

"I'm not hungry."

She grabbed my wrist. "You're shaking. Come sit." She pulled me toward the chair, and I was too tired to resist. An urge to vomit pressed at the back of my throat. I held onto the seat to steady myself, and barely felt the prick of the needle Karen pressed into my fingertip.

"No." Lightheadedness engulfed me, and my stomach killed. I wanted to get the hell out of there. I tried to get up but Karen pressed me down with one hand as she tested the glucose strip in the other.

"Hold on, I'm waiting for the number. Johnny, help."

I was going to throw up any minute, and I started thrashing around on the chair. I wasn't sure what was happening but powerful hands held me down, and when I looked up, Johnny loomed over me. When had he gotten so strong?

"Oh, God," Karen cried. "You're over six hundred! No wonder you look like a train wreck." She lifted my shirt and jabbed a needle into the left side of my abdomen. Over the rush of blood in my ears, I heard her say "Get an ambulance to thirty-three Mt. Vernon Avenue."

"No," I moaned. No longer in control of my muscles, I slid down the chair.

As Johnny transferred me to the floor, Karen balled up her jacket and stuffed it under my head as a pillow.

Don't vomit, I kept repeating.

"Is he okay?" Fitch peered down at me, and Itch came up next to him.

I realized the guys were no longer arguing. *Damn.* My collapse couldn't have come at a worse time. They wouldn't want a band member who couldn't last one rehearsal. *Sayonara, band dreams.*

"He's diabetic," Karen snapped. "And he hasn't been checking his blood glucose."

I couldn't keep my eyes open, but maybe that was a good thing. I wouldn't have to face her wrath.

She said, "Shoot, I forgot water. You guys got any?"

Some time later, she lifted my head, and water dribbled into my mouth. It tasted so good, I didn't even care that it was warm.

The nausea lightened—maybe the insulin was kicking in. I opened my eyes. "Where's Weston?"

Itch glared. "He's off doing what he always does when he doesn't get his way: baking his bong. Sorry we didn't get to play together."

"It's my fault." I grimaced.

"You were doing great—you jumped right in, before you…" Itch chewed on his lip. "Do you like the song? I wrote it."

I managed a smile. "'Gaijin Dream'…I really felt the guy's longing for the girl."

Itch lit up.

"What does *gaijin* mean?" I asked.

"It's a Japanese word for Westerner."

Two paramedics hustled in. Karen barked orders, and soon they wheeled me on a gurney to the ambulance. I'd been through this before.

A few hours later, they rolled me from the ER to a hospital room. They'd had to admit me since my blood glucose wasn't coming down quickly enough. The day just kept getting better.

The huge hospital room looked suspiciously similar to Alejandro's from a two years ago. They'd stuck me with two IVs, which now stood next to my bed. Despite my protests, the nurse had also added a catheter to the mix. Irritation tightened my throat.

Karen's arms crossed her chest. "You've been through high BGs before. How could you miss the signs?"

"I thought it was the heat." I looked down as I replayed my first and last band rehearsal. "And I was kind of swept up in the moment."

"Me, too," Karen said. "I felt like I was in an episode of VH1's *Behind the Music.*" She sighed. "I shouldn't have let them distract me from checking in on you."

It wasn't her fault, and I felt like a selfish jerk. She was just trying to do her job. I looked up at her guilty eyes. "Sorry I've been a pain in the ass."

The deep line in her forehead smoothed out.

"Interesting friends you got there," Johnny said. He pinched his forefingers together and held them between his pursed lips like he was inhaling from a joint.

"I'm not sure about this, Mateo," Karen said. "Our boss won't be happy if he finds out we allowed illegal drug use right in front of us."

I exhaled. "Thanks for not making a scene. But don't worry, I'm sure the guys won't want me after all this."

"I've heard you play," Johnny said. "You're good."

I stilled.

"They'd be lucky to have you," he added.

A nurse came in to run some tests on my blood and urine, and I knew that would happen about a thousand more times before they discharged me.

After she left, Johnny straightened and seemed to listen to his earpiece. "Oh."

"What?" I followed Johnny's gaze to the door.

When two Secret Service agents entered, my eyes widened. "Mr. Frances?" What was Joey's dad doing here? Then my mom darted into the room, and I groaned. "You didn't have to come, *Mamá*."

"Of course we did!" She bustled over to the bed in her formal red dress and leaned down to hug me.

"*We?*" My voice sounded weak.

More agents preceded Dad, and if that wasn't enough, Alejandro came in next. *Awesome.*

Mom glared at me. "Karen told me you haven't been checking your numbers."

I tried to find Karen in the sea of agents now populating my hospital room, but couldn't. *Traitor.*

"You're not managing your illness well," Mom continued. "Do you want to stay in college?"

My jaw unhinged. "You'll make me leave Highbanks?"

"Sylvia." Dad draped his arm across her shoulders. "*Tranquila.* Let's not be rash. Great to see you, Matty."

I nodded at Dad, who looked tired, even in his dapper tuxedo. Was it possible his black hair had grayed a little more in the one week since I'd seen him?

Mom rifled through her giant handbag and drew out a package of tissues. She took one and dabbed under her eyes.

Shit. She was crying.

"How're you feeling, best man?" asked Alejandro, assessing me.

I nodded. "Better."

"I'm glad, buddy. Want to make sure you're fit for the wedding." He grinned.

When my dad smiled, too, I let out a breath. "Thanks for coming, guys."

"Of course we're here!" Mom sniffed. "And we're not leaving till you get the pump."

"Come again?" I sat up. Could I retract my gratitude? "You told me that was *my* decision."

Mom shook her head. "Not the way you've been dealing with your illness. *Denying* your illness. This has to stop, *niño*. We can't fly here every time you have a problem."

"Nobody *asked* you to come!"

"Sylvia, sweetheart." Dad guided her to the lounge chair in the far corner of the room. "It's been a long day."

My teeth clenched as I watched my parents murmur to each other. I was so sick of Mom telling me how sick I was.

Alejandro's eyes lifted to the ceiling. "Ignore her. She gets like this when she's had wine."

"She drinks wine?" That was news to me.

"Only when she has to attend events with Sherri Nichols."

Despite my anger, my mouth twitched with the beginnings of a smile. Dad almost hadn't picked Bill Nichols as his VP because Mom hated his wife. She thought Sherri was a stuck-up bitch.

"They were having a dinner for some head of state—who can keep track—and Mom had to sit next to Mrs. Nichols the whole time." Alejandro snorted. "She probably was grateful she had to leave."

"Yeah, so she could yell at me about the damn pump."

Alejandro shrugged, and I expected him to chime in about how I needed it. But he just stood there. I noticed Joey's dad by the wall, and when he saw me looking at him, he smiled and waved. I nodded at him. Living under protection sucked, but at least Mr. Frances could take care of his family because of it.

My brother spoke up. "Could I ask a question?"

"Yeah."

"I know you have concerns about the pump. What's your biggest one?"

I looked down.

"If you don't want to tell me, that's okay," he added.

"What if…" I sighed. Then I lowered my voice. "What if a girl's undressing me, and she sees that thing? Instant turn-off."

Alejandro studied me for a moment.

Did he think my reasoning was stupid? Immature?

"Wow," he finally said. "That makes total sense. No wonder you've waited."

I gaped at him.

"But, Matty, think about this. If something like that turns her off, she's not the right girl for you. You don't want a girl who disdains the very thing that keeps you healthy."

I let that sink in.

"Besides, when she's undressing you, she won't be looking at your side." His gaze drifted down to my crotch, and he smirked.

My eyes flew open. Had Mr. A+ Alejandro just made a sex joke?

"Matty!" Lucia cried from the doorway. Her long, wet hair hung over her volleyball themed T-shirt, which read *Sorry, Princess…Not Even Cinderella Could Get to This Ball*. "I came as soon as my match ended."

I groaned as more agents filled the room.

"Did you win?" asked Alejandro.

"Of course," she scoffed.

"Luz got eighteen kills!" Dane said as he crutched in.

Why the hell was *he* here? My breath caught when I saw Jessica and her dad come in next. *¡Chin!* I didn't want her to see me looking like a sick weakling. I tried to sit up in bed.

Lucia must have seen the panic on my face, because she leaned in to whisper, "Sorry. Dane insisted on coming once he heard you were sick."

"You okay, Teo?" Dane asked. Jessica hung behind her brother, watching me. The circles under her eyes looked even darker than yesterday.

I nodded. "I'm good."

"Mr. DuPont," Dad said as he stepped forward and shook his hand.

"It's Patrick, Mr. Pres—"

"Call me Adolfo, please. And you remember Sylvia."

Mom smiled at him. "Is Lois here, too?"

"No, she sent me to visit Dane and Jessie. Guys, come here." He waved them over.

Mom gasped when she saw Dane's crutches. "Ay, Dane. *¿Qué pasó, niño?*" Instead of giving him a chance to reply, she moved on to Jessica. "Jessie, you're at Highbanks, too!" Jessica seemed to tense when Mom scooped her up in an embrace.

My cheeks warmed. Mom sure was a hugger.

"You had high BG?" Lucia asked me.

Alejandro answered, "Over six hundred."

I rolled my eyes. Privacy was impossible with the Secret Service involved.

"I bet your body's just adjusting to a new environment, new stressors," Alejandro said. "That's why your numbers have been so up and down."

Hmm. That sounded plausible. And I didn't seem to have as much time to bother with test strips in college.

"That sucks, Matty." Lucia patted my hand.

I swallowed. "Mom said I have to get the pump or they'll make me leave Highbanks."

Lucia's mouth dropped open. "She *did?*"

"Dad won't let her do that," Alejandro said. "Don't worry."

Lucia rested her hand on my shoulder. "Are you thinking about the pump?"

I clutched the sheet. "Maybe. This…" I gestured around me. "This could still happen, you know. It doesn't prevent blood sugar crashes."

"But it makes it easier to monitor things, right?"

Alejandro nodded. "Right."

"Alex," Dad said. He beckoned for him. "We're talking wedding over here. Where's the reception?"

Alejandro joined the discussion between my parents and the Monroes.

Lucia sat on my bed, and the coconut smell of her wet hair floated toward me. "Don't do this for Mom, or Dad, or me, or Alex. Do this for yourself."

I frowned.

"You quit sports for Mom's sake," she continued. "That wasn't right. But the pump benefits *you*, right? Makes it easier to go to class, run on the treadmill, play guitar with your buddies?"

I wondered if I would've made it through today's rehearsal if I'd had the pump.

"It's okay to take care of *you*," Lucia said.

I stroked my jaw.

Dane materialized by the bed, towering over me as he balanced on one foot.

Lucia popped up and leaned into him. "You must be exhausted from your crutches."

"No fucking kidding." He managed to wrap one arm around her.

She whispered something in his ear, and a huge grin broke out. I wondered what she'd said. Judging by her soft blush, it was something sexual. As they turned to the side, Jessica approached.

I tugged the sheet to make sure the catheter was hidden from view. "I didn't want you to see me like this."

She looked down, and her blond ringlets fell over one cheek. She wore white shorts, and my eyes trailed down her long, toned legs. "I didn't want you to see me like this, either," she said.

Like what…*beautiful?*

Her mouth quivered, and her eyes glistened. Was she about to cry?

"Are you okay?" I asked.

She blew out a breath, and I thought I smelled alcohol. "You're the one in the hospital, and you're asking *me* if I'm okay?"

"*Sí*," I stared into her eyes. When she looked away, I squeezed her hand. "Jess. Are you okay?"

She turned back to me, eyes wide, blinking rapid-fire. Her chest rose with a long breath. "No." Her hand tensed in mine, like it cost her to admit that. "I'm not doing so great. I've had a rough start here."

"I'm sorry."

She slumped. "Thanks."

I let go of her hand. "It's not, um, it's not been easy for me, either."

Her pretty blue eyes came up to meet mine.

"I'm not managing my diabetes well here. *Mamá's* right." My jaw tightened. "Looks like I have to get an insulin pump. A fucking pump."

"Oh." She blinked at me. "So…a fump?"

In an instant, I grinned. "Yeah, a fump." How in the world did she get me to smile? "A fump, near my rump."

She giggled, and it was the cutest sound. "It goes on your butt?"

"Nah." I patted the area above my hip. "The needle goes in my side, I think. And I wear the pump in my pocket, or clipped to my belt."

"Sounds like carrying a cell phone," she said.

I'd never thought of it that way. "The fump's got my pancreas on speed dial."

She giggled again. I wouldn't mind having *her* on speed dial. But I didn't even know her number. As her light chlorine scent washed over me, I felt my body reacting. *Holy crap* — the catheter tube shifted next to me. I folded my hands together over the sheet to hide my growing problem.

"Could I get your number?" I blurted.

She flinched, and her eyes got big.

Idiota. I shouldn't have asked that, but my dick had no self-control. "Or, uh, I could give you mine? You could decide if you want to call, or text, or…"

She pulled her phone from her pocket. "Let me turn it on."

"Why'd you turn it off?"

Her head stayed down as she licked her lip. "Um. Battery's, uh… dying."

Was she lying? Something felt off. I caught a glimpse of her phone lighting up with incoming texts as it vibrated in her hand. "Oh, no," she whispered. Her hand shook as it floated over her mouth.

"You're getting texts you don't want?"

She seemed to freeze and wouldn't look at me. I got the sense she was scared, but I didn't know why.

I tried to make my voice as gentle as possible. "Why don't you block them?"

"Huh?" Her glassy eyes blinked at me.

"You can block a number, right?"

Her lips parted. "You're brilliant. Why didn't *I* think of that?"

She just called me brilliant? The catheter levitated off the mattress.

After tapping on her phone several times, she looked up at me with a dazzling smile. "Okay, tell me your number, Teo."

9

Jessica

★ ★ ★

I grumbled as I read through all the questions I had to answer for Dr. Valentine. When I looked around the sports medicine waiting room, a man with his arm in a sling stared at me.

This blows. My appointment was scheduled to begin in ten minutes, but I hadn't realized I'd have to answer so many invasive questions beforehand. My head hurt. I wished Dane was here to help me, but he had class on Mondays.

What is the reason for your visit today? My face flamed as I wrote, *Positive drug test.*

After a bunch of questions about athletic injuries, school, and family, there was a symptom checklist. Insomnia? *Check.* Appetite loss? *Check.* Low energy? *Check.* Impaired sport performance? *Check.* Impaired school performance? Not checked, due to the aforementioned insomnia. My late nights at the studio meant I'd already finished art projects due next week.

What are your goals for counseling? That one stumped me. I was here because I had to be, but I thought it'd be rude to write that. When Mom had been a psychologist, she used to complain about court-ordered clients giving her a hard time. I didn't want to make things difficult for Dr. Valentine.

I don't want to feel so tired, I finally wrote. But then I thought about all the times I'd nearly jumped out of my skin when someone startled me the past week. *I don't want to feel so jumpy.* Though my drooping eyelids told me I was still tired. Maybe I shouldn't have crossed that out. How could I feel jumpy and tired at the same time? It made no sense.

Fuck it. It was just stupid paperwork. *Why am I obsessing over these asinine questions?* I gave the packet to the receptionist and returned to my seat. A nurse or somebody called a name, and the man with the sling followed her down a hallway.

Now I was alone. The TV played ESPN, but I didn't care to hear the commentators argue over Highbanks football's ranking in the national polls. One guy said Highbanks had played pansy opponents, so we didn't deserve a high ranking. The other guy told him he was just jealous. I thought they were both fuckknobs.

I pulled my phone out of my backpack. Thank God Blake couldn't text me any more. I was so grateful that Mateo had mentioned blocking him. The fact I hadn't thought of it myself showed I wasn't thinking clearly.

But there was another text I'd avoided answering since this morning.

Where are you? It's unacceptable to miss practice.

My stomach clenched as my headache pounded. I hated when coaches were mad at me. But I just hadn't been able make it to practice this morning. It had been such a relief not to hear from Blake all weekend that I couldn't force myself to face him at the pool. *Wimp.*

When I'd told Mackenzie I wasn't going to practice this morning, she'd stared at me like I was crazy. And maybe I was. My nightmare about the shadow pursuing me, yanking my ankle to pull me into him, had certainly made me feel that way.

Instead of responding to my coach, Kathy, I scrolled through my contacts to get to the Rs. I searched for Mateo, but didn't find him under Ramirez. Then I remembered he'd told me to list his number under his Secret Service nickname in case anyone stole my phone. I tapped the contact for *Roberto.*

He'd invited me to text him, and I wondered if I could. I pictured Mateo in the hospital bed, looking tired and sad. I didn't like anyone to touch me, but when he'd held my hand, I hadn't felt scared. I hadn't jumped. He felt safe, somehow. Maybe it was seeing him so vulnerable, hooked up to IVs. Or maybe it was having Johnny and Karen nearby. Johnny had always been there for me. I held my breath, then typed a text.

It's Jess. Feeling better?

His response came a second later.

**You texted! Yeah, thanks.
You in class?**

I chewed my lip. I didn't want to admit where I was. So embarrassing.

No. You?

**It's time for Music Theory,
but I'm not going.**

Oh. Is your blood sugar still too high?

It's fine now but they vary my routine for security.

I felt myself making a face.

So you can't go to class some days?

Yeah.

That sucks.

**Well, it's not too bad.
At least I get to hang with my cat.**

It was adorable that the Ramirez family had a First Cat. Mateo added:

**But I don't get to see some cool guys
from theory class today.**

His text made me think of Van from my 3D art class.

*Burning question for you.
Guys with man buns: straight or gay?*

LOL, random. Straight for sure.

My lips parted. I hadn't expected such a definitive answer.

*Really? What if he teaches yoga?
Gay or straight?*

**Hmm. That's tougher.
Does he have a lisp?**

I suppressed a grin.

You're awful.

**You're the one who asked.
WHY did you ask, by the way?**

*There's a guy in my 3D class.
Trying to figure out if he's flirting.*

**Tell him you're not interested.
You don't like ambiguously gay men.
You need to stay away from him,
from all man buns.
They're dangerous.**

I giggled.

"Jessica?"

I looked up and saw Dr. Valentine waiting for me. She held my packet of paperwork.

"Oh, hi." I gathered my backpack and stood. My laughter disappeared as my headache returned.

She smiled as she shook my hand. "Please follow me."

As we walked down a hallway, I typed a quick good-bye to Mateo.

The soft yellow light of her office made it feel homey. I gawked at the bursting bookshelf. "You've read all these books?"

"Well, no." She shrugged. "Someday, I hope."

There was a framed photo of a big gray cat with mean green eyes on one shelf. "So you have a cat, too."

She nodded. "You have a cat?"

"No. Mom's allergic." She appeared confused so I added, "I was just talking to someone who has a cat."

"Ah. Please have a seat." I settled into the sofa while she took a chair across from me. "I suppose there'd be no cat in the White House if your mother had won."

"No way. She wouldn't even let my dad get a dog."

"What kind of dog does your dad want?"

The conversation was easy so far—not the interrogation about drug use I'd expected. "Well, he really wanted a Weimaraner like the artist William Wegman paints. But Mom shut him down — said those dogs were too big. So then he wanted a dachshund like Pablo Picasso had, but Mom wouldn't go for that, either."

"Too bad. You wanted a dog, too?"

I considered her question. "It probably wouldn't be fair to the dog, considering how much my mom travels. And it'd starve, too. Once my dad gets going on a painting, he's kind of closed off from the world."

"Has it been a while since you've heard from him?"

"He's here, actually."

Her eyebrows lifted. "In the waiting room?"

"No, at Dane's apartment. He's painting." Dad had set up a little studio in the guest bedroom and painted all day Sunday. He'd claimed I was his muse. "He doesn't know I'm here. He, uh, doesn't know about the drug test."

"Ah. Do you plan on telling him?"

"Hell, no."

She didn't seem fazed by my answer. "How do you think he'd react? Is he strict?"

"Nah, he'd be cool. Mom's stricter than him, but they're both pretty chill. I just don't want them getting the wrong picture of me."

"What picture do you want them to get?"

I felt like she could see through me. "That I'm a hard worker, I guess. A good swimmer, a good student. Not bad at art."

She gestured to the papers I'd completed. "Says here you're an art major." When I nodded, she frowned. "That'll be a tough major for a swimmer."

"They already told me they didn't think I could do it."

"What do *you* think? How's it going so far juggling art and swimming?"

I shrugged. "I won't get a four-point-oh like Dane, but I can make it work. You see Dane, too, right?"

Her facial expression didn't change. "Now would be a good time to review confidentiality." She launched into a diatribe about privacy in counseling, and asked me to sign a release to Michelle Farris, the athletic administrator.

"How old were you when you started swimming?" Her hands were poised over the keyboard of her tablet.

"Six."

She typed in my response. "That sounds young."

"Not really. You need a lot of training to swim fast. Dane and I basically lived at our neighborhood pool every summer. He was already on the team, and they needed a girl my age for the relay, so they recruited me."

"Dane swam, too?"

"Yeah, but he quit when he was eleven. Said the sport wasn't violent enough."

She smirked. "What do you love about swimming?"

I blinked. No one had asked me that in a long time. "The water's just a special place, you know? I feel light and powerful at the same time. And I'm good at it." I squirmed. "Sorry, that sounds arrogant."

"Not if you can back it up." She grinned. "You're on a full scholarship?"

I nodded.

"Sounds like you *can* back it up. How do you like the Highbanks pool?"

"It's pretty good." The hairs on the back of my neck bristled as I remembered Blake coming up behind me on deck two days ago.

"What is it?"

I flinched, then looked at her. "What?"

"You look sort of scared."

I swallowed. "Nothing."

She studied me for a moment. "How do you like your coaches?"

"They're great." I sighed. "They probably don't like *me* so much, though."

"Why not?"

I shrugged. "The whole reason I'm here."

"Yes, the drug test. We'll get to that."

Can't wait.

"I hear the training's intense for your sport. How's that going?"

"My club team trained really hard, so I'm used to it. I should be swimming faster."

"What's holding you back?"

The thought of Blake at the other end of the pool squeezed my chest. "I'm…tired."

"You mentioned on the paperwork that you haven't been sleeping well. When did your insomnia start?"

"About a week ago." *The night after the party.*

"Are you having trouble falling asleep?" I nodded, and she continued, "Trouble staying asleep? Waking up early?" I nodded again. "Do you have worries that keep you awake?"

"Not really. I just can't sleep. So I stay at the studio late, make myself super tired, then collapse."

"So, you're avoiding sleep?"

I shrugged. "I guess."

"Are you having nightmares?"

My heartbeat spiked as I felt the clammy presence of the shadow behind me. "Yeah."

"About what?" She stopped typing and looked at me.

I swallowed. "Not sure. Someone's chasing me."

"Is it a recurrent nightmare?"

"Uh, variations on a theme, I guess."

"Have you…Have you experienced something traumatic in your life?"

My chest hurt, and it was hard to breathe. Blake hovering over me, trapping my arms over my head as he licked between my breasts—

"Jessica? Are you remembering something?"

I sucked in a breath and licked my dry lips. Blake had said *I'd* come on to *him*. Then why was that memory so frightening?

"Have you been through a traumatic event?" she repeated.

I fought to push Blake's probing eyes from my mind. I didn't want to talk about him, and consensual sex shouldn't have been traumatic. But she still stared at me expectantly—I had to give her something.

"My mom. She…when she was running for president, there was a plot to bomb her bus. I had nightmares after that."

"Wow, that's awful. Is that what you were remembering just then?"

"Yes," I lied.

"Do you replay those memories in your mind sometimes?"

"I haven't in a while. Johnny—he was my Secret Service agent—he stopped the bombing. And it didn't bother me as much once Mom lost. But the nightmares began again, about a week ago."

"When you started at Highbanks," she said.

I nodded.

"Sometimes painful memories get triggered, and you re-experience the trauma like you're back in the past. Your heart races, it's hard to breathe, you feel sick, you can't sleep…"

My eyes widened. She was describing my life.

"Are you feeling on edge? Easily startled?"

I nodded.

"Sounds like you're having PTSD symptoms again. Post-traumatic stress disorder. You're feeling unsafe, like there's a threat to kill your mother."

My mother had nothing to do with me feeling unsafe, but Dr. Valentine seemed so certain that I didn't want to question her. I certainly didn't want to discuss my night with Blake.

"Re-experiencing trauma feels horrifying," she said. "You want the memories to stop, but you can't get them out of your mind."

Absolutely.

"And that's where drugs come in."

I looked up. *Here we go.*

"People who have flashbacks may abuse drugs to avoid the memories, dull the pain. Let's talk about your substance use. When's the last time you drank alcohol?"

Why was she asking about my drinking?

When I didn't answer, she added, "I know you're underage, but you won't get in trouble for answering. This is a no-judgment zone. I just want to get a sense of the role substances have in your life."

Hmm. "I drank on Saturday, after the game. With my dad." *And last night, too.* I'd smuggled some of Dane's liquor back to my dorm room. But I didn't want to admit that.

"How often do you drink?"

"Like once a week. Or less."

"So a standard serving is twelve ounces of beer, about five ounces of wine, or a shot of liquor. How many drinks do you typically consume in one night?"

I shook my head. "I don't know, like two or three."

"How many did you have on Saturday?"

I remembered swigging straight from the bottle. I'd never done that before. "Um, how many glasses of wine are in a bottle?"

"Between four and five. You drank a bottle of wine?"

"My dad had a little." I heard defensiveness in my tone. I probably sounded like an alcoholic.

"What made you drink more than usual for you?"

"I thought it would help me sleep better."

She pressed her lips together. "Common myth. Alcohol helps you fall asleep faster, but it interferes with REM sleep. It worsens the quality of your sleep. Marijuana impairs sleep even more."

"Oh." No wonder I felt even more tired today.

"Do you typically drink alcohol when you use marijuana?"

"I only smoked once."

She squinted like she didn't believe me.

"It's true! Last Friday was the only time I've ever smoked."

"Okay, and did you drink alcohol when you smoked?"

"Yeah."

"How much?" she asked.

"One beer—well, like, one and a half beers, and a vodka tonic."

"Sounds like your usual amount."

I considered how drunk I'd felt. "The vodka was strong, though."

"I see. Did you make the drink?"

"Um, no." My legs began to shake.

"So you're not sure how many shots were in it."

My airway constricted, and I couldn't speak.

Her head angled to one side. "If you'd never used marijuana before that night, what made you change your mind?"

The trembling progressed up my body. "He said freshmen don't get tested."

"He?"

"Blake," I whispered.

Her voice gentled. "Who's Blake?"

I couldn't look at her. "A swimmer. A senior. We were at his house."

"You were with friends?"

"My teammates. Mackenzie and Elyse." I looked up. "They won't get in trouble, will they?"

"This isn't about getting people in trouble. What happened?"

"I had a beer, and it was gross. Mateo was there." With a faint smile, I remembered his cute little dimple.

"Mateo Ramirez?"

"Yeah, Dane's friends with him." I paused. "Blake brought me a drink." My smile vanished as I recalled accepting the vodka tonic. Had he *drugged* me? No—I would've tasted it, right? My entire body shook. "And he was kind of mean to Teo, so he left."

She blinked. "Blake left?"

I wish. "No, he…" I could barely swallow, my throat was so dry. "Blake took me to his room." I heard my heartbeat in my ears, a rapid cadence. "He rolled us a joint." I cringed. "I didn't want to smoke, but…he's a senior. I didn't want to be a naïve freshman. It was stupid. *I* was stupid."

"Where were Mackenzie and Elyse?"

"I don't know." I wished they'd seen me go up the stairs. I wished they'd stopped me. My nose stung with impending tears.

"How did the joint make you feel?"

I closed my eyes. "Man, I was tired. It was too much, the alcohol and the pot together. I was really drunk. I'm so stupid." A lump of regret lodged in my throat.

"Jessica?" I opened my eyes to find her leaning toward me, watching me. She hadn't typed in a while. "What happened next?"

Her look of concern got me. I had no chance to fight the tears that started flowing. "We had…sex." I looked down as I clenched my fists.

"That upsets you?" She handed me a box of tissues.

"Well, yeah. I barely knew him."

"The sex was consensual?"

Startled, I looked up. "Yes. It had to be."

"Why's that?" she asked.

"He texted me the next day. He said I threw myself at him. I just can't remember."

"Sounds like you were too drunk or high to give your consent."

"But I must've agreed." My hand trembled as I dabbed a tissue under my eye. "Why would he keep asking me to go out? Why would he keep texting? He's pushing me to be together now. I don't want to be rude, but I don't like him. I just want to forget that night. But he keeps texting me nonstop. It was so bad I had to block him."

She looked a little green.

Is my story that awful? "What's wrong?"

She shook her head. "Jessica, what do you think happened that night?"

His smile loomed over me, tensing my body like a coil. The frenetic beat of my heart made it hard for me to get air. *Your pussy's so tight*, he'd told me. A shudder crept up my spine. "He said I forced myself on him."

"Do you believe him?"

No. I realized I didn't believe a word he said. Somehow I said it out loud: "No."

"Then what do you think happened?"

Chills bloomed on my skin as I flashed back to that night…

Spots had crowded my vision as I'd tried to crawl away from him. *"Oh no, you don't."* His big hand had squeezed my ankle and dragged me back. *"No,"* I'd cried. My chest had vibrated with fear.

I'd forgotten that part of the night. No wonder my ankle had been bruised. I wished I'd never remembered.

My heart raced. Was I having a heart attack? I clutched the arm of the sofa as a wave of nausea rolled up my throat. I knew what had happened. I'd known all along. When I gathered enough air in my lungs to speak, I said, "He raped me."

The word made my skin crawl.

Dr. Valentine sat back in her chair. "Is that what you're having nightmares about?"

"H-H-He's pulling me back. I'm trying to escape. Oh, God." Tears spilled down my cheeks.

"You just remembered that?"

I nodded. Shudders vibrated through me.

"You're doing great. Good job sharing that with me. What do you notice about your breath right now?"

I gasped for air. "I'm not breathing."

"Let's practice some deep breaths, then. In…" She inhaled through her nose and nodded at me. "Out, two, three, four. In…out, two three, four."

My body kept shivering as I tried to breathe to her count. I wiped under my nose.

"May I see Blake's texts?"

That was an odd request, but I rummaged through my backpack for my phone. "If he's texted since Mateo told me to block him, I can't see those texts."

"Mateo knows about the rape?"

My eyes widened. "No. Nobody knows. *I* didn't even know until just now."

"Memory works that way. It's not foolproof."

"You're saying I might be wrong? He *didn't* rape me?"

"*Something* happened that night, or you wouldn't be reacting this way. Let's take our time with this. First, let me read the texts."

I handed her my phone and wondered why the texts were so important.

Her mouth tightened as she read. In the silence, I became aware of the ticking clock. She seemed to force a swallow before she looked up at me.

"I attended a drug-prevention conference a month ago."

Her eyes narrowed. Was she angry?

"One of the presentations that stuck with me was called The Weaponization of Alcohol."

"Okay?" I had no idea what she was talking about.

"It covered how sexual predators use alcohol and other drugs to incapacitate their victims. They might get the girl drunk, slip a roofie in her drink, or use other drugs to mess with her mind. Maybe they almost strangle her to stop her oxygen supply, make her memory even cloudier. Then they rape her."

Revulsion closed my throat.

"The next morning, they text to cover their tracks. 'I love you,' they might say. 'Can't stop thinking about you.' Or, 'I know you want me, but it's not a good time in my life for a relationship' — tricking the victim into thinking it was consensual."

Holy shit. "I think I'm gonna be sick."

She stood and dragged a wastebasket in front of me. "It's okay. You're experiencing the fight, flight, or freeze response. It's not dangerous, just unpleasant."

Unpleasant? Hello, understatement. I held my head as I rocked on the sofa. *Don't barf. Don't barf.*

"Keep breathing. Tell me what colors you see in my office."

I sniffed and looked up. "Maroon, khaki, white lights." She'd strung Christmas lights around her door even though it was September.

"What do you hear?"

I stilled. "The clock ticking. People talking in the hallway."

"What do you taste?"

"Um…Nothing, really. I haven't eaten anything today."

She frowned. "You didn't eat before or after morning practice?"

I took a shaky breath and started crying again. "I didn't go."

"Oh." Her face softened. "Because he's at the pool."

A sob escaped, and I covered my mouth.

She opened a desk drawer and handed me a protein bar.

"But I don't want to get sick."

"Food will settle your stomach. And you may be too agitated to notice your hunger, but your body needs fuel to deal with this trauma. To manage your emotions. Go ahead and take a bite."

I closed my eyes as I bit into almonds and bittersweet dark chocolate stuck together with…something. The bar didn't taste very good, but I kept eating anyway.

"It's tempting to avoid practice. Avoidance goes hand-in-hand with PTSD." She eyed me. "But avoidance interferes with healing and with reaching your goals. I know swimming's important to you. Are you in danger if you attend practice?"

I swallowed. "No. He can't hurt me as long as I'm not alone with him."

"Are you ever alone with him?"

"I've refused his invitations." I shuddered. "I haven't let him get me alone."

She nodded. "Your body knew. Your brain hadn't caught up yet, but your body knew what happened. It's like a trauma book I've read: *The Body Keeps the Score.*"

Yep. Blake one, me zero.

She typed away as I finished the bar. I felt my heartbeat start to decelerate, and my headache returned. I wished I had time for a nap.

"How are you feeling?"

"Tired." I drank from my water bottle.

"I bet. That was a lot to share with me today, but it needed to happen. To tell your story is to heal."

Could I heal from this? That seemed like a fantasy.

"I'd like you to get checked out by your team physician." She gave me a business card. "You can meet with Dr. Cabela here at Sports Medicine, and she'll run some tests. Do you want me to talk to her first?"

I tensed, knowing exactly what type of tests she was referring to. "No."

"That's fine, as long as you're honest with her. You did good today." She smiled at me. "We're out of time, but I want to meet with you again, help you deal with what happened to you."

Oh, crap. I had to talk about this again? Would more memories surface? I didn't think I could handle it.

"I know it's scary," she said, probably watching my freak-out cross my face. "But sharing your memories decreases their intensity. I want to teach you some ways to sleep better and get through flashbacks. For now, practice some deep breaths three times a day. Use your five senses to notice the present. And I'll show you more next time, okay?"

I had to face what had happened. I didn't want to, but I knew I had to. "Okay."

As we scheduled for next week, I sat up. "You won't tell Dane about this, right?"

"Right. I don't have your permission."

"And Ms. Farris? You won't tell her?"

"Not unless you want me to. But you might consider reporting the sexual assault to the school."

I gasped. My headshakes were rapid-fire.

"You had an uncontrollable thing happen to you, but you're in control of this, okay?" She nodded. "This is your private information. I won't act without your permission."

"Okay." I exhaled. I hadn't felt more exhausted in my life.

On my way out, I said, "Just a heads up: Dane wants to see you again. Good luck with that."

"Why do you say it that way?"

"He's a handful."

She smiled. "What's he like as a brother?"

"Very opinionated." I remembered his hug on Saturday and felt a lump in my throat. "He's protective, too. But not in an overbearing way."

"Sounds like a keeper. See you next week."

10
Mateo
★ ★ ★

She texted me! I almost jumped up for a happy dance but managed to stay put on the TV room sofa. I didn't want one of my agents to come in and catch me acting like an idiot. Johnny had already given me crap for checking my phone ten times an hour since Saturday night.

How was I supposed to focus on my stupid music theory textbook after she texted? We had a quiz next week, but all I could think about was Man Bun making the moves on Jessica. Was it too late to switch into her art class to block him? And since her last text had been an abrupt good-bye, how long did I have to wait to text her again?

After thirty minutes of rereading the same paragraph about pentatonic scales, I tossed the textbook to the ottoman. Escuincle lifted his head from his curled-up position on the sofa. His eyes opened wide.

"Está bien, gato."

He lowered his head since I'd told him things were cool. He probably understood Spanish better than English after growing up in my house. When I walked out of the room, I heard a thump behind me and knew he was following. Lucia had been upset that he stayed by my side, even when she was home. *What can I say?* The cat had discerning taste.

I passed the office on my way to my bedroom, and Karen called, "Mateo?"

"Yeah?" I stepped inside to find her on the computer.

"How's it going?"

"Great!"

She leaned back. "What's got *you* so chipper?"

I hadn't realized my elation was visible. I'd felt the same way when Jessica told me I was brilliant for suggesting she block unwanted messages. I wondered if Man Bun was the guy bothering her with texts. Seemed I had to worry about him *and* Suave Swimmer Shithead.

"Would you mind telling me your BG?" Karen asked.

"Sure." I reached for the monitor in my pocket. "Ninety eight."

She beamed. "It's working great."

I had to admit it was nice not to have to stick myself every time someone wanted to know my blood glucose level.

"How intrusive does the pump feel?"

"Meh…" I could feel the small tube under my skin. "It was kind of uncomfortable last night. Woke me up when I turned over in bed."

"I think that's a normal adjustment. But you won't know it's there in about a week."

I hoped she was right. The Ramirez clan had returned to DC yesterday morning, and I didn't want them to have to make an emergency trip again anytime soon, or ever. Escuincle weaved through my legs, so I picked him up and asked, "Where's Johnny?"

Her eyes flashed with mystery, and she looked back at the computer monitor. "He's on an errand."

What's that *about?* Before I could leave, Karen turned back to me.

"Oh, Frank said Lucia will be home before seven for dinner."

"Please tell me you're not cooking."

"So ill-mannered." She shook her head. "We're getting Thai takeout."

My fist pumped. "Score!"

I headed into my bedroom but stopped short once I saw the empty spot near my dresser. *Damn.* I'd come in to work on a song, but we'd left my guitar at the warehouse in our rush to get to the hospital. I hoped I could get it back. I felt naked without it.

But I did have my electric keyboard, so that would have to do. I settled into my bed with the keyboard in front of me. No sooner had I turned it on than a streak of black flashed over the keys.

"Escuincle!"

As he turned, he swiveled his butt in my face. Then he pranced the other way across the keyboard, leaving a trail of dissonant notes in his wake.

I scooped him up and placed him on the floor. "No, brat." This interference was why I preferred my guitar when writing songs.

I'd already landed on a title for my new song, and after grabbing my notebook, I wrote on top of a blank page: *Find You*. Filling my head were Lucia's pep talk from last week and nonstop thoughts about Jessica.

I played a couple of chords, then sang, "*They say college is the time to find yourself.*" *Not quite right.* I jotted down some words, but movement at the foot of the bed drew my eye. Two black ears crept over the footboard.

"Squinkyyy," I warned. The ears descended from view. He was in full stealth mode now.

I erased the first line and sang another version. "*University is the time to find yourself.*" I scowled. That still didn't sound right. As I tapped out a melody, a black paw shot up to pounce on the C key.

"Ow!" Squinky's sharp claws had snagged my pinky finger. I leaned over to find the mischievous cat perched by my foot where it hung over the bed. His green eyes peered up at me as his tail swished. "You are not a piano player!"

His meow suggested he disagreed. I grumbled as I got up and opened the top drawer of my chest. I pulled out a crinkly bag, and the meows increased in volume. He knew what was coming. I moved his folded blankie from my floor to my bed—with Escuincle hot on my heels—and poured out a few of his favorite treats. He'd crunched through all three of them before I could settle back down near the head of the bed.

"Stay." I pointed at the blanket.

Meow?

My mouth in a firm line, I kept pointing. "*Stay.*"

He seemed to sigh, then circled the blanket a few times before stretching out on his side. He licked his mouth and began the serious business of grooming himself. I loved when he licked his paw and rubbed it over his face to wash it.

I exhaled as I observed his bedtime routine, knowing he wouldn't bother me once he fell asleep. I wrote the first stanza:

They say
University is the time
To find yourself
But I don't want to find myself
Just want to find you

The keyboard was actually a good fit for the rollicking melody. After scribbling two more stanzas, I wrote the refrain. As I sang this faster, peppier section, I craved my guitar.

You're so fine
Wanna find you
You'll be mine
Gonna find you

Escuincle's head lifted, and a moment later I jumped as I noticed movement in my doorway. When the hell had Fitch and Itch arrived? And who'd let them in?

"Chimichanga, that's catchy," Itch said as he waltzed in. "Who are you singing about?"

"What?"

"You're obviously singing about a girl." Itch nodded at the keyboard. "Or a guy." He splayed his hands. "Not that there's anything wrong with that."

Wearing a Cubs hat I hadn't seen before, Fitch grinned as he came in, too.

I stood. "What're you guys doing here?"

"You forgot your guitar," Fitch said. He set down my case and reached out to pet my cat.

Escuincle growled at him, and Fitch stole his hand back.

"Easy, Squinky." I patted the raised fur on his back.

Itch tilted his head. "What's your cat's name?"

"Escuincle. Spanish for brat."

The brat padded across the mattress toward Itch, who leaned down to scratch his ears. The sound of purrs filled the room.

"Hey." Fitch scowled. "I've got three cats at home. Why doesn't she like me?"

"It's a he," I said. I was trying to figure out the same thing. Why the preference for Itch over Fitch?

Itch puffed out his chest. "All pets like me. And Squinky and I have the same hair."

He was right. Itch's fluffy, black hair was the same texture as my cat's. Fitch's baseball cap hid his lighter brown hair. I started laughing.

"It's the baseball hat." I gestured to the Cubs logo. "Alejandro played baseball, and Escuincle hates him. You remind him of my brother."

"Well, I ain't takin' off my hat," Fitch said.

Itch rolled his eyes. "He even sleeps in that damn thing."

"Do not."

"His blue hat smelled so bad, I made him wash it," Itch told me.

"At least *I* shower," Fitch countered.

I shook my head at Itch. "You're still not showering in the dorms?"

"Uh." He grimaced. "I caved, finally. But you can be damn sure I'm wearing flip-flops in there. Who knows what bacteria and fungi grow on that skanky communal tile." Itch glanced at Fitch. "Or underneath the rim of that ball cap." He sprang for the Cubs hat and ripped it off his head.

"Give it back!" Fitch yelled.

Itch held the hat above his head. With their height difference, it was tough for Fitch to reach it, even when he jumped. Itch tossed the hat to me, and my eyes widened when Fitch came to get it. I tucked it behind my back, and Fitch reached around to grab it. Ears back, Escuincle hissed at him, which made Itch double over with laughter.

"The cat's like Secret Service, too!" he cackled.

Fitch kept grabbing for his hat, but I eluded his groping hands. I could tell he was getting pissed off and was just about to return his hat when he shoved me to the bed.

"*Oompf.*" I felt a tearing sensation and reached for my belly.

Fitch jumped off me. "Are you okay?"

My fingers touched the tip of the tube, which had ripped free from my abdomen. *Damn pump.* I wasn't sure what to do.

"Everything okay here, Mr. Ramirez?" Johnny asked from the doorway.

It all clicked as I rolled up from the bed. "Thanks for bringing my friends here, Johnny."

"Least I could do." He nodded. "Mr. Kahanawke and Mr. Fitcherson thought they'd return your guitar in class, but you weren't there, so they called me."

"Sorry, man," Fitch said. His hat had found its home again. "You're still too sick to go to class? Then I tackled you — not cool."

I shook my head. "I didn't go to class for security reasons. I'm fine now." I felt wetness from the tube leaking onto my shirt. "But Johnny, could you ask Karen to come in? I think the tube came out of my pump."

"Sure thing." He zipped away.

Itch stared at me. "You have an insulin pump?"

"Yeah. You know about them?"

"This girl in high school had one. But yours didn't work so well on Saturday, huh?"

"I didn't have it then. I just got it at the hospital." I lifted my shirt to study the injection site. "It's gonna be pretty gross to change out this sucker." I could already smell the burned-plastic odor of the leaking insulin. "You guys should hang out in the TV room."

"Nonsense," Karen said as she swept in. "This'll be quick." She set down an alcohol swab and other equipment for my pump.

"I'm real sorry." Fitch winced. "I didn't mean to hurt him."

"We needed to change the cannula tonight, anyway," Karen said.

I opened the alcohol swab and swirled it over the skin to the side of my belly button. Karen handed me the infusion set, and I took a deep breath before pressing it into my skin. I felt a slight burn from the needle, but it didn't sting as much as insulin injections. Far less frequent, too. Why hadn't I gotten the pump sooner? Sometimes I was too stubborn for my own good.

"Want to change your shirt?" Karen asked.

I looked up at Fitch and Itch and grinned. "I guess *I* smell now, too."

"We can rename our band Smell It, Bitch," Itch said.

My eyes shot up. They considered me part of their band?

As Karen left, she said over her shoulder, "I'll put out some snacks for you guys in the kitchen."

I peeled off my shirt and got a new one from the drawer. As I slipped it on, I asked, "Hey, what's the name of your band? You never told me."

"Witch," Fitch said.

I lowered my chin and peered up at them. "Weston, Itch, and Fitch. You seriously combined your names?"

"Don't be a hater," Itch said. "It's tough coming up with a band name."

Especially when weed's killed all your brain cells. "Did Weston go back to Cincinnati?"

"He had to get back to work." Fitch frowned at Escuincle, who glared at him from the bed. He picked up one of the framed photos on my bookshelf. "Hey, is this you with the vice president's kids?"

"No, PQ's kids. Uh, Paula Quinlen, Secretary of State. Where does Weston work?" I couldn't imagine him holding down a job.

"He's a bartender," Itch said.

I squinted. "Don't you have to be twenty-one to do that?"

"He's twenty-five, actually. Killin' it reaching the life goals." Itch darted around me to grab my notebook from the mattress.

"Hey!" Feeling like Fitch trying to get his hat back, I lunged for the notebook. Itch held it high, but I caught a corner in my grasp. I tugged, but Itch held tight. "Give it to me, klepto."

"Easy, Ramirez." His tone was light, but his grip was strong, and I didn't want my notebook to rip. "If you want to be part of this band, we need to see what you got."

I let go in an instant.

He turned to one page and read aloud:

When I was five
My world turned sour
From too much sweetness
In my blood

When I was five
Not my finest hour
Alone in my tower
A sugar flood

Didn't think I had
A reason to hope
A reason to plan
To become a man
Till I met you

The room was quiet. They'd flayed my heart open before them, and I was dying to know if they'd stab it.

Fitch broke the silence. "That's really sweet, Mateo."

Itch sniffed and pretended to wipe a tear. "*So* sweet," he cooed.

My eyes narrowed.

"Just playin' with ya," Itch added.

My shoulders lowered, but I was still nervous about their opinion.

"Dude. You got it bad for her," Itch said. "Who is it?"

"It's…you know." I reached out to pet my cat. "No one who'd be into me. Just a girl in my imagination."

"Uh-huh." Itch eyed me, then flipped to the front of the notebook. "How many songs have you written?"

"Around fifty."

His gaze snapped up, and Fitch sucked in a breath.

"*Fifty?*" Fitch asked. He marched over next to Itch. "What's that one?" He pointed to the page.

Itch read:

Hey, chica! Where did you go?
Don't wanna fly this thing solo
But you're running away like a track star
The distance between us, it's too far

"Have you recorded any of these?" Fitch asked.

"A couple of years ago." I shrugged. "The quality's not great."

"Let's hear it," Itch said.

My hands shook as I opened my laptop and searched for "Hey, Chica!" on my songwriting software. What would they think of this one? The Latin beat filled the room.

Itch's foot tapped along. "Love what you did with the guitar riff. I gotta try that." He knelt by my guitar case. "May I?"

I hesitated. "Just be careful."

"Of course." He unclasped the case and slung the strap over his shoulder.

"I'll be right back." Fitch dashed out of the room. When he returned a minute later, he held two wooden spoons.

Itch leaned back and put his hands over his face. "Don't spank me, Mama! I'll be good, I promise."

"You deserve to get your ass beat, son," Fitch said. But instead of attacking his roommate with the spoons, he scuttled into the bathroom off my bedroom and emerged with an empty cleaning bucket.

"Resourceful, isn't he?" Itch said.

Resourceful at what? But when Fitch flipped the bucket over on my desk and tapped it with a spoon handle, his makeshift drum set materialized.

"Let's do this," Itch said. He gestured to my keyboard. "Count me in."

Evidently Escuincle had determined that Fitch wasn't too much of a threat, because he returned to his blanket. I sat on the bed and readied to play the melody. Tingles of excitement zinged up my spine. We were about to play *my* music. *Live.* I prayed it didn't sound like shit.

I said, "One, two, three, four…"

My song came alive with Itch's guitar skills and Fitch's exotic spoon beat. The clap of the wood on the bucket almost sounded like maracas. I pictured long, toned legs, a playful smile, and curly blond hair as I sang:

> *Hey, chica! Come conmigo*
> *And baby, why don't we go*
> *Down under the bridge to the water*
> *With you it can only get hotter*

Fitch jumped in to harmonize each time we hit the hook, and he amazed me with his intuitive harmonies on only his first listen to the song. The guys made the song ten times better—I couldn't wait to play all of my songs with them.

I looked up to see Karen and Johnny in the doorway, listening. Johnny maintained his typical stoic expression, but Karen's smile seemed wistful. Were those tears in her eyes? As we kept playing, she ducked out. I wondered what was going on with her.

At the end of the song, I held up my hand to signal them to stop. The last notes reverberated in the room. I looked at Itch, who stared at me. Fitch grinned.

"Fantastic," Johnny said. "You guys sound great together."

"Thanks, Johnny." I was pretty sure I was blushing. Or maybe my face was flushed from the high of playing.

Itch shook his head. "Your voice is…"

I held my breath.

"So *good*, dude!"

I breathed out and grinned.

"It's, like, smooth, but…" He punched his fist. "Commanding. You've got stage presence, man."

"He's much better than my sorry vocals," Fitch said. "Think we got a new backup singer for Witch."

I stood. "No way—your harmonies were sick, Fitch."

He didn't appear to hear my compliment, though, since his attention was focused on Itch. They shared a cryptic look.

Karen reappeared. "Want some snacks, guys?"

"Let's play another one," I said.

"Mateo, you should probably eat," she said.

I frowned, but Itch pushed me to the doorway. "Go. Fitch and I need to talk. We'll meet you in there in a sec."

I wished they wouldn't leave me in the dark. I followed Karen to the kitchen.

"You okay?" I asked.

"Sure. Remember to administer a bolus before you eat."

Nice blowoff. She'd set out carrots, triangles of pita bread, and hummus on the kitchen table. I slid the pump out of my pocket. "Two units, you think?"

"Probably three." She took the pump and helped me calculate how many units of insulin I needed.

I was scooping red pepper hummus onto a carrot stick five minutes later when my boys came in.

"Sweet kitchen," Itch said.

Fitch attacked the snack.

"Actually, the whole house is amazing." Itch scanned the open space. "When're we moving in?"

Fitch chuckled. "You wish."

Itch gestured to the swipe of hummus on the corner of Fitch's mouth. "Can't take you anywhere." He turned to me. "Maybe I can come over for showers once in a while?"

"Negative," Karen said as she walked out of the kitchen.

I crunched a carrot. "What were you guys talking about?"

Itch pulled apart a pita. "You." He popped a piece in his mouth.

I tensed.

"We want you to be part of our band," Fitch said.

"Really?" Butterflies fluttered in my gut.

"Fitch." The edge in Itch's voice froze the butterfly wings mid-flap. Did he not agree?

Fitch patted his shoulder. "It'll be okay." He nodded at me. "Welcome to the band, Mateo."

I couldn't wait to tell Jessica. This would be the perfect excuse to text her, right?

11
Jessica

★ ★ ★

As we finished another practice from hell — I'd managed to make all five of them since my therapy session — my brother crutched onto the deck, trailed by his athletic trainer. *Why is he here?* And why was he wearing a swimsuit?

When I dragged myself out, I was relieved to see the men's team still practicing on the other side of the pool. I kept closer tabs on the length of their practices than my own.

"What're you doing here?" I asked Dane.

"He needs to burn off some energy," said Tina, his athletic trainer. "Can he swim with you?"

"But my practice is over."

"C'mon, Jess," Dane said. "I'm going crazy without exercise."

"And making everyone *around* him crazy," Tina added.

Dane glared at her, then looked back at me. "I hadn't thought of swimming until Dr. Valentine mentioned it. And Tina says it's okay as long as I don't push off the wall with my broken foot."

"I'm sure your coaches won't mind if Dane gets in," Tina said.

I noticed Mike erasing the whiteboard. Kathy appeared to be lecturing my teammate, Emma, who'd been late to today's first practice after oversleeping. I didn't envy her. I'd gotten the same stern sermon after missing Monday's morning practice. Kathy had told me if I screwed up again, she'd tell my parents about the drug test.

Elyse sauntered over. "You gonna introduce me to your brother?"

"Hey." Dane nodded at her. "I've seen you around. You're a senior, right?"

"Yep." She squeezed water from her long, black hair as she looked up at him with a seductive smile.

"Elyse, this is Dane," I said. "He already has a girlfriend."

Her mouth dropped open. "I know that, of course. Everyone in America knows that. He kissed Lucia on national TV."

Dane rolled his eyes.

"But he has some friends on the team he can set me up with, right?" Elyse asked. "Volleyball guys are *hot*."

Dane raised his chin. "Yes, we are."

Now *I* was the one rolling my eyes. Then I froze in place as my breath caught. Fear tickled up my spine. *The body knows the score.*

"Dane Monroe, what's goin' on?" Blake said from behind me. Oh God, did my brother know him?

"Hey." The uncertainty in Dane's voice answered my question.

I turned to see Blake extend his hand. "Blake Morrell."

As they shook hands, I noticed Blake was even taller than Dane. Though Dane currently slouched a bit over his crutches.

"What happened to your foot, man?" Blake asked.

"A weight got dropped on it."

Blake chuckled. "Ooof."

When Blake's wet hand cupped my shoulder, my heart went into overdrive. My gasp drew Dane's attention, and I tried to remember to blink. What had Dr. Valentine told me? *Breathe.* I felt my chest vibrate as I exhaled.

"Do you swim as fast as your little sister?" Blake asked, squeezing my shoulder.

Dane stared at Blake's hand, then straightened to his full height. "I haven't trained for ten years."

"Too bad. I could use some competition in the sprints." Blake's fingertips pulsed into my skin. I wanted him off of me. "Sure don't get any here."

Elyse stepped closer to me. "So humble, Blake." She wrapped her arm around my waist and tugged me toward her, away from him. His hand dropped off.

Thank God. I closed my eyes. His lingering touch seemed to sting.

"I need to get in," Dane said. He looked at Blake. "Catch you later." His smile seemed obligatory—the same one Mom gave when shaking the hand of a particularly odious Republican.

"Sure. See ya, Jess, Elyse."

My shoulders lowered after he left.

"What's up with you?" Dane asked.

I swallowed. "Nothing."

"Do you know him? Why'd he touch you like that?"

My breaths picked up speed.

"He thinks Jessica will be his next conquest, I bet," Elyse said. "But she's smarter than that."

I wished I'd been smarter than that.

"He's such a creep," Elyse said.

Dane tilted his head. "Really? Why?"

"Ugh." She shook her head. "I heard he slept with the entire field hockey team."

"That's ridiculous," Dane said. "Can't be true."

Elyse shrugged. "And when one or two of them wanted nothing to do with him, he wore them down till they said yes."

"Stay away from him, Jess," Dane ordered. "You don't want to be associated with a man ho."

Where were you two weeks ago, brother?

"I agree with Dane," Elyse said. "He's bad news." She hugged her body. "I'm freezing—gonna hit the showers. Have a good swim, Dane."

Dane nodded.

"Let's go, Monroe!" Tina called. She'd been chatting with my trainer, Zeke. "I don't have all day."

Dane glowered at her, but he did crutch toward the blocks. He beckoned me. "Stay around and make sure I don't drown."

"You'll be fine."

"I haven't swum in years. And I need a ride to Luz's after this, too."

I groaned. "You're such a pain in the ass. Will your foot heal, already?"

"No shit. I'm ready to pitch these suckers into the deep end." He gripped his crutches.

"Don't do it. I'm not getting them from the bottom."

He handed them to me and gestured for the goggles in my hand. "Can I borrow those?"

I grumbled but handed them over. "Want my cap too, to protect your pretty blond hair?"

"Too unmanly." Perched on one foot, he dove into the water with hardly a splash and emerged from a perfect streamline. His freestyle looked a little rough at first, but then he eased into a rhythm. He dragged his injured foot, though even without a kick, he only needed about ten strokes to reach the opposite end. After four lengths of the pool, he clutched the gutter and looked up at me. "Christ," he panted. "I'm so out of shape."

"You don't look bad, actually." I set his crutches down on the deck and sat on the starting block. "Keep going."

He frowned before pushing off with one foot. His long, powerful strokes mesmerized me. I didn't notice my coach, Kathy, standing next to me until she spoke.

"Your brother, right?" She watched him push off at the opposite end.

I nodded.

"I didn't know he was a swimmer."

"He quit when we were kids."

"Do you play volleyball, too?"

"I tried." I remembered my flailing limbs when I'd played in seventh grade. "But I'm too uncoordinated."

She laughed. "Swimmers aren't so good on land."

We watched Dane for another minute or so, and she said, "Great fly set today."

I smiled. "Thanks. It was tough."

"You were up for the challenge, though. Your energy was better."

I nodded, and she patted my shoulder as she walked away. Now that she mentioned it, I *had* slept better the past two nights. Nightmares hadn't woken me up in a panic.

After Dane finished, I got dressed and walked to retrieve his sweet Beemer. Mom had said I could also get a BMW next year when I was allowed to have a car on campus. I drove to the turnaround near the pool, and Dane settled into the passenger seat.

"Why couldn't Dad drive you to Lucia's?" I asked.

"Oh fuck, forgot to tell you. Dad texted me while you were at practice. He's heading to DC."

"What?" My stomach sank. "He was gonna take me to dinner tonight."

"Sorry. Mom says she needs him for something." Dane looked at his phone. "Dad's plane probably hasn't left yet. Let's call him." He pressed a button on his phone, and I heard ringing through the hands-free connection in his car.

Dad answered. "Dane, did you talk to Jessie?"

"I'm here, Dad." My voice quivered, and I swallowed. How pathetic was I that I didn't want my dad to go? I needed to get my shit together and act like an adult.

"Aw, Jessie, sorry I have to leave. But your mother called—she needs me." Urgency laced his voice. "That stupid Ashton's trying to cut the NEA budget again. Last time I was able to rally the art world to get him to stop."

Terry Ashton was a Republican senator my mom hated. Their budget battles were epic. I felt Dane's eyes on the side of my face, so I tried to put on a brave front. "That's okay."

"Honestly, I got to see you and Dane only about five minutes a day, anyway," Dad continued. "Your schedules are insane."

Dane snorted. "Welcome to the life of a student-athlete."

"But no matter how busy you get, we want to hear from you. Your mom wants you to call her, Jessie."

I gulped. I'd been avoiding Mom's calls, responding later with brief texts instead. I didn't want her psychologist skills to detect what had happened.

"They're telling me the plane's ready." Dad was likely flying on Grandpa's private jet. "I better go." His voice lowered. "Really great to see you both. I'm…sorry I haven't been around more. I'm so proud of you."

He made me want to cry. He shouldn't have been proud of me.

"Dane, I hope your foot heals quickly. You'll be back out there soon."

I glanced at Dane and saw his jaw tick. "Thanks, Dad."

"And Jessie, hang in there. Freshman year's tough, but you're doing great."

My throat burned.

"Well…" Dad paused. "Good-bye."

"Bye," Dane and I said together.

Dane shook his head after the call ended. "Fucker doesn't know how to say I love you."

"But he does," I said. "Love us."

Dane sighed. "You get him better than I do. You were always closer to him."

"And you're closer to Mom."

He looked out the car window. "He sounded so proud that Mom needed him." We passed the football stadium. "Their relationship's still fucked up. Do you think they'll make it?"

"I don't know." I thought about the many divorced parents of my high school friends. "Guess all they can do is keep trying. If they get divorced, we'll survive."

Dane scowled.

"What?"

"It's not that easy, Jess. It'd suck for our family to split apart. Do you know how shitty holidays would be if they divorced?"

Holidays? How could he think that far ahead? I could barely make it through today, much less entertain the idea of Christmas in four months.

"Turn right here," he said. I'd visited the greenhouse two years ago when Dane had lived there, but this was my first time driving.

I wondered about Dane's reaction to our parents' troubles. "Why do you care so much? You don't have any control over what Mom and Dad do."

He blew out a breath. "I feel like Mom and Dad have to make it. If they split, it throws doubt over my relationship with Luz."

My eyebrows lifted. *That* sounded insightful.

"At least that's what Dr. Valentine says," he added.

Ah. "But you and Lucia have your own thing. You're different from Mom and Dad."

"Also what Dr. Valentine says."

I said the same thing as my psychologist? I wasn't sure if I should feel pleased or scared. "You saw her?"

"Yesterday. Dad took me, but can you drive me next week? You have to see her again, right?"

"Did she tell you that?" I demanded.

"No, but I figured she made you schedule again when you didn't gloat that you were done with counseling."

My eyes narrowed. "I see her Wednesday at nine."

"Perfect. My appointment's Wednesday at ten. We can hang out in the waiting room during each other's sessions."

"But I have class at eleven."

"No problem. I'll finish early. Take a left at the stop sign."

I couldn't believe he'd roped me into confessing about counseling *and* driving him to his appointment. "You know, I'm kind of busy. I don't have time to chauffeur you everywhere."

He was quiet for a moment. "I'm sorry, okay? I hate this, too, but I don't have anyone else to ask. Josh doesn't have a license, and Luz can't drive me because of her agents. It wouldn't be cool for Secret Service to drive me everywhere on the taxpayer's dime just because I'm injured."

He had a point. As we neared the ranch-style mansion, Dane exhaled.

"No media out front. Hallelujah."

"Have they been here?" I cringed. Last thing I needed was a camera in my face with wet hair and no makeup.

"Yeah, last week. They were excited when Teo arrived, but the shine's worn off, I guess."

Teo. I hadn't even thought about the possibility of seeing him. I looked in the rearview mirror and frowned at my pale complexion.

When I pulled up to the gate, Dane said, "Press the buzzer."

A moment later a male voice boomed, "Hello, Monroes."

"Hey, Frank," Dane said. Once the gate opened, Dane pointed to the far end of the driveway. "Park over there."

"What do you mean?"

He dipped his chin, then held up his hands at ten and two like he guided a steering wheel. "Press the gas pedal, brake, then put the car in park. You can do it, li'l sis. I have faith in you."

"Fuck off."

He laughed. He loved when he annoyed F bombs out of me.

"I thought I was just dropping you off," I said.

"No, you're coming in for dinner. Luz invited you when I told her Dad was leaving early."

"What am I, a fucking mind reader? Thanks for telling me."

"Whoa. Down, girl." He held up his hands in surrender. "I'm telling you now. You want to come?"

I chewed my lip. "Wait a minute." I rummaged in my backpack for some pressed powder and lip gloss. Dane snickered as I applied both. "What?"

"Nothing." He got out of the car, and I joined him as he crutched to the front door.

An agent with curly blond hair—shorter and tamer than mine—answered the door with a smile.

"Hey, Allie." Dane reached out to fist-bump her.

"Come in, Dane." She shook my hand as we entered. "Officer Allison Largent, Jessica. Welcome."

"Thanks."

Dane looked around. "Where are Luz and Teo?"

"Lucia's in the kitchen, and Mateo's still at class."

That information deflated me, but maybe Mateo would return soon. I followed Dane toward a spicy scent.

The fan above the stove whirred, but Lucia must have heard Dane's crutches because she wheeled around and grinned. "You made it!" As she bopped over to him for a hug, I read her black volleyball shirt:

GOOD GAME
GOOD GAME
I HATE YOU
GOOD GAME
GOOD GAME

"That shirt's obviously meant for Bridgetown," Dane said as he released her and collapsed onto a kitchen chair.

"Obviously." Lucia smirked. "We don't play them till October, but we're gonna Hulk-smash 'em. Hey, Jess!" She came over and enveloped me in a hug, too. Her hair was also wet, and she smelled like coconut and cilantro. "Thanks for driving Dane. Do you like *chile relleno?*"

I glanced at Dane.

"Sylvia's recipe?" he asked.

Lucia nodded.

"You'll love it," Dane told me. "It's *muy picante.*"

I didn't like super spicy food, but I plastered on a smile.

"Want me to chop something for you?" Dane asked Lucia. "I'll be your sous chef."

They grinned at each other like idiots, and Lucia leaned down to plant a scorching kiss on his lips. I backed into the counter, wishing I could disappear.

"You can make the salad." Lucia straightened. Dane moved to get up, but she held out her hand. "I'll bring the fixins to you, cripple." She set vegetables and a cutting board in front of him.

I bit my lip. "Can I help?"

Lucia shook her head. "You're our guest! Here, let me get you a drink. Water okay?"

I nodded. I was always so thirsty after practice. She gave me water with a slice of lime.

"How was your swim?" Lucia asked Dane.

Dane looked up from chopping tomatoes. "Brutal. I only managed a thousand."

Lucia's head retracted. "Isn't that a lot?"

"How many yards did you do today, Jess?" Dane asked.

"Seven thousand for afternoon practice, and four thousand this morning."

Dane shook his head. "Almost seven miles. That's why I quit your crazy sport."

"*¡Hijole!* I thought volleyball practice was bad," Lucia said.

Dane grinned. "Volleyball's much more fun than swimming, especially with shagging balls."

He'd told me once that collecting volleyballs from around the gym and scooping them into the basket was called *shagging*.

Lucia looked down at the avocados she chopped, but I could tell she was blushing.

"That's why we love volleyball, right, Luz?" Dane's eyebrow cocked. "We love to shag balls."

Her face turned red, and she shifted her eyes in my direction. "Dane!"

And *that* was my cue to leave.

I wandered into a TV room, marveling at the massive flat-screen and cushy sofa. When I passed by an office, I noticed Allison sitting in front of a computer. She waved at me, and I tensed.

"I'm just looking around."

"Go for it. We've already done a background check on you." She laughed.

If a few thousand more Californians had voted for my mother, I could've been a resident instead of guest at this house. What would that life be like? Would it be better? A sob pressed up my throat. Secret Service wouldn't have let me get raped, that's for sure.

I passed a bedroom and backtracked to peek inside. I knew it was Lucia's when the smell of coconut hit me. The pale yellow duvet and khaki walls appeared cozy yet modern. I wondered how often Dane slept in the queen-size bed.

The guitar case leaning against a dresser in the next room clued me to its inhabitant. Curled on top of Mateo's bed was a beautiful black cat, with eyes the same color as the sage green duvet. "Hi, kitty." I crept into the room. When the cat didn't shy away, I lowered next to it. I offered my hand to let it sniff me, then scratched its ears. It leaned into my touch, so I stroked down its shiny fur. The low rumble of purrs soothed me, and I closed my eyes.

Accumulated swimming miles pressed down on me. That hellish butterfly set had scorched my shoulders, and I'd struggled to drag myself out of the pool. But Dane waiting for me on deck had been rather novel. I hoped he'd come to more practices. His presence had comforted me, made it slightly less awful when Blake touched me…

Deep blue eyes hovered over me, too close. When I pressed back against the mattress, he chuckled. The smell of booze and sweet smoke on his breath turned my already queasy stomach. He swallowed my whimper with a forceful kiss. The boozy smell invaded me, swirled down my throat. My whole body tensed, and I tried to push away, but I was too weak. He grinned at me. "Relax, baby." I couldn't breathe. He shoved my turquoise shirt up to my neck and cupped my breasts through my bra. "Delicious." He nuzzled down to lick between my breasts—

"His name's Escuincle."

I bolted from the bed, and Mateo leaped back. His huge eyes told me I'd way overreacted to him entering his own room. *Shit.*

"Sorry." He gripped the straps of his backpack as he stared at me.

My chest heaved with strained breaths. When I touched my collarbone, I felt wetness. I looked down and noticed splashes of tears on my skin. My hands darted up to cradle my hot, wet face. *Fuck.* "Sorry." I panted. "I shouldn't be in here."

"Nonsense." He peeled off the straps of his backpack and set it on the floor. "You're always welcome. Squinky likes you." He pointed to the bed.

I looked to my side and found green eyes staring at me. The cat stalked closer and rubbed his cheek against my leg. My hand trembled as I scratched between his ears.

Mateo smiled. But his smile vanished when his gaze floated to the far wall, where some sort of medical equipment littered the dresser. He crossed the room and swept the items into a drawer. When his back was turned, I plucked a tissue from the box on his desk and dabbed my face. Thankfully he hadn't said anything about my tears.

"He's a good judge of character, you know." Mateo turned back around.

My heartbeat finally slowed down. "Yeah?"

"He's like deputy Secret Service."

As he stepped closer, a light sandalwood scent wafted in my direction. He picked up the cat and gently flipped him on his back to hold him like a baby. *Adorable.*

"How was your day, Squinkster?"

A shadow crossed the doorway, and I looked up to see Johnny gawking at me. He straightened and nodded. "Miss Monroe."

"Hi, Johnny. What's up?"

"I, uh, heard voices, and didn't know you were here."

"Yeah." I slid my hands into the pockets of my capri pants. "Lucia invited me for dinner, I guess."

A smile lit up Mateo's face.

Johnny said, "Excellent," and moved down the hallway.

Escuincle struggled against Mateo's elbow, so he set the cat on the bed. Mateo fidgeted as we stared at each other.

"How's your fump?" I finally asked.

He looked down. "Fine."

He didn't say anything else, and I tried to think of another topic. "How was class?"

"Mmm. Confusing. The book we're reading in English is kind of over my head."

"What is it?"

"*A Portrait of the Artist as a Young Man.*"

I nodded. "James Joyce—I read that in high school. Very confusing. But my dad helped me understand it better."

"Really? Will you explain it to me? I'm totally lost." He gestured to the foot of his bed. "Want to sit?"

I swallowed, then sat on the mattress. When he sat near his pillow and gathered his cat into his lap, a thrill zinged up my spine. It felt different—illicit, more exciting—to be on his bed with him so close.

Mateo scowled. "I mean, Joyce goes on describing hell for about twenty pages, and I feel like *I'm* in hell reading it."

I laughed. "Don't remember that part."

"Do you believe in hell?"

"Um…" If hell existed, I knew a tall swimmer who belonged there. "Not sure. Do you?"

He leaned in. "Don't repeat this to my mom, but no. I don't believe in hell. She'd probably tell me I was *going* to hell for thinking that."

"Your family's pretty religious, huh?"

"We're Catholic rock stars. Team Jesus and all that."

The roll of his eyes made me smile. "Do you believe in heaven?"

"I do." His gaze scanned up my body and met my eyes. My breath quickened, but not from fright. The intimacy of his stare flustered me. I tucked my hair behind my ear.

He shifted on the bed. "Why do I feel the need to lay a cheesy pick-up line on you?"

"I'm not sure."

"How 'bout this one. Did you fall from heaven, baby?"

I tensed.

"'Cause you're an angel," he finished. His grin faded as he kept looking at me. "Did I say something wrong?"

I blinked and shook my head. "No. Just…" I blew out a breath. "Just don't call me baby."

"Oh. Sorry."

The stiffness in his shoulders made me regret opening my big mouth. "It's not your fault. Tell me another one."

He looked uncertain.

"Another bad pick-up line," I said.

He stroked Escuincle's fur as he licked his lower lip. His mouth was rather sexy. I imagined his plump lips pressed up to a microphone as he sang, and felt myself grow warm. After what Blake did to me, I was relieved I could still feel turned-on by a guy.

"Okay, got one." He sat up. "If you were a laser, you'd be set on stunning."

I groaned. "Star Wars humor."

"Oh, here's another—my brother Alex told me to use this. On a scale of one to America, how free are you tonight?"

I shook my head, but smiled. Figured the son of the president liked that line.

He was on a roll. "If I could rearrange the alphabet, I'd put U and I together." He dipped his chin and looked up at me with a seductive squint.

"Good thing N and O are already side by side," I said.

His jaw dropped. "Nice comeback, wench!"

I laughed.

"What's so funny?"

I turned to see Lucia standing in the doorway holding a dishtowel.

"She just put me in my place," Mateo growled.

"I knew I liked you, Jessica." Lucia winked at me. "Dinner's ready, guys."

Mateo and I stood. He gestured in front of him. "After you, Miss Laser."

As I followed Lucia to the kitchen, I felt Mateo behind me. I wondered if he was looking at the seat of my white pants. If so, I hoped he thought my ass was stunning. Because it was.

12
Mateo

★ ★ ★

What a cute butt! Her white pants showed off a delicate curve flowing from her lower back to her endless legs. In contrast to the thick glute and hamstring muscles of a volleyball player, Jessica's physique was all long, lean lines. She moved with grace, like a dancer. A *tall* dancer.

"Teo!" Dane boomed as I walked in behind Lucia and Jessica. He sat at the kitchen table with his crutches propped on the wall behind him. "When did you get home?"

"A while ago — we were hanging in my room." I noticed cheesy goodness on the plate Lucia served him, and I inhaled hot spice. "Please tell me that's *chile relleno.*"

"*Sí, hermanito.*" Lucia set a plate on the table across from Dane. "Here's yours."

"Yes!" I bounced on my feet, then played an air guitar solo — an ode to my favorite dish. When I looked up, Jessica smirked at me. *Whoops. Must act cooler.*

"You can sit here, Jessica." Lucia placed a plate between Dane and me.

Jessica circled the table. "Thanks."

"Wait!" I hustled behind her and pulled out her chair. She giggled as she took a seat.

I sat as well, then Lucia set her plate next to Dane's. "Okay, everyone has a beverage, got the salad dressing…" She stood behind her chair and surveyed the table. "Anyone need anything?"

"Nope," Dane said. "Let's dig in."

But Lucia didn't take her seat. She stared down at me with raised eyebrows. "Ahem."

Why wasn't she sitting down? She tapped her chair and kept looking at me expectantly. *Oh!* I jumped up and held her chair as she sat. "Madam." I bowed.

Dane shook his head.

After I poured ranch dressing over my salad, Dane said, "I'll take that." I handed it to him. Discreetly, I checked my blood glucose and administered a bolus of insulin from my pump.

Jessica took a bite of her salad, but I went straight for the *chile* while it was still steaming. *Yum.* I'd been asking Lucia to make this since I'd moved in, but her volleyball travels had kept her too busy. Maybe I could bug my mom to teach me the recipe for the times Lucia was out of town.

Dane ate with impressive speed, pausing only to say, "This is awesome, Luz."

"I agree." I shoveled in another bite.

"So what were you guys doing in your room?" Dane asked with a glint in his eye.

Thanking the love gods for bringing this blond beauty to my bed. But I couldn't say that. Corny pick-up lines filled my head, like *Nice pants—they'd look better on my bedroom floor.* But I didn't want to say those out loud, either.

"We talked about Joyce's *Portrait of the Artist as a Young Man,*" Jessica said.

Dane looked as if that was the last thing he'd expected his sister to say. "Really? That book's vile. I remember suffering through it in English class."

I nodded. "Amen, brotha."

"It's not that bad," Jessica said. "It's got some good themes."

"Like what?" As I took a sip of sparkling water, I remembered our conversation. "Hey! You promised to explain it to me. Don't leave me hanging."

Jessica ate a cheesy bite, and it looked like she forced a swallow. She grabbed her water and took a long gulp. "It's fiction, but Joyce said it's more like an autobiography about becoming an artist. He led a tortured life, and he transformed his pain into his writing. Art's all about emotion—especially painful emotion. Suffering is essential for art. You have to suffer to produce good work."

I thought about what she said. To label my music as art was a stretch, but I wondered if that was true for me. Most of my songs were about frustration and longing, not exactly suffering—like my struggle with diabetes, or pining for Jessica. I couldn't believe she was right here, in my house. I didn't ever want her to leave.

"Intriguing." Dane blinked. "That's deep. But how'd you come up with those themes from that garbled mess of a book?"

"Dad told me." She shrugged. "When we read it in high school, I complained about being completely confused, and he explained how suffering connects to art. Dad said maybe I hadn't suffered enough to understand it."

"Who knew Dad could be so insightful." Dane nodded. "With the privileged lives we lead, probably none of us has suffered like that."

"Or maybe some of us should've produced art masterpieces by now," Jessica muttered.

We all stared at her.

"What do you mean?" Dane asked.

She started, and fear filled her wide eyes. "Nothing. I, I don't know what I'm talking about." She looked at her plate, and her upper lip trembled. I saw her hand twist in her lap. She seemed so sad! I fought the urge to take her hand and stroke it.

After we ate in silence for a few moments, Lucia piped up. "I think that applies to sports, too."

"What does?" Dane asked.

"You need to suffer to be successful. Maybe not *suffer*, but experience adversity. Adversity's important for success in sports. Take the team that's undefeated in the regular season. How often do they win the championship?"

Dane shook his head. "Not as often as they should."

"Well, there you go," Lucia said. She pointed to Dane's foot. "You've got your adversity right there. Once you heal, you're gonna be tougher than ever."

He gazed at her, and a slow smile spread across his face. "Love you, Luz."

She reached to cup his chin. "Love you more." She leaned in for a kiss.

The intimacy of the moment made me squirm. Part of me felt uncomfortable witnessing their kiss, and part of me craved that depth of love. Would I ever find that?

I noticed Jessica also focused on our siblings. When she turned to me, the solemnity in her eyes seemed to ease. Then her face lit up in an alluring smile.

Did the sun come out, or did you just smile at me?

I wondered why she was grinning. Was she happy for her brother because he'd found someone? Did she want that kind of love, too? Did she want a relationship at all? She hadn't eaten much of her *chile*, but she took another bite. Mesmerized, I watched her glossy, pink mouth accept the fork. My mouth moved in time with hers, like I was taking my own bite.

"Matty," Lucia said.

I snapped out of my daze and looked at my sister. She and Dane smirked at me. *Quit being so obvious.* "Yeah?"

"How's your music coming along? Have you had much suffering to inspire you?" She grinned as she took a bite.

"*Good* things are inspiring me." Lucia glanced at Jessica then back to me when I added, "Fitch and Itch invited me to be part of their band."

Lucia's mouth dropped open. "Congratulations!"

"Great news, Teo," Dane said.

Jessica coughed, then fanned her mouth. "You know somebody named *Itch?*"

"His name's Ichiro. He's part Japanese."

Her eyes flashed with pain as she touched her lips.

I leaned toward her. "Are you okay?"

"Too…hot." She reached for her glass of water.

"Lucy!" I glared at her. "You made these too spicy."

She eyed my empty plate. "You and Dane didn't seem to mind."

"Eat the avocados." Dane gestured to the slices on Jessica's plate.

Lucia frowned. "No, have some sour cream. That'll help."

"You're both wrong." I ran to the fridge and poured Jessica a glass of milk. "This will tame the fire in your mouth."

"Thanks." She gulped it down and grimaced. "It still burns."

"Give it some time," Dane said. "Fuck, my sister's a culinary wuss."

As Lucia stood, she shook her head. "You were exactly the same way the first time you ate Sylvia's recipe."

He scowled. "*Cállate.* Don't want to lose my spicy street cred."

"You are very strange, Danish," said Jessica. Her smile was back, and all felt right in the world.

"Danish?" Lucia tilted her head.

Jessica's grin broadened. "Apple Danish. He hates when Mom calls him that."

His eyes narrowed at his sister. "*Voy a matarte.*"

I'm going to kill you, he'd said. I started laughing.

"We've been together two years and this is the first I'm hearing this nickname, Danish?" Lucia gave an evil smile as she carried her and Dane's plates to the sink.

"I wish you could unhear it," he grumbled. "Euchre, anyone?"

I chewed the inside of my cheek. I didn't know that game. I took Jessica's plate over to Lucia.

"Dad just sent a new board game I want to try," Lucia said.

I pouted. "He sent you *another* gift?" I pointed to her volleyball shirt, one of many Dad had given her. She was so spoiled.

"*Tranquilo.* It's for you, too, since you live here. It's called The Game of Things."

"Sounds thrilling," said Dane.

"Oh, hush. You'll love it. Matty, do the dishes, and I'll get the game set up in the TV room."

Bossy much? I backed away from the sink. I was about to protest until I saw Jessica watching me, her big blue eyes tracking my moves. I didn't want her to think I was a petulant child, so I opened the dishwasher.

Dane looked at me. "Want some help?"

Jessica stood. "Yeah, let me."

"Nonsense." I waved them away. "You're our guests. Stay there." Jessica sat back down. "Catch up with texts if you want."

The Monroes took out their phones as I loaded the dishwasher. I watched Jessica from the corner of my eye. I hoped she wasn't texting SSS or Man Bun. Finding a way to spy on her, I grabbed the cutting board I'd just washed and returned it to its cabinet behind her. "So, who are you texting?"

She looked up from her phone. "Mackenzie. She's my roommate."
Praise Dios.

"She's jealous I'm here. She said the dining hall sucked tonight."

I wiped down the counter. "Is she a swimmer, too?"

"Yeah. She swims butterfly. She's from Australia." Her eyebrows lifted. "She didn't even know my mom ran for president!"

"Wow." I rinsed out the dishrag.

"To be fair, I know zilch about Australian politics," Jessica added.

I nodded. Neither did I.

"You know Mom's going to Canberra next week though," Dane said.

Jessica looked at him. "Really?"

"She's talking to their parliament about mandatory voting. She wants to see if that'll float here."

Lucia entered the room. "No way that'll happen. The game's all set up, guys."

"Don't you believe voting is our civic duty?" Dane asked.

"I do, but I don't think people should be forced to vote."

Dane grabbed his crutches and stood. "Let me guess—this is Adolfo's opinion that you've adopted."

Lucia once told me Dane had called our dad "Adolf" when they'd first met. I wondered if he'd whip that out now.

"This is my own opinion that my dad happens to share." Lucia's hand found her hip. "It's about the role of government—it should be smaller. Government shouldn't force people to vote. And you think exactly the same way as your mom, so spare me the hypocrisy."

"We just want to help people do their civic duty."

Lucia's face reddened. "By fining them if they don't comply? You and your mom want to force people to do all kinds of things in the guise of 'helping' them."

"At least we're not 'helping' other countries by invading them and stealing all their resources," Dane responded.

"We aren't invading them!" Lucia railed. "We're fighting terrorists. Thank God my dad has the balls to take out those ISIS butchers."

Chin, she was mad. Jessica's wide eyes met mine when I glanced at her. She seemed frozen in place as she watched their spat.

Dane crutched forward. "Maybe if he'd think with his head instead of his balls, America wouldn't kill so many innocent people."

"We're trying to *stop* the murder of innocent people!"

"Whoa!" I shouted. Lucia and Dane turned their glares on me, and I swallowed. "Stop the argumentertainment, guys. Thought I'd get away from this crap when I left the White House."

Dane kept glaring. "One-sided crap, you mean. Your dad's whole staff badmouths Democrats on the daily."

"As if your mom's staff wouldn't hate on Republicans if she was prez?" Dane shut his mouth, and I continued, "Dude, you just told Lucy you loved her a second ago. Why all the nasty?"

"She can't say stuff like that!" Dane fumed. "She knows it pisses me off."

"She did go kind of Alejandro on you," I agreed. I wondered if Dane could handle my honesty. "But you've been extra bitchy lately. I don't know if it's your foot or PMS or—"

"You don't know what it's like to be injured as an athlete," Jessica said. "I was out a whole month with a shoulder problem, and it sucked."

What really sucked was her pointing out that I was the only one of us who wasn't a superstar athlete.

"But Matty knows better than any of us about dealing with a chronic health problem," Lucia said.

Piteous silence filled the air. *Damn diabetes.*

Jessica sucked in a breath. "I'm sorry, Teo—I didn't think about that."

I hated the embarrassed look in her eyes. "No, you're right. I'm not an athlete. I don't know what that's like. But I *was* around Alex after elbow surgery, and he was a total *pendejo.*"

"Oh shit, you're comparing me to Alejandro?" Dane scrubbed his jaw. "I must be acting like a *complete* asswipe."

A laugh erupted from Lucia, and she covered her mouth.

Jessica looked at me. "Your brother's an ass?"

"He's not that bad. He's gotten better since he started dating Maddie."

Dane nodded. "Everything changed when he got laid."

"You're so crude, *gigante*." But Lucia snuggled into his chest.

Dane tucked her closer. "Sorry," he whispered.

"*Lo siento*," she replied.

Jessica's mouth quirked. "Aw. Much better, you two. I won't have to separate you now." Her condescending tone amused me.

"Are we playing this game or what?" I cocked my head toward the TV room.

We sat at the card table to the side of the sofa. Lucia had torn strips of paper and piled them in front of each chair, along with a pencil for each of us.

"Okay." She pointed at the stack of cards. "One person takes a topic card and reads it to everyone, like 'Things that scare you.' Then the other three write down something that scares them. The reader blindly judges the best response, and whoever wrote it gets to keep the card. The winner's the person with the most cards at the end."

I silently read the instructions to the game as she spoke. "Says here, 'The true object of the game is fun, not winning.'"

"I don't do anything just for fun," Jessica said. "I want to *win*."

Dane high-fived her across the table. "Competition runs in our blood. Way to go, Monroe."

Lucia and I shook our heads at each other. *What am I getting myself into?*

"It *is* fun," Lucia said. "My team played this in Florida, and Brianna laughed so hard, she cried."

Dane scoffed, but he took a card off the top of the stack. "I go first. Ready, bitches?"

Lucia nodded. "Bring it."

"This is perfect." Dane snorted as he read, "'Things you shouldn't say in group therapy.'"

I frowned at the strip of paper. I'd never been in group therapy, though my mom had nagged me to attend a diabetes support group when I was younger. I'd wanted nothing to do with it. But if I had attended, what would've freaked me out? I wrote my response.

Dane accepted the folded strips of paper from Lucia and me, then looked at Jessica. "Hurry up."

"Give me a second." Her eyebrows pulled together, creating an endearing indent between her eyes. She scribbled something, then handed the paper to her brother.

"Let's see what we got." Dane scrambled the pieces of paper before unfolding one. "Things you shouldn't say in group therapy: 'I'm not secretly recording this on my phone. I promise.' Yikes."

That was mine—I hoped it won. People had posted tons of videos of my family online over the past two years, and I would die if they ever secretly recorded me in group therapy.

He unfolded another. "'I only had sex with my dog once.' What the fuck?" Dane grimaced. "What kind of fucked-up group therapy is this?" He unfolded the last one. "'My group therapist keeps her blinds open all night in her first-floor apartment.' Oh. *Ew.* That's creepy to the max." He stilled. "That last one's the winner."

"Yes!" Jessica threw her arms in the air in a victor's pose.

Her brother looked her up and down. "You're twisted, Jess."

She gave him a sweet smile. "Thank you." She snatched the top card and read, "'Things cats are secretly saying when they meow.'"

I channeled my inner Escuincle and wrote what he would say.

Jessica sat up taller and read the first response. "'You don't even know how many times I've planned your death.' Ha, good one." She unfolded another paper. "'I found Nemo…delicious.' Aw. Poor Nemo." She grinned before she read the last paper strip. "'You're late, slave.' Another good one." She thought for a second, then nodded. "I'm going with Nemo."

"Holla!" I did a chair dance in celebration. Maybe I was kind of competitive, too.

"That's *so* wack," Dane said. "Jess only chose the Disney reference because you're both baby freshmen."

Lucia grinned. "Dang, you're competitive, Danish."

"Teo, read the fucking card," he growled. "I'm getting this one."

"You got it, Apple Strudel." I picked the top card. "'Things that would make golf more exciting.'" The uber-tall people at the table gave me blank stares. "Wait, let's change it to volleyball. Things that would make volleyball more exciting."

Lucia frowned. "You can't just change it like that."

"Why not, rule follower?" Dane elbowed her. "I like this one."

"Fine, whatever. Things that would make volleyball more exciting." She chewed on her eraser as she stared at her paper.

Dane's intense vibe put me on edge, but Jessica's little grin relaxed me. Our hands touched as she passed me her strip of paper, sending a spark up my arm. Had she felt it, too? She looked down, but then peeked up at me with a soft smile. *Dios.*

Once I had the three papers, I opened the first one. "'Full contact, no net.'" *Boring,* I thought, and unfolded the next paper. "'Naked volleyball.'" I smiled. "It's got potential. Okay, last one: 'The court's on an electric grid, and players get zapped if they make an error.' Wow. Rough crowd." I looked up and studied each of the three. Which had Jessica written? *Please, let this be hers.* "Gotta go with electric ball zap."

"Yee-hah!" Jessica leaped out of her chair and circled her forearm like she was swinging a lasso. "That's two for me, zero for you, brother."

Lucia had told me Dane was an awful winner—he gloated like no tomorrow—and apparently his sister shared that trait. I'd never seen Jessica so lighthearted.

"Son of a bitch," Dane hissed. "Sit your ass down."

Apparently he was an awful loser, too.

"Naked volleyball sounds kind of bouncy, uh, jiggly," Lucia said.

Dane nodded. "Maybe for those of us who are well-endowed."

"Gross." Jessica perched on her chair and plucked a card from the pile. "Things you shouldn't do in the shower."

Jack off. Jack off. Jack off, was all I could think. I'd done my fair share of solo shower sex since seeing Jessica again a few weeks ago.

"Let's see what we got," she said a minute later as she read, "'Take a dump.' Really, Dane? That's disgusting."

His head retracted. "That's not mine!"

"It *so* is yours." She opened the next one. "'Sing in a chipmunk voice.' Hee hee. I like that one. And third, 'Lick the tile.' *Eueh.*" She tucked one of her curls behind her ear. "The chipmunks win, of course."

"Thankyaveramuch." My Elvis impersonation sounded lame.

Dane's eyes darkened.

Lucia frowned at me. "You guys suck. You have a Jedi mind connection or something." She turned to Dane. "I'm never inviting your sister over again."

My breath caught in my throat before I realized she was joking.

Jessica's eyes flared as she held up the card. "But you only win if you sing like a chipmunk."

"Yeah?" I blinked at her. I wasn't prepared for a performance.

"Do it." She nodded.

I aimed for the highest falsetto I could muster and squeaked, "*Me, I want a hoooola-hooooop.*"

They all cracked up.

"Definitely don't sing that in the shower, Matty," Lucia said.

"Yeah, it sounds like someone's squeezing your balls," said a male voice from behind me.

I spun around in my chair. "Itch!" Fitch stuck his head out from behind his roommate. "Hey, Fitch." I stood. "What're you guys doing here?"

"We had band practice tonight, remember?" Fitch said.

I inhaled. "Crap, I forgot!" Weston couldn't make it this time, but I was supposed to meet them at the warehouse after dinner. Jessica's heavenly presence had thrown me off.

"No worries." Itch gestured to the front of the house. "We called Johnny, and he came to pile our equipment in the SUV. We can practice here." His black eyes checked out my three companions. "What're you playing?"

"The Game of Things — it's dumb." Lucia said. "Matty and Jessica are kicking our butts, so I'm out."

I frowned. "Already?"

"I've got morning practice tomorrow." When she stood, she was the same height as Itch, and he gaped at her as she stuck out her hand. "I'm Lucia, Mateo's sister."

"Ichiro." In a star-struck daze, he shook her hand.

"And this is Ryne Fitcherson." I pointed to my classmate in the royal blue Cubs hat. "He plays drums."

Lucia smiled at him. "Hi, Fitch."

When Dane hopped up on one foot, Itch's eyes widened. Dane crutched over to Fitch. "Your parents named you after Ryne Sandberg?"

Fitch looked up at Dane, who was over a foot taller than him. "Best second baseman ever."

"I know!" Dane grinned. "He's my grandfather's favorite player."

As they rattled off baseball statistics, I noticed Jessica standing to the side. I walked over and slipped my fingers through hers. "Want to meet the guys in my band?"

Her hand tightened in mine, but she nodded. "Sure."

"Hey, Itch." I brought her over to him. "This is Dane's sister, Jessica. She's on a swimming scholarship here."

"Nice," he said. "What year are you?"

The prettiest pink colored her cream skin. "Freshman. You, too?"

"Yeah. You stuck in a dorm, or in a sweet house like this one?"

"I'm in Canfield," she said.

He flinched. "That's one of the oldest dorms at Highbanks! The showers must be disgusting."

She chuckled. "I won't be licking the tile any time soon."

Itch paled.

I laughed. "At least no one's taken a dump in your showers, right?"

"Yuck." She shoved my shoulder.

"Hey, Jess." Excitement laced Dane's voice. "Fitch's dad caught a foul ball hit by Ryne Sandberg at Wrigley! Grandpa would be so jealous."

"Really?" She stepped over and joined their conversation.

Itch appraised me with a Cheshire-cat grin.

"What?"

He leaned in. "Now I know who inspires your love songs."

13

Jessica

★ ★ ★

D r. Valentine smiled at Dane and me. "Hello, Monroes." Her
voice was low, presumably to avoid others in the waiting room
overhearing her.

When I didn't get to my feet, Dane nudged me. "Your turn, ganja
girl."

"You're hilarious." I glared at him as I followed the psychologist
to her office.

"Does Dane tease you a lot?" she asked after we sat.

"Yes." I looked at the ceiling. "Stoner Sally's another of his favorites."

But she didn't crack a smile. "If he only knew the whole story."

My lips pressed together. "Which he won't."

"You don't want him to know?"

I shook my head. I didn't want anyone to know what Blake had
done to me. It was disgusting.

"How have you been feeling?"

"So much better."

Her head tilted like she was surprised. "You have?"

"Um, I've had fewer nightmares, I guess. Or maybe I don't remember them as much."

"You don't have to tell me you're all better just to please me, you know. You've been through a lot. How are you really feeling?"

I pondered her question. "I'm still jumpy, and my sleep isn't great. I…don't want to think about that night. But when I hang out with Mateo, it's not as bad. He relaxes me or something."

"You've been spending more time with him?"

A light feeling entered my chest as I recalled that ridiculous game we'd played almost a week ago. Mateo had texted that he wanted to play again, calling it Game of Things: The Squeakquel.

"Occasionally."

I wished he'd been with me last Saturday night after the football game. My smile faded. Maybe I would've acted more responsibly then. He wasn't as stupid as I was.

"You saw Dr. Cabela?" asked the psychologist.

My face flamed. The gynecological exam with my team physician hadn't been fun, but I'd gotten through it. I wouldn't know about HIV for another couple of months, but the other tests had come back negative, thank God. "Yes."

"Good job. You didn't avoid it."

Yay for me.

"So is there anything in particular you want to discuss today?"

I swallowed. I wasn't sure what to say. She would probably want to hear about Saturday night, but I didn't want to admit how I'd behaved. "Uh, I didn't do so hot on my psychology test yesterday."

"That sounds disappointing. What happened?"

"I tried to study, but I couldn't focus. I kept thinking about…" I snuck a glance at her. "You know."

She nodded. "Flashbacks to the trauma."

Fucking flashbacks.

"Let's talk about trauma some more, okay?" She waited for my nod. "It can feel like you're going crazy when you're here in the present, but your mind's back in the past, reliving the trauma through flashbacks or nightmares. So why does that happen? I use a metaphor to explain it.

"Imagine a screen door in your brain." She held up her hand and spread her fingers. "When we feel threatened, hormones like adrenaline and cortisol flow through the screen to mobilize our response to the threat." She mimed the hormones flowing through her fingers. "The fight or flight response is important for our survival. But when something traumatic happens—say, sexual assault, severe car accident, physical abuse—the body can become overwhelmed. Hormones fly through the screen so fast that they bust a hole in it." Her other hand flew past her face to mimic the speedster hormones.

She studied me. "You following okay?"

"So far, yes."

"Good. The trauma ends, but the trauma survivor is left with a hole in her screen. So anything that reminds her of the trauma—a person, a place, a certain smell—"

There had been weed at the party on Saturday, and the scent had freaked me out.

"—can trigger the hormones to zip through that hole in the screen, making her feel like she's back in time. It's hard to distinguish the past from the present. Her heart races, her chest tightens, her body freezes."

"Exactly." The word came out breathy. "That happened Saturday night."

"What were you doing at the time?"

I bit my lip and stayed silent.

After a beat, she said, "It was frightening, huh?"

I nodded.

"There are techniques you can learn to help you return to the present when you're experiencing flashbacks or nightmares. They're called grounding skills. First, what do you notice about your breathing right now?"

When I exhaled, I realized I'd been holding my breath. "It's not great."

"That's normal—part of the fight, flight, or freeze response. An important grounding skill to calm your body is diaphragmatic breathing."

She taught me how to breathe into my belly, which eased the trembles vibrating through my chest.

"You can also use your five senses to observe the present moment. I mentioned this last time. What do you hear?"

"Your voice."

She smiled. "What does my voice sound like?"

"Um, it's a little lower than most women?" When her brows pulled together, I added, "But not manly or anything."

She grinned. "No judgment here. Grounding skills involve observing nonjudgmentally—observing without judging as good or bad. For example, I might notice myself getting angry when my computer crashes. If I judge that observation, it'd be, 'I *shouldn't* be angry about this.' But the goal is just to notice without judgment, like 'My face feels hot when I have computer problems.'"

I had listened more carefully to her voice as she spoke. "Your voice goes up and down a lot." I held up my hand and let it undulate like a dolphin riding the waves. "It's expressive."

"Huh. I've never noticed that before, but that makes sense because I'm an emotional person."

"You are?" I'd been told I was emotional, too. "You must hate it."

"I used to. I'd get all embarrassed when I cried, and I'd try to shove down my feelings. But it didn't work so well."

Bummer.

"Our feelings are part of who we are. Feelings are not to be suppressed or fixed—they're to be acknowledged."

I let that sink in.

"Are you emotionally sensitive, Jessica? Do you feel things deeply, express emotions more easily than others?"

"I think so." My club coach, Gary, had often claimed I overreacted to bad swims and team drama.

"How does that help you?"

I shook my head. "It doesn't *help* me. It turns me into a basket case."

"Really? What's your major, again?"

"Art." She nodded but didn't say anything, so I asked, "And?" She still didn't speak. "You're saying my emotional sensitivity helps my art?"

She shrugged. "You tell me. When have you created your best art?"

I'd been shocked by my first college critique of the curlicue sculpture I'd made two weeks ago in my 3D class — the one representing my nightmares. Man-bun Van had been one of many who'd loved it. Professor Schneider had taken me aside after class and said, "*You're clearly a student to watch. Excellent job.*" And, I'd won an award in high school for the painting I'd created after Mom lost the presidential election. She'd cried when I gave it to her. *So much sadness and longing, but hope, too,* she'd told me. Maybe Dr. Valentine and James Joyce were right: the deeper the emotions, the better the art.

"I see what you're saying," I told her.

"So what else do you notice?" she asked. "What do you taste?"

I ran my tongue across my teeth. "Scrambled eggs."

"Have you been eating more?"

"I'm trying."

"Well done. And what do you smell?"

I sniffed. "Maybe coffee?"

She took a sip of hers and nodded. "These are all grounding skills. Take deep breaths, observe with your five senses, and reorient your mind to the present by repeating statements like…" She glanced at her watch. "It's Wednesday, September twelfth, at nine twenty-six a.m." She looked at me. "Go ahead, say it."

I repeated the date and time.

"I'm an adult," she said.

When she kept looking at me, I said, "I'm an adult."

"I can use my voice to stand up for myself."

I repeated that as well.

"I want you to practice these skills, Jessica. They won't stop the flashbacks right away, but over time they'll help you cope better, get back to living your life. I've got a handout for you in case you don't remember." She opened a file cabinet and handed me two pieces of paper. "Here are some sleep tips, too."

"Thanks." I folded the papers and stuffed them in my backpack, hoping Mackenzie wouldn't find them and ask about them later. She'd seemed mad at me lately, and I didn't want my issues to push her further away. I'd already been avoiding our dorm room because of her questions about Blake. She couldn't understand why I didn't want to date him. The thought of that made me want to puke.

Dr. Valentine watched me, and I shifted on the sofa. Was I supposed to talk?

"I'm wondering," she said, "have you thought about reporting the rape?"

My heart hammered. Since I'd figured out what had really happened only about a week ago, I hadn't yet decided what to do. I just knew I didn't want anyone close to me to find out. They'd view me differently. "Do you think I should?"

"I want it to be your decision. We can definitely talk through the pros and cons."

I licked my lip. "What're the cons?"

She tapped her notepad. "The way things happened, I'm guessing you don't have any physical evidence, right? Other than the texts, which probably won't make a case."

I gulped and shook my head. The bruises on my wrist and ankle had faded, and my shower the next morning hadn't helped my situation, either. If he had drugged me, I hadn't taken a drug test until the athletic department had forced me to. I inhaled. "The drug test. Would it show if I'd been roofied?"

"How much time had elapsed since the rape?"

"It happened on a Friday night, and I was tested the next Wednesday."

She shook her head. "I'm guessing the drug would be long gone by then. And if there was a sedative in your urine sample, Ms. Farris would've told you."

My stomach twisted. *He's going to get away with it.*

"You asked about the cons. When it becomes a he-said-she-said case, the prosecutor might not press charges on your behalf. I'm not an attorney, mind you, and I don't know all the specifics — just what I've experienced with other clients. Even with a rape kit, sometimes the guilty go free. Plus, the survivor can feel re-traumatized in the process. Her honesty will be questioned. It can get ugly."

I grimaced. "Why would *anyone* report it, then?"

"The chance for justice. The opportunity to speak your voice, to tell your story. It can be a way to seize back the power that was stolen from you. For some survivors, reporting the crime is a path toward healing. When others know, they can support you better. And there's one more pro I can think of." She met my eyes. "Reporting may decrease the chances the perpetrator will offend again."

Oh, God. I knew she was going to say that. The fear that Blake would hurt someone else — maybe a teammate, maybe a friend — absolutely haunted me. I'd feel horrified if he did this again because I hadn't spoken up.

"It won't be on your shoulders if he rapes another woman." It was almost like she'd read my mind, and I looked up. "*He's* responsible for his behavior, not you. You should only report if you're ready."

"What if I never report?" My voice sounded small.

"Life goes on. Some survivors decide not to pursue the legal route. But I don't think it's a good idea to keep it a secret from loved ones."

My chest tightened. "Why?"

"Like I said, they can't support you if they don't know what happened. You've been all alone in this, Jessica. You don't have to be alone."

I felt tears press at the back of my eyes, and trembling in my lips.

"You said you haven't been acting like yourself, right? People who love you are probably worried about you."

Where was my cheerful disposition? *I've lost so much.* The thought started the tears flowing.

She handed me a box of tissues. "I'd be crying, too. It's okay to cry." She waited while I wiped my nose. "Have people expressed concern about you?"

I sniffed. "Elyse."

She squinted.

"She's my teammate."

"What has made her concerned?"

I wondered if I'd get in trouble with my coach if I admitted the reason. Dr. Valentine had said this was a no-judgment zone, but could I trust her? I balled my hand into a fist. "Elyse chewed me out on Sunday. For…drinking too much Saturday night."

She didn't even blink. "I see. How much did you have?"

"Not sure. I blacked out."

"So a lot, then."

I cringed as the cloying sweetness of peach schnapps came to me. It had tasted even worse on the way back up. I wished the vomiting had been part of my blackout that night.

"Were you…?" She paused. "Safe?"

"Yes. We were at Elyse's apartment, and she took care of me. Apparently I made a mess in her bathroom and spent the night in her bed. She was pretty ticked off."

"And worried?"

I nodded. "She said two blackouts in less than a month is bad. And I guess at some point in my drunkenness I told her about my positive drug test, so that also made her nervous."

"Jessica, I'm concerned, too. You're at risk for additional traumas right now, and alcohol only increases the risk."

I shrank back into the sofa. "*More* traumas?"

"We need our emotional brain—our amygdala—as an alarm system in order to protect ourselves. But PTSD is a raging fire in your amygdala. It over-fires so much that it's like a fried circuit board, and it doesn't work well to detect danger. Some people get sexually assaulted multiple times as a result."

Once is quite enough, thank you very much.

"What made you drink so much that night?"

"Some guys were there—not swimmers, or I wouldn't have gone. They were NARPs."

She angled her head to the side. "NARPs?"

"Non-athlete regular people. Highbanks students."

She smiled at the lingo.

"Anyway, they were smoking weed. As soon as I smelled it, I…" My body tensed.

She nodded. "You started remembering the rape."

"I didn't want to think about it."

"So you drank yourself into oblivion."

I winced. "Sorry."

"Now you have your grounding skills to practice, so you don't need alcohol. But you *do* need more support to get through this. Could you tell Elyse about the rape?"

I remembered what she'd said about Blake and the field hockey team. She'd either think I slept around or that I was stupid to be alone with him. I shook my head.

"Your roommate?"

I shook my head again. Mackenzie thought Blake was perfect.

"How about Dane? It'd be nice to have family on your side."

I sighed. "I've thought about telling him, especially after he thought Johnny, of all people, hurt me."

"Who's Johnny?"

"He's Mateo's Secret Service agent. He protected me before the election."

"Oh, right. He's the one who stopped the bombing plot."

"Yes, and he's a really good guy. Dane questioning if he'd raped me is ludicrous. But my brother's getting closer to the truth. He knows I've been acting weird, and he's trying to figure out why." The creepy feel of Blake's hand on my shoulder made me tremble.

"Would it be better to tell him yourself than for him to stumble onto the truth?"

I swallowed, and the tears started again. "Probably. But I'm scared to tell him. What if he goes after Blake?"

She exhaled. "Men often want to attack the perpetrator, but we could explain that it would make things worse. Dane's in the waiting room. Want to bring him in here so I could help support you both?"

"I would tell him *here?*" My eyes opened wide.

She nodded. "It's one option. No pressure."

Dane had stared at Blake's hand on my shoulder. *"Why'd he touch you like that?"* he'd asked later. How would he react if I told him the reason? He'd be shocked, for sure. Would he judge me?

"Telling others is a way to challenge the shame you're feeling," Dr. Valentine said. "Part of you thinks this is your fault, right?"

"I was drinking, and then I smoked weed. I let myself be separated from my friends." Tears spilled down my cheeks.

"You could've consumed twenty beers alone in a bar, and you still weren't asking to be raped. This isn't your fault. This is the perpetrator's fault. You may not see that now, but you will over time. And Dane could help you understand it's not your fault."

Oh, God. My hands trembled with the realization that I wanted to tell Dane. I was scared of his reaction, but I needed to tell him. As awful as my positive drug test had been, it had forced me to meet with the sport psychologist. And telling her about the rape had already helped me. Would it help to share it with my brother, too?

"Would you like to go get him from the waiting room?"

I looked up. After a beat, I nodded. I grabbed a fresh tissue and wiped under my eyes before I walked down the hallway.

With his headphones on and eyes glued to his laptop, Dane didn't notice me until I was right next to him. He started, then took off his headphones. A slow smile spread on his face. "She got you to cry, huh? She's good at that."

I pressed my lips together, but more tears flowed. I took a seat next to him.

His smile faded. "What's wrong?" He looked at his watch. "You've got another ten minutes. You sure it's my turn?"

I noticed he'd been watching his soap opera, but I was too overwhelmed to give him shit about it. "She wants…" I cleared my throat. "We want you to come back and join the session. I need to tell you something."

His smile had disappeared, replaced by a deep crease between his eyebrows. He stared at me for a few moments, then closed his laptop and stuffed it in his backpack.

I reached out. "I can carry your backpack."

"No." He slung it over his shoulder and got to his feet. He crutched toward the office, and I followed him. My heart shuddered.

"Welcome, Dane." Dr. Valentine pointed him to one side of the sofa, and I returned to my seat on the other.

"What's going on?" He looked from her to me. His long legs stretched out in front of him.

She nodded. "Jessica and I have been discussing an incident we thought you should know about." Her warm eyes landed on me, and she dropped her chin like she was saying, *You can do this.* "Are you breathing, Jessica?"

No. I let out air like I was an overinflated tire.

Dane's bright eyes scrutinized me, and I ran my hands down my thighs. My mouth felt dry.

"Something happened?" he prompted.

"Yeah." My endless tears had saturated the tissue I clenched, and he reached for the box to offer me more. I took a few to sop up the leakage.

"Whatever it is, it'll be okay." He patted my arm. "I'm here for you."

His kindness made me cry harder.

"Oh, Jessie." He clasped my wrist, and he inched toward me, but then turned to Dr. Valentine. "Can I hug her?"

"It's up to Jessica," she said.

"No." I splayed my hands out. *Get your shit together.* "I'm stalling. I just need to tell you this."

He pulled back but kept a close watch on me.

I sucked in a shaky breath. "The first night I was here…" My ankle twitched. "I went to a swimmer party."

He nodded. "Teo went, too."

"Yes." *Sweet Teo.* If he'd stayed, maybe I wouldn't be here now, choking out words. I tried to swallow. "There was a senior there. It was his house."

Dane seemed to tense. "That guy I met at your practice, uh, Blake?"

Hearing his name made me freeze. I looked at Dr. Valentine.

"You're doing great, Jess," she said.

I closed my eyes, took a breath, then forced them open. "He got me a drink."

Dane stilled. His mouth parted as he stared at me.

"W-W-We smoked weed in his room."

His face lost its color as his jaw lowered. I watched his fists clench and his eyes taper into slits. "Motherfucker. He *raped* you."

I flinched, but after a second, I nodded.

The energy sparking off him filled the office. "I knew it." He sat up taller. "I fucking *knew* something happened to you. But I was too blind—too wrapped up in my own shit—"

"Dane." Dr. Valentine shook her head. "You couldn't have known."

"I *should* have known!"

I pulled away from him, making myself as small as possible.

"Son of a bitch! I'm gonna fucking kill him." He scrambled to his feet and lunged for his crutches.

Dr. Valentine stood as well. "Dane, sit back down."

"I'm outta here."

"You can't leave." She tried to block him, but he was too fast, even on crutches. He'd already made it out the door by the time she reached it.

"Get back in here, now," she called. Her icy voice sliced through me.

Holy shit. It had all happened so fast, I barely felt my feet as I stood. I came up behind Dr. Valentine and looked over her shoulder through the open door. Dane spun around to face us but still appeared ready to bolt.

A man stuck his head out of an exam room down the hallway. "Need any help, Carly?"

"Thank you, Dr. Finnegan. You played football in college, right?" She pointed at Dane. "Block him if he tries to leave."

"Just try it," Dane said as he sized up the big man.

"Dane, if you leave, I have to warn the athlete you're coming to get him."

Whoa. She would warn Blake?

Dane's mouth dropped open. "You wouldn't do that!"

"I will. This is a Tarasoff situation if I've ever seen one."

His eyes blazed as he seemed to consider her threat. "Fuck." After a minute, he crutched back into the office and collapsed on the sofa.

The psychologist closed the door and took her seat. I sat back down as well.

"What's Tarasoff?" I asked.

She nodded at my brother. "Dane?"

His chest heaved, and he blew out a breath. "It was this court case in the seventies. A guy told his therapist he wanted to kill a woman. The therapist didn't tell anyone about it, and when the guy killed her, the court ruled that therapists have a duty to warn potential victims."

"Well said." She kept her eye on him. "You paid attention in class."

"Yippee." Bitterness laced his voice.

She turned to me. "Remember how I told you one exception to privacy was imminent danger of harming self or others? Blake is one of the 'others' in this scenario."

"He deserves to have his fucking heart ripped out," Dane muttered.

"That may be true, but *you* won't be the one to do it, young man."

His heart ripped out? I gawked at my brother and psychologist. When had they become so barbaric?

Dr. Valentine shook her head. "I should've known you'd try to fly out of here and avenge your sister."

Dane grunted.

"You know you can't do that. It won't help Jessica if her brother's in prison for murder."

"I get it, okay?" Dane rubbed his hand over his face. He looked toward me. "You're going to the police, right?"

I recoiled. "Um..."

His eyes got huge. "Of course you're going! The fucker *raped* you. You can't let him get away with this."

His fists were clenched again, and a vein pulsed in his neck. I knew he wouldn't hurt me, but I still felt scared. I turned to my psychologist for help.

"You look frightened, Jessica."

I nodded. At least I'd stopped crying.

She looked at Dane. "You want your sister to feel scared of you?"

He stared at his shoes. "No."

"Then calm your shit down."

A very inappropriate laugh almost escaped me when he hung his head lower. This was too much damn drama for one day. I was about to lose it.

"Jessica had something out of control happen to her, Dane." Dr. Valentine sank back in her chair, now that he seemed less explosive. "She needs to be the one in control now. *She* decides whether or not to report—not you."

"But—"

"And we all know what could go wrong if she reports this to the university or law enforcement," she continued, cutting him off. "Your mother's the one spearheading legislation to protect sexual assault survivors. Too often they get raked over the coals when they come forward. It's not a decision to be made lightly."

It was quiet for a few moments. Dane still seemed pissed off, but not like he was going to run out and hunt Blake down. I felt confused. Why wasn't I angry like him and Dr. Valentine?

She smiled at me. "Looks like you're doing some thinking over there."

"Oh. Um, I don't know. I guess I'm confused. Dane's really mad, but I'm..."

He looked at me.

"Numb?" she said.

I nodded.

Dane asked, "You're *not* angry?"

I chewed on my lip. Was I?

"It's normal for survivors not to be aware of their anger at this point. That'll come later, most likely. Jessica's too mad at herself to be angry at the perpetrator."

"What the fuck?" Dane looked baffled. "Why're you mad at yourself? The guy's huge—taller than me, even. You couldn't have fought him off."

"She may've been drugged, too," Dr. Valentine offered.

Dane's fists curled, and his arms trembled. He took a noticeable deep breath.

"I showered," I said, and my tears started again. I remembered the game we'd played: *Things you shouldn't do in the shower.* My throat burned as I thought of a new response: *Destroy key evidence.* "I screwed up."

A line appeared on his forehead.

"I wasn't sure what he did to me," I admitted. "I was stupid." The tears were hot on my cheeks.

"Oh, Jessie, don't cry." His eyes shone like he was fighting tears himself.

I'd never seen him cry, and I didn't want to start now. I clenched my teeth and looked at the clock. "I'm sorry we ran into your session. Do you want me to wait in the lobby?"

His eyes bugged. "My stuff is infinitesimally less important than this." He looked at his watch. "Crap, it's ten forty. We need to get you to class."

"It's okay. I'll skip it."

"No avoidance, Jessica," Dr. Valentine chided. "You did so well today confronting your fear, telling Dane. And Dane won't fuck it up by going after the guy, correct?"

He scowled. "Correct."

"I want to reschedule with both of you." She looked at me. "We needed to figure out some things today, but we'll get back to your memories of that night. I want you to tell me your memories in as much detail as possible. It'll help get you unstuck."

Sounds terrifying. But I nodded.

"And Dane, I know you're feeling helpless right now. Your injury only increases the helplessness." She gestured to his crutches. "But you knowing what happened is a tremendous help to your sister. You can be on her side, supporting her. She won't feel so alone."

He blinked as he twisted his mouth to one side.

"In particular, Jessica needs your support not to drink alcohol."

He still looked close to tears, and he didn't respond.

She scheduled appointments for us as we stared blankly at each other. "You'll both heal from this," she promised.

I hoped she was right.

14
Mateo
★ ★ ★

"Luz!"

I paused the treadmill and removed my earphones. Was that Dane's voice?

"Luz!" he yelled again. I heard a thump on the stairs. He wasn't coming down here, was he?

I hopped off the treadmill and jogged over to the basement stairwell. When I looked up, Dane loomed above, his head almost touching the ceiling as he maneuvered down the stairs on his crutches.

"*¡Dios!*" He stopped at the sound of my voice. "What do you think you're doing?"

"Is Luz down there?" he panted.

It was then I noticed wetness on his cheeks, and my stomach dropped. Dane was *crying*? What awful thing had happened to make him cry? I climbed the stairs. "She's at class."

"She's supposed to meet me here." He swiped at his face as he breathed hard.

"Then I'm sure she'll be here soon. C'mon." I grasped his elbow but almost let go when I felt his arm shaking. This was not cocky, foul-mouthed, bigger-than-life Great Dane. I wasn't sure who this guy was. "Let's go to the kitchen and wait for her, okay?"

He sniffed and looked down. "I should've been there for her."

The crack in his voice hit me like a volleyball to the gut. He should've been where? Was my sister okay?

"*Vámonos,*" I said. "Can you turn around?"

He gathered his crutches in one hand and hopped in a circle on his good foot. I hovered on the step below to make sure he didn't fall. When he crutched back up to the kitchen, Johnny was waiting for us.

"Dane, you need to tell us when you're coming over," he said. "Karen was about to start the home invasion protocol."

"I reset the alarm!" Dane hissed.

Johnny backed up when he got a look at Dane's tears. "Oh." He slid his hands into his pockets. "Is, uh, everything okay?"

"No. I need to see Luz. *Her* agents know I'm here."

I took Dane's elbow again. "Have a seat at the table. I'll get you a glass of water." I helped Dane into a chair and retrieved a glass from the cupboard. As I filled it, I noticed my agent still standing there, fidgeting. "It's okay, Johnny."

He watched us for a moment, then left.

After I gave Dane his water, I dashed into the TV room and searched for the box of tissues that typically lived there. *Chin*, where was it? I sprinted to the bathroom and grabbed another box. As I hustled back to the kitchen, I realized Dane's desperation was making *me* desperate.

"Here you go."

Dane glared at the tissues but yanked one so he could blow his nose. "So damn stupid." The tissue ripped in his hands. "I *knew* she was acting weird."

"Lucy?" I asked.

He shook his head.

"Who?" I sat next to him. "What happened?"

He kept looking down. "Can't say."

"But you'll tell Lucy?"

"No." His voice quivered. "I, I didn't know what else to do. Where else to go." He let out a derisive sound from deep in his throat. "I know where I *want* to go. But I fucking can't. Can't take matters into my own hands, as much as I want to." His shoulders slumped, and it looked like he started to cry again. "I have to see Luz, that's all."

My gut clenched as he spoke. I'd never seen him like this. I rubbed the back of my neck and felt a light sheen of perspiration from my jog. "You texted Lucy to meet you here?"

"Yeah."

"Is there anything I can do?"

His glassy eyes narrowed as they met mine. "What exactly are you gonna do, Teo? You're fucking eighteen. You can't make this better. No one can."

Ouch. I was about to tell him I was almost nineteen when I heard the beep of the front door alarm, followed by Lucia's voice.

"Dane! I saw your car—did Jessica drive you?"

Dane flinched but didn't answer her, didn't call for her. What was his deal? He'd been so eager to see her a second ago.

"We're in the kitchen!" I yelled.

She rushed in and saw us sitting at the table. "How'd you get here, Dane?" Her eyes widened. "You *drove* here? On your injured foot?"

"I had to. Jess needed to get to class." His voice cracked again.

"*Idiota.* You'll delay your recovery." She stepped toward him, then gasped. "You're *crying?*"

He clenched his fists. "I need to talk to you. I…don't know what to do."

"*¿Qué pasó, gigante?*" She leaned down to hug him.

He pushed her away and got to his feet. His eyes darted to me and back to Lucia. "Let's go to your room."

"Dane, what's wrong?" It sounded like fear in her voice.

"Please." He snatched more tissues and tucked them in his pants pocket. "Your room."

Lucia stared at me after he crutched off. "Do you know what's going on?"

"No idea." I took Dane's still-full glass to the sink. "I was on the treadmill when he flew in here in a panic. Have you ever seen him like this?"

She swallowed. "Once, when he was a sophomore. I hope his parents are okay."

"Why wouldn't they be?"

"Forget I said anything." She headed toward her bedroom.

As I placed the glass in the dishwasher, I reviewed what Dane had told me. He hadn't mentioned anything about his parents that I could recall. But he had said he *"should've been there for her"* and *"she was acting weird."* Who was he talking about? His mother? He'd alternated between freak-out and fury, and I was totally confused.

My hand turned the basement door handle, and I froze. The cheers at Highbanks Arena filled my ears. At Lucia's volleyball game a couple of weeks ago, Jessica had bolted to the bathroom, leaving Dane and me to stare at each other with confusion. He'd shrugged and said, *"She's been acting weird since she came to school."*

He hadn't been referring to his mother a minute ago, but to his *sister.* Was Jessica okay? My fluttering heart told me I had to find out. I crept toward Lucia's bedroom.

Her door was still slightly ajar—our agents preferred we didn't close our doors all the way if we didn't have to. I backed against the wall closest to the opening and eavesdropped on their murmurs.

"…ever been so pissed off you want to do something bad?" asked Dane.

"Like what?"

He muttered something.

"*Kill* someone?" Lucia drew in a sharp breath. "You're scaring me. Tell me why you're so upset."

"Can't."

"This is about Jessica, right?"

Dane paused. "Why do you say that?"

"Because I know where you were this morning. And you're not denying it, so this *is* about Jessica."

"Fuck." He blew out a breath. "You know me too well. I wish you'd figured things out better that night, though. I should've been there."

"What night?"

No answer.

The bed squeaked, and Lucia said, "Here, lie on your belly. You're so tense." More sounds of shifting on the mattress, followed by a moan.

"Lower," Dane said.

I hoped to God I was listening to a massage and not my sister having sex.

"Ohhhh. Right there." He moaned again.

After a beat, she said, "Tell me why you're so troubled. What happened with Jessica?"

"She'll kill me if I tell you. I'm already dead if she finds out you know she failed the drug test."

Jessica had tested positive for drugs? *Intriguing.* That didn't seem like her. I leaned closer to the door.

"Only because I dragged it out of you when you wouldn't let Frank drive you to therapy," Lucia said. "Did you find out why she smoked pot?"

I heard a choking sound, followed by harsh intake of air. Dane crying made me feel sick. It just wasn't right. I wished I could help him feel better.

"Oh, GD. *Mi gigante.*" Lucia's soothing voice kept murmuring little words of comfort as I imagined her rubbing his shoulders.

A creak behind me caught my attention, and I spun around to see Karen frowning. *Busted.* Her eyebrow cocked, questioning my obvious invasion of privacy. When she didn't move, I exhaled and walked back to the basement. Espionage was difficult when living with government agents.

I picked up my earphones and resumed listening to my music homework as I settled back into my jogging warm-up. Alejandro had written my workout today—an easy warm-up followed by all-out sprints. He'd gotten all geeked out about a cycling study showing three twenty-second sprints were just as good for the heart as forty-five minutes at a moderate pace. I doubted such a short workout would do anything for me, but to shut him up, I'd said I'd try it.

When I switched over to sprints in a few minutes, I'd have to change my audio selection to music for some motivation. Maybe I'd listen to Twenty One Pilots, a local band that was making it big. I liked their lyrics.

But at my current level of distraction, my sprints were going to suck no matter what music I chose. I kept thinking about Jessica. What had turned Dane from a stoic jock into a weepy character from *Days of Our Lives*? Something bad must've gone down. Real bad.

Dane had said he wanted to kill someone. Someone Jessica knew? Who would he want to kill? I knew *I'd* want to kill anyone who tried to hurt her. She was so pretty, so spunky. Well, she'd seemed that way at the party that first night, at least. After that, she'd turned spacey and unhappy. She'd jumped out of her skin or gone off on me randomly a couple of times. Then she'd told me she was sorry for being a mental case.

"I've had a rough start here," she'd said at the hospital. Why? She'd seemed fine at the party. When I'd gone for it and given her my number, she'd had to turn her phone on first. Her hands had trembled as text messages poured in. Had she been scared of them?

Who'd texted her? Though I'd wondered about Man Bun, she'd joked about him—he was probably harmless. And maybe gay. So was it Suave Swimmer Shithead? At the volleyball game, I'd asked her about him. As I thought about it, that had been one of her freak-out moments. She'd yelled at me, then apologized, calling herself a bitch. She could never be a bitch in a million years.

Wait a minute. SSS had been at the party. The party was when she'd changed. *"I want to kill someone,"* Dane had said. Was it swimmer guy? Had he hurt Jessica? A surge of dread filled my chest, spiked my heart rate. I ripped off my earphones.

I pressed the emergency stop button on the treadmill and dashed up the stairs. Once I reached Lucia's room, I shoved open the door.

"Matty!" Lucia looked up from her position, straddled across Dane's naked back. Thankfully she was dressed. "Have you heard of knocking?"

Dane must've noticed my wild eyes, because he said, "You're mad at me, right? Sorry for snapping at you. It was misdirected anger." He grimaced. "My specialty."

My head shook double-time. "No. I'm here about the tall swimmer guy. Suave Swimmer Shithead."

Dane's head shot up, and his eyes bulged.

"He hurt Jessica." I swallowed. "Right?"

From the expanse of his wide eyes, I knew I'd hit on the truth. My breath caught in my throat. I wished I'd been wrong.

"What?" Lucia turned Dane's shoulder toward her, bringing his chest off the mattress. "What swimmer guy?"

Tingles of horror climbed up my spine. "What'd he do to her?"

When Dane's eyes welled up in tears, I stepped back. I was about to get sick.

"The worst…" He took a shuddering breath. "The worst thing a guy can do to a girl."

No. With zero control over my body, I backed out of the room and closed the door. *No.* The tremble in her hand when I'd held it… her sheer terror when she'd looked at her phone…*No.*

"I should've been there for her," Dane had said. His words flooded me. I understood what he meant now. I understood the devastating depth of his guilt. It was my guilt, too.

"Johnny!" I shouted.

He was next to me in a second. "What's wrong?"

"You gotta take me to Jessica's."

"No!" Dane yelled. Lucia's door opened, and he filled the doorway, balancing on one foot. "No way you're going over there. She'll never forgive me for telling you."

Dane's tears had stopped, but Lucia's had begun. Her eyes glistened as she nudged around him and looked up. "But you didn't tell him. Matty figured it out on his own."

"Figured out what?" said Johnny.

I darted into my room and grabbed a long-sleeved running shirt to throw on over my tank top. What else did I need? With Dane's shouts in the background, I couldn't think. I looked at my bed. Jessica had scrambled off the mattress when I'd come in the other day. She'd stared at me like I was an ax-wielding attacker, which had puzzled me then, but made too much sense now. No wonder she'd been so scared.

"Don't go," Dane said when I emerged from my room.

Johnny looked from Dane to me. "What's going on?"

"I have to go." *I have to see her.*

"Dr. Valentine said she needs to be the one in control now. Not me, not you." Dane glared at me. "You can't crash her dorm room like this. She might not even be there this time of day. She went to class a little while ago."

My phone. Where was my phone? I zoomed into my room and scooped it up. When I looked at the time, I ticked through her schedule, which I'd memorized. With the hope they wouldn't think I was a crazy stalker, I returned to the hallway and said, "Her class just ended." I pulled Johnny's arm. "She should be there."

Dane now leaned on his crutches, and he pointed one at me. "Don't do it."

"I have to. C'mon, Johnny."

Lucia sniffed. It hurt me to see her crying, but I didn't have time to comfort her. I had to get to Jessica.

"Jess needs someone right now," Lucia said. She circled her arm around Dane's waist and leaned into him. "Let Matty go. You've seen them together. He's good for her."

Dane's jaw muscle squeezed as he looked to the side, but he tucked her in closer to him. "Fuck."

I took that as a sign he wouldn't stop me, and I headed to the garage. I felt Johnny on my six. He pushed his hand against the car door before I could open it.

"Mr. Ramirez, Karen's not here. She had to meet with the backup team. Tell me what's going on, or I'm not driving you."

I sighed. "I can't. Just…please. Please, Johnny. I know you care about Jessica, too. I need to see her." I blinked quickly. "Please."

He assessed me for a few long moments.

"Do you know where her dorm is?" I asked.

"Of course." His eyebrows lowered. "Karen won't like this."

"She'll get over it." I reached for the door handle and exhaled when he let me open it. "Just tell her my blood sugar was low. I wasn't thinking straight and made you drive me."

He started the SUV with me in the backseat behind him. "What *is* your BG?"

"Really?" Was he going to get on my case, too? I wasn't the one who needed help here.

He nodded. "Really."

I did a quick test. "It's fine." Okay, it wasn't fine — my BG was kind of high. I administered a quick bolus as we drove through the gate. Happily the media had lost interest in me once I started classes. Maybe they were too busy slamming my dad for decreasing public assistance and increasing border security. At least that's what Alejandro had told me.

The number of pedestrians increased as we neared campus. Many of them wore light jackets even though it was September. It was a cloudy day, and I was glad for my long-sleeved shirt. But envisioning what Jessica had gone through still made me shiver.

"Could you drive faster?"

He didn't respond, though it did seem like we picked up speed.

My mind drifted back to high school, thinking about Iris. Joey and I had befriended Iris in music class, but mysteriously she'd stopped talking to us a few weeks later. When we'd confronted her about it, she'd yelled about staying out of her business. But months after that, Iris had confessed to Joey that she'd been raped. She'd wanted Joey to tell me because she couldn't do it herself. I'd been shocked, but Joey had told me to play it cool. When we'd started hanging out again, Iris had said she wished she'd told us sooner. She'd said keeping the secret was almost worse than the rape.

"I have an uncle," Johnny said.

When he didn't elaborate, I met his eyes in the rearview mirror.

"He has diabetes, too."

Why hadn't he told me that before? "Uh, sorry."

"He got really sick a few years ago. Almost lost his foot."

I closed my eyes. One of the White House physicians had tried to scare me with stories like that, but I didn't want to think about it now. I needed to focus on Jessica.

"I don't want that to happen to you. I asked Karen to keep close tabs on you."

I opened my eyes and saw him studying me. "So it's your fault she's on my case all the time?"

He shrugged. "She has her own reasons for that."

"Like what?"

His mouth tightened. "Not my story to tell. Just don't want you to think Karen's the bad guy all the time."

"She's not the bad guy, I know." I frowned and patted the pump in my pocket. "Now that I'm used to the pump, everything's okay. I probably should've gotten it sooner."

His eyebrows flew up.

"But don't tell Karen I said that."

He smirked. "Your secret's safe with me."

We had to wait for students taking their time in the crosswalk. Scrolling through their phones as they walked slowed their progress.

"You're pretty worried about Jessica, huh?" He kept his eyes on the road.

"Yeah."

"What's got you so worried?"

I studied the back of his head, his short, blond hair in a military cut. I'd already said I couldn't tell him. "I see. You tell me one of your secrets so I'll tell you mine? Don't think so."

"That's not what I'm doing."

Uh-huh. Damn Secret Service.

He pulled the SUV into a loading zone next to a rundown brick building. Itch hadn't lied when he said Jessica's dorm was one of the oldest on campus.

Once we exited the car, a couple of students gawked at me. One snapped a photo. *Shit.* I was used to the unwanted attention going to class, but what would they think of me entering a dorm? Would they connect me to Jessica? Social media attention was the last thing she needed.

"You stay close to me, got it?"

I nodded and followed Johnny to the side entrance. I noticed a swipe pad—the door must've been locked—and wondered how we'd get in. But then he pulled an ID card from his pocket, and presto, the door opened. *Awesome Secret Service.*

"She's on the second floor." He led me up the stairs.

"Have you been here before?"

He kept climbing. "It's my business to know these things."

That was cryptic. When we walked down Jessica's hallway, I wondered why characters from *Frozen* lined the walls.

Johnny stopped and tilted his head toward room 220.

I gulped. Now that I was here, I had no idea what to say. I only knew I'd felt a driving force to see her, to try to help her. But there was probably no way I *could* help her. I clenched a fist, then rapped my knuckles on her door.

"Go away, Dane!" Jessica called.

Dios, she was here. Part of me was thrilled and part terrified. "It's not Dane." I chewed my lip. "It's Mateo."

The door wrenched open, revealing blond curls that shot out in all directions. Bedhead? She looked adorable. Her tired eyes bounced from me to Johnny. "What're you doing here, Teo?"

"I wanted to see you." The words that I'd had trouble saying that first night now spilled out of my mouth. What if I'd said them then? *I wanted to know you. I wanted to hold you.* Would she want me? Could she ever want me after what SSS had done?

She swallowed, then flinched at a sound down the hallway. I looked to see one of her hallmates sticking her head out of her room. The girl's eyes got big as she stared at me.

"Can I come in?" I asked.

"Um…" She glanced at an unmade loft bed, which I figured was hers, then back at me. Her roommate wasn't home.

"Please?" I jerked my thumb toward my guard. "Johnny's staying outside."

He grunted like he disagreed, but after he leaned in to scan the room, he stepped back.

She blinked at me for a moment. "Okay, I guess."

I let out a breath as I entered.

"Bye, Johnny." She closed the door.

Shirtless men covered her roommate's wall, and I stepped closer to read the names on the posters. They were all more muscular than me. "Who're these guys?"

"Australian footballers. Mackenzie's a little obsessed."

I examined one poster — the guy looked like an underwear model. "He's pretty ugly, huh?"

Her mouth twitched. She glanced around the room as she fidgeted with her sleeve. "You can, um, sit there." She pointed to a small sofa beneath her bed.

I hoped she'd join me, but she pulled out her desk chair to face the sofa. Before she sat, I rushed over. "I'm crashing your room. *You* sit on the sofa — I'll take the hard chair."

"But you're my guest."

"Uninvited guest. You should sit under that cool-ass painting. That's you, right? Did you paint that?"

She shook her head. "My dad did."

"I love it. The water looks alive. Go ahead, you sit on the sofa."

She frowned, but seemed too tired to argue. Once she'd collapsed on the cushions and I sat on her desk chair, she studied me. "So, why are you here, uninvited guest?"

My heart thundered. I'd stalled long enough. But how could I start this conversation? "Why're there *Frozen* characters all over the walls?"

"Dorm bonding." She rolled her eyes. "Every wing has a theme, and my RA's a huge Olaf fan." She smirked. "I guess the li'l snow-guy *is* kind of cute."

I remembered one of Olaf's lines as I studied her: *I'd totally melt for you.*

"So you were on the treadmill?" She stared at my bare legs.

I hoped she didn't think they were too thin. She wore jeans so I didn't get to see her beautiful legs. "Yeah. I'd just started my workout."

"Where's your fump?"

I reached into the pocket of my shorts and took it partway out, but then tucked it back in. I didn't want my stupid pump to be our topic of conversation.

"Why'd you stop your workout?" she asked.

Butterflies flitted in my belly. I knew I had to man up and tell her why I was here. "Dane came over."

She started, then twisted her hands in her lap. "What'd he want?"

"He was…upset."

The only part of her that moved was her eyelids as she blinked at me.

"He was crying," I added.

She looked away, and I noticed her sharp jawline as she swallowed.

I ran my hands down my thighs as I tried to ignore the tightness in my throat. "I've never seen him cry before. It was hard to watch."

"Did he say anything?" Her voice seemed shrill. She closed her eyes and clenched her teeth like she was fighting with herself. "About why he was crying?"

"He wouldn't tell me."

Her eyes opened, and she let out a breath.

But I figured it out. Would saying that out loud destroy her? It seemed like keeping her secret was far more destructive, and I needed to apologize for not being there for her. I wanted her to know I was on her side. I wanted her to know she could trust again.

"Dane didn't tell me," I said. She met my eyes. "But I figured out the truth."

It looked like she'd stopped breathing.

"The swimmer guy raped you."

Her eyes opened wide as her mouth formed a frightened circle. She didn't move.

I gentled my voice. "That's what happened the night of that party, right? I'm so sorry."

She bolted off the sofa, and her eyes flared at me. "How'd you know that?"

I leaned back in the chair as I watched her fists clench. "You've been acting so scared since the party. I'm sorry I left you there. You were drinking. I should've taken care of you. This must be awful for you."

"You don't know anything." Her fists trembled. "You don't know what it's like. What're you here for? To tell me how stupid I am?"

"No." When I got to my feet, she backed away from me. Her fear made me sick.

Johnny's voice came from the hallway. "Need help in there?"

"We're okay," I called. That was a lie. She looked anything but okay.

She covered her mouth. "Does Johnny know, too?"

"No." I waited a moment. "But Lucia overheard me talking to Dane."

"Great, just great! Why're you here, Teo? To tell me I should've known better?" Her voice shook, and she pushed her fingers into her riot of hair.

"Jess, no." I fought the urge to go to her, to take her in my arms. "I just want you to know you're not alone in this."

She inhaled a staccato breath, and her face crumpled. She started crying.

"You've kept it secret, and you've been all alone." My chest hurt watching her cry. "*Que sepas que estoy aquí.*"

"I-I-I don't know what that means." She sniffed. "Dane's better at Spanish than me."

"I want you to know I'm here."

Her shoulders sagged as her anger deflated, replaced by endless hurt and loss.

She sank into the sofa and drew her feet up on the edge of the cushion. Her forehead rested on her knees.

I could hear her sobs, and they were killing me. "Can I...?"

Her choppy breaths made her chest jump up and down as she looked up at me with glimmering eyes.

"Can I sit next to you?"

She nodded. Her tears kept flowing, darkening the knees of her jeans.

I didn't know what to do as I slid in beside her. She'd been angry, then had shied away from me. But sitting here doing nothing wasn't right, either. I placed my right hand between us. After a moment, I raised my arm, let it hover over her, then took a risk and cupped her opposite shoulder.

I exhaled as she leaned into my touch. She kept crying. When she nudged toward me and twisted around, I wasn't sure what was happening. In a flash she'd curled up in my lap, her right cheek on my collarbone and her hands folded together under my chin. Her legs extended from my lap, and her feet pressed against the opposite armrest.

Cautiously, I wrapped my arms around to cocoon her in my hold. Her hair smelled like chlorine and fresh flowers. She'd bestowed a beautiful gift by crawling into my lap, and I didn't want to screw up her trust in me.

She began to cry harder. I tried to think of what my mother would say when I was scared during a diabetes crash. "*Tranquila*," I murmured, closing my eyes. I smoothed my hand down her hair. "Things will get better, Jess." She probably didn't believe that now, but I hoped it would be true.

I could've prevented all of this pain, if I'd only stayed at that party. If only I hadn't left. Her cries sliced into me, piercing my heart.

Pressing her cheek to my chest, I rocked her. Her tears kept coming, but I wouldn't let myself cry. She cried enough for both of us. "*Tranquila.*" I held her tight as we rocked together.

15
Jessica

★ ★ ★

With only ten seconds rest, I barely had time to look up to the spectator area of the natatorium before my next two-hundred-yard repeat. Mateo still sat there, flanked by his agents. His concentration seemed intense as he scribbled in a notebook. Wondering what he was working on, I pushed off the wall in a tight streamline and began an undulating dolphin kick.

It had been two weeks since he'd discovered my secret, and he hadn't missed an afternoon practice since. A couple of days he'd arrived late from class, but his steady presence had calmed me all the same.

I came up to lane leader Elyse's feet on the freestyle and finished right behind her.

"You go first," she panted.

The senior captain wanted me to lead the lane? My shoulders lifted with surprise, but there wasn't time to debate. I pushed off the wall to begin the next individual medley swim. Butterfly wasn't my best stroke, but I was pleased to notice Elyse nowhere near me as I turned on my back for the second fifty. After backstroke came my best stroke—breaststroke—and I extended my lead before bringing it home with a fifty freestyle.

"Good, Jess," Kathy shouted as I finished the fourth two hundred. I glanced at the pace clock and breathed hard while waiting for the sendoff. "Make number five your best one."

A surge of energy pulsed through my limbs, keeping me high in the water with a nice rhythm for the butterfly. I maintained a snappy tempo for the backstroke, and worked on aggressive thrusts in breaststroke. After I finished the last of the eight lengths with freestyle, I hugged the wall and panted. From the other side of the pool, Kathy smiled.

Mateo no longer looked at his notebook, but instead stared at me. I couldn't read his expression.

"Nice, freshman," Elyse said when she finished the set. Her chest heaved as she smirked. "No wonder Dane's kicking ass. You both got chlorine in the genes."

Dane had attended every morning practice since that fateful therapy session. At first my teammates had ogled him in a speedo, but then they'd been awed by how well he kept up after years away from the sport.

"Fifty cool down!" Kathy called once the rest of my lane had finished.

As I swam easy backstroke, I thought about Dane and Mateo's sudden interest in swimming. It was pretty obvious they'd colluded on a schedule to monitor me and keep me safe. Whatever they were doing was working—Blake hadn't approached me for some time.

In the showers, Elyse didn't even ask before she grabbed my shampoo. Mom had sent me expensive salon products that Elyse coveted, and I was happy to share my family's largesse. I'd also finally answered a few of my mother's calls. She seemed to sense something was off with me, but she hadn't pressed too hard. And Dane had promised to keep his mouth shut after acknowledging he was to blame for Mateo catching on to the truth.

Elyse scrubbed her black hair. "Why's Ramirez at every practice?"

"I already told you." I squirted some conditioner onto my palm. "His agent Johnny intercepted some threats against my family, so he wants to keep watch over me. And where Johnny goes, Teo goes." *A damn clever lie, if I do say so myself.* Mateo had texted it to me when I'd told him my teammates were asking why he was always around.

"But why're terrorists threatening your family?" She rinsed her hair.

"Hellooo? My mom's a high-ranking senator."

She massaged conditioner into her hair. "But she voted against the war on ISIS."

I shrugged. The terrorists thought all Americans were infidels regardless of what we did.

"Why wouldn't they go after President Ramirez? He's the one pushing to destroy them."

I turned off my shower and squeezed water from my mass of curls. "Why do you think Teo and Lucia have guards around the clock? It'd make a terrorist's day to kill the president's family." As the words left my mouth, my stomach flipped. What would I do if something happened to Teo?

The feel of him holding me as I bawled had stayed with me for two weeks. He wasn't a big guy, especially compared to Dane, but his hold had felt big. His *heart* was big. Whenever I felt scared now, I thought of him. His fresh scent of soap. His long fingers smoothing my hair. His sexy Spanish words.

I was clasping my bra when Mackenzie closed her locker. "Hey, roomie. You coming to the dining hall with us?"

"Yep."

"Ace." She leaned against her locker and watched me pull on my shirt. "So, are you dating that bloke? Mateo?"

I hid a grin. "No."

"You sure? He's defo into you."

I wondered if I was "defo" into him, too. I sure thought about him a lot.

"Well, see ya at dinner." She followed Kaylee and Emma out of the locker room.

When I got to the lobby, Mateo and his agents were waiting for me, just like after every practice. Teo wore flip-flops, raggedy jeans, and a long-sleeved red polo shirt. The color looked so good against his dark complexion.

It wasn't a surprise when he asked, "Want to come over to the greenhouse?"

I'd turned him down every time—I just didn't feel ready. And I didn't want to talk about the rape with Mateo, Lucia, or Dane. Rehashing it with Dr. Valentine was bad enough.

"I'm meeting the girls at the dining hall."

He nodded as his smile wavered.

"But you could join us if you want?"

His eyes widened. "Sure!" Then he looked at his red-haired agent, Karen. "Can we do that?"

She glanced at Johnny. After a beat, he nodded.

We fell into step together as we emerged into the cloudy coolness of late September. It had rained earlier in the day, and my shoes had gotten soppy walking to class. Mateo's agents walked behind us.

His fingers played with his collar. "What's the dining hall like?"

I gawked at him. He'd never been? I watched Johnny speak into his comm-link before we crossed the street, and realized Mateo probably had missed out on a lot of college experiences. I'd have to change that. "Substandard food. Don't get too excited."

"At least I won't have to cook tonight."

"Good point." I didn't know how Elyse and my other upperclass teammates found time to shop and cook with our busy practice schedule.

"You were killin' it at practice today," he said.

I smiled. "Thanks." That had probably been my best practice at Highbanks. The fire in my belly had finally rekindled. Hot damn, I wanted to make the Olympic team.

"What's it called when you keep switching strokes?"

"Individual medley, or IM."

"You're really good at that, huh?"

I shrugged. "It's one of my best events. I like the variety."

"Hmm. Kind of like playing different instruments."

I'd never thought of it that way before. "Great analogy! I know you play guitar because I saw one in your room. Anything else?"

"Eh, I dabble a little in piano and keyboard. Tried bass guitar a few times. And Joey taught me how to play the flute, but I suck."

"Is Joey one of your bros from high school?"

He shook his head. "She's my best friend."

She? I wasn't expecting that one. He studied my reaction, so I tried not to show my alarm, but my mind raced. He had a female best friend? What did she mean to him? Had they dated? Kissed?

Had another chick gotten to those sweet, plump lips before me? I aimed for a nonchalant tone. "Tell me about her."

"She's really gifted. She goes to Berklee." When I tilted my head, he added, "It's the top music school in the country."

"Oh. Did you think about going there?"

"I didn't audition because my parents wanted me to go here, for security. But I probably wouldn't have gotten in."

He'd lost a lot when his father had won the presidency. Maybe it wasn't so bad that Mom didn't win. All the stares we were getting on our walk across campus certainly wouldn't be welcome twenty-four seven.

"Do you and Joey, uh, talk much?"

"We text." He grunted. "She told me she met someone already. He's a cellist."

Thank God! I couldn't suppress my grin. When he caught it, he smiled right back at me. *Damn!* He knew I was relieved.

I scrambled to change the subject. "What were you writing when I was swimming?"

"A song." His expression changed, and his pace slowed.

"Was it a sad song?"

He kept frowning. "A stupid song."

What does that mean? "Will your band play it?"

"No. This one's just for me." He brightened. "But I hope they'll play some other songs I wrote. Maybe I'll get to sing backup. We rehearse on Saturday."

"So you're a vocalist, too." I nudged his shoulder. "Very skilled, *Señor* Ramirez."

He smiled at that.

"And I still haven't heard you sing."

"Well, I haven't seen you swim in a meet."

"But you *have* watched me practice." I swallowed. "Thanks for being there for me."

He nodded. "*Siempre.*"

Always. That word sounded a thousand times sexier in Spanish.

He looked at my hand like he wanted to hold it, but quite a few students stared at us as we reached the dining hall. Instead, he opened the door for me.

We entered the Tudor-style building, and I handed the worker my university ID. "Four swipes," I told him. I waved away the money Mateo tried to give me. "I got this. It's on my meal plan."

"But I can't let my date pay for dinner!"

I grinned. "We're on a date?"

"Of course." He smirked.

There was a flash, and I watched a girl lower her phone. When she saw me look at her, she spun around and ran back into the dining hall. *Awesome.* Our photo would be on Twitter in a heartbeat. I hoped my wet hair wasn't too wild.

"Miss Monroe, we won't let you pay for us," Johnny said.

I took back my ID from the worker. "Too late, Officer Zucko." I heard him grumble behind me as I picked up a tray and utensils. I arched an eyebrow at Mateo and gestured for him to get a tray, too. "Okay, dining hall virgin."

His eyes flared.

"Here's how it works. Get whatever you want — salad bar, sandwich, Italian, Mexican, Chinese — then meet me in the dining area. I'll find my girls and get seats for everyone." I noticed the agents were still empty-handed. "You guys need trays."

"We'll get Mateo settled and may eat later," said Karen. "No need to find us seats."

"Tsk. You'll miss out on negative-five-star cuisine."

Mateo chuckled.

I headed to the salad bar while Mateo roamed around the large kitchen area. Every student tracked his moves, and the kitchen workers lit up when he passed their stations like they were begging him to choose their food. He ambled past the Mexican station, but it was no surprise when he slid a couple pieces of pizza onto his plate. Typical college boy fare.

Mackenzie sidled up to me as I scooped cottage cheese onto my salad. "I *heard* you brought him to dinner. Good on ya!"

Apparently word had traveled through the dining area with the speed of a fraternity food fight. "I felt bad for turning him down all the time. Hope you guys don't mind if he sits with us."

"No worries." She aimed a lecherous look at Johnny. "Who's that blond bloke in the suit?"

"You sure like the blond boys, don't you?" I remembered that swimmer she'd crushed on at the party our first night here. I felt myself tense, but I forced a deep breath. *It's September twenty-sixth. I'm in the dining hall.*

"Eh, Christian's cactus."

"What?"

"He's dead to me—keeps blowing me off. But that bloke's tastier, anyway. More mature. Who is he?"

"Teo's Secret Service agent." I'd once held a candle for Johnny too, in high school before I'd met my boyfriend, Duncan. It seemed like a lifetime ago. When Mackenzie gave me a quizzical look, I added, "They protect the president and his family." I drizzled vinaigrette, then picked up my tray. "Save us some seats?"

She nodded.

As I waited in the pasta line, Mateo approached with his agents behind him. He pointed to my tray. "That looks good. Where's the salad?"

I angled my head to the left. "What do you want to drink?"

"Surprise me."

Once I gathered a bowl of bow-tie pasta and meat sauce, I filled two glasses with ice water and two with lemonade. I was so thirsty that I downed a glass of water and refilled it as Mateo finished building his salad. "Ready?"

We walked into the dining area, where about three hundred students watched us. Probably half snapped photos with their phones.

"Sorry," Mateo whispered.

I saw Mackenzie wave from the corner. "We'll have to bring you here more often so the shine wears off."

His mouth quirked. "Yes, we will."

As we moved through the gauntlet of gapers, I glanced at his tray. "Their Mexican's not *auténtico* enough for you, *chile relleno?*"

"That's not it. Figured I'd stick with something safe after your warnings. Even *they* can't screw up pizza, right?"

"Don't be too sure." I set my tray down, and Mateo followed suit. His agents split off and stood on either side of the table with their backs to the wall. "This is Mateo, everyone. Mateo, this is my roommate, Mackenzie. And Kaylee and Emma are freshman swimmers, too."

"Hey." His shy smile made my heart melt.

Emma's eyes rounded as we sat. "What's it like for your dad to be president?"

"Emma!" Kaylee scowled at her. "I'm sure everyone asks him that. Come up with something original."

I watched Mateo look down at a device in his hand, held under the table, and realized he was doing something to his insulin pump. I averted my eyes to give him some privacy.

"I bet it sucks to be protected by Secret Service all the time," I mused.

He put the device back in his pocket.

"Right, Teo?"

He looked up. "Totally."

I, however, didn't mind them at all. I could let my guard down when the agents guarded Mateo and me.

"The blond one can protect me anytime," Mackenzie said.

Mateo laughed and held up his finger. "Now *that* was an original comment."

I dug into my pasta as he took a bite of pizza.

"Not bad." He chewed. "Mackenzie." He cocked his head toward her. "I hear you're from Australia."

She nodded.

"What city?"

"Melbourne."

I watched her beam and realized I'd never bothered to ask her that. I'd been too wrapped up in my selfish PTSD quagmire to get to know my roommate. I vowed to do better.

"So, I saw your posters," he told her.

"He was in our *room?*" Her mouth popped open. "You've been holding out on me, roomie." She returned her attention to Mateo. "Why were you there?"

We shared an uncomfortable look, and I licked my lip.

"My agents wanted to check on Jess," Mateo said. "Her family's been getting threats."

I let out a breath. I'd forgotten the cover story for a second.

"Is your family okay?" Emma asked me.

The concern in her eyes sent a stab of guilt through my chest. "Yeah, we'll be fine."

"Who's your favorite football player?" Mateo asked Mackenzie. "I mean, all of 'em are hideous looking, so I hope at least one plays well."

She shoved his shoulder, which made Johnny step closer. "Pig's arse! David Zaharakis from Essendon is the bloody best."

"Good to know."

Kaylee spoke up. "Hey, why's your dad so war-hungry? He's gonna get people killed by declaring war on ISIS."

Wow. I hadn't known she cared about politics.

Mateo set down his pizza slice. "I think Congress is the one that declares war."

"But your dad pushed for it. He's dead wrong."

He shrugged. "You're entitled to your opinion. It's a free country." He turned to Mackenzie. "So what makes this Zaharakis guy so great?"

Kaylee's nose wrinkled as Mateo turned his full attention to Mackenzie. The way her mouth hung open after Mateo failed to take her bait wasn't flattering, and I held up a napkin to hide my smile. Dane had told me Alejandro was even more strident than Lucia in defending conservative beliefs, but evidently Mateo didn't follow in their footsteps. I was glad about that. Swimming and school kept me too busy to care much about politics, so if Mateo sought a debate partner, he'd find me lacking.

I'd polished off my pasta and was halfway through my salad when Mateo said, "What do *you* swim, Emma?"

"Backstroke." She grinned. "And IM." Her grin faded. "I'm not as fast as Jessica, of course."

"Well, who is?" The gleam in his eye put my heart in a tizzy.

"Right?" Emma said. "She had the fastest two hundred IM time in the nation last year."

Mateo turned to look at me. "Seriously? You didn't tell me that."

"Just in high school." I felt my face flush. "There are faster American swimmers, especially in long course."

"What's long course?" he asked.

Kaylee set down her fork with a clang. "You don't know?"

Mateo looked at me with uncertain eyes.

"How would he know that, boofhead?" Mackenzie scowled at Kaylee. "He's not a swimmer. His sister's an ace volleyball player, though. Bet he knows heaps about volleyball."

"Yeah," I said, proud my roommate was defending Mateo. "Like shagging balls." Mateo's eyes widened as he looked at me again. "Do you know what it means to shag balls, Kaylee?"

My blond teammate shook her head as Emma giggled.

"Teo?" I looked back at him. "Will you educate us?"

He placed his hands in his lap. "Put the balls back in the basket at the end of practice."

"Bloody Yanks," Mackenzie muttered. "That's not what it means at all."

Mateo and I grinned at each other. I realized nobody had answered his question.

"By the way, long course is a fifty-meter pool—the distance they swim at the Olympics. In college, we swim short course, or twenty-five yards. Lots of flip-turns."

He nodded.

I watched Johnny step forward to intercept two male students who approached.

"Yo, Mateo!" A guy in a blue jacket poked around Johnny so Mateo could see him wave.

Johnny pushed them away from the table.

"We just want to say hi," the short guy huffed. "We're with the College Republicans."

"Really?" Kaylee made a face. "They exist?"

Karen spoke to Johnny. He looked back at us with a frown, but moved aside so we could see the students. "Stay back here," he ordered.

"Hey." Blue Jacket waved at Mateo. "We're with the Highbanks University Republicans. It'd be so rad if you joined us. Will you come to our meetings?"

"Um…" His nervous eyes darted toward me, as if *I* could help him with this.

"H-U-G-O-P dot com," the short guy said. "Check us out."

Mateo still didn't answer.

"Sorry, gentleman," Karen said. "Mr. Ramirez can't attend meetings due to security protocol."

Blue Jacket's head drooped.

But Short Guy perked up as he stared at Mateo. "Dude, your dad rocks."

"Uh, thanks?" Mateo looked at me again, and I grinned.

"Takin' it to ISIS, man!" Blue Jacket thumped his chest twice, and I read the saying on his shirt: *Turning ISIS into WASWAS.* He then jabbed two fingers in a peace sign like he was channeling his inner rapper.

Celebrating war while showing the peace sign? I scratched my head. Dane would have a *lot* to say to this guy.

"Good to meet you guys," Mateo said before Johnny shooed them away. He took a bite of pizza as I drained my lemonade.

Emma leaned in. "Do you have to deal with that all the time?"

"Not really." Mateo shrugged. "The students in my classes don't really notice my agents anymore. And the media's stayed away for the most part."

"Yeaahhh." Karen came up to the table and winced. "Not so much."

"What do you mean?" I asked.

"The backup team's on their way, and campus police is outside," Karen said.

I sat up straighter as silence blanketed our table.

"They're keeping all the reporters from crashing the dining hall."

Mateo watched my reaction as he asked, "Reporters?"

"Seems you two are all the rage on social media," Johnny said.

Kaylee thrust her phone in my face. "Oh my God! There's a picture of you." She stole her phone back and read, "Love at first bite." She rolled her eyes. "Mateo Ramirez joins Jessica Monroe at campus dining hall."

"Is this Dane and Lucia part *dos?*" Emma piped in, also reading from her phone. "Ducia fans, make way for Jessteo."

Mateo groaned as he looked at me. "Sorry, I didn't mean—"

"It's okay." I patted his arm. "Not your fault."

Mackenzie said, "At least Jessteo's better than Massica."

With her accent, the word sounded like *massacre.* I laughed as Mateo shook his head.

"Must be a slow news day," Karen said. "Listen, our vehicle's still at the pool. Want to wait for me to grab it or take a police escort to your dorm?"

I asked, "Why don't I just walk back to the dorm alone?"

"They're gonna hound you," Mateo said.

I considered that, and agreed with him. "Then why can't *we* walk?"

Johnny frowned. "Too many reporters—they could follow us. Wouldn't be safe. Don't you remember protocol, Miss Monroe?"

I should've recalled all of the security rigmarole since it had only been two years. But I'd get a refresher course if I kept hanging out with Mateo. I thought about him holding me and being there every practice, and I knew he was worth it.

"Are you finished?" he asked, gesturing to my tray.

"Yeah, but you still have some pizza left."

"Nothing ruins your appetite like paparazzi." He looked at Johnny. "How about the police option? It'll get us there fastest."

As Johnny spoke into his comm-link, the thrill of evading the media pulsed through my bloodstream. The back entrances, Secret Service whispers, and goading questions of my mother's presidential run came back to me. My heartbeat kicked up as Mateo touched my arm.

"You ready?"

I nodded.

We were about to stand when Mackenzie grasped my wrist. "This means you're no longer with Blake, right?"

I flinched and ripped my arm away from her. Where the fuck did that question come from? Blood rushed in my ears, and I fought for air.

"You okay?"

Mackenzie's voice sounded far off.

"Did I say something wrong?" she added.

A flash of blue eyes feasting on me. *"Get wet for me, baby."* My skin tingled, and my hands shook.

"Jessica." Mateo's voice, low and calm, was in my ear. "Can I hold your hand?"

I blinked, then nodded. His warm fingers entwined with mine.

"Do you think you're having a flashback?" he whispered.

I stilled and closed my eyes. "I-I don't know. Maybe."

"What do you hear?"

The pounding reverberated in my chest. "My heart."

"Good. Are you breathing?"

No. My shoulders had almost reached my ears, and I lowered them as I exhaled.

"What do you smell?"

My nosed wrinkled. "Gross food."

He chuckled. "*Sí,* I think you called it 'substandard.' What else do you smell?"

"Something woodsy. Maybe your cologne?"

His hand tensed. "Do you like it?"

I breathed in his scent and nodded. *Very much.* When I opened my eyes, he was smiling at me. I squeezed his hand and tried to smile back. Then I looked at my teammates, who gawked at me. Scanning the dining hall revealed that most of my fellow Cougars were also staring, looking ready to pounce. A few tables away, every student sitting there had their cell phone cameras trained on Mateo sitting so close to me. But he didn't pull away.

"How 'bout we blow this joint?"

I nodded. "Yes."

Mackenzie asked, "Are you okay?"

"Yeah. Sorry. I'm good." I tried to look normal.

She didn't exactly seem convinced, but she didn't ask me anything else.

Somebody had bussed our trays, so I let go of Mateo's hand and reached for my backpack.

"Want me to carry that for you?" he asked.

I noted his backpack strap on his shoulder. "But you have one, already."

"Got two shoulders." He pointed to illustrate.

Johnny frowned at Mateo as he extended his arm. "I'll take that for you, Miss Monroe."

"Right." Mateo grimaced.

What is going on? "Guys, I got it. I think I can carry my own backpack. Jeez." I forced a smile at my teammates. "See ya in the morning."

"Bye," Emma said.

Karen led the way. Mateo's hand drifted toward me, then he stole it back. He fidgeted with his backpack as he looked toward the exit.

Johnny cleared his throat, indicating we needed to get a move on.

I realized why Mateo was suddenly aloof: he didn't want to breach my privacy any more than he already had. He didn't want it to seem like we were a couple if I wasn't ready for it. *Screw it.* What difference would it make if there were a few hundred more photos of us together? When I reached for his hand, he gave it to me quickly. We walked out together, our heads held high.

He whispered, "Sorry 'bout that. My backpack's bulletproof, so Johnny makes me wear it over both shoulders."

Whoa.

Flashing cameras and shouted questions assaulted us as we jogged to a waiting police SUV.

"Mateo! Are you and Jessica together?"

"What do Dane and Lucia think of your relationship?"

"Will you have a double wedding with Dane and Lucia?"

That one got us laughing as we reached the vehicle. Johnny sat next to the campus police officer in the front seat while Mateo, Karen, and I hustled into the back.

The officer pulled away. As the reporters' chatter faded in the distance, he glanced at Johnny. "What took so long? We were ready to go five minutes ago."

My face burned as I looked at my lap. *I freaked out, and Mateo had to talk me down.*

When Mateo squeezed my hand, I realized he was still holding it. "Thanks for driving us," he told the officer.

"My pleasure, Mr. Ramirez. I'm Officer Whitworth, if you need anything."

"Thank you, sir."

I looked at him from the corner of my eye and smirked.

He knocked my hand into my thigh and whispered, "What?"

I whispered back, "You gonna salute him, too?"

His eyes narrowed. "At least I don't have parsley in my teeth."

I gasped and fumbled for my phone in my pocket. When I bared my teeth for the camera and found no sign of green, I glared at him.

"You totally fell for it," he cackled.

We arrived at Canfield Hall, and I bounded out of the car. Fortunately the media hadn't figured out where I lived yet, but they probably would soon. Mateo jogged up next to me, with Karen on his heels. Johnny stayed back at the police car, conferring with the officer.

When I unlocked the door to my room, I looked at Mateo. "Okay, um…"

"Have a good night." He backed up a step but held my gaze.

His eyes seemed soulful, like he felt ten different emotions at once. Did he see me as damaged? Did he pity me? Did hanging out with me make him happy? Did he want to kiss me?

"Want to come in?"

"Yeah."

We left Karen in the hallway and set our backpacks down. I touched the thick fabric of his and hoped he wouldn't ever need its protection from a bullet. My fist clenched as my chest tightened.

"Will Mackenzie be home soon?" he asked.

"Maybe." I cleared lotion, deodorant, and makeup from the dresser and shoved them into a drawer. Keeping my back to Mateo, I swallowed, then sighed. "Sorry I had a meltdown back there."

He came up behind me. "You did great. But why on Earth did your roommate bring up his name?"

"I had the same question." I shook my head as I turned to face him. "I haven't told her what he did to me, though, so it's my fault."

He inched closer. "It'd be tough to tell anyone, I bet."

I was so relieved I hadn't had to tell him. Maybe Mackenzie would figure it out on her own, too. He sure seemed to know how to help me through my worst moments.

"Did Dane…" I blew out a breath. "Did he tell you what to say to me if I started panicking?"

He nodded.

"Thank you."

"*De nada.*"

"It wasn't *nothing.* It meant a lot." I twisted my hands together. "One stupid question from Mackenzie and I go psycho." A guttural sound escaped my throat. "I wish it was over with. I wish I didn't have to think about what happened."

"Me, too." After a beat, he added, "Dane told me you're not reporting it?"

I chewed my lip. "Do you think…that's bad?"

"I think it's your decision."

"You didn't answer my question."

Mateo sighed. "Do I want to see the douchebag fry for what he did? Of course I do. But mostly I want you to get your life back. If reporting helps you move on, maybe you should."

"I'm not sure it would help me move on." My throat constricted.

It was quiet between us. Mateo came closer and curled my fingers in his. Those dark eyes watched me as his thumb caressed my knuckles. "Well, I hope you get your act together, at least by the time we have our double wedding."

Just like that, I giggled. I wrapped my arms around his waist and pressed into him, so grateful for his presence in my life. It took a moment before his arms enveloped my back. But when he tucked me closer, I melted into him. I rested my cheek on his collarbone and drank in his soothing scent.

I wasn't sure how long we hugged, but at some point I decided he probably needed to get back to his life instead of focusing so much on mine.

"I should let you go." I stepped back. He gazed at me like he was checking my mental stability. "You need to rent your tux, and I haven't even started looking for a wedding dress."

His eyes flashed surprise a second before he unleashed a huge grin. "Maybe if Dane's not ready for a double wedding, he could be our flower girl instead?"

"Ha, ha, ha!" I shuddered at the image of Dane tossing flowers out of a basket as he crutched down the aisle.

His grin faded as he studied me. "So you'll be okay, then?"

I nodded. "Good luck at band rehearsal on Saturday."

His eyes smoldered, and he brushed his fingers down my cheek. I leaned into his gentle touch. We held there for a minute before he grabbed his backpack.

Once he left, I turned around and pressed my back against the door. My heart rate shot up, but it wasn't from fear. It was excitement. It was being near Mateo.

We hadn't even kissed, and the reporters were already marrying us. I looked at my palm and smoothed my fingertips over my skin, remembering the warmth of his hand in mine as we'd hustled past the cameras and microphones.

Maybe we should give them something to talk about.

16
Mateo

★ ★ ★

Girl needs protected
Her memories affected
But I get rejected
So stupidly, I leave

Unfeeling ass, I leave

Pedal to gas, I leave

She's biting her wound
Ascending, the moon
I don't like this tune
So stupidly, I leave

Futile fool, I leave

Heartless tool, I leave

And now what can I do
To help her get through
There's nothing; it's true
The time to act's overdue

Because I left

I left.

M y eyes closed as I finished singing. If only I hadn't let that Blake guy intimidate me, I wouldn't have left Jessica in his arms. His creepy arms. I wanted to rip them out of the sockets.

There was a knock on my bedroom door, and I flipped over the page of lyrics. "Come in."

Lucia stuck her head in the room. "Hey."

"Thought you were at practice." She usually practiced the morning of her Saturday-night match.

"Coach didn't make us stay to watch video, thank God."

When she came in and closed the door, I tensed. *Bad news?*

"You got a minute?"

"*Sí.*" I looked at my phone as she sat in my desk chair. "But I have to meet the band at noon."

She nodded, then stared at my guitar, saying nothing. I tried to figure out what she wanted to discuss. Her T-shirt featured a horse-drawn carriage with a volleyball pumpkin perched atop wheels with long spokes.

Cinderella went to the ball
And then she spiked it over the net

"Sorry I didn't come to your match last night," I said.

"Oh." She blinked. "That's okay. You don't need to go tonight, either. I'm sure you have better stuff to do."

Actually, I was waiting to hear back from Jessica about tonight. She'd said she was going out with her roommate, but I hoped she'd change her mind and hang out with me. The explosion of our photos in the media had made it impossible to keep her out of my mind, especially with everyone asking if we were dating. When I'd denied it, people either thought I was hiding the truth or I was stupid for not being into her. As if I wouldn't be into such a beautiful studette.

"That song you just played...it's about Jessica, right?" Lucia asked.

I flinched. "You could hear the lyrics? I was trying not to sing too loud. Don't want the agents to know."

"I kind of listened outside your door. Sorry."

I supposed I couldn't be angry with her about that, since I'd done the same thing.

Lucia fiddled with the hem of her shirt. "How's she doing?"

"Um…" I realized Lucia hadn't seen Jessica since finding out about the rape. "Good, I guess. Unless someone mentions Shithead's name. Then she shuts down."

"Must be awful." She sighed. "I've thought about calling her, or going to her dorm, but Dane said she needs space. I just want to give her a hug, you know?"

I knew the feeling well. I wanted to spend every second with Jessica, but I didn't want to suffocate her. I didn't want to push her too hard. And Dane's advice had seemed to work well a few nights ago.

Lucia examined me. "You blame yourself, then?"

My throat clenched. "I was there. I saw him give Jess the damn drink."

"But you couldn't have known." She shook her head. "Dr. Valentine told me we shouldn't blame ourselves. She said we're feeling helpless, and blaming ourselves is a way to regain control."

"Wait." I squinted. "You blame yourself, too? How's it *your* fault?"

"Don't you remember that night? Dane wanted to go over there, but I told him not to. *¡Fui una estúpida!*"

Recalling how I'd spent the night laughing with Lucy and Dane after I left the party, I felt the urge to throw up. "It might've been too late, anyway."

Her mouth trembled.

"It's not your fault, Lucy. Not Dane's fault." I exhaled. "Not my fault either, I guess." My jaw clamped. "The only one to blame is Suave Swimmer Shithead — the one person who skates free, with zero consequences."

Lucia's eyes narrowed. "It's not right. But if I were in Jessica's shoes, I wouldn't want to report it, either."

I shook my head. *So freaking unjust.* Dad had said one reason he got into politics was to fight for justice. And here was a travesty playing out before us, with nothing I could do about it. My dad was the most powerful man in America, but I couldn't involve him — not without Jessica's permission.

Lucia stood and cupped my shoulder. "I'm really glad you're there for her, *hermanito*."

"I'm not sure I'm doing anything." I frowned.

"You are. Dane says you mean a lot to her. At least *I* feel better, knowing she has you."

I patted her hand. "*Gracias.*"

"I'll let you get to your band buddies. That going well?"

I shrugged. "The lead singer's an ass, but he lives out of town. Itch and Fitch are cool. Itch has a crush on you, by the way."

She blushed. "The short one?"

"No, the taller Japanese-Mohawk guy, Ichiro."

She rubbed her hand across the back of her neck as she pursed her lips. "Don't let Dane know."

"Really? Might be fun to watch his reaction when I tell him he's got competition."

She didn't smile. "He's got enough on his plate right now, Matty. And he's eager to hurt someone to avenge his sister. Don't let your friend be the one to take the fall."

Point taken. After watching Jessica disappear inside herself at the mere mention of Shithead, I could relate to Dane's desire to vent his rage.

Thirty minutes later, Johnny led the way into Fitch's uncle's warehouse. This time the temperature was cooler. With October only two days away, there was a hint of autumn in the air. As I passed by rows of lockers, I noticed the heat wasn't the only thing missing. The skunk smell of Weston's weed was also absent. I thought he would be here tonight.

I turned the corner to find Fitch and Itch setting up their equipment. No sign of the sullen mumbler. "Where's Weston?"

They shared a look.

Fitch said, "He won't be joining us today."

"Or ever," Itch added with a wide smile.

Huh?

"You don't have to look so happy about it." Fitch tugged at the bill of his hat and glared at his roommate.

"C'mon, Ryno. You just feel bad because your moms are friends."

Fitch raised his chin. "His mom's the reason we moved to Cincinnati!"

"Guys." I set down my guitar case. "Want to tell me what's going on?"

Itch nodded at me. "You're our new lead singer."

I froze.

"All right!" Johnny said. He slung his arm across Karen's shoulders. Her grin matched his, which made them look like proud parents.

"Come again?" I asked.

"Dude." Itch approached and thumped me on the back. "You're it. Weston's gone."

"What happened to him?" I was beginning to thaw out, but this shit still felt unreal.

Itch pointed to my guitar. "When I read your lyrics…then heard you *sing*, I wanted to kick West out right away. But Fitch wasn't on board."

Fainting at our first rehearsal like a swooning chick probably hadn't impressed our drummer.

"It's not that I don't want you to be our lead," Fitch said, taking off his cap and running his hand through his hair. "It's just…My mom's best friends with West's mom. When my parents split, my mom wanted to get the hell outta Chicago. His mom took us in. She did a lot for us."

I held up my hand. "I get it. You guys don't have to choose me over him."

"But we do." Itch nodded. "This has been building for a while. West forced it, though—threw down the gauntlet. He said he wasn't coming up here to rehearse any more because he didn't want to deal with cops." He glanced at my agents. "He told us it was either you or him."

And they chose me? *Dios.*

Fitch came over, looking serious. "We want *you*, Mateo. Your songs are way better, and you're cooler to hang with. Will you be our front man?"

I looked back and forth between them, trying to play it cool, but my massive smile betrayed me. "Hell, yeah."

We somehow knew to jump together to execute a sweet three-way chest bump, which made us laugh when we landed. And my pump didn't dislodge this time.

"Just don't start mumbling the lyrics or get addicted to weed," Itch warned.

No way that would happen. Dane had told me SSS made Jessica smoke a joint that night, probably to manipulate her into keeping quiet about the rape.

Itch bounced on his feet. "We don't have to work around West's bartending schedule now. We can book a gig!"

Holy shit.

Fitch fiddled with an amp while Itch strapped on his guitar. I tried to remember to breathe.

"This means we need to play more to get ready," Itch said.

Fitch jabbed his drumstick in my direction. "No forgetting rehearsal because of some girl."

I winced as I knelt to unbuckle my guitar case. They continued to give me crap about that night I hadn't shown up.

"You still claiming you're not with Jessica?"

I looked up at Itch. "Yep."

"Whatever." Itch took on a dreamy look. "Speaking of lovely, long-legged ladies, how's your sister?"

"Out of your league, *amigo*." I strummed my guitar and began singing "Let It Go" from *Frozen*.

Fitch grinned as he threw his hat back on and added a drumbeat. Itch's bass guitar joined in next, morphing the song into a thumping rock ballad. I didn't know all the lyrics, but it didn't matter. Together we created a new, edgy vibe for a Disney song, of all things.

Fitch's dark eyes lit up. "We should totally do a cover of this!"

Nine hours later, I leaned back against the seat of the SUV. But I wasn't tired. I was exhilarated. Johnny had gone out for food twice, and we'd done great work composing a tentative playlist. I looked at my phone and frowned when I saw two missed texts from Jessica. The first one was a casual question about what I was doing, but the second, which had come just a few minutes ago, sounded more urgent:

Where are you?

I typed:

**Driving home after rehearsal.
Where are you?**

Her reply came at once.

At Elyse's. Come get me?

Yes.

My stomach flipped. "We need to pick up Jessica."

"Where?" Karen frowned from the driver's seat.

I waited for Jessica to text me the address and relayed it to Karen.

"Negative. That's a busy section of off-campus housing on a Saturday night."

"She needs me."

She blew out a breath as we rolled to a stop at a light. "Why?"

I felt Johnny's stare from the seat next to me. "She just does. Please? I'll stay in the vehicle. It'll be safe."

Her fingers drummed the steering wheel as Johnny typed on his phone.

"You need to turn right at the next light if we're picking her up," he said.

"So you agree with this?" She hit the gas when the light turned green.

Johnny nodded. "Sure. But it's your call."

I held my breath as we approached the next light, and I exhaled when Karen turned right. My fingers tapped my phone.

On our way.

After we snaked through crowded streets to arrive at a duplex, Karen left the car idling between rows of parked cars on either side of the street. She reached for the door but Johnny said, "I'll get her."

"No, you won't." Karen opened her car door. "You're not exactly objective about this. Stay with the car—I'll be quick." She left.

Johnny's jaw ticked, and I said, "What'd she mean about you not being objective?"

He swallowed. "Because I used to protect Jessica, I guess." He kept looking out the window at the duplex.

"Did you like protecting her more than me?"

He swiveled to look at me. "Of course not." He seemed to think about my question. "Being on the presidential detail is different. So many agents—I'm just a cog in the wheel. Protecting Miss Monroe made me feel more useful."

"You *were* useful. You saved her life."

"An overstatement. I did my job."

A low-riding car barely squeezed between rows of parked cars and our SUV. Its horn blasted over the thumping of rap music. "Get outta the road!" the driver yelled as he drove away.

Johnny ignored them. "You care about Jessica."

After a beat, I admitted, "Can't get her out of my mind."

"Don't screw it up, Ramirez."

I smirked. He cared about her, too. Dane had told me Jessica outgrew her crush on Johnny from a couple of years ago. Apparently he could tell me about competition for my girl, but I wasn't allowed to return the favor.

I sat up when Karen exited the house sans Jessica. She opened the car door.

"Miss Monroe's in a room upstairs, and she won't come out." Karen looked at me. "She said she needed *you*."

"I'll go with him," Johnny said.

Karen climbed back into the driver's seat. "Fine."

Johnny led the way into the house with me on his tail. The interior was rather dark, but I could tell from the loud music and glow of cell phones that quite a few people were here.

"Mateo." A girl with long, black hair reached for me, but Johnny shook his head as he stepped between us. "Oh, sorry." She inched back. "I'm Elyse, the team captain. Thank God you're here."

"Jess is upstairs?" I asked.

"My room." Elyse mounted the stairs two at a time, and we followed her. She stopped outside a closed door. "We were having a good night—she was sticking to her two-beer limit—when suddenly she's got a vodka bottle in her hands."

I cocked my head. "Two-beer limit?"

"She asked me to help her not drink too much. But then she wouldn't listen. She freaking screamed at me when I snatched the bottle from her."

"Sorry 'bout that. Did something happen?"

"I have no idea. She bitched out Mackenzie, too. We threw her in my room to shut her up."

I'd heard all I needed to hear. I knocked but there was no answer.

"Your Jalapeño's here," Elyse called.

I looked at Johnny. *Jalapeño?*

The door opened to reveal Jessica's blotchy face and glassy eyes. "You came." She stepped into my arms, and I held her tight. Her entire body trembled. I smoothed circles on her back until she seemed to settle.

"So you're not yelling at *him*, too?" Elyse said.

Jessica let me go and looked down. "Sorry."

"What happened, Jess?" I asked.

She clasped my hand and drew me into the room. After taking a quick scan of the interior, Johnny closed the door and stayed outside.

The room was decorated in shades of lavender and smelled like a sexy perfume. When she sat on the bed, I eased down next to her. Her hands twisted in her lap.

"We were supposed to party here all night. But then they wanted to go to the swimmer house, and I…"

His house. Her emotional explosion made sense now. I cupped her hands in mine and stroked her soft skin.

"Mackenzie and Elyse are mad at me."

"They'll come around."

She sniffed. Blond ringlets hid one side of her face, and I wanted to tuck them behind her ear. "At least Elyse got the vodka away from me before I could drink it."

So that was why she didn't seem drunk. "Want to ditch this place?"

She nodded.

I waited for her to blow her nose, then opened the door to find Johnny lingering in the hallway.

"*Vámonos*," I said.

"You stick by my side," he told me, then turned to Jessica. "And you stay right behind us."

Elyse bounded up the stairs and stopped short when she saw Jessica. "Well, *you* look better."

"I'm so sorry!" Jessica engulfed her in a hug. "I'll stop with the crazy town, I promise."

"You've definitely used up your crazy quota." Elyse let her go, then pointed her finger at me. "Take care of her, mister."

I smiled at her bossy tone. "Yes, ma'am."

Her hand darted to cover her heart, and she stage-whispered to Jessica, "He's adorable."

My face felt a little hot, but when Jessica smirked at me and said, "He is," the rest of my body caught on fire.

"Okay, you two." My agent took my arm, and we hustled down the stairs.

When we arrived at the car, Johnny pleased me by sitting shotgun, leaving the backseat to my date and me.

Okay, so we weren't technically on a date.

"Can we hang out at your place?" she asked.

Definitely a date. "Sure." I nodded at Karen. "To the greenhouse, Jeeves."

"That's Master at Arms Kennedy to you," Karen said.

When Jessica looked at me, I explained, "Karen used to be in the Navy."

"Oh." We were quiet the rest of the ten-minute drive.

When Jessica and I walked into the house, I gestured to the kitchen. "Hungry?"

She shook her head.

"Um. Want to watch a movie?" Maybe we could cuddle.

Another head shake. "I want to hear your voice."

My stomach twisted.

"Will you sing for me?" She motioned to the guitar case in my hand. "C'mon. You've held out on me long enough." Without waiting for me, she marched to my bedroom.

I hurried to catch up. "But I've been singing all day. My voice might—" I halted inside my bedroom door. She held Escuincle to her chest with her nose buried between his ears. His tail swished as purrs rumbled from his throat, and it almost looked like he was grinning. She closed her eyes and let out a little moan. It was the sexiest damn thing.

"Your voice will be fine." She set the cat on the bed and lowered herself next to him. After she scooted back to rest against the wall, Escuincle surprised me by climbing onto her lap. "Señor Squinks and I want a show. *Vámonos.*"

How could I argue with that? I took out my guitar, then seized up with nerves. I had no idea which song to choose. "What do you want to hear?"

"Anything. What about that song you wrote at my practice a few days ago?"

No way I'd choose that song—the one Lucia had overheard. I didn't want to remind Jessica about that night, or about my failure to protect her. I remembered I'd written a less obvious song yesterday that could work. It might be a risk, showing how much she consumed my mind. *What if she doesn't feel the same about me?*

But I had to go for it since I didn't know when I'd have such a stunning girl in my bedroom again.

Her eyebrows lifted when I closed my door.

"This is a private performance," I said.

"Ooohh." She leaned closer to my cat's rotating ear. "Aren't we lucky?"

Fitch had added an off-kilter drumbeat when we'd rehearsed the song earlier today, and I silently counted to the staccato beat. I closed my eyes and inhaled a deep breath. *Here goes nothing.*

Trust
Is a hard-to-earn thing
Just
Try to keep listening

Swallow
Down all of the unjust
Hollow
My chest, my heart will bust

Reach
Out to take her hand
Teach
Me to be a good man

The slight rasp to my voice actually worked for this song. I was about to continue when I watched her back peel off the wall, her eyes expanding.

"What?" I asked.

"Not sure...Is this a song about me?"

I had to be honest. "It's one of them."

"You've written other songs about me?"

Only about a hundred. I put my guitar back in its case. "Does that freak you out?"

A smile slowly spread, crinkling her eyes. "I like it. I want to hear more."

Was I ready for her to know for sure how I felt about her? "Then you'll have to come over another time. The guys wiped me out today."

"Your voice didn't sound tired at all."

"Thanks." I slid my hands into my pockets. "I was trying to remember what my instructor taught me about breathing."

"What kind of breathing do they teach singers?"

"Deep breathing—I think it's called diaphragmatic?"

She snorted.

I stared at her as I crossed to sit near my pillow. "Did I say it wrong?"

"Oh! No, I was laughing because my 'instructor' taught me diaphragmatic breathing, too."

I cocked my head.

"And by instructor I mean psychologist," she added.

Sí. Dane had mentioned the breathing technique. "You're supposed to take deep breaths when you're…having flashbacks?"

She stroked Squinky's fur. "Or when I wake up from nightmares."

That sounded dreadful.

"I bet petting this little brat would help me fall back asleep."

I shrugged. "He probably interferes with sleep more than he helps it."

"Maybe we'll have to test that out one day."

She stared straight at me as she spoke, awakening my lower body. I shifted to adjust myself. "What else, uh, what else did your psychologist say would help you in bed, er, sleep?"

"Dr. Valentine told me my brain's sending alarm signals to my body, making me tense and edgy. She said I should get massages to calm down my muscles, but I haven't had time."

Dios. She led me right there. My heart raced as I contemplated sharing my next thought. "Would you like me to give you a massage?"

She dipped her chin and looked up at me. "Do you know how?"

"Hell no. I'm no massage therapist."

She laughed. "I've never had a massage, so it's not like I'd know the difference."

"You've never had a massage? They're awesome." I used to get them monthly at the White House. I rose to my feet and pointed to my pillow. "Um, here. Want to lie down on your stomach?"

She hesitated.

"Only if you're up for it," I added. "No pressure."

Her blue eyes met mine. "That song you sang? I do trust you, by the way."

I let out a breath. "I'm honored."

To back up her words, she set Escuincle on the floor, kicked off her shoes, and extended her body toward the headboard. The mattress was extra long, but there still wasn't much space left at the foot of the bed once she'd stretched out. Her head lifted from the pillow. "Am I supposed to take my clothes off?"

Hijole. Blood rushed to my groin. *Absolutely,* I wanted to say. Instead I sat next to her shoulder and stroked her hair.

"That would be the perfect ending to the perfect day, but we shouldn't rush things."

"I guess you're right." She lowered her cheek to the pillow.

I chewed my lip as my hands hovered over her shoulders. I was really doing this? I touched the base of her neck as gently as I could, but she still jumped.

"Sorry!" she said.

"*Tranquila.* It's okay." I lifted her hair to one side and smoothed my fingers down her neck, fanning out to her shoulder blades. Her muscles felt tense as hell. "Now would be a good time for those deep breaths."

She nodded, and I felt her torso rise beneath my hands.

"You don't like it, we stop. No problem."

"It already feels good." She closed her eyes and sank into the mattress.

Buoyed by that feedback, I began working her shoulders through her royal-blue shirt. The scent I'd noticed in Elyse's bedroom lingered on her skin, and my body responded to the smell and the touch.

"Mmm," she purred when I moved to her shoulder blades. Her sated sound turned me rock hard.

Her body was lean with soft curves thrown in at just the right places. She was firm and muscular, yet still feminine. Still a complete turn-on. Would she think I was a pervy masseur if she knew how hard I was?

Escuincle watched us for a while, then hopped up on the bed. He pranced over to her and stepped onto the slight slope of her jean-clad bottom.

"Squinky." I frowned. "Get down."

She giggled. "Is he sitting on me?"

"Yeah. Do you want him off?"

"Nah." He began kneading her lower back with his paws, and her giggles increased. "My first human *and* cat massage."

"He was weaned early," I explained. "Sometimes he kneads Lucy and me, too." The feline masseur was busy down below so I slid my fingers up her neck to bury them in her thick hair. Damn, I loved her curls. When I massaged her scalp, she stopped giggling. She sank into the pillow. Her breathy moan was a shot to my groin.

I drew circles with my index fingers on the back of her head, and she seemed to sway under my touch. The sound of her slow breaths filled the room, filled me with satisfaction. I relaxed her as she excited me.

Escuincle hopped down and curled up by her hip.

Kneading behind her ears, my fingers skated down along her jaw.

"So." Her voice was lower than normal. "What made your day perfect?"

I paused until I remembered my earlier comment. "Fitch and Itch kicked out their front man."

"Really? What does that mean?"

I shrugged. "Guess I'm the new lead singer."

She bolted upright, somehow without disrupting the cat. "Oh, my God! That's great news, Teo." She threw her arms over my shoulders and squeezed me tight.

Though I'd been stoked when my bandmates had told me the news, that feeling was nothing like the elation I experienced in her arms. Her celebrating my good fortune multiplied it into a billion bucks.

We sat hip to hip on the bed as we embraced. I felt the softness of her breasts pushing into my chest. She lifted her head from my shoulder and looked into my eyes. Up to this point, our hugs had felt peaceful, comforting. But the charge in the air and the lively sparkle in her eyes seemed different this time. My throat was a desert, and swallowing didn't help.

"Now you're not relaxed anymore," I said.

"To be honest, your massage didn't relax me very much."

"I told you I was winging it."

"Oh! It's not your technique."

I searched her face for a clue.

She gave me a sly smile. "It's the massage therapist." She leaned closer, our noses almost touching. "He's turning me on."

I opened my mouth to suck in a breath, and in a flash her lips were on mine. *Dios*, she was kissing me! I closed my eyes and savored her silky mouth. My hands wove through that glorious hair as I deepened the kiss. She tasted like mint, with a lingering hint of beer, and I drank her in like a thirsty traveler.

She kept kissing me as she lifted up and moved one leg across my body to straddle my lap. Her heat burned into me. My erection pressed against her through our jeans, and my eyes flew open to see her reaction.

"Hmm." A smile played over her mouth. "Feels like I'm not the only one who's turned on."

She scooted closer and shifted her body with a slow grind against me. I was about to come right there.

"*Chica,*" I panted. "I've had it bad for you for a long time."

"I'm honored, Teo." Her blue eyes deepened. "The first time we met, I thought you were so cute."

"*Cute?*" I leaned back with a scowl.

She grinned. "Back when you were just a boy. And I was just a girl." Her grin vanished. "A stupid girl lately." Her face fell. "I've done some things I regret. I, I lost my way somehow." She tossed her head and blinked a few times. "But anyway, now you're a man. A *hot* man."

That sounded way better than *cute*.

"A man who's helping me find my way back. I don't know what I would've done without you." She pressed her warm lips to mine, and this kiss was silkier, slower. Her hands raked through my hair as I massaged up and down her spine. I was melting like Olaf into a puddle on my bed.

She held me tight as she opened her eyes, an inch from mine. "Thank you. *Gracias.*"

"*Siempre.* Anything for you."

She looked behind her at my pillow, then back at me. "Could we…Could I stay here tonight? I mean, not to…" She swallowed.

"I could hold you as you fall asleep?"

She let out a breath. "Yes. Please."

I found some pajamas for her in Lucia's room and checked my blood glucose as she brushed her teeth. After I got ready for bed, I came out of the bathroom to find her lying on her side with Escuincle curled up against her belly. She stroked his fur as she smiled at me.

I'd never wanted to get to bed faster in my life.

For a moment I wondered what Johnny and Karen would think about Jessica sleeping over, but I pushed that thought aside. No other guy my age had to worry about that crap. I climbed behind her and curved into a spooning position, then drew the covers over us.

"Can Squinky breathe?" she asked.

"Yeah. He'll probably leave at some point."

She sighed. "He'll be outta there for sure if I have a nightmare."

"No nightmares." I kissed her shoulder and tucked her closer. "This is a nightmare-free bed."

"Good." I heard a smile in her voice. She snuggled into my chest.

I thought there'd be no way I could fall asleep with the girl I'd been dreaming about a reality in my bed. But when her breaths steadied, I felt my eyelids droop. The drain of a long band rehearsal seeped into me.

"*Te quiero,*" I whispered. Her warmth filled my body as I drifted off to sleep.

17
Jessica

★ ★ ★

Mackenzie and I laughed as we entered our dorm room. After a few days of awkwardness and me trying to apologize without revealing anything, she'd finally forgiven me for yelling at her two weeks ago at Elyse's. I was grateful. We'd just finished an intrasquad meet — frosh vs. varsity — and our team (the freshmen and seniors) had crushed the sophomores and juniors.

"You're celebrating with me tonight, right?" Mackenzie asked as she flung her backpack onto the chair.

My laughter died. I took off my jacket and fluffed my wet hair. "Actually, I'm going over to Teo's. We're teaching him how to play euchre."

"Jessica." Her eyebrows lowered. "You're no fun anymore."

"Sorry." I winced.

She looked into the mirror above her chest of drawers as she drew on eyeliner. "So Teo's not there for one meet and you go through withdrawal?"

Dane and Lucia had attended my meet — Lucia had a rare weekend break from volleyball, and Dane wanted to show off his sans crutches ambulatory status — but Mateo had spent his Saturday afternoon at band rehearsal. He was freaking out about having only two weeks to get ready for their first gig, which had been scheduled for the last weekend of October.

Mackenzie started applying mascara. "You defo need a bangaroo with him."

I wasn't sure of the exact definition of *bangaroo* but it definitely seemed sexual. I blushed, thinking about sex with Mateo. We hadn't progressed beyond kissing and touching, but I sensed more was coming. And I could *defo* get on board with that. I just hoped I wouldn't have a flashback.

I plugged in my hair dryer as Mackenzie continued with her makeup. "What about you?" I asked. "Still no dice with Christian?"

She pouted at her mirror. "He's living up to his name."

"Huh?"

"He's a choir boy. No bloody bangaroos with him."

I looked at a reflection of one of her alpha-male posters in my mirror. "Bummer," I said.

"No worries. Got my eye on another bloke." She rubbed her lips together after applying lipstick.

"Really? Who?"

She paused. "Why do you want to know? You have Mateo."

That seemed like a strange response.

"Don't want to jinx it," she added. "He's prolly out of my league." She turned on her hair dryer, which drowned out further conversation.

I shrugged and turned on my own hair dryer, attaching a diffuser to keep my curls from going berserk. My hair was almost dry when a chill went up my spine, despite the hot air. I clicked off the dryer and turned to Mackenzie, who had moved on to flat-ironing her sleek brown hair.

"The guy you like…is it Blake?" Saying his name made me sick.

She met my eyes in her mirror, then set down the flat iron.

When she didn't answer right away, nausea coiled in my gut.

"What if it is?" She blinked. "You don't own him."

Oh, God. "I know I don't. This isn't about me—it's about you." My voice shook. "You shouldn't be with him, Mackenzie. He's a bad dude."

"No, he's not. But even if he is, maybe I like bad boys."

No, no, no. "Trust me, you won't like him. He...didn't treat me well. He's not right for you, either."

"So I'm not good enough for your sloppy seconds?"

She hadn't heard a word I'd said. My heart seemed to vibrate, sending trembles through my core.

"That's not what I'm saying!" The tightness in my chest made it tough to breathe, and I clutched my desk chair for support.

"What's your deal?" She stepped closer. "Why've you been acting so weird?"

I hoped my attempts at deep breaths weren't too obvious. I felt sweat bead at my temple.

"Like, why'd Elyse stop you from drinking the other night?"

I forced a swallow down my constricted throat. "I'm not supposed to drink."

"Why not? All swimmers party."

I stepped around to sit in the chair, shoving my hands under my legs to stop their quiver. "I failed a drug test."

Her eyes widened. "For what? When?"

"The first night we were here. The party at the swimmer house." My voice quivered on that last word, and I closed my eyes. "Blake gave me a joint. I should've said no."

"*Aaahhhh.*"

I opened my eyes to see her nodding.

"So *that's* why you don't like him. You're a hornet in a bottle—angry at him because he got you in trouble."

"No, it's more than that." *Much more.*

Her head cocked as she waited for me to continue.

I couldn't tell her about the rape. I wasn't ready. If I told her, she might blab to others, which might force me to have to report it to the police. What if she didn't believe me? Or what if she told Blake I'd figured out that he raped me? Would he try to come after me? Threaten me? "I...I can't tell you."

"It's not *his* fault you smoked, you know." She went back to her flat iron.

Clearly she liked Blake. She was on his side, and she wouldn't believe me. "I know that. I shouldn't have done it."

I wished I hadn't. But if I hadn't tested positive on that drug test, I wouldn't have met with Dr. Valentine. Maybe I would've still thought I'd had consensual sex with him. Maybe I'd be with him.

I shuddered. "Don't let him take advantage of you."

I watched her eyes narrow in her mirror. "But you're the one who dumped him." She turned and stared at me. "Why are you so jealous?"

I was about to tell her I was anything but jealous when my phone buzzed. Teo and his agents were outside the dorm waiting for me.

She grabbed her small purse and headed for the door.

"Mackenzie, wait."

She halted, but wouldn't look at me.

"Where're you going?" I asked.

"Elyse's."

I exhaled. Elyse would watch over her. "Please. I know I'm not making sense, but please believe that I'm not jealous. I, I just don't want you to get hurt."

When my phone buzzed again, she looked at the door. "I think I can handle myself."

"I know you can—"

She walked out.

"Ugh!" I groaned at the closed door. *It's not you I don't trust.* My heart galloped, and I covered my face. What to do? I texted Mateo back, threw on some makeup, and jogged to the SUV.

Mateo grinned as I climbed in, and I tried to relax my mouth when he leaned in for a kiss.

"Turquoise looks great on you."

I looked down at my long-sleeved shirt beneath a shaggy white vest. "Thanks."

"It's not as much bling as that sequin one. Maybe when it gets warm again, you'll wear it?"

My airway compressed. "I threw it away."

He waited a beat, and I watched his eyes as he realized that particular shirt held bad memories for me. "Oh. Right. Sorry."

Johnny drove the car toward the greenhouse as I stared at my phone. *Should I text Mackenzie? Do I have a prayer of convincing her to stay away from Blake?* My cheeks puffed out with a long sigh. *Probably not.*

"*¿Estás bien?*"

I looked at Mateo, whose face had filled with concern. From the driver's seat, Johnny seemed to be waiting for my answer, and I didn't want to say anything in front of him. *Pull it together.*

I pasted on a smile. "Fine." I ran my tongue over my teeth. "Just thinking about the best way to teach you euchre, Teo. We'll be an awesome team."

He smiled as his hand slipped into mine. "Dane's been trash-talking me all week."

"He's a little competitive."

"Just a tad."

"What'd he say?"

He scrolled down his phone. "Here's a good one: You suck more than a suck machine set on 'suck a lot.'"

My brother was so juvenile.

He kept reading. "Get your popcorn ready, 'cause I'm gonna put on a show."

And arrogant.

"Here's my favorite, though." He smirked at his phone. "Let me get you a menu, because you're about to get served."

"Well done for working volleyball slang into it." I had to grin. "How'd you respond?"

"Fitch helped me come up with 'Get the marshmallows ready, 'cause, baby, I'm on fire.'"

I chuckled. "Niiiice. How was rehearsal?"

"So good. We wrote a new song. I've never composed with other musicians before." His eyes lit up. "It was totally organic, totally synergistic."

When had he become vegan Reiki master?

"How was your meet?" he asked.

"Our relay rocked. Elyse swam back, I did breast, Mackenzie fly, and Emma free. My individual events were a little off, but we have five months of training before NCAAs in March."

He considered that. "So you didn't win IM and breaststroke?"

"No, I won." I'd won by a lot, but I didn't want to boast. "But my times could've been better."

He shook his head. "You sound like Lucy. Maybe you're being too hard on yourself."

"Tell me this: are you ever completely satisfied with the songs you write?"

His mouth puckered. "Touché."

When a text vibrated my phone, I looked down. It was from Elyse.

Mack says you're not coming over?

I tensed. I hadn't thought about Blake for five minutes, but now my worries for Mackenzie came rushing back.

Sorry—thought I told you I'm going to Teo's.

Oh, right. We'll miss you, chica!

Miss you, too.

I nibbled on my lip as I typed another text.

Would you do me a favor?
Would you watch over Mackenzie?

Why?

My teeth clenched.

She likes Blake.

Ew.

Elyse had always seemed wary of Blake. I aimed for a lighthearted response, ignoring my hammering heart.

I know, right?

Mateo was studying me, so I said, "Elyse is bummed I'm not coming over."

"That sucks."

"Mackenzie's pissed at me, too." A twinge of fear hitched my breath. *Should I tell Mateo my roommate has the hots for Blake?*

"But you just spent all day with them, right?"

I nodded.

"Don't they realize you need some time with your boyfriend?" His dimple appeared when he smiled at me.

He'd started referring to himself as my *boyfriend* two weeks ago, after our first kiss, and my heart fluttered every time he used the word.

He deserved my trust. I cupped my hand over his ear and whispered, "Mackenzie told me she wants to be with Blake."

His eyes got big.

"So I asked Elyse to watch over her tonight."

He nodded. "Good idea. Do you need to be there?"

I thought about it for a moment. "No, it's okay." I smiled at him. "I want to be with you."

His grin lasted all the way to the greenhouse.

"Good, no media," Karen said as we approached the gate.

I exhaled, and Johnny punched the gate code.

Karen held the front door open for us, and I ran inside, right into the wall otherwise known as Dane. He gave me a bear hug and studied me when he let go. "What's wrong?"

I wished they'd stop treating me like a cracked teacup. "Nothing."

"Jessica!" Lucia swooped in to hug me as well. "So happy you're here."

At least she didn't ask me what was wrong.

"Do I get to hug little Monroe, too?"

I looked up and noticed a tall, sandy-haired Californian: Dane's best friend. "Hi, Josh."

He gave me a lazy smile and scooped me up.

"Hey, now," Mateo said when Josh held me a beat longer than was appropriate. Did Josh know what had happened to me?

He let me go and chuckled. "Chillax, Teo. Don't mean to make the moves on your wife before the double wedding."

"Dude," Dane said. "Shut up already about that reporter's dumbass comment."

Lucia's face fell. "*I* didn't think it was dumb."

Dane stalked toward her and hauled her over his shoulder, which made her screech. "You're right, Luz." He patted her bottom. "Not dumb at all."

From her upside-down position, she lifted her head, eyes shining. "C'mon in, guys. Let's start the game."

"Eager, aren't we?" Dane teased, but he led us into the TV room where a card table was set up.

Josh took a seat at the square table and dunked a tortilla chip into salsa.

I counted five people for a four-person game. "Josh is playing, too?"

"He'll be my partner." Dane nodded. "You and Teo can team up to play the same hand until he understands euchre."

My hand flew to my hip. "Teo's smart. He doesn't need me."

"But he's a Ramirez. He needs extra help." Dane shrugged. "I know how hard it was for Luz to learn the game."

"Ooooh." Lucia's eyes flared. "Wedding's off. Good thing you're not my partner, because I'm going to *annihilate* you."

He cocked one eyebrow. "Bring it."

I looked at Mateo, who shook his head. My brother and his girlfriend had *issues*.

I dug into my purse as Lucia slid into the seat next to Josh.

"What're you looking for?" asked Dane.

"A tissue," I said. "You have a little bullshit on your lip."

To my side, Mateo cracked up. He cradled my cheek and drew my face toward him for a kiss. *"Perfecto."*

"I'm gonna remember that line," Lucia said as she got us drinks.

Mateo dragged over another chair. We sat side by side across the table from our partner, Lucia, while Dane and Josh had the seats perpendicular to us. When I felt Mateo's body heat, I was glad Dane had paired us up.

I watched Josh guzzle sparkling water and wondered if he'd rather have a beer. He and Dane were both of age, and Lucia was about to turn twenty-one. I hoped my emotional issues weren't interfering with their fun.

Four drinks and a bag of chips later, I pointed to the jack of diamonds in Mateo's hand. "That one."

He turned to me and whispered, "Isn't that the most powerful card?"

I liked him whispering in my ear. His sexy voice sent tingles through me. "Yeah. Let's be aggressive," I whispered back.

"Hmm." His mouth twisted, but he led the card.

I noticed Lucia hiding a smile and knew I'd made a good choice. She was probably loaded with the trump suit of diamonds, and it helped to know her partner, instead of her opponents, had the granddaddy diamond.

"That's an *estúpido* lead," Dane said.

"Dane, I get so emotional when you're not around." Mateo tilted his head. "And that emotion is happiness."

Josh laughed. "Bam."

"Why're you all ganging up on me?" Dane sulked.

"Aw." Lucia rubbed his shoulder. "Poor little *gigante*. Dishes it out but can't take it."

She trumped our next lead, and we won all five tricks — two points for our side. Josh was about to deal the next hand when my phone buzzed with a text from Elyse.

Uh-oh. Blake just showed up. Creep.

My fingers flew over the phone.

At your place?

Yeah.

I wasn't sure how to play this without telling her everything. All I knew was I had to stop Blake from hurting my roommate.

Is Mackenzie still there?

**She's talking to Blake now.
He's got his hands all over her.**

Oh my God. Oh my God. Oh my God.

"Hey." Mateo's arm wrapped around my waist. "What's going on?"

I looked up to see the cards dealt and everyone staring at me.

"Who're you texting?" Dane asked.

I blinked at him, frozen.

Mateo's hand pressed into my thigh. "You're trembling. What's wrong?"

Blake was going to rape Mackenzie. And I couldn't stop it. He'd ruin her just like he ruined me.

"Jess!" Dane's voice made me flinch.

Mateo unlatched my fingers from my phone and stole it away. "She's texting Elyse." After a few seconds of reading, he looked up. "*¡Cabrón!* Blake came over to Elyse's. He's making the moves on Mackenzie."

"Holy fuck." Dane scrambled out of his chair, with Lucia a second behind him.

"Who's Blake?" Josh asked, looking confused.

So he didn't know. I couldn't move.

"What should we do?" Dane asked.

Johnny jogged into the room. "We should go over there."

As he stood, Mateo's jaw dropped, mirroring my own shock. "Were you eavesdropping?"

Johnny swallowed and looked at me, his mouth in a grim line. "I've known for a while."

My eyes welled with tears as I darted my gaze to Mateo.

"Mateo didn't tell me," Johnny said. "I figured it out."

Tears washed over me, but it didn't matter that he knew about the rape. Mackenzie was all that mattered now.

"Please," I breathed. "Please help her."

"Yeah." Johnny nodded. "Karen, we need you!" He typed on his phone as he waited for her.

Mateo took my hand and drew me to my feet, gathering me against him in a tight hug. Over his shoulder, I watched Karen fly into the room.

"Morrell's about to strike his next victim," Johnny told her.

She nodded, seeming unfazed by the news.

My body shook uncontrollably.

"Wait," Dane said. "How do you know he'll try something tonight?"

"Call it my spidey sense," said Johnny. "We need to get over there to stop it."

Dane's hand fisted. "If something's going down, I'm going in."

"No." Johnny looked at him. "You need to stay here with Lucia until her agents return from a meeting. And we might need an inside man—someone Morrell doesn't know." His eyes landed on Dane's teammate. "Josh, you're it."

Josh rose to his feet, eyes wide.

"We need your help to stop Blake from hurting Mackenzie," Johnny said.

Josh gaped. "He's gonna hurt her?"

"He might drug and rape her."

"How do you know?"

Johnny glanced at me. "He's done it before."

I watched Josh's eyes, and when they flickered with sadness, I knew he'd put the pieces together.

"More than once, we think," Johnny added.

I felt like I was about to be sick, and Mateo tensed next to me. "What do you mean, more than once?" His tone was sharp.

"I talked to campus police," Johnny said. "There've been a few Title-Nine reports to the university about girls who suspected they were raped. But none of them pressed charges—probably because they couldn't remember much. We're not letting this happen again." He turned to Josh. "You in?"

"Hells yeah."

Johnny made for the door. "We'll brief you on the way. Mateo, you're with us. Maybe you can get Josh up to speed en route."

"*Sí.*" Mateo nodded.

Johnny beckoned for me. "Jess, you too. Let's go."

My fear must have shown because Johnny said, "It's okay—you'll stay in the car. We need you to keep Elyse in the loop. Bring your phone."

Mateo reached for my hand. "We gotta stop him from hurting her."

I nodded and let him propel me forward, following Johnny and Josh.

Lucia caught my elbow. When I looked at her, she was crying. "*Ten cuidado.*"

Be careful. I wished I'd heeded her advice my first night here.

"Motherfucker!" Dane yelled. "I need to be there!"

Karen held out her arm. "Stay with Lucia." She hurried Mateo and me toward the door.

Mateo sat between Josh and me in the backseat. He kept hold of my hand as he briefed Josh on what Blake, Mackenzie, and Elyse looked like. Then he told him skeletal details about the worst night of my life, more than a month and a half ago. Had it really been that long since I'd been raped? Since I'd lost my sense of peace, my easy trust?

"Jessica."

I found Johnny's eyes in the rearview mirror.

"You need to text Elyse. Tell her to stay calm. If he tries anything before we get there, we need her to stop him."

My breaths came fast and hard. Mateo squeezed my hand. *I can do this. I can do this.*

On our way. Keep an eye on Mackenzie.

Ok?

I paused. Elyse needed to know what kind of douche we were dealing with.

Blake did something to me.
He's a bad guy. Please watch him.

It took her a while to respond.

Ok.

We weren't far from her house now. When my phone rang, her name popped up on the screen. "Yeah?"

She sounded breathless. "I'm in the bathroom. I-I-I think I saw Blake put something in Mackenzie's drink."

"What?" I straightened, and Mateo shifted next to me.

"I was writing a text to you, and I kept deleting it. Then I looked up and saw him pour something in her drink."

"Oh my God."

"What?" Johnny asked as we lucked into a parking spot not too far from Elyse's house.

"What should I do?" Elyse cried. "She doesn't know."

"Does he know you saw him do it?"

"Don't think so."

My stomach twisted as I announced to the car: "Elyse thinks Blake spiked Mackenzie's drink. You gotta get her. You have to help her."

"Shit," Karen said. She looked at Johnny. "I'll go in."

He sat still for a moment, but when Karen reached for the door handle, he grabbed her elbow. "No! We can't barge in there."

Elyse chirped in my ear, "Do you want me to get the drink?"

"Do you want Elyse to get the drink?" I asked.

"No," Johnny said. "Don't get the drink, and don't go in." He turned to look at me. "We have an opportunity to stop Morrell for good."

I gulped.

He stared at me. "We need Elyse to call the police, report what she saw."

Police? My chest squeezed.

Johnny added, "Josh goes in, makes sure Mackenzie doesn't get hurt, gets the drink before campus police arrive."

When I paused, Mateo said, "It's a good idea, Jess. The spiked drink is evidence they can use to stop Shithead."

"Time's ticking," Johnny said. "I've already got Officer Whitworth on standby. I'll tell you his number."

Everyone in the car stared at me, and I nodded. "Yes." Then I told Elyse, "We need you to call campus police. Tell them you saw Blake spike the drink." I relayed the number to her and hung up.

Karen twisted around to look at Josh. "We need that drink. Morrell will try to destroy it when the police arrive. You and Elyse have to get Mackenzie and her drink away from him, okay?"

I couldn't believe it when Josh actually smiled. "No problem, dude."

"So you're good with the plan?" Johnny asked.

Josh pointed to a couple of houses down from us. "That one, right?"

Johnny nodded. "Yep. I'll text Elyse before we go in."

Josh left, and it wasn't long before a Highbanks police car pulled up next to us, its lights and siren off. Karen jumped out to speak to the same officer who had driven us away from the prying paparazzi at the dining hall.

Johnny turned to us. "Jess, give me your phone so I can text Elyse."

I handed it over.

"You two, don't you dare leave the vehicle, or I'll tell the president you had premarital sex."

With that he slammed the car door, and I looked at Mateo, who stared back, wide-eyed. The tension of the moment snapped, and I let out a giggle.

His eyes got even bigger as a smile stretched his mouth. *"Loca,"* he said.

"I know. I'm insane."

"This *situation* is insane."

"*Sí.*" I watched Johnny and Karen confer with Officer Whitworth and another campus police officer. After they talked for a minute or so, Johnny and the officers sprinted toward Elyse's house. Karen stayed by the hood of the SUV.

"It's happening," I whispered.

He nodded.

Mateo's arm was still around my shoulders, and I liked the circles his thumb traced on my collarbone.

"I'm scared," I admitted.

"I won't let him hurt you again, but it's okay to be scared." He tucked me in closer. "I was scared when Alex was shot."

I turned to look at him. "Of course you were."

"I thought he was going to die, and the last thing I'd said to him was something mean, like he'd never understand me, or something like that. But then he made it."

I patted his hand. "I'm glad."

"Will you…" He shook his head. "Never mind."

"What?"

He ducked his head. "I'm the king of bad timing here, but will you be my date for the wedding? For Alex's wedding?"

"Of course."

That cutie-pie dimple creased his cheek, and he pressed a kiss to my temple. He started singing, his voice low and steady. "*Where it began…*"

It took me a verse or two to recognize Neil Diamond's "Sweet Caroline." But when he got to the refrain, he sang, "*Sweet Jessica.*"

How was I smiling on a night like tonight? I pressed into him and inhaled his sandalwood scent.

When he finished the song, Mateo prayed softly in Spanish. I tensed into a ball of fear, and it seemed like neither of us breathed for five minutes. The front door to Elyse's house finally opened, and a tall, dark-haired man emerged. I knew that body. My heart kicked up, and I inhaled sharply.

"Wait a minute." Mateo squinted out the window. "Hey, he's in handcuffs!"

I blinked, then noticed Blake's arms tight to his sides as Officer Whitworth pushed him toward the police car. Toward us. I froze.

"Look at me." Mateo cupped my chin. "Tinted windows. He can't see in here."

I shuddered. "O-Okay." People streamed out of the house, watching Blake being hauled away. He held his head high, like the arrest was merely an inconvenient mistake, which infuriated me.

You can't hide what you did any more, Blake. What had Mateo called him? Suave Swimmer Shithead. *Not so suave anymore, asshole.*

Blake glanced at the SUV before the officer pressed down on his head to put him in the car. *Good riddance.*

Once the police car left, Josh and Elyse bounded toward us. Josh's eyes were bright as he opened the car door next to me.

"Fuckin' A, we got it!"

I looked to where he pointed — a glass in an evidence bag held by two more campus police officers talking to Johnny. When had they arrived?

"You got the drink?"

Josh high-fived Elyse. "We got it!"

"We're awesome like that." Elyse smirked.

"So we know it was spiked for sure?" asked Mateo.

"Had to be. Blake lunged for it when the cops crashed in," Elyse said with a wicked grin. "But Josh tackled him." Her grin faded when she looked at me.

"Where's Mackenzie?" I sat up. "Is she okay?"

"The EMTs are with her," Elyse said. "She's sleepy and disoriented."

My hand covered my mouth.

Mateo stared at the house. "I don't see an ambulance."

"They came around the back," Josh said.

I looked at Elyse. "Will you go with her to the hospital? I'll be there when I can."

"You got it." She hesitated, then leaned into the vehicle to hug me. "I think we need to talk."

I sniffed. "We do. We will. Thank you so much."

She let me go.

"You'll be okay, Little Monroe," Josh said as he hugged me, too.

I think he's right. I'd expected to feel intense shame with so many people finding out about the rape. Instead, I felt relief. I could breathe again, knowing Blake wouldn't hurt anyone tonight.

Elyse turned to walk back to the house.

"Hey, I'll go to the hospital with you." Josh fell into step beside her.

"Interesting." Mateo watched them return to the house. "Is Elyse single?"

"Yeah, but doesn't Josh have a girlfriend?"

He smiled. "He was moaning the other night about not having one decent date his entire college career."

Johnny appeared at the open car door. "They're booking the perp at the campus police station." He turned to look at curious students who'd left the house, some of them now walking toward the SUV. His gaze landed back on me. "I want to stop there before he lawyers up. You'll stay in the car, but I have a few words for Mr. Morrell. Is that okay with you, Jessica?"

My lips parted as I blinked at him. I didn't know how to answer.

"What will you say to him?" Mateo asked.

Johnny stepped closer. When he took my hand, my nose burned with impending tears. He'd just added my roommate to the list of important people he'd saved. "You don't want to report what happened to you, right?"

Through my blurry tears, I watched a guy approach us, but Karen stopped him from coming closer. The guy was a swimmer who lived with Blake. What would my team think if they heard about the rape? They'd never forget it. Never look at me the same. Something I'd had no control over would haunt me for my college years and beyond. It had already stolen almost two months of my college career.

"No."

Johnny nodded. "But you don't want him to do this to anyone else."

"That's my worst fear," I sobbed.

Johnny nodded. "Mine, too. I'll ensure that won't happen, okay? Give me some time alone with him."

I shook away my tears. "Do it. But then I need to see Mackenzie." A spiral of anger tightened in my belly. How dare Blake try to hurt my roommate? I didn't know what Johnny was going to do, but I hoped he'd beat the shit out of him.

He squeezed my hand and closed the door. He and Karen bounded into the front seat, and we sped off.

"Turn off your comm-link when you go in there," Karen said quietly.

"No." Johnny's grip tightened on the steering wheel. "It'd put Mateo at risk. We need an open line to the backup agents."

I chewed on my lip. "You're not going to get in trouble for this, are you?"

Johnny looked at Karen but didn't answer.

"No, Johnny." My shoulders seized, and Mateo took my hand. "Don't do it. I'll, I'll report the rape."

"You won't have to. It's all right. It's my honor to do this for you, Miss Monroe." He pulled into the police parking lot and hopped out.

I watched him jog into the station.

After a minute or two, Karen removed her earpiece. She twisted to look at me. "Do you want to hear this?"

I glanced at Mateo, whose soulful eyes blinked back at me. "Up to you," he said.

"Okay." I laced my fingers through Mateo's and braced myself as Karen adjusted something on the earpiece. She rested it on the seat between us. I hadn't realized the audio could be amplified like a speaker.

Through the earpiece, I heard what sounded like a steel door close.

"The perp's probably in cuffs, in an interrogation room," Karen explained.

"Mr. Morrell." Johnny's voice was crisp. "I'm with US Secret Service."

Fainter was Blake's voice. "You can't be here."

"Oh, but I can."

"I'm not talking to you without my attorney."

"Good, because I don't want to hear your bullshit lies and excuses. I'm the only one talking." Johnny paused. "You're done hurting women, Morrell. You're done with drugging them, raping them. And how do I know this?" There was a rustle, then his voice lowered. "Because no matter what happens in court after tonight, I'm going to track you the rest of your life. My Secret Service friends will help me. You even *look* at a woman wrong, and we'll take you down. You won't know where we are, but we'll be there. It's what we do."

"Fuck you," Blake said.

"Fuck yourself, you pompous asshole."

Mateo's eyes widened, and I was equally surprised. I'd never heard Johnny drop the F bomb before.

"You destroy lives just to get off," Johnny continued. "You probably never think about it again, unlike your victims. They never stop feeling afraid. They will never be the same. They will question themselves, blame themselves, hate themselves, all for something *you* did. You've skated scot-free for years. No more. You're the one this will stay with now. *You'll* be the one on edge, always looking over your shoulder. You'll never be free of the shame and helplessness. How does that feel?"

Blake either said nothing or we couldn't hear him.

"Your raping and pillaging days are over, my friend. And, as they say, may God have mercy on your soul. 'Cause I sure as fuck don't."

There was a thumping, maybe a pounding on a door, and Karen drew the earpiece back toward her.

"Dios," Mateo said.

Dios *indeed. What a night.* I slumped against the car seat and closed my eyes. Tears leaked out the corners. But I wasn't crying from fear or loss this time.

"You're shaking again," Mateo murmured.

My eyes opened, and when I smiled, Mateo seemed surprised.

"It's all right." I let out a long breath, letting go of the past. "They're happy tears."

His smile was tentative at first, then grew wider as he realized I was okay.

We were okay. I lunged to maul him with triumphant kisses.

"Whoa!" He laughed as I pushed him against the seat. I covered him with insistent kisses, and his mouth surged against mine, hot and honeyed. His fingers pulsed through my hair.

I vaguely heard the driver's door open and Johnny chuckle, probably at the sight of our make-out session in the backseat.

"Guess she liked what you told the perp," Karen said.

Guess so. Lightness filled my chest as I hovered over Mateo. I was free.

18
Mateo
★ ★ ★

Dane's piercing whistle blasted my eardrums, but I felt too excited to complain.

Jessica was swimming the two hundred individual medley in her first dual meet, two weeks after Blake's takedown. When she swam the breaststroke leg, her lead increased even more. Then her powerful freestyle strokes, sleek and strong, propelled her home through the water.

She finished the race, and I looked up at the scoreboard.

"She's lane four," Dane said, helping me make sense of the numbers.

"Is that a fast time for her?"

"Anything under two minutes this early in the season is great, so yeah."

She placed her hands on the deck and pulled herself out of the pool. Water gushed down her body as she removed her swim cap and shook out her hair. Beneath her black suit, her toned legs went on for days. What would it feel like to have those legs wrapped around my body? I fanned my face with the meet program. Was it hot in here?

Next up was a short sprint—only two lengths of the pool—and Jessica's teammate Emma won the women's event. It appeared to be a strong freshman class for Highbanks. The men's fifty freestyle was about to begin when Dane and I looked at each other.

"Was this—"

"—the fucker's event," he answered.

I swallowed. But there was no super-tall shithead behind the blocks. Blake's coach had kicked him off the team once word of his arrest got out. He was charged with second-degree assault for spiking Mackenzie's drink—thank God she was fine. Even though the charge seemed solid, especially since the police had found a vial of tranquilizer in Blake's pocket, Johnny had initially told me Blake planned to fight to stay at Highbanks. His situation had changed when two field hockey players came forward with accusations that he'd drugged and raped them last spring. The news had sickened me, but hadn't been a total surprise. Blake had hired a good attorney and was out on bail. According to Johnny, he'd left for his parents' house in Nevada.

After the men's fifty freestyle, there was a break in the meet. I turned my attention to the ongoing competition in the diving well while Dane texted Lucia, who was in Minnesota for a volleyball match. As a Highbanks diver executed about ten flips and three twists off the high board, I got a text of my own:

Get your ass over here.

I grinned. Itch didn't mince words.

No can do. She still has breaststroke left.

**Get your mind off her boobs
and haul your buns over here, son.**

We had our first gig tonight, and Itch wanted to rehearse more, but I'd decided not to miss another swim meet. Besides, we were ready. Jessica had listened to our playlist and said we sounded awesome. But I had one song planned that she hadn't heard yet.

Need to save my voice for tonight.

Your voice is fine, Mariah Carey.

He knew I couldn't stand her voice.

Be there soon, Jock Itch.

It's only our entire music future, Feo.

Grr. Why did Spanish for *ugly* have to rhyme with my name?

About an hour later, Jessica prepared to swim her second individual event—the two hundred breaststroke. She stood behind the blocks, stretching and shaking out her muscles. Perched on one leg, she reached behind her and tucked her foot to her bottom to stretch her quad, then exchanged feet to stretch her other leg. She clasped her hands together behind her and bent over, her hands pulsing over her head. Her obvious flexibility took my mind in naughty directions.

"Go, Jessica!"

I looked behind me to raise my eyebrows at Karen.

She seemed to blush. "What? There's nothing wrong with cheering."

Next to her, Johnny smirked.

Dane unleashed another ear-torturing whistle.

"Dang, Dane!" I tugged my earlobe. "I need my hearing for when Fitch counts me in tonight."

He shrugged. "Nobody says you have to sit right next to me."

When I scooted away, my agents shifted behind me. But that brought me closer to a spectator who started snapping photos of me with his phone, so I slid back next to Dane. "At least teach me how to do that whistle," I said.

His smile was smug. "Take your pinky fingers." He drew his pinkies toward his mouth, making a V with the point near his lips. "Fold the front part of your tongue back, and press your fingers on your tongue. Then blow, baby, blow."

I watched him fold his tongue and insert his fingers. The piercing noise he created still made me jump.

"Now you try."

My brow furrowed, but I folded up my tongue and stuck my pinky fingers over the fold. My first try barely produced a squeak, which made Dane laugh.

"*Cállate.*" I tried again, this time with my fingers angled more to the side.

"Better." He nodded.

I was determined to get this right. Before my third try, I breathed into my belly and pushed my fingers together. The screeching whistle that exploded startled even me.

Jessica's gaze darted up to the stands, and when she saw me lower my hands from my mouth, she grinned. Her thumbs-up sign made me proud.

Dane thumped my back. "Well done, Teo—you're a natural. Should've predicted that with your singer pipes."

My tall girlfriend stood heads above her competitors as she stepped up on the block. The crowd quieted before the start. Once the beep sounded, she rocketed into the water and emerged ahead of everyone to take her first stroke.

"She's got an awesome underwater pullout," Dane said.

"What's that?"

"Here, watch this." He pointed to the other end of the pool, where she turned and pushed off underwater. "In breaststroke, the underwater pullout is when you take one pull and one kick before you surface. I made sure Jess's legs are really strong, so she crushes her walls."

"You trained her?" I asked.

He nodded. "Back in my high school gym, I used to set her for hours. Her coordination's shit—she could never get a good hit—but all those jumps really help her off her walls." His chest puffed out.

I watched her torso rise and surge forward with each stroke for eight lengths. She was so powerful, so fluid, so elegant in the water. It was no surprise when she touched the wall first, about five seconds before Pittsburgh's top breaststroker.

I megaphoned my hands around my mouth. "Way to go, Jess!"

She looked up at me and waved. She barely seemed winded.

Seven hours later, *she* was the one cheering for *me*. We'd just finished playing "Hey, Chica," and the small crowd gathered to see us produced an impressive volume of claps and cheers. Jessica raised her fist and shouted "Yeah!" before high-fiving Elyse. Mackenzie was also there, hanging out with Dane, Josh, Emma, and Kaylee. Johnny stood to the side of the stage, surveying everyone, with Karen and the backup agents stationed around the club.

I grabbed the microphone. "Thanks for coming out tonight! We're Sugar High."

"Woohoo!" someone yelled.

Next on the play list was a song I'd written a couple of years ago: "You Steal Me." When we got to the refrain, Fitch went nuts on the drums.

> *You break me*
> *I'm broken*
> *You take me*
> *I'm token*
> *You steal me*
> *You feel me?*
> *You steal me*
> *Fucking steal me*

I couldn't believe people were dancing. To my music. To a song I'd written. I'd never felt so high—I never wanted the song to end. But when it did, the cheers whisked away my insecurity like insulin flushing sugar from my blood.

"That's Ryne Fitcherson on drums!" I turned and gestured to my bandmate, who boosted his Cubs hat high to acknowledge his fans.

We started our rock version of "Let it Go," and I watched people's faces light up once they recognized the fairy-tale melody. Their laughter seemed to enliven their dance moves. But I frowned when I looked at Jessica and saw a guy grooving next to her. He'd swept up his brown hair in a little bun. Who the hell was that? *Oh, no*—it was Man Bun! I almost botched the lyrics as I watched their interaction. Was he flirting with her? Was he gay? The way he shimmied his body next to hers kept me guessing.

"Thanks for hanging with us at The Library!" I said at the end of the song. It was a popular campus bar that didn't get students in trouble when their parents asked where they'd been—and one of the few bars featuring under-twenty-one nights on Saturdays. "We're taking a short study break."

There were actually groans of disappointment!

"What the fuck?" Itch hissed when I turned to unstrap my guitar. "We had two more songs planned before our first break."

"I'm thirsty, anyway." Fitch stood. Sweat dribbled down his neck.

"Get me some water, will you?" I asked. "I gotta check on Jessica."

Itch rolled his eyes as background music came on.

I hopped down from the low stage and made a beeline for my girl. Johnny wasn't far behind me, of course.

"You sound amazing!" She threw her arms around me and kissed my cheek. I felt happy in an instant.

"I knew you'd be a hit," Dane said. He fist-bumped me.

"Thanks, GD."

"This is Van." Jessica pointed to Man Bun. "We're in the same art class."

My mood plummeted. I tried not to glare at him as I lifted my chin in greeting.

"You guys swaggin'!" Van hauled a short girl with purple hair to his side. "I was just telling Tara you're the best campus band we've heard."

She bounced up and down. "Sugar High's on fleak!"

Elyse laughed, and Josh leaned in to say something to her—maybe about *freshmen.*

Jessica said, "So Van and Tara are together."

She caught my eye and smiled. *Mystery solved.*

Mackenzie stepped closer to me. "That was shit hot, Mateo."

"Thanks. How are you?" She looked a little tired.

"Eh, not too bad, mate. My parents are coming next week to help with stuff."

She probably didn't want to say so, but I surmised her parents would help her deal with the prosecutor's office. I felt sad that America had made an awful first impression on her.

"I never got to say thank you." She reached her arms around me, and I hugged her back. Over her shoulder I saw Jessica smile as she blinked quickly.

"Here's your water." Fitch thrust a bottle at me after Mackenzie let me go. He and Itch joined the conversation, and soon we were back on stage.

"This song's for a special girl," I said. My gaze started at Jessica's long black boots, floated up her black leggings, and crested to the soft curve of her breasts pressing against her shirt. Her blue eyes popped against her denim top. She ran her hand through her curls as she grinned at me. "It's called 'Curl.'"

Itch led with his bass guitar, and Fitch added a slower drumbeat. I hoped taking the speed down a notch wouldn't upset our fans. *Fans?*

I was getting way ahead of myself. I strummed my guitar and looked into her clear, vibrant eyes.

Curl
The shape of your blond hair

Girl
Your look that strips me bare

Unfurl
Our story, if we both dare

Oh, oh, oh, oh, oh, oh
You take me high and low

Curl
Up next to your heat

Girl
Caught by your heartbeat

Unfurl
Fists against the sheet

Oh, oh, oh, oh, oh, oh
You take me high and low

My voice started deep, climbed when I sang "high," then fell when I sang "low." Kind of what was happening in my jeans—only there was no falling back down. As Jessica swayed to the beat, her eyes locked on mine. I'd never seen her look at me that way before. Her gaze pulled me closer, scorched me with its heat. Her lips parted, and her chest swelled with each breath. Was she breathing hard for me? *I* felt breathless for her. Not a good thing when I was the lead singer.

The rest of the set was torture. I had to look away from her during several songs in order to remember the lyrics. But inevitably my eyes would find hers again, and everything around us blurred. After we played our last song, the cheers kept going, even louder than before. More people had shown up during our set, jamming the dance floor and bar.

Johnny approached as I unhooked my guitar from the amps. "We need to get you out of here."

The bar owner was right behind him. "Awesome, guys. When're you playing again?"

Itch, Fitch, and I shared a huge grin.

"We'll be in touch," said Johnny. He frowned at me as I took my time stowing my guitar in my case. "Let's go."

"Not without Jessica." I straightened and looked for her in the crowd.

He shook his head as he took my elbow. "She's meeting us by the back exit, horndog."

Damn, I loved Secret Service. "See ya, Fitch and Itch."

Johnny hustled me to the rear of the bar, where a backup agent blocked patrons from following us. The students still got plenty of photos with their cell phones. I knew video of my performance was probably already all over the Internet—I hoped I didn't sound out of tune.

When I reached the door, Karen stood next to Jessica. She handed me a sandwich. "You need this?"

I peeked at my pump and nodded.

"Eat while you wait here," she ordered. "I'll get the car."

After she left, Jessica and I stared at each other. Johnny was probably somewhere behind me, but I wasn't thinking about him. I focused on the soft blush of her creamy cheeks. My mouth felt dry. "So you're coming over?"

She licked her lip. "Is that okay?"

"Perfecto." When I inched closer, she inhaled. Her lip was wet, and I longed to suck it. She blinked at me, her expression intriguing and inciting.

"Vámonos," said Johnny from behind me.

I placed my hand on the small of her back, and we jogged out into the chilly night air. But I didn't feel cold.

After I shared the sandwich with Jessica in the backseat—and Karen forced another one on us—Jessica turned to me.

"Your band name's Sugar High?"

I studied her face. Did she like it? "For now. We almost had a smack-down trying to decide."

"Really? What else did you consider?"

"Fitch wanted it to be Ritch, for Ramirez, Itch, and Fitch."

Her head tilted. "Isn't combining your names kind of lame?"

"That's what *I* said! So then I suggested Honey's Sweet." She gave me a blank look, and I scowled. But I couldn't be mad at her for failing to recognize an old-man song. "It's from 'Forever in Blue Jeans' by Neil Diamond."

"Oh!" She nodded. "I like that."

"Yeah, but Fitch thought it was too obscure. And from that look you just gave me, he's right. Then Itch came up with Sugar High."

"High for Highbanks?"

"Yeah. And at my first rehearsal, I passed out from high blood sugar. They'll never let me live that down."

"I remember that." She looked sad, then brightened. "Plus, Itch is so hyper, it's like he's on a sugar high."

I nudged in. "And you make me high, sugar."

I felt her grin against my lips as we kissed.

Jessica grabbed my hand when we arrived at the greenhouse, and I followed her like a happy puppy into my bedroom. Once I closed the door, she was on me.

She pinned my shoulders against the door as her mouth smooched all over mine. I tasted turkey from the sandwich and inhaled her soft, alluring scent. My hands slid down to her hips to draw her closer. Her fingertips skated along my collarbone and began to unbutton my black shirt.

I thudded the crown of my head against the door when her lips skimmed down my neck and suckled on my exposed chest. *Dios.* All the blood drained from my head. I fumbled for the buttons of her shirt. She pushed off of me with a smirk and ripped open the top snap below her collar. Quick tugs on the remaining snap buttons left her denim shirt on the floor, revealing a lacy pink bra and the soft contours of her lean abdomen.

Beautiful. Her milky skin called for me. I unbuckled my belt and tossed it to the side as she unzipped her boots. I nuzzled her neck and breathed in her skin. She smelled sexy and fresh. "Can't get enough of your perfume."

"Thanks. Elyse let me borrow it."

"What's it called?"

She ran her hands through my hair. "Squeeze, I think."

"Like this?" I tucked her into me, wrapping her so tight that our bodies suctioned together. I couldn't get close enough to her. Her skin felt like velvet under my touch.

Her hands pressed into my spine, like she felt the same consuming hunger. "You're strong," she murmured.

I *felt* strong in her arms. Our energy sparked, infusing me with excitement. But when she reached in to unbutton the rest of my shirt, I froze.

"What's wrong?" She leaned back and searched my eyes.

Chin. I wished I'd had some alone time in the bathroom before she'd started removing my clothes. I swallowed and felt my heart pounding. *Just do it.* Unbuttoning the shirt, I looked down as I slid it off my shoulders. It pooled at my feet. My naked torso revealed the ugly insulin pump.

Her soft fingers lifted my chin, and I looked into her eyes. But I didn't see disgust or uncertainty there. She gazed at me with the kindness she'd always shown, and the same hint of desire her eyes had held all evening.

"You're so fit." She traced the curve of my pectoral muscle, which was nowhere near as defined as Alejandro's. "I love your body."

She did? I studied her, but saw no sign of dishonesty.

I held my breath when her hand trailed down to rest on the tape covering my infusion set. "What do I need to do?"

"I…I'm gonna disconnect the pump."

"Okay." She smiled at me.

I turned toward my chest of drawers to prepare an alcohol swab. When she came up behind me, I stilled. Her wet lips pressed kisses down my neck and back, flowing like liquid down my spine. Tingles electrified my arm, and my hand trembled as I removed the infusion set.

Once I'd placed the pump on top of the chest, I spun around and clasped her face, needing her mouth on mine again. In between kisses she unzipped my jeans, which relieved some of the building pressure. But my body jolted when she reached in my boxers and touched me. *Pressure's back.*

She grinned when my eyes practically rolled to the back of my head. "Take off my bra?"

I was eager to comply. Soon I had her perky breasts cupped in my hands, her taut nipples pushing into my palms. She tossed her head back as I fondled her soft skin. "Ahhh."

She tugged down her leggings, and when she stepped out of them, I noticed the curves of her strong calves. My eyes slid up the line of muscle on her long thighs. There were those sculpted legs that gave her great "walls." Doing all kinds of things to my blue balls.

Standing only in her pink panties, she reached for my jeans, shucked them down my legs, and dispatched them quickly. My boxers tented as I raised an eyebrow. "You've got great speed."

"Oh, yeah?" She turned to pull down my covers, then arranged herself on my bed with her arm propped at the elbow. Her blond curls tumbled over one breast. "I've got even better endurance."

Holy Lord. I tried to remember to breathe as I indulged in her gorgeous body. "I'm keeping the sensor in," I said, pointing to the circle of tape near my hip. "So don't be too rough with me."

She laughed and stretched out on the bed like she slept there every night. *I wish.*

I climbed in next to her, and my hand skimmed up her thigh as she feathered my lips with weightless kisses. When my fingers progressed toward her panties, she deepened her kisses.

"Yes," she breathed, and I touched her wetness. She gasped, then moaned as my fingertips moved over her. She cheered me on with her words and her body.

And I was about to explode, but I didn't want to push her too fast.

"You're ready for this?" I asked her.

Her eyes opened, and she stared at me for a moment. "I've done this before."

My heart seized. She must've felt me tense because she said, "No, uh, I didn't mean with *him.*"

Dios. We both knew who she was talking about.

"I had a boyfriend in high school. We…um…"

I withdrew my hand from her panties.

"Duncan and I tried…" Her face pinked as she averted her eyes. "Well…"

Just who was this Duncan? What a stupid name.

"What about you?" she asked, looking right at me.

My eyes widened.

"Have you ever been with a girl?"

I squirmed. "So, I told you about Joey, right?"

Her eyes tapered. "I thought you said she was a friend."

"She was! She is. It's just…" How could I explain this? "We knew we didn't feel that way for each other, but we didn't want it to be awkward the first time with someone we *did* have feelings for. We just helped each other out, you see."

She looked unconvinced.

"Joey's dating a guy at Berklee. You've got nothing to worry about."

The tension faded from her eyes. "I better not. 'Cause I'm very possessive of my rock star boyfriend."

The fierceness in her gaze got me hard again. "And I'm possessive of my swim star girlfriend." I pressed into her hot mouth, moving against her, trying to relieve some pressure but only making things more intense with the friction of our bodies. Her hands whisked my boxers down my legs, and I returned the favor by peeling down her panties as our tongues collided.

Her mouth skated down the center of my chest, then veered toward my pump. I held my breath, but inhaled when her warm breath hit the area just below the sensor tape. When she kissed my skin, I shivered.

I lunged for a condom in the drawer of my bedside table, and Jessica tried to help me slide it on. We were both so excited that it took several attempts — and countless laughs — before we got it right. Despite our earlier confessions, it was obvious we were both inexperienced. But as soon as I entered her, our bodies knew what to do.

We rocked together, and I couldn't believe how good she felt. Her roving hands and soft moans told me she was into it as well. I let her lead, and that was fine by me. *Ecstasy.* It wasn't long before the heat deep in my belly detonated as I came. It was even more mind-blowing when her legs squeezed around me a second before her entire body shuddered. Her eyes closed, and her breaths came fast and short. I could feel our hearts racing together.

I held her as our synchronized breaths began to slow. She opened her eyes, gazing up at me with a look that zinged straight to my heart. A look that felt like love. "How do you say *wow* in Spanish?"

I smirked. "How 'bout *increíble?*"

"That'll do." Her cheeks were flushed, her eyes bright.

I drank her in. "I didn't think I could get higher."

"What?"

"Earlier tonight, at The Library—they actually liked the songs I wrote. They danced. They cheered. It was the best feeling. I never thought I'd feel as amazing as I did in that moment. But then…"

Her mouth curled into a grin. "Are you saying I'm a better high?"

"The best." I kissed her smile. Eventually I let her go to take care of the used condom, and when I returned to the bed, my fatigue hit me.

Her eyelids drooped as well. She accepted me back into her arms. "This means a lot to me, tonight. Thanks for swimming in my lane."

I considered what she was saying. Had it helped her to make love after what she'd been through? I aimed for a light response. "Thanks for not letting me drown."

"*Siempre.*" She kissed my collarbone.

I felt like I *would* drown if I ever lost her. I hoped we could stay together no matter what lay ahead. It meant so much for me to be there for her, to help her. Just like she was there for me.

I looked into her eyes. "Everyone plays guitar alone, but we can play side by side."

She gazed at me for a long minute, then swallowed. "I like that." She closed her eyes and snuggled into me.

A few minutes later, I ignored a soft rattle at the door. But when it happened two more times, I groaned.

Her eyes flew open. "Johnny's not coming in here?"

"No." I sighed. "Brat Cat wants in."

"Awww. Let him in."

I rolled my eyes but got up. A leering whistle sounded behind me, and I turned to see her ogling my butt.

"Sugar, you are one sexy muffin," she cooed.

I smirked on my way to the door. Escuincle bolted in once I opened it a crack. He skidded to a stop as he stared up at the mattress. "He's not used to seeing you in my bed." When she raised the sheet and exposed her luscious, long legs, my breath hitched. *But I could get used to seeing you in my bed. Real fast.*

"C'mon, Squinky." She thumped the mattress.

Soundlessly he leaped, then circled a few times before curling up by her belly button. Her light giggles lifted my spirits. "His fur tickles."

I turned off the light. "*I'll* show you tickles." I barreled back into bed, and she squeaked and snickered as I tickled the hell out of her. She retaliated to my apparently sensitive bottom and had me laughing as well. Escuincle darted out from the sheet to the end of the bed, glaring at us until we settled down.

"He disapproves of our tickle fight," I said.

She traced my jaw with the faintest of touches. "He'll get over it."

We faced each other with our heads on the pillows, our legs tangling under the sheet below. I pulled the blanket over us and stared into her eyes.

I was almost asleep when Jessica started in my arms. "Your fump," she said. "You need to reconnect it, right?"

Her eyes glittered in the darkness, and I had trouble getting a breath. This girl...it was like God made her for me. I gave her a peck on the lips then left the warmth of our cocoon to take care of things.

When I slid back under the sheets, I tucked her closer. *"Gracias."*

19

Jessica

★ ★ ★

"Love what you've done with the place," Mom said.

I tilted my head. "Really?"

"Yes!" She pointed to the space beneath my lofted bed, where I'd hung a string of white lights that reflected off the silver and blue of the mermaid girl. "Patrick's painting looks remarkable."

Dad grinned.

"And living in the dorm *is* an important part of college life, you're right," Mom said. "Much better than off campus with Dane."

The thumping hip-hop music from my neighbor's room made me doubt that. Mackenzie had just left for the library after meeting my parents, but if she'd been here she would've busted into a kinetic tribal dance, shimmying in front of her favorite football player. I would've probably joined her and laughed my butt off. She and I had been a lot freer with each other since sharing what we'd been through.

Looking in the mirror, I fiddled with my hair as my mother lowered herself onto the loveseat under my bed. Dad stood near my desk, flipping through my art history textbook.

To show my school spirit for Lucia's volleyball match later tonight, I pulled the sides of my hair back into a maroon barrette with a cougar design. Highbanks was about to host the NCAA finals, which made it fortuitous that the home school had qualified. I'd never seen Dane so nervous.

"You sure you have time for the game tonight?" Dad asked me.

"I told you I'm done with all my finals."

He shook his head. "But it's only December eighth. Finals just started. I'd be pulling all-nighters by this part of the semester."

I shrugged. "Can't pull all-nighters and make morning swim practice. I had to work ahead on my projects."

"Unbelievable." Dad smirked at Mom. "She gets that drive from you, Lois."

Mom's frown made it appear she didn't take that as a compliment.

"I'm going to make this work." I dabbed some pressed powder on my nose. "Nobody thinks I can major in art *and* swim. I know I can do it, though."

"That's a great attitude, honey." Mom's eyes were still tight. "But make sure you have some fun along the way. You seemed so stressed out whenever we talked this semester."

I swallowed. I hadn't mustered the courage to tell them about Blake, despite Dr. Valentine's encouragement. "I *do* have fun." I turned to my parents. "Mateo makes me laugh all the time." Our recent euchre victory over Dane and Lucia came to mind, bringing with it a smile.

"Seems rather serious between you two," Mom said.

Maybe it was serious. And awesome. And thrilling. I didn't even care that the press hounded me almost every time I went to the greenhouse. Being greeted by Mateo's shy smile and soft kisses made it worth it.

"You haven't had much time to get to know him," she added. "You might want to slow things down."

I scowled at her.

"Associating with the son of the president carries a high price. I've already put our family in the limelight, but you're ripping away all privacy when you're with Mateo. Fame steals freedom."

"I'd hardly say I'm famous." I applied the orange-flavored lip gloss Mateo loved.

"But Mateo is. And signing a record deal will only multiply his fame."

My lips parted. Mateo had just learned about a record label showing interest a couple of days ago. Itch had almost had a coronary.

"How'd you know about that?"

"Jessie." Dad lowered his chin. "Your mother gets national security briefings daily. Of course she knows that."

Duh. And she'd also found out about Blake's arrest soon after it had happened. I'd played it cool when she'd called and asked if anyone besides Mackenzie had been affected on my team. At least Mom hadn't brought up the subject with Mackenzie earlier.

"Dane dates a Ramirez, too. Do you ask him these questions?"

"Dane's a lost cause. He's closing off his options too early. I can't *believe* he…" Her voice faded off. "Anyway, he's a senior, about to graduate. You just turned nineteen."

With all that had happened this semester, I felt way older than that.

"You're going to grow and develop and change. Don't tether yourself to one boy—"

"*Tether* myself?" The word disgusted me.

Mom noticed my grimace and held up her hand. "Sorry, that came out wrong. What I'm trying to say is choosing a partner's a big deal. Committing to someone with a life-long health condition…"

When my jaw unhinged, she shut up. "His *diabetes?* You're holding that against him? Something that's completely not his fault?"

Dad set the book on my desk and joined Mom on the loveseat. When he reached for her hand, she sighed.

"Maybe that's unfair, but look at the statistics, Jessica. Mateo may be fine now, but down the road he has a higher risk of blindness, neuropathy, stroke…"

"He's got the best health care there is, and he takes good care of himself." I folded my arms across my chest. "And I'm not perfect, either."

Dad's eyebrows pulled together. "What're you talking about, Jessie? Any guy would be lucky to have you."

"If anything, I'm the lucky one. Teo's been there for me." A lump lodged in my throat. "I don't know if I would've made it without him."

"What do you mean?" Mom searched my eyes. When I pressed my lips together so I wouldn't start crying, she looked across the room at

Mackenzie's posters. Mom tapped her chin. "What Mackenzie went through had to be rough on you. I knew I should've visited when I heard what that monster did to her."

Damn it. I hadn't cried in weeks, but here came the waterworks.

"Oh honey, I'm sorry," Mom said. "I should've been here."

Dad stood and pushed my desk chair closer to the loveseat. Then he rubbed my shoulder and guided me into the chair.

I sniffed. "It's okay you weren't here. I'm not crying because of that."

"Then what's making you upset?" Dad asked.

I frowned. "I hate you saying mean things about Teo."

"Mean?" Mom said.

I realized how juvenile I'd sounded. How could I make them understand what he meant to me? I drew in a breath. "He's not just some boy I have a crush on. He's more than that. We've been through a lot together."

Mom's eyes narrowed. "Please don't tell me you're pregnant."

Dad's eyes got huge.

Despite my tears, I barked out a laugh. My hand darted to my mouth as I kept snickering. My mother was a big believer in birth control, but I hadn't told her I'd started taking the pill a month ago. "Um, *no.* I'm not preggers."

Dad looked upward in apparent relief.

Blake could've gotten me pregnant, though. The thought killed my laughter in a second. Thank God my HIV test had recently come back negative as well. "Mateo helped me." I exhaled. "He helped me heal from a trauma."

My psychologist mother sat up—I knew that would get her attention. "What trauma?"

I glanced at Mackenzie's side of the room, then back at my parents. "Blake Morrell." I was proud my voice didn't shake when I said his name. But the lump in my throat hardened as I watched Mom's chin quiver. She shrank back on the loveseat. She'd heard too many horror stories from her psychotherapy clients, and she probably knew what was coming.

"Mackenzie wasn't his first victim."

Dad was slower on the uptake. "What are you saying?"

Mom leaned forward and took my hand, which made me start crying again. "He...he drugged you?"

It was difficult to speak. "I think so."

Dad gasped and took my other hand. "Oh, God, Jessie."

"Did he...?" Mom had begun crying, too.

Could my parents handle it? Dr. Valentine had said they could, but I wasn't so sure. I was about to find out. "He raped me."

"Son of a bitch." Mom closed her eyes, and tears squeezed out.

Dad clutched my hand. "I'm so sorry."

"I'm doing much better now." I didn't have a hand free to wipe my nose, so I sniffed. "I've been meeting with the sport psychologist—"

"Carly Valentine?" Mom exhaled when I nodded. "She's been so good for Dane. Did he tell you to see her?"

I swallowed. "I sort of got mandated to see her. For a positive drug test." Mom's eyes widened, and before she could ask more, I added, "Blake gave me a joint that night. I shouldn't have smoked it." Just like I shouldn't have accepted that drink from him.

"When did this happen?" Dad asked.

I looked down. "The first night I was here."

Mom let go of my hand as her voice rose. "And you're just telling us *now?* Over three months later?"

"Lois." Dad frowned at her.

"Sorry." I blinked. "It took me a while to figure out what happened. I...I couldn't remember, and then when pieces of it came back to me, I didn't want anyone to know."

Mom blew out a breath. "That's the shame talking. But this isn't your fault."

"I know that, Mom." I hid a smile. *What a shrink response.*

"You're having nightmares? Flashbacks? Hypervigilance?"

More psychologist questions. "Not any more. I got some things off my chest when I wrote him a letter, even though I didn't send it. Then, when he got arrested, it was like a load off my shoulders."

Mom studied me. "I haven't heard anything about you making a police report."

"I don't have to. I was with Mateo when we found out Blake was about to hurt Mackenzie, and Johnny made sure she was okay. Then

Johnny told Blake that whatever happened with the charges against him, Secret Service would watch him for the rest of his life."

Mom's eyes grew round. "Wow. Johnny did that?"

"Yeah. And when Blake's arrest got out, two other athletes came forward. Elyse and I got them connected with Dr. Valentine—I hope they'll be okay, like me. I'm ready to put this behind me. I thought about reporting, but the media would go crazy if they found out who I was. It'd draw way too much attention to you and Dad."

"Jessica." Mom sighed. "This is exactly what I was saying about fame. Don't let our family's stature dictate how you live your life."

"But Mom, I don't *want* to make a report. The only reason I would is so Blake can't hurt anyone else. Johnny made sure he won't."

Mom shook her head. "He's done so much for our family. I have to say that having Johnny near you is a definite bonus of dating Mateo."

"So Mateo knows what happened to you?" Dad asked.

"He figured it out. He listens to me. He *cares* about me. He's been so amazing—he's really helped me. I don't think about Blake much at all anymore, especially when I'm with Teo."

Mom assessed me. "You *do* seem rather calm about the whole thing. You must've done some good work in therapy."

I leaned back. That was one of the nicest things my mother had ever said to me. "Thanks. But I wouldn't be here without Teo. He's so kind and smart. And have you heard him sing?" I pressed my hand to my heart. "*Dios*, his voice takes you to a different place."

After a beat, Dad chuckled, and Mom exchanged a look with him. Her eyes tapered.

I wrinkled my nose. "What?"

"Don't say it." Mom held up her hand.

Dad smirked. "Our daughter has found love."

"Ugh." Mom looked to the ceiling.

"How is love a *bad* thing?" I demanded.

Mom rubbed her temples. "It's been *so* difficult not saying anything to Dane about Lucia's politics. Two whole years I've kept my mouth shut. What helped me get through was hoping you'd find a nice liberal boy. Or girl. Now those hopes are dashed."

"I'm not *gay*, Mom."

Her mouth turned down at one corner. "You sure?"

"You'd rather me be gay than with a Ramirez?"

Dad laughed. "Every parent has dreams for their child." He squeezed my hand. "I know we can't control who we fall in love with. I wouldn't have chosen the daughter of a real estate mogul as my first pick." He let go of my hand and caressed Mom's cheek. "But I'm so glad I did. And grateful she gave me another chance when I fucked it all up."

Mom seemed to soften as she looked in his eyes. "The real estate mogul wasn't thrilled when I fell for the poor artist." She kissed his hand. "But *I* was."

They looked like they were about to christen my loveseat. Evidently they'd taken my news better than expected. "Um, do I have to see this?"

Mom grinned at me and got to her feet, with Dad not far behind. "Group hug!" she hollered. I scoffed at the idea. But when we held each other, I closed my eyes and said a silent thank you to my psychologist for nudging me to tell my parents. No more secrets—only relief. It was over.

Mateo lit up when we made our way to the roped-off seating area in the arena. There were countless Secret Service agents mingling with the First Family and their entourage, and likely many more I couldn't see. My boyfriend, followed by Johnny, came up to us.

"Good to see you, Mateo." Mom shook his hand.

Mateo fidgeted. "You too, Senator Monroe."

Dad reached out to shake his hand, but instead drew in Mateo for a hug. "Thank you," Dad said before he let him go.

"Uh, sure." Mateo looked at me with questions in his eyes.

We'd picked up Dane on our way to the arena, and Mateo fist-bumped him. Dane gave him a shaky smile. "Yo, Teo."

"Lucy's going to play great," Mateo told him.

Dane exhaled. "My nerves are that obvious, huh?" He looked down at the teams warming up. "Typically I'd do a few jump serves and get it out of my system. This spectator thing sucks balls."

"It's not so bad." Mateo gestured to the stands. "We have some seats for you over here by my parents." He rested his hand on my back, right where I liked it, and guided me in that direction. "You look incredible," he whispered.

His touch zinged tingles up my spine.

As we passed Johnny, I smiled at him. He aimed the faintest of smiles back at me while maintaining his professional façade. He then looked behind me and nodded at my parents. "Senator Monroe, Mr. DuPont."

I heard Mom tell him, "We owe you."

Dane reached Alejandro and his fiancée first. I'd only seen photos of Maddie, and she looked even prettier in real life. Her defined jaw and muscular body conveyed her athletic talent, but her full lips and high cheekbones competed with runway models'. I liked her curly hair, too. She and Alejandro made a striking couple.

"How's my groomsman's foot?" Alejandro asked Dane as they shook hands. His wedding was only one week away.

Dane nodded. "Stronger than ever. Ready to kill it on the dance floor."

"So modest," Maddie said with a grin. She perched on her tiptoes to hug Dane.

Alejandro smiled at me. "So *this* is the girl Matty can't stop talking about."

Mateo draped his arm across my shoulders. "Jess, this is Alex and Maddie."

"Hi." I gave a little wave, which made Maddie laugh.

"How's the national team?" Dane asked Maddie as he sat next to her.

Mateo and I squeezed between my parents and Alejandro. Then the announcer told us to rise. Mom and Dad stopped chatting with Mateo's parents to stand for the national anthem.

I smiled when I saw Elyse and Josh together across the arena. They'd been dating over a month now, and I was proud I'd had a role in bringing them together.

The music started, and I nudged Mateo. "Will you sing?"

He lifted his hand to cover his heart and smirked at me. "No."

"What if I do this?" I also placed my hand over my heart.

He pursed his lips. "You drive a hard bargain, *chica*." He began to sing the second verse.

That low, smooth voice made my legs clench. Was it hot in here?

"We should've had *you* sing the national anthem, Mr. Record Deal," Alejandro told Mateo after we took our seats.

"Nah, this is Lucy's night. Besides, 'The Star Spangled Banner' is tough! My instructor said I'm not ready for that kind of range yet."

So modest. And I wasn't being sarcastic.

Mateo held my hand during the team introductions. "Did you know Wrigley Field was the first place they sang 'The Star Spangled Banner' at a sporting event?"

"Nope. Fitch told you that, huh?"

"Along with five hundred other useless facts about the Cubs." He shook his head. "Wrigley's also the first ballpark to let fans keep the foul balls they catch."

"…but military spending is way up," my mother said.

I looked over to see her and President Ramirez deep in discussion.

"ISIS has given us no choice," he said. "They're every bit as dangerous as the Nazis. You've seen what they've done to women, Lois. This is a human rights issue. We have to stop them."

"Not at the expense of poor and disabled Americans," Mom countered.

"Despite ramping up the military, we've decreased the national debt for the first time in years. That'll help the economy, which in turn will help the poor."

She shook her head. "Americans are suffering from these insane budget cuts."

"We all have to sacrifice to rein in massive government spending. You're right," he said.

"I don't see *any* sacrifice when it comes to funding your juggernaut military."

The referee's whistle brought me back to the reason we were here. I looked to my left to find Mateo watching me.

"Sorry," he whispered.

"For what?"

He cringed. "My dad gets kind of heated."

"Like my mom doesn't? They disagree on everything."

"Hopefully they'll agree about us being together."

I wasn't about to share my mother's unfounded doubts about him. I wondered how his parents viewed me. "Hope so."

"What…" He bit his lip. "What'd your dad thank me for?"

I took a deep breath. "I told them. About Shithead."

He squeezed my hand. "How'd they take it?"

"Shockingly well. Especially when I told them what Johnny did." I looked to the other end of the row, where Johnny stood surveying the arena, protecting Mateo. Protecting me. I drew Mateo's hand to my mouth and kissed his knuckles. "And how you've been there for me."

"You've been there for me, too."

Dane leaped up. "Yeah, Luz!"

"Whoops." Mateo looked at the court, where the first game was in full swing. "I better watch this."

Lucia bounced the ball behind the baseline. When the ref blew the whistle, she tossed it up and blasted a jump serve. The libero on the other team shanked it off the court. *Point, Highbanks.* Lucia rattled off five more screamer serves before there was a side out.

"I've been working with her on her serve," Dane said.

Maddie shook her head. "I think Rez deserves at least *some* of the credit."

Thanks to Lucia's impressive kills, Highbanks won the first game. But Penn State roared back to win game two. In the huddle during a time out, Lucia's coach got red in the face.

"Take a chill pill, Holter," Dane muttered.

In the third game, Highbanks' libero made an impossible dig and passed the ball right to the setter.

"Way to go, Kaitlyn!" Mateo hollered.

Lucia went up for a hit, but the opposing blockers stuffed the ball back on her side of the net. The setter somehow got her hand under the ball, and another Highbanks player passed the blooper up to Lucia, who lunged and plopped a little dink over the net. Penn State dove for the ball and kept it in play. The crowd kept *ooh*ing over each improbable save. Lucia jumped in sync with the middle hitter to block the next hit back into Penn State's court, but the back row player passed it to their setter again. The Penn State middle hitter spiked a quick hit, but once again, Highbanks defense got the ball up.

"Whoa," said Mateo.

My mouth also hung open as I watched the never-ending volley. Lucia went up for another hit and managed to avoid the block by slamming the ball down the line. Not even the best player in the world could've dug that ball. *Point, Highbanks.*

President Ramirez shouted, "*Excelente*, Lucia!"

"Kill!" Dane yelled, his voice dripping with bloodlust. He high-fived Mateo, then ripped one of his trademark whistles.

Mateo grinned at me before he unleashed a whistle of his own. It wasn't as loud as Dane's, but still respectable.

"Matty!" I looked over to find the president giving his younger son a thumbs-up.

"Just wait." Mateo rolled his eyes. "Dad's gonna ask me to teach him how to whistle like that."

I laughed. *That* I would like to see.

Lucia was on fire. Her mix of cross-court and line hits with dinks kept the defense guessing, and she also made some stalwart blocks. At the end of game three, Highbanks led two games to one.

"Oh my God," Maddie said. "They could win the national championship."

Alejandro nodded as he patted her leg. "They *will* win!"

Looking as excited as his brother, Mateo vibrated next to me. "All they need to do is take the next game, right?"

I nodded.

"Do you think they'll do it?" The flecks of gold in his brown eyes captivated me.

"Your sister's on fleak tonight, so yeah."

He grinned as he kissed me.

Game four started with Penn State up, but Highbanks chipped away at their lead with some butt-kicking serves. When Lucia's block banged the ball straight down to the court, I saw a blur to my right. I gaped at my dad, standing and shouting, "You show them, Lucia!"

He looked around and must've seen people staring, because he was back in his seat in a second. President Ramirez thumped him on the shoulder. My suave, gray-haired father bellowing at a sporting event? It was the most uncharacteristic thing I'd ever seen. Mom caught my eye and shook her head. We shared a small smile.

Mateo nodded. "Now I see where you and Dane get your competitiveness."

My head tilted. "All this time I thought it was from my mom."

Lucia kept playing out of her mind until we were all on our feet for match point. The cheerleaders got the entire crowd clapping in unison as Kaitlyn served. Penn State got off a good hit, but Kaitlyn passed the ball to the setter, who back-set it to another of Lucia's teammates. Her spike careened to the floor untouched. *Win, Highbanks.* Lucia tackled Kaitlyn, and the rest of the team rushed in, arms in the air, heads thrown back in victory.

The crowd went nuts. Mateo grabbed me in a hug, and we kissed amidst the chaotic noise and energy like it was New Year's Eve in Times Square.

I watched all the celebrations around me with a warm glow and a stupid grin on my face. This was the culmination of three years of hard work for Lucia. Good things were happening in Mateo's music career as well. I hoped Dane and I would also reap the benefits of our efforts one day.

"Outstanding." Maddie stared at the court. "That was a thing of beauty—Rez outdid herself. I hope my national team coach was watching tonight."

They presented the team trophies while photographers snapped endless photos.

Most of the spectators had left when one of the photographers said, "Let's get a Ramirez family photo." He gestured for the First Family to come down onto the court.

"I think it's time for us to head out," Dad said.

Mom and Dad hugged Dane, then turned to me. Mom eyed all the agents mulling around. "Looks like you'll be okay here. You're in good hands."

I imagined Mateo's hands roving over my body. *Yes, I am.*

"You're stronger than I knew. I'm so privileged to be your mom." She stepped in and circled her arms around me. Her heels brought her to my height. I smelled her familiar perfume, but something felt different. Instead of mother and child, we were like two adults hugging. I appreciated her support, but I didn't feel quite as needy as when I'd lived at home. Highbanks felt more like my home now.

Dad hugged me next. "Love you, Jessie."

"Love you, too."

"So Dane will drive you home after the wedding?" Mom asked.

I nodded.

"It'll be so great to have everyone home for Christmas." She beamed.

I watched them walk away and thought about the holidays. Our celebration would be short because my flight to Florida was scheduled for the day after Christmas. Two weeks of hellish training loomed ahead, but at least we'd swim in the sunshine.

On the gym floor, Lucia gripped the massive NCAA trophy while her family surrounded her for the photo—her parents on one side and brothers on the other. It was an impressive group. Their dark hair and toothy grins shone in the arena lights. Even brooding Alejandro smiled for the camera.

Maddie approached and grumbled, "Figures they win *after* I graduate."

"You'll just have to win the Olympic gold medal to make up for it," I said.

She grinned. "I like the way you think, Monroe. Maybe you'll be there with me, representing Team USA."

"That would be a *dream!*"

With the photo shoot over, Mateo's brother leaned in to say something to him. Mateo looked up at me, his eyes darkening, then spoke to Alejandro. What were they saying?

"Want to give me any advice for handling a Ramirez man?" I asked.

Maddie laughed. "Hmm…" She blinked a few times. "When he gets pissy, just wait it out. His passion will show through."

"I don't think I've ever seen Teo in a pissy mood."

"You're still in the infatuation stage, huh? Matty's different from Alex, but everyone gets irritable now and then."

I considered her response. What would he be like when he was bitchy? Weirdly, I looked forward to finding out. Mom was right that I hadn't known him very long—something I needed to rectify. I had no idea how I'd last almost a month without seeing him over winter break.

Secret Service guided Maddie, Dane, and me down to the court. From the corner of my eye, I saw Lucia launch herself into Dane's arms, and their frantic kisses made me blush. But when I noticed Mateo's parents watching the PDA, they didn't seem embarrassed. Mrs. Ramirez rested her shoulder on the president's lapel. He tucked her closer.

Mateo and Alejandro walked toward us.

"What were you two talking about?" I asked.

Beneath Mateo's blush, his dimple appeared.

Alejandro chuckled. "I'm happy you're coming to the wedding, Jessica." His lips brushed my cheek. Then he took Maddie's hand. "Hey, we better get going. It'll already be past midnight by the time we get to your dad's."

"Right. Bye, Matty. Good luck, Jessica." She winked at me.

They left with Alejandro's agents.

"Why'd she wish you good luck?" asked Mateo.

"She was sharing the finer points of handling a Ramirez man."

He squinted. "Yeah? What'd she say?"

I curled his long fingers around mine and stepped into his space. "Love him, she said. Love him, embrace his passion, and he'll be yours forever."

"I always liked Maddie." He caressed the back of my neck and pulled me close for a soft kiss.

20
Mateo
★ ★ ★

"**W**hat the fuck were you thinking, Jake?"

I stopped in my tracks. That was Alejandro's voice? I'd *never* heard him drop a swear word, much less the big mother of them all. Jake's response was muffled, so I opened the door to the pastor's office and peeked inside. My brother didn't notice me because his glare was riveted on his best friend, Jake, who backpedaled away from him as he spoke.

"…thought this would be the best time," Jake said.

"At my *wedding?*"

Jake's black tunic wrinkled as he bunched the hem in his hands. His Marine dress uniform looked far superior to the stupid tuxes my brother and I wore.

"Weddings are happy times," Jake explained. "I thought you wouldn't be so mad if I brought her now."

"Think again, *¡cabrón!* My bride has bad blood with Nina. Don't you know that?"

Jake looked up. "Nina might've mentioned something…"

Eyes wide, I stepped into the room. "You brought *Nina* as your date to the wedding?"

When Jake nodded, I laughed.

"*Cállate*, Matty." Alejandro scowled at me.

My head shook as I kept laughing. "Nina, the girl who moved in on Maddie's ex—maybe even while Maddie was still with him?" I couldn't believe Jake was so stupid. "Nina, *Dane's* ex from freshman year?"

"Fucking hell." Jake looked at Alejandro as he pointed at me. "Get Matty outta here. This is between you and me."

"No, I want my brother here." Alejandro nodded at me. "He knows what's what. He can see you're sticking a knife in my back by bringing Nina to my wedding. To Maddie's wedding."

"*El Niño*, you know I don't want to hurt you. But I've kept quiet long enough. The truth has to come out."

Alejandro squinted. "Just how long have you and Nina been together?"

Jake shrugged. "Couple years."

"What?" My brother's eyes bulged. "Where'd you meet her?"

"At a bar near Highbanks." Jake studied him. "After…after you got shot."

Alejandro ran his hands through his hair.

"She's a great girl, once you get to know her," Jake said.

"A great girl?" Alejandro's hands dropped to the side. "Did they nerve gas you in Afghanistan? Your brain lacks oxygen."

"My brain's fine, asshole. Nina is just misunderstood. She had a rough home life, but she's better now. We're good for each other."

"I kept wondering why you've been avoiding me." Alejandro's voice warbled as he looked away from Jake. "I thought I did something wrong."

Jake sighed. "Sorry. I know I've been shitty. And it's crap timing, but I don't want to lie about her any more."

"*There* you guys are." Dane came into the office. His gaze bounced from Alejandro to Jake to me. "What's going on?"

Alejandro blew out hot air. "Guess who's sitting in a church pew, waiting for the ceremony to start?"

Dane cocked his head.

I took a deep breath. Dane was even more of a hothead than my brother. I watched him as I said, "Jake brought Nina as his date to the wedding. She's his girlfriend."

Dane's eyes flashed with shock, narrowed with anger, then crinkled with amusement. "Fuckbiscuit." He looked at Alejandro. "That sucks, man. How do you think Maddie will take it?"

"Not well. Those were bad memories from her senior year." Alejandro eyed Dane. "Maddie doesn't deserve this. I don't want anything marring her wedding day."

Dane shook his head. "Me neither." He glared at Jake. "What the fuck were you thinking?"

I smirked. Those words sounded much more natural coming from Dane.

"Nina's sorry for what happened when you were together," Jake told Dane. "She has many regrets."

Dane held out his palm. "Save it. My maturity wasn't stellar in that relationship, either. But Luz and I have moved way past that." He turned to Alejandro. "So, do we wait until Maddie sees Nina? Maybe she won't notice her till the reception. Or do we tell her now?"

He tapped his thigh. "She doesn't like surprises."

Maybe because her mother walked out on her when she was a baby. I frowned.

"Matty, will you tell her?"

I stepped back as the three stared at me.

Alejandro added, "I'm not supposed to see her before the ceremony, and you have a good way with her. Will you?"

This best man thing was becoming more of a pain in the ass by the moment. I'd slaved over my speech for days after finals ended. But I nodded.

Karen waited for me outside the pastor's office. She followed me to the Sunday School room, where the female contingent of the wedding party waited for the ceremony to start. I knocked and called, "You decent?"

Lucia opened the door. "What're you doing here?"

"I have a message for Maddie."

She gave me an odd look, but let me in. Soon tall women in festive gowns surrounded me.

I smiled. "Ladies, lookin' good." Jessica struck me as the most stunning in her red off-the-shoulder bridesmaid gown, but I didn't want Maddie, Lucia, or Maddie's Highbanks basketball friend Tamisha to feel bad about me saying that out loud. Jessica was a last-minute substitution for Maddie's national team teammate, who was out with an ankle sprain.

"Thanks, Matty." Maddie fidgeted with one of her dangling earrings. "What's up?"

"I come bearing good news and bad news," I said.

Maddie's pinned-up hair drew attention to her long, elegant neck, and the bobbing of her throat as she swallowed. "Hit me with the bad news first."

"Well, uh…" There was no easy way to say this. "Jake's date for the wedding is Nina."

Lucia gasped, and Maddie's chin dipped.

"They've been together since Alex got shot," I continued. "Jake avoided telling Alex because he knew he'd be mad, and he was right. Dane thinks it's crappy, too. But Jake didn't want to lie any more."

Maddie's head lowered, and Lucia sidled up to rub her bare shoulder.

"What'd Dane say about it?" Lucia asked me.

"That you and he have moved way past the Nina situation."

A slow smile grew on my sister's face. "He's right."

Maddie watched her, then rolled her shoulders back. "You know what? I've moved on, too. Jake can have Nina—God help him."

"You tell him," Jessica said with a determined look in her eye. Lucia had shared her prior dealings with Nina one night after euchre.

Tamisha arched an eyebrow. "And what, pray tell, is the *good* news?"

I grinned. "My brother found someone to tolerate him for the rest of his life. Thanks for taking him off our shoulders, Maddie."

"Amen," Lucia added.

Alejandro's agent, China, popped her head in the door. She wore an all-black business suit. "Ceremony's starting in five, people. And don't worry, we've got this place air-tight."

Secret Service had managed to keep the media out of the church, though they hovered like hangry wasps right outside. Not many weddings involved metal detectors at the church entrance.

I pressed a kiss to Jessica's cheek and whispered, "Your beauty isn't supposed to upstage the bride's."

"Shh..." She gave my shoulder a light slap as she grinned. "By the way, that tux sure is *cute* on you."

My eyes narrowed, which made her giggle.

"Girls only," Lucia said, shooing me away.

"Okay, okay." I held my hands out as I backed through the door.

After I told the guys Nina's presence was a non-issue, I joined them near the altar for the start of the ceremony. I noticed Braxton, Maddie's older brother, sitting between his mother and father. He'd reportedly declined Maddie's request to be a groomsman because he said he hated the spotlight. However, Alejandro had told me it was probably more about their political differences. Maddie hadn't wanted more than three bridesmaids and groomsmen, anyway, so Alejandro hadn't forced the issue.

The wedding music started, and first down the aisle was Jessica. Dang, my girl rocked jewel tones. Her fiery red dress hugged her curves just right—the last-minute alterations had evidently been a success—and sent flames of arousal licking up my body. A curly tendril of blond hair had escaped her up-do. I wanted to boing that curl. And after that, I wanted to bonk *her*.

Everyone stood when Maddie walked down the aisle on the arm of her father. Her strapless off-white dress highlighted her muscular arms and slim waist. I glanced at Alejandro. His beaming smile made me wonder who'd stolen my morose brother and stuck a grinning *idiota* in his place.

Maddie's hometown pastor and our priest from Houston, Father Jim, had agreed to officiate the ceremony together. When Maddie paused just in front of Alejandro, the pastor said, "Who gives this woman to be married to this man?"

Though Maddie's parents had married other people in the past year, her mother stepped up next to her father. "Her mother and I do," Mr. Brooks said.

Maddie joined the grinning *idiota,* and the ceremony began. I kept stealing glances at Jessica, and one time I caught her looking back at me. We maintained eye contact during the reading of a verse. I'd often zoned out when Mom had made me attend mass, but hearing words from the Bible while looking into Jessica's divine blue eyes made me listen better. The gravitas of the moment struck me. Alejandro and Maddie were committing to each other in front of God and friends and family *for the rest of their lives.* Could I ever do that?

Alejandro nudged me. I looked at him, and he gestured to my guitar stand at the side of the altar.

"Move your ass, Teo," Dane whispered.

Whoops, missed my cue. I cleared my throat as I stepped up and walked to my guitar. Bob Dylan might've written the song I'd chosen, but Neil Diamond had sung it best at the White House. A few strums of my guitar, then I began a jazzed-up version of "Make You Feel My Love."

I directed the lyrics to Jessica, feeling the warmth shining in her bright eyes. *I'd do anything for you, Jess, to make you feel my love.*

When I returned to the line of groomsmen, my dad nodded at me, his dark eyes gleaming. Mom was crying, of course. Next came the vows. This time I paid attention and had the rings ready for my brother.

The ceremony moved quickly after the vows, and soon Father Jim lifted his hands. "May I present Madison and Alejandro Ramirez!"

Everyone applauded as my brother and his wife scooted down the aisle. *They did it. They really did it.* I didn't have much time to ponder the momentous occasion before Jessica grabbed my hand to accompany her back down the aisle.

"Let's get to the reception," she whispered. "I'm *starved.*"

I had to keep my swimming star well fed. Karen gave her a snack to placate her while we snapped photos at the church. Then limos carried us off to a downtown Cleveland hotel not far from Lake Erie. Maddie had said the lakefront was fun in the summer but too cold to check out in December.

As we waited for dinner to be served, I took out my pump.

"How do you know how much insulin to add?" Jessica asked.

I explained how the pump helped me calculate, but we replaced talking with shoving food in our mouths once the servers set down our plates at the head table. Given the elegance of the hotel ballroom, the quality of the meal didn't surprise me. The whipped pesto potatoes were particularly delicious.

Maddie's family didn't have much money, so my parents were footing the bill, but Alejandro insisted he'd pay them back once he started earning a salary as an orthopedic surgeon. I, on the other hand, had no qualms accepting money from my parents. I had my eye on a sweet guitar I was hoping to receive as a Christmas present.

Later, on my way back from the restroom, I passed by a table filled with Maddie's family. I paused. "Braxton?"

Maddie's brother rose and shook my hand.

"Or should I call you Dr. Brooks, like my professors?" He'd just finished his doctorate in political science.

"That *is* music to the ears, but I probably need a job first. Speaking of music, you killed that Dylan song at the church."

I admired his dreads. "Thank you."

He looked across the ballroom, and I followed his gaze. Nina stood out in her hot-pink dress as she danced with Jake.

Braxton stiffened when I caught him staring, and he looked back at me. "Good luck with your band, Mateo."

"Good luck finding a job."

He nodded.

The DJ gave me a questioning look once the song ended, and my heart thumped. I returned to my seat a second before he announced, "Your attention, please. Time for a toast from the best man."

A smattering of applause greeted me as I stood and accepted the microphone. Lucia looked up at me with gratitude, her hands pressing together under her chin. She'd been too nervous to give a maid-of-honor speech and had asked me to speak for both of us. As I looked over the sea of wedding guests staring at me, agreeing to take one for the team seemed like a bad idea.

"Thank you for being here tonight. I know it means a lot to Alejandro and Maddie to share this moment with you." Jessica's smile bolstered my confidence. "My sister Lucia was supposed to attend the University of Texas on a volleyball scholarship." I paused and tried not to scowl as I thought about the next line I'd written, but Jessica had made me delete: *Thank God the Texas coach had an affair with a player, or Lucia never would've made it to Highbanks.* Jessica had told me a reception was hardly the place for such a remark. When I looked up and saw the President of the United States watching me, I conceded that she was right.

"But Alejandro and I are blessed that our sister chose Highbanks instead. Because if Lucia hadn't played for the Cougars, she wouldn't have met Dane. And today's awesome celebration wouldn't have happened, because Alejandro never would've met Maddie."

Amid the *aww*s in the ballroom, I silently added, *And I wouldn't have met Jessica*. We'd deleted that line, too, preferring to keep our relationship private—as private as it could be in a twenty-four-hour news cycle. I caught her little wink and continued.

"We're from Texas, but Lucia and I have found a home in Ohio. Alejandro has found a home here, too, thanks to Mr. Brooks and Mrs. Williams." I nodded at Maddie's parents and stepparents. "I've learned a lot about Ohio, like how people love to spell the state name." As I raised my fist, I shouted, "O-H!"

"I-O!" came the resounding shout, accompanied by cheers and laughs.

Jessica grinned at me. She'd suggested inserting that.

I shook my head. "Y'all need *help*."

More laughs.

"It's hard for me to admit, but I've always looked up to my big brother." I found his dark eyes and locked on them. "Alex is cranky sometimes, and opinionated all the time, but what shines through is his integrity and compassion. I know where he stands, and that's right behind me. He's the responsible one in our family. He's got my back."

His hand drifted up to cover his heart.

I blinked a few times. "His career-ending baseball injury motivated him to pursue orthopedic surgery, so he can help other athletes. But I suspect another motivation to enter medicine was to take care of people like me. I saw how much it hurt him when he couldn't take away my diabetes—couldn't stop the disease from changing my life."

His fingers tapped on his chest as he nodded.

"Now Alejandro is directing all that caring and intensity on Maddie." I looked at her and smiled. "Lucky *you*."

She chuckled along with the others in the ballroom, then kissed Alejandro's cheek.

"Your academic and athletic talent drew him in from day one, Maddie. But I know he will lift you even higher, because that's what he does. He wants others to succeed just as much as he drives himself to achieve. He got that from our father."

Dad tilted his head and gazed at me with a hint of curiosity in his eyes, like he was seeing me in a different light. *Yep, Dad, your youngest is all grown up now.*

"And Maddie, thank you. Thank you for becoming part of our family. *Gracias* for loving my brother. You've challenged him to become a better man. You've softened his rough edges. I already have one amazing sister, but I'm thrilled to have another. Both of you can spike a volleyball like nothing I've ever seen."

Maddie beamed at me.

"But which one is better?" shouted a guy from the back of the ballroom.

I couldn't see who had spoken. "Dude, you think I'm stupid enough to answer that?"

My aunt's laugh was louder than the rest. *Tia* Mari and my mother nodded their approval.

"Please join me in toasting the newlyweds, Alejandro and Maddie." I lifted my glass of champagne, and everyone in the ballroom did the same. "*Salud, amor, y dinero, y tiempo para disfrutarlos.* Health, love, and money, and time to enjoy them."

"*¡Salud!*"

"Cheers!"

I clinked Jessica's glass, then handed the microphone back to the DJ and took a seat.

"*Fantástico,*" Jessica said. Her eyes glittered. "Itch is right—you got stage presence, cute boy."

"Don't call me cute."

She laughed and leaned in. "Sugar, you're hotter than the bottom of my laptop."

I cringed. "That's awful!" I tried to think of a worse pick-up line. "Do you have a map? I just keep getting lost in your eyes."

Her eyes rolled, and she took a sip of champagne. Her wet lips called for me. "I'm participating in the Sexual Olympics multiple-orgasm relay race, and my partner just died of exhaustion. Would you help me out?"

My gaze darted around us to make sure nobody was listening, but it appeared everyone focused on the newlyweds' first dance. *Dios.* I mustered a glare at her. "*Which* partner?"

She giggled.

"Congratulations!" I said. "You've been voted Most Beautiful Girl in This Room, and the grand prize is a night with me."

"Ooh, aren't *I* lucky?" She batted her eyelashes. "Mom thinks I'm gay. Can you prove her wrong?"

Karen tapped me on the shoulder. "They want the wedding party to join them on the dance floor soon."

I was sure Karen had overheard Jessica's last pick-up line, but her poker face told me she'd ignored it.

"Sure." I took Jessica's hand and led her to the edge of the dance floor. When we arrived, I spoke in her ear. "I'd be happy to prove your mom wrong."

Her eyes blazed.

I heard a raised voice and looked to the corner of the ballroom, where Jake gestured wildly as he spoke to Nina. *Uh-oh.* I hoped Nina's drama wouldn't infect the reception.

Lucia's laugh drew my attention. She and Dane lingered next to us, and to their other side were Allison and China. Allison wore a classy white business suit. I hadn't realized until she stood next to China that they'd coordinated outfits. After my dad had made sure they didn't get in trouble for their relationship, they'd married a year ago.

Karen and Johnny were right behind me. Nothing had been said, but I'd suspected Dad had learned about Johnny's involvement in the Blake situation and had protected *his* job, too.

I watched my brother and his bride on the dance floor. Alejandro's moves were smooth and confident, and Maddie looked up at him with rapture. I wondered if they'd practiced, or if Alejandro was just a natural. Probably the latter — he excelled at everything he did.

"What do you think, Mateo?" Karen asked.

"I think it's pretty sweet, all of this." I looked over my shoulder at Johnny, then at Karen. "Thank you for protecting my family."

Karen started, like what I'd said surprised her. A soft smile spread on her face.

"Our pleasure," Johnny said.

After the dance, Jessica and I stood in line at the bar. As I accepted two cokes, I noticed Jake and Nina talking to Dane and Lucia.

"I wonder how *that's* going." I nudged my head in their direction.

Jessica sipped her drink as she watched them. "Dane looks pretty relaxed."

He wrapped his arm around my sister's shoulders. "So does Lucia."

We danced some more, then stood off to the side to catch our breath. Allison and Johnny stood next to us.

"Is Light in place?" China asked as she approached Allison.

Allison nodded. "Yeah, she's where she needs to be."

"Wait," Jessica whispered. "Light's a person? Who is it?"

"Lucia," I said. "Light is her code name."

She thought about that a moment. "Oh! The English word for Luz."

"*Sí.*"

She eyed me up and down. "*Me gusta.*"

I took her hand and pulled her closer. "I like what I see, too. What's your room number, hot stuff?"

Her eyes got big as she sucked in a breath. "What if your parents catch us?"

"They'll survive. They'll probably be too busy to notice, anyway. Have you seen the looks my mom's been giving my dad on the dance floor?"

"Weddings *are* an aphrodisiac," she said, then pouted. "And I won't get to see you for almost a month after this."

"Yeah, about that." She tilted her head, and my heart fluttered. "Dad said I could visit you in Boca."

She gasped. "You're coming down to Florida for my winter training?"

"Is that okay?"

"Room five twelve," was her instant response.

This damn reception couldn't end fast enough.

"Ladies and gentlemen," the DJ said, "Please direct your attention to the head table."

Was it time to cut the cake? *Wait*—they'd already done that.

But it was Dane and Lucia in the spotlight, not the newlyweds. Lucia's forehead creased as she looked up at Dane. He shook out his hand in an uncharacteristically nervous gesture. When he knelt and removed a volleyball from under the curtained table, I knew something was up. A volleyball at a wedding reception?

Dane handed the ball to Lucia. She stared at it for a few moments. Then her head shot up, eyes wide.

When he lowered to one knee, I heard gasps in the room. As he extracted a small box from his pocket, I realized my jaw hung open.

He held up the open box, and the ring flashed in the overhead lights. Lucia clasped her hands together and blinked like crazy.

"¡Sí!" she cried with a little hop.

Dane jumped up and engulfed her in a hug as everyone clapped.

Jessica bounced up and down, her face bright. "I had no idea!" She ran over to Dane and Lucia.

"Unbelievable." I shook my head, still in shock.

Alejandro grinned at me and pulled me in for a side hug. "Isn't it great?"

"You're okay with Dane proposing on your wedding night? Isn't he stealing your thunder?"

"Not at all. Here, Mrs. Ramirez will tell you." He signaled for Maddie, and she snuggled into his side. "Dane asked Maddie and me about proposing at our reception, and we thought it was an excellent idea."

"I'm so lucky to see my best friend get engaged," said Maddie.

Dad and a couple of agents joined us. "And I'm lucky to see my daughter get engaged. Well done, you two." He hugged Alejandro, then kissed Maddie on the cheek.

"¡Dios mio!" Lucia walked toward us with her eyes glued on the rock on her finger.

Maddie bounded up to her and squealed as she wrapped her in a hug. Jessica joined Maddie in admiring Lucia's ring.

"What does it say on the volleyball?" Alejandro asked after he shook Dane's hand.

Dane handed him the ball, and my brother read in Spanish, "My love for you will never die, Luz. You are my light, my life, my love, and I want to spend all my days with you."

Alejandro tossed the ball up and set it over his head.

"Not bad, Ramirez," Dane said. "But you need to position your hands like this…" As Dane showed him a few setting tips, Maddie and Lucia joined them.

Dad and I watched the two couples—one married and one planning to be married. He surveyed the scene like a well dressed emperor, a half-smile on his face.

"You knew," I said, and Dad looked at me. "You knew Dane would propose."

"Of course I knew, Mateo. Dane did the right thing by asking for my permission first. Just like you're going to ask Mr. DuPont before popping the question to Jessica."

My mouth dropped open.

"In ten years," he added.

My mouth closed. "Ten *years!* But Lucy's only twenty-one."

Dad shook his head as he chuckled. "I know, I know. I'm getting old, but not as wise as I ought to be by now. My kids will do what they want regardless of what I tell them. And that's the way it should be, I guess. Your brother and sister have done well for themselves, and I know you will, too."

"Thanks, Dad."

"Looks like all three of you will marry liberals." He grunted. "Proof that love really does make you *loco.*"

I laughed. I was definitely crazy in love with Jessica.

"I'm proud of you, Mateo." Dad thumped my shoulder.

An agent said, "Mr. President?" Dad stepped away to confer with him.

The volleyball rolled toward me, and Dane loped over to scoop it up. He fist-bumped me. "Dang, son, that was one sweet speech. You're definitely in the running for my best man."

"Who's my competition?"

"Josh, of course."

I smiled. "I guess he's earned a spot."

When one of my favorite Neil Diamond songs started, I grabbed Jessica's hand. "Hello, I'm a thief, and I'm here to steal this dance."

She snorted and followed me onto the dance floor. "Yesterday's Songs" had a slower seventies beat, and I tucked her into me. Her light, sweet scent floated over me as I savored the feel of her body in my arms. Yesterday's pain and sadness would fade over time. But the good things would remain, like my love for her, and her love for me.

I paused my soft singing to whisper in her ear. "*Chica*, my love for you will never end."

SPECIAL NOTE FROM THE AUTHOR

As I wrote *Spiked*, news broke about a sexual assault by a college swimmer in the United States. The story sickened me on many levels—as a swimmer, woman, and mental health advocate. This novel is a work of fiction, but as a psychologist, I have worked with survivors of sexual assault and other traumas. It is up to each survivor to determine the best path forward. Though the character Jessica Monroe chose not to report her rape to the police, reporting can be helpful for many survivors. And whether or not a person chooses to report, telling someone about the trauma is often a way to reduce shame and begin healing.

If you've endured a trauma, help is out there. I encourage you to find a competent therapist with whom you can build trust.

psychology.tools/ptsd.html
deploymentpsych.org/content/insomnia-tools

~Jennifer Lane

ACKNOWLEDGMENTS

When I wrote *Blocked*, I hadn't planned to start a series. I'd only wanted to create an opposites-attract sports romance, and who could be more oppositional than conservatives and liberals? In America's heated political climate, I wanted to represent both sides fairly and leave it to the reader to decide who won the presidency.

But then, reader response amazed me. I'm so grateful to readers who took the time to tell me what they loved about *Blocked*. And, I understand those who were angry about the evil cliffhanger and hoisted pitchforks outside my window. *hides*

So I decided to continue with the Ramirez and Monroe families in *Aced* and *Spiked*. I may write a novella featuring naughty Nina in the future, but for now the series is finished. I thank my wonderful teammates for making *Spiked* possible.

Nicki Elson, critique partner and friend. I'm so relieved I can vent and laugh with you about the wild world of publishing. Your assistance with the suspense element of *Spiked* was especially invaluable, and my editor was impressed by the "squeaky clean" manuscript you critiqued!

Jessica Royer Ocken, editor *magnífica*. You have improved my writing ten-fold. I'm impressed by your skill, speed, and support.

Coreen Montagna, book designer. I can't tell you how many compliments I've received on your cover designs, and I appreciate your fine attention to detail.

Mitsy Princell, PA. It's been a blast watching you build your author assistant business. Thank you for celebrating my books.

Nelly Guajardo, Spanish and diabetes consultant. I know you have a special place in your heart for boys named Mateo, and I have a special place in my heart for you! Thank you for your assistance, *chica*.

Yelania Velasco, Spanish consultant. Gracias for your help, *amiga*. (Any remaining errors are mine.)

Nic Roach, Australia consultant. We met through our love of *Prison Break* (I'm so stoked for the show's return), and I'm grateful for your help with Mackenzie's character.

Swimming teammates at Kenyon College, especially my best friend: Gwynn Evans Harrison. After moaning for years about my characters rooting for the Chicago White Sox, you finally bullied me into including a Cubs fan in my novel. I hope Ryne Fitcherson represents your fervor well. (And thanks for the Wrigley Field tour!)

ABOUT THE AUTHOR

Get psyched for romance with psychologist/author (psycho author) Jennifer Lane! By day she's a therapist, and by night she's a writer. She can't decide which is more fun.

Jen loves to create sporty heroines and hot heroes in her college sport romances. Volleyball wonder Lucia Ramirez found her love match in *Blocked* despite the glaring political spotlight aimed on her family. In *Aced*, the second book in the Blocked series, it's her brother Alejandro's turn to get lucky in love. *Spiked* (Blocked #3) features Lucia's younger brother Mateo and launches in October of 2016.

A swimmer and volleyball player in college, Jen writes swimming-based romances as well: *Streamline*, a military mystery, and the free New Adult novella *Swim Recruit*.

Stories of redemption interest Jen the most, especially the healing power of love. She is also the author of The *Con*duct Series, a romantic-suspense trilogy that includes *With Good Behavior, Bad Behavior,* and *On Best Behavior*. She will return to romantic suspense with her next novel, *Twin Sacrifice*.

Ultimately, whether writing or reading, Jen loves stories that make her laugh and cry. In her spare time she enjoys exercising, attending book club, and visiting her sisters in Chicago and Hilton Head.

Visit Jen at:

JenniferLaneBooks.blogspot.com
Facebook.com/JenLaneBooks
Twitter.com/JenLaneBooks
Pinterest.com/JenLaneBooks
Instagram.com/JenLaneBooks

www.ingramcontent.com/pod-product-compliance
Lightning Source LLC
Chambersburg PA
CBHW071309170626
46809CB00001B/387